£1 80

Havock Junction

Joe Donnelly has published five previous novels. He is a journalist by profession who has won several awards for investigative work, including Reporter of the Year award. He divides his time between writing novels and journalism, and in his spare time he draws cartoons and climbs hills, tries to fish and plays guitar enthusiastically and badly. He lives with his family in Dumbarton, near Loch Lomond and the Scottish highlands. Most of his books have been centred on this part of the world and based on Celtic mythology.

Joe Donnelly

HAVOCK JUNCTION

ARROW

Published by Arrow Books in 1996

1 3 5 7 9 10 8 6 4 2

© Joe Donnelly 1995

The right of Joe Donnelly has been asserted under the
Copyright, Designs and Patents Act, 1988 to be identified as
the author of this work

First published in the United Kingdom by
Century, 1995

Arrow Books Limited
20 Vauxhall Bridge Road, London, SW1V 2SA

Random House Australia (Pty) Limited
20 Alfred Street, Milsons Point, Sydney,
New South Wales 2061, Australia

Random House New Zealand Limited
18 Poland Road, Glenfield
Auckland 10, New Zealand

Random House South Africa (Pty) Limited
PO Box 337, Bergvlei, South Africa

Random House UK Limited Reg. No. 954009

A CIP catalogue record for this book is available from the
British Library

Papers used by Random House UK Limited are natural, recyclable
products made from wood grown in sustainable forests. The
manufacturing processes conform to the environmental
regulations of the country of origin.

ISBN 0 09 952701 4

Printed and bound in Germany by
Elsnerdruck, Berlin

To Mary.
For many reasons,
including her navigation on some of these roads.

All of us, when things go wrong, have sometimes found ourselves on roads where luck and light is hard to find. Many people believe the *Ley Roads* actually exist and that possibility, of course, is for the reader to decide. The characters of *Havock Junction* however are completely fictional.

I'll see you in hell first.

The words were still ringing in her ears. Spat out words, cat-snarled, hot with venom.

Patsy Havelin tried to shake them off, shuck them away from her, keep her mind on the present and her eyes on the road. Ahead of her, the rain pounded on the black surface, heavy rain that hit so hard the splashes were halogen-white coins spinning by the million. Above her, clouds rolled past, fast and black and heavy, tumbling across the night backlit by pulses of greasy lightning which gave them a sickly tinge of green.

The car sat at a steady sixty, as fast as she dared risk on this road for fear of aquaplaning on the puddles and losing the grip of traction, sending the car into a spin. God knew it was hard enough to keep a grip on herself. The wipers fought the torrential rain drumming hard on the glass. The wheels hissed on the wet road and pulled violently to the left of the camber every time they caught a nearside slick of water. White beams picked out the silver rods of rain for only a few yards before they were swallowed in the thunderstorm, forcing her to sit hunched over the wheel, eyes straining, too scared to go faster, too downright afraid to slow down.

Patsy Havelin was in a desperate hurry. She was flying for her life and for her sanity. She hated driving at night, hated driving in a storm. But this night she had to drive, and she had to drive fast. Behind her the children snuffled, half asleep but unable to settle. She reached and tilted the mirror, risking a glance. Peter was huddled against the nearside door, an arm around little Judith who was tucked in against his chest, thumb in her mouth, her pale face a white smudge in the dark. Despite her anger and the drained, washed-out exhaustion that follows great fear, she was able to summon a ghostly smile. It was just like Peter to have that protective arm around his sister. He'd been the man of the house for too long, and that had been too long ago.

Overhead, in front of the car, lightning flickered a juddery dance deep inside the thunderhead. One blue line jolted from the bottom of the heavy cloud-base and stabbed to the ground just beyond the range of where the headlights picked out the cat's-eye reflectors. A second later the thunder hit in such a blast the whole car shook with the concussion. Judith whimpered in fright. Peter mumbled low and soothing and they both fell silent. Out on the road, the lightning jittered along the top of the crash barrier in the phantasmic St. Elmo's fire, writhing and twining like supercharged blue serpents. She drew her eyes away from it, but the image still spun and twisted in her vision, dopplering down from purple to orange afterburns. The car raced onwards, too late to stop. The blue-fire came sparking out from the barrier, reaching out for her. Instantly she felt the static charge in the air, felt the hairs on her arms and the fine down on the back of her neck creep with sudden eerie tension. The battened-down fear that she'd held in tight fought to break free again and she clamped her teeth on her lip, biting down hard enough to feel pain.

Then the lights went out and suddenly she was driving in pitch darkness. The engine cut out and whined in protest slewing the car to the nearside, heading towards the crash barrier and the writhing electric snakes. Patsy slammed the stick into neutral, sightless in the night, heart hammering, fright clenching at her belly. The offside wheel hit something on the road, *judder-bump*, a cat's-eye set in the surface and even blind she knew that meant she was in the centre, straddling both lanes. She held the wheel steady, unaware that her knuckles were standing out white as bone.

Then she was past the blue fire. She sensed it in her own skin even before the lights came back on again. She eased back on the pedal and the engine juddered in low protest before it caught, revving up quickly as she stepped on the fuel to try to maintain her speed. The car had veered into the fast lane, close to the far kerb, though she hadn't heard the rumble of the road reflectors. When the full beams blared, all she saw was the big sign off to her left but she was already hauling hard on the wheel and the sign whipped past before she could read it. She brought the car back to the inside, allowing herself to breathe again, heart begin-

2

ning to slow when a monstrous roar blared right beside her. She jerked on the wheel, overcompensated and felt the back tyres slide just enough to give that sickening roll in her belly, then managed to wobble onto the straight again.

A huge black truck hauled up alongside, wheels kicking up spume only two feet from where she sat rigid, paralysed with fear.

The scream came inside her head. *Oh dear God, help us.*

The truck's horn blasted again, a ferocious beast in the night and its air brakes coughed like a hunting panther. Its weight shuddered the road surface and the air-shock of its passing rocked the car, swinging Patsy from side to side as the suspension tried to even out the buffeting. The movement wrenched the belt on the rib just under her breast, sawing the edge against her. The rig pulled away, close, too close, but it was pulling away and the swelling terror, the certainty that they'd been caught out on the road, subsided, leaving her numbed.

The big truck roared on. Its tail-lights glared at her, orange tiger-eyes, diminishing in the distance until they were blurred by the rain.

'Shouldn't be orange,' Patsy muttered to herself, trying to focus her mind on something, anything at all, to get her concentration back. Fright and anger were armwrestling for control while real fear, *mother fear*, prepared to take on all comers. She shoved them all away from her, knowing she couldn't crack, not yet. Not before she got Peter and Judith and herself home safe.

The truck had come from nowhere. She hadn't seen its lights. Its great menacing shape had just appeared beside her, horn blasting. Had there been lights or had it been driving as blind as she had when the lightning had traced the barrier? She tried to think, tried to recall the stab of light in her mirror. She'd have seen that, she told herself. Patsy shook her head. She'd been concentrating on the road, trying not to hit the farside crasher. It didn't matter now; it was gone and it hadn't been *them*.

She took a deep breath and drove on.

The car hissed on the wet, keeping at a steady sixty while overhead the thunder rolled across the sky and the lightning stuttered and stabbed. She drove on and the cat's-eyes flickered in the light of the beams, night animals glare-blinded on an empty road. They brought back the searing memory and she blinked it away, feeling herself shudder. The counter clicked up the tenths of the miles as she headed for home and away from what had happened.

'Mum?' Peter's voice was low, just loud enough to hear, the way he'd always spoken when Judith had been asleep as a baby. She felt the smile try to come back, buoyed on a surge of mother love. She angled the mirror again, just to have another look at them. Judith was awake. Her eyes were just dark hollows in the shadow.

'Yes, *Trouble*?' She'd called him that when he'd been small and fast as a cat, mischievous as all hell. She hadn't called him that in a long time. In the mirror, he gave her a tired grin and her heart did a soft flip.

'Where are we?'

'We're on our way home.' *Home and safe. Back together again. Please God, let us get home safe.*

'Are we going the right way?'

'Sure we are,' she said, though in truth, she wanted to be surer than she herself was. She'd been looking out for the road sign for the past five miles, hoping to get her bearings on this unfamiliar road. She'd passed it without a chance to read it, unsure of whether she'd taken a wrong turning somewhere in the last twenty miles. To herself she cursed the storm and that bastard of a trucker who'd scared the living daylights out of her and almost sent her spinning off the road. She still couldn't recall having seen his headlights.

'Why do you ask?'

'I don't know,' Peter said. She looked in the mirror and their eyes met. His brow had those two vertical furrows that showed he was trying to puzzle something out. 'It's just that. . . .' His voice trailed off.

'Just what?'

She glanced again, saw him look down at his sister, noticed the little motion of his shoulder as he squeezed her closer. He didn't want to say anything that would upset her, Patsy could tell that much.

'It's just, well, it doesn't *feel* right.'

'What doesn't?'

4

'I don't know. It doesn't feel like the right way.'

'It feels fine enough to me, honeybun.' Another pet name from the far past. 'It feels hunky-dory, just you wait and see.'

He was a bright kid, a smart boy. She hoped he wouldn't hear the lie in her voice, the mother-lie of comfort. In herself, this road didn't feel right at all. Nor hunky-dory. He could probably pick up all those doubts radiating out from her. *Home and safe.* She kept the words right up at the front of her mind, also able to see them winking like a welcoming sign picked out in neon, and she tried to believe in them. But the sense of pursuit still crawled up and down her spine and the sensation of danger scratched on the inside of her skull.

'Listen, just let me drive for a bit and then we'll stop and get a bite to eat and a nice hot drink. I promise we'll stop at the first station along the road, and then we can ask to make sure. But try to let Judy get some sleep, huh?'

Her son pulled his sister back against him. His eyes stayed fixed on hers until she had to look away and watch the road. His face was pale, and a little too thin, though that could have been her imagination, contrasting on the deep shadows under his brows. He'd grown some in the last few months, despite what he'd been through, so it could just be normal. He sat silent and she felt the questions in his eyes, questions she didn't know how to answer.

The missed sign didn't matter, she tried to assure herself. All roads lead to Rome, all roads lead to *home*. She forced the fears down deep and tried to think where she was going, where she was taking her children. Patsy Havelin was driving away from a nightmare and the white lines between the cat's-eyes stuttered like tracer bullets as they speared past the car and the rain drummed like shrapnel against the windscreen.

They travelled in silence for another five miles along the bleak and empty road until she saw the winking lights ahead through the grey veils of rain. Patsy fished the rag of chamois from the door-pocket and wiped the glass with two deft back-and-forth swipes, leaned forward over the wheel and peered ahead. There was little to be seen, even at full beam. She touched the brakes lightly and felt the drag of the belt as the car slowed. A few yards further on she could make out the shape on the road and the swing of the orange lamp. It glowed the same colour as the tail-lights on the truck that had almost batted her off the road. Off to the left, out of direct vision, there was a faint and flickering glow, somewhere beyond the straggle of roadside scrub. She got a strong whiff of burning oil on the damp air and she slowed some more until the silhouette resolved, became solid, became a man in uniform. He was holding the flashlight aloft, swinging it in a high arc. The wind whipped the tail of his coat like a loose sail. The flat peaked cap registered on her tired brain and Patsy felt a sudden sag of relief.

The car edged forward, stopped within a few feet, two tyres crunching on the grit of the hard shoulder. The man lowered the light, holding it in front of him and she saw it wasn't a flashlight, but a yellow roadside hazard beacon. He came round to the driver's door and planted his hand on the front, just above the wheel arch, leaning in towards the window. A pearl-chain of droplets swung in unison on the edge of the visor. Patsy rolled the window open.

'What's happening, mummy?' Judith's voice was small and sleepy. Peter mumbled something and the pair of them fell silent again.

'Road's a real mess,' the man said, hunching down to peer in the window. She could hear the rasp of the cold night in his voice. A flurry of wind whipped in heavy raindrops over his shoulder, cold and wintry on her cheek. The damp air smelled of tar and exhaust fumes and burning. There was another smell, sour and tart, which she couldn't identify.

'What's wrong?' Patsy asked. The man was close, leaning too far in. But he was a policeman. At least he was wearing a uniform. In the dark, she couldn't make out the badge on his cap.

'Big pile-up two miles ahead,' the voice told her. 'Driving too fast in this weather.' The man's face was in shadow. She could smell his breath, as greasy as the diesel fumes she'd caught moments before. The hairs unexpectedly started to prickle again on her neck.

'And this bit o' trouble here,' he said, drawing back as if sensing her alarm. He jerked a thumb, just a black motion and a swing of the lantern. She leaned back.

6

There was a narrow space in the scrub beyond the shoulder where the embankment flattened out then dipped a little to what might have been a pasture but was just a field of black. The light showed the white ends of torn and broken branches where something big and heavy had gone through. Just in front of them, a section of the barrier was crumpled and ripped like a tin can. The edges gleamed orange in the light. Through the space she could now see the burning car side-on, lying nose down in a small gully. Flames were licking up from the skeleton of the gutted framework, defying the downpour.

'Is anybody hurt?' Patsy asked, while inside her she felt the urgent, flaring need to be away from here, away from the burning car. She didn't want her children to see this, but more than that, something was scratching at her senses, down below the level of conscious thought.

'Fraid so, miss,' the man said, turning back towards her. 'Too late for those down there, even if the fire brigade was here, but they're held up along the road with the other lot, and that's a real mess, I can tell you.'

He gave a low chuckle. 'There's blood and guts and bits of bodies all over the place.'

Peter's breath drew in sharply.

'Excuse me, officer,' Patsy said quickly, reaching a hand behind her to squeeze her son's knee. 'These children don't need the details.' Alarm bells were now jangling inside her.

'On a road like this, they'll get plenty,' the man said, chuckling again, low and hollow, like a tide in a deep cave. 'It's a bad night to be out here at the junction.'

'Is the road blocked ahead?' She forced the question out, despite the urgent clamour of her instincts shrieking at her to get her foot down on the pedal and drive on.

'Completely. It's like a junkyard, and you don't want these kiddies to hear the screams, that's for sure. They'll be going on a while yet.'

She recoiled as if she'd been slapped, unable to believe what he was saying. Judith whimpered.

'You'd better take the slip. It's only a mile ahead. Junction 13. Fine piece of road.'

7

Patsy fought against the need to close the window and get the car moving.

'Where does that take me to?'

'Oh, you'll always get back on the road again. No fear of that.'

He pulled back again and Patsy got another glimpse of the burning car. It was as if he'd deliberately moved to give her a better view. She couldn't help but turn towards the red glow. The rain had eased just a little. She could see the tyres rimmed in flames and the oily smoke swirling up in rolling billows, black as the night, but tinged pink with the heat. There was a low growling noise as the flames gushed from the crumpled engine block. She tried to draw her eyes away, but the glare held them and a movement close by the dented rear made her turn further. Another man stood in the glow of the flames. Beyond him, on the far side of the car, she caught a glimpse of another face. She looked again, at first unsure of what she was actually seeing. A pair of hands, pale in the light, were raised in the heat.

The enormity of it struck her like a blow.

People had died in that smash. Only minutes ago people who had been alive and driving on this road had gone tumbling off the verge and had died. And someone was hovering down there, warming his hands on their flames. A low groan of disgust escaped her. She began to turn her head away from the sight. Her eyes panned the burning car, reached the front end where the flames were growling and gobbling at the fuel, when she froze. Her eyes clicked back to the passenger window.

Behind the cracked glass, she could see another figure, just a black shape, a head and shoulders, a hand reaching up to hammer slowly at the window. Behind it, another movement. A small thing pressed against the glass. A glimpse of a wide mouth, a scream drowned and unheard in the snarl of fire.

Oh my god. The words came out in a hiss of breath.

There were people in the car, people trapped and burning in the flames.

She jerked back, garroted by the image, shaking her head to fling the appalling picture from her mind. It must have been a trick of the flames, a trick of the flickering light, she tried to tell herself. It had to be. Nobody could be in the midst of those flames and still be alive. Yet she could still see the movement, the pale and twisting motion behind the smoke-stained glass and somewhere deep inside her she knew that what she was seeing was true.

'Something wrong, miss?' The voice came back, low and rasping in the cold air. She sensed the chuckle beneath.

'It's. . . .' she started to say. 'I . . .'

Of a sudden she knew she had to be away from here. The mental alarm bells were now clamouring so powerfully her head felt as if it would split. Patsy shoved herself back against the seat, taking deep breaths to fight down the overpowering revulsion and dreadful fear.

'Here, let me help you,' she heard the man say. She turned to the window, still pressed against the seat-back. With no warning at all, he leaned right inside, head and shoulders looming towards her. His greasy breath filled the car, sour and stale and somehow rotten.

'What do you think you're doing?' she blurted.

The man's hand reached fast, but almost casual. It touched her neck, cold and clammy, then without hesitation it slid down inside her shirt. She gasped in utter shock, frozen to stone in an instant, hands still clasped on her knees. The silent brutality of the invasion was so overwhelming she was unable even to breathe.

The man laughed, low and throaty. His fingers cupped her breast and scraped over the skin, dragging goose-bumps to the surface. It found her nipple and wedged it between two fingers. She felt every nerve of her body twitch and shrivel. He squeezed hard and a sharp bite of pain flared on her breast.

The pain broke her paralysis. Even in the crest of the shock she moved quickly. Her right hand reached up to heel the courtesy light and her left grabbed his wrist. It was thick and meaty and covered in coarse hairs. She pulled it upwards, feeling another twist of pain there as her breast tugged free of his rough grip.

'Just thought I'd give a hand,' he said, sounding more animal than human. He laughed aloud this time, right in her face and the stench of his breath almost made her gag. She squirmed away, batting him with her elbow. Behind her Judith let out a wail and huge fear erupted inside her.

9

The children.

She had to get them away from this maniac. Away from the burning bodies. Away from the man who warmed his hands on a funeral pyre.

'Get away,' she heard herself shout. Her elbow caught the man's cheek and his head jerked back, spilling his hat off. Judith cried out in alarm but Peter was up behind her, scrambling to get over the seat.

'Get off, you,' he bawled, punching out at the big hard hand. 'That's my mother. Get your hands off.' He was forcing his way between the front seats. Patsy shoved him back.

The man reached in again and batted Peter with the back of his hand. Patsy heard the thud and heard the squawk of pain. Peter went bowling backwards and crashed against the far door. The hand groped behind the seat and made a lunge for Judith.

'C'mon, baby,' the grunt was barely comprehensible now, 'You gotta come with me, kid.'

Patsy screeched and beat desperately at the arm reaching past her shoulder. It was like hitting a piece of wood. The foul animal smell was thick and choking, the musty scent of an old pig sty.

'Leave her alone,' Peter shouted high and fierce. The man laughed, no longer sounding like a man. Judith was screaming, a strange ululating sound, pitiful and terrified. Patsy hammered uselessly at the reaching arm then realised how futile the fight was. She twisted suddenly and shoved Judith right to the far side, away from the groping hand, then spun back. With one hand she turned the key and heard the engine start first time. The other worked frantically on the winder. The glass caught under the man's elbow and he grunted in surprise. In the glow of the blinking hazard light, she saw his face for the first time.

He wasn't a policeman. His coat was ripped at the shoulder in a tattered gash through which poked stuffing like horsehair. In that brief glance, when shock had stretched time out, every detail etched into her. The man had a long, grey face, and a wide, almost dog-like nose. He was grinning, or grimacing with effort, mouth pulled back over narrow and blackened teeth. As he pulled back, the hazard lamp cast moving shadows over his face and for an instant his face seemed to writhe and change.

But it was his eyes that hooked into her mind and made the panic soar.

They were animal's eyes, glittering orange in the light, as orange as the crash-lamp reflecting in their corners. They were night-hungry feral eyes. They glared savagely and Patsy's inner voice yammered at her.

Not human! Not human.

The shadows twisted and worked on the long face, making the skin crawl and run like wax. Patsy pumped on the handle, feeling it grind up against the reaching arm. From outside the car, the shape grunted again like a bear in a cave, like a beast in a cage.

She got her other hand to the wheel, stamped on the accelerator and felt the car shoot forward. Outside, just beside her ear, the grunt turned into a wolfish howl then soared to a screech.

The hand banged twice against the windscreen, hard slaps that would have felled her, then it was dragged out. Patsy still wound on the handle, forcing the glass up further. Something ripped harshly and the shriek became a high squeal filled with sudden pain. A crack like a bullet-strike ricochetted inside the car followed by a metallic jangle and then the man, the *thing*, whatever it was, had gone, and she was speeding along the road. Behind her she saw a shadow lurch on the road and in the wing mirror, she saw the snaking red flames of the burning car.

She floored the accelerator and the car bolted forward into the rain.

11

Broadford House.

That was where they'd fled from. Driving in a panic, Judith whimpering, Peter's face a pale oval in the mirror while the hoarse shouts of angry men and the high screech of pain were ringing in her ears.

Broadford House, a gaunt stone building on the edge of a moor, on the shore of a black loch somewhere in Scotland. She'd never been there before, until this one night in the dead of winter. It stood, slitted windows and crumbling balustrade, a few miles outside of a town. *Levenford.* There was a familiar sound to it, which she couldn't place, but with the name came an odd shivery notion of wrongdoing.

The old house fit with that notion, matched this strange place. It was unfamiliar territory, this hilly country where the grey skies scoured the teeth of jagged ridges and where veils of drizzle dragged themselves across the rolling purple moorland. The single-track roads, dotted with mangy black-faced sheep, coats grey in the drenching rain, took all her concentration as they zigged and zagged mile upon mile with only an occasional small lay-by serving as a passing place for the rare car travelling in the opposite direction. Carrick Thomson, her brother-in-law sat beside her, a solid, supportive presence. Behind them, the man with the white beard sat quietly, occasionally humming to himself. He'd told her what she had to do and that was why she was heading through the murk of a Scots winter. The man called McGregor travelling in the van ahead, had pulled into a village with a discordant name peeling on its rusted signpost, a hamlet set in a notch on the loch shore. A woman with a weathered face as grey and forbidding as the sky had served them tea and hard scones. This was a strange place, where the slow-quick accents of the local folk sounded almost like a foreign language. Their eyes sized up every stranger, measured, evaluated then dismissed. On again after the tea and uneaten scone, with Patsy striving to keep the old van in sight while the wipers battled at full power against the rain while the fear and the urgency gnawed at her.

Broadford House was where she'd found her children. This was where Paul had taken them that dreadful day in the summer, where the nightmare had started in the full sunlight, with a warm eddy riffling the summer-bright pom-poms of marigolds. Nightmares did not always come in the gloom of night, in those dark, still waters of sleep. Bad dreams could be born, like grotesque and evil foundlings, in the clear light of day, in the wafting scent of sweet-peas and lilac and in the lazy buzzing of honey-bees. The nightmare for Patsy Havelin had begun in the sound of the car door slamming closed, in the silence from the front garden where the children had been playing, in the sinking twist in her stomach that had made her come hesitantly round the side of the cottage – *should have run, should have known* – and in the sickening lurch of understanding that her children were gone.

She should have known it, should have trusted her own instincts and the bleak dreams that had been some sort of prescience. She should have realised it from the dark-eyed stares, the hungry looks of the gypsy people who'd watched them from the shadows beyond the garden.

That feeling of foreboding had stayed with her since the first of the awful dreams when she'd seen the blood splatter on the stone. She'd thought she was losing her mind, but now she knew. There was a part of her that was aware on the finest, instinctive level. There was a part of her mind that could see what her other senses could not perceive. An awesome black threat had been crowding into her.

It had taken a long time to get to that bleak moorland road.

Carrick Thomson and McGregor had done the finding. Her brother-in-law was a good man. As the bad dream lurched on, draining her of the will to do anything, he'd told her he loved her and she hadn't been able to work out whether he wanted her, or whether he was just stating a fact. Now she knew. He'd been a rock through all of this, someone to cling to, solid and dependable and as hard as the granite rocks that now poked up through the peat. Despite the divorce, he'd stayed a friend at a time when she'd had few enough, because he'd seen what was happening to his own brother, maybe even before she herself had become aware of the changes.

It had started three years before, when Patsy had her hands full with Judith who'd had a poor start in life, and Peter who'd been a sunny little boy, but was charged with enough mischief for several more. Really it had started before that because Paul had been looking for something else, something more than he'd had or achieved. She'd been too busy, too involved in the small routines to notice. She'd been too willing to trust in the present, to believe in the evenness of her life; too sure of the harmony.

Paul hadn't been a bad man, not then, she told herself, more to save her own sanity than for anything else. He'd just not been a very good one. He'd been too much of a gladhander, a small-town lawyer on the make.

He'd been a handsome young man with an easy smile when they'd met in his final year of the law degree. He'd a way about him, as her mother had observed. He could charm the pants off anyone, her friends had told her with a hint of warning in their description. She'd ignored that and he'd charmed her, with that lazy smile and knowing eyes. The charm hadn't faded, at least not to those pillars of society whom he'd wanted to impress, but she rarely felt its focus. There were dinner parties where she felt as if she was an accessory, pretty enough and harmless enough, but she'd felt left out at those parties, accepting the compliments on her cooking, but always feeling excluded from his work, not admitted into his world. She'd kept his suits pressed and his shirt collars white, and a couple of times he'd left purpling bruises on her chest and arms when the children were in bed and when something she'd done had met with his disapproval.

She'd needed punishing. That's what he'd said, dark-eyed and glowering, and at that time she'd come to accept it, almost believe it. *Wasn't hindsight a good teacher*? It gave her that wonderful 20–20 vision with which she could pick out the flaws and the faultlines the way she could see the mat of hairline cracks under the sheen of glaze on her wedding china when she angled a plate to the light. Hindsight angled herself to the light, turned the spotlight on her marriage and the hairline cracks widened to fissures and chasms.

She must have been blind, she could tell herself afterwards. Too close to see clearly, too conditioned to think of herself as a real person and not just an appendage to charming Paul's career.

On the road to Broadford House, sitting in the passing place while a tractor trundled by, its driver just a grey slick mound inside the steamed-up cockpit, she thought about the theft of her life.

Bastard.

It was not a word she used often, and when she did, it came whispered, through clenched teeth as if she could bite it back, or just bite anyway.

The children were in appalling danger, she knew that now, and it had been his greed, his twisted desires that had put them in peril. If he caused them hurt, she'd kill him, that she knew.

He'd hurt her before. In small ways at first. Just an embarrassing pained look at times when they were in company, at one of the posh faculty dinners when he thought she hadn't used a word in *quite* the right context, had laughed a little too loudly. It was the look which told her she was letting him down, giving the wrong impression to important people, that he had married below his intellect. She didn't know it was the look any hurt wife could recognise in the clarity of hindsight.

Patsy remembered the flush of colour in her cheeks when she felt the heat of his disapproval, not knowing what it was she'd said or done.

Someone, a fairly well-known barrister she recalled, had been sitting opposite her, eyes twinkling with that hint of practised suggestion, enjoying her attention as he told a racy anecdote about a circuit judge and a well-known weatherman. She'd laughed, because it had been a funny story, made a joke about a trough of low pressure, just the kind of thing which would have had them in stitches in college. She'd turned and seen that blank shadow flit across Paul's eyes and she'd felt it drag over her, a cold, damp dishrag of disapproval.

The sounds of the dinner table had faded around her. Somewhere off to the side someone had laughed hollowly and she'd felt it directed at her. Her eyes flicked down, feeling awkward,

15

as if she'd used the wrong spoon, a steak knife for fish. She'd sensed the clench of apprehension under her ribs and the uneasy bewilderment of knowing she'd made a mistake yet couldn't understand what that mistake had been.

They'd gone home in silence, with Patsy driving and Paul smouldering, the scent of too much wine and an overlay of whisky on his breath. She'd paid the babysitter who lived along the lane, hands fumbling uncertainly for the notes in her purse. She'd turned and he was gone. In the bedroom he'd banged his hip on the chair in what would otherwise have been the comic trouser-dance of the drunk, but she hadn't laughed, which was just as well. The sharp pain had freed his tongue and he'd used it like a whip. The exact words were blurred in the distance, but she'd remembered him saying something about letting herself down, and him as well. The barrister, the one with the confident eyes and the double-barrelled name was a close friend of the senior partner, and didn't she think she should just listen politely while those more important, legally qualified people could speak without interruption.

It took him half an hour to get round to the real nub of it. Didn't she think, he'd asked in that dry, long-suffering tone that had flattened out his voice, that she'd given *double-barrel* a real eyeful with that dress?

Patsy had blinked twice, completely bewildered.

'You know what I'm talking about,' Paul had rasped. 'Look at yourself, hanging out all over the place. He must have thought he was getting a real come-on.'

She'd whirled to face the mirror and felt herself flush again. The dress was low-cut, but no lower, no more revealing than anyone else's had been. One button had popped, just the one, and as she looked down she could see the dark harpoon of her cleavage.

'Yes, he must have thought you were real easy meat,' Paul had said. 'Just want to give him a little look, eh?'

Patsy shook her head. 'No, it wasn't. . . .' she stammered, hating herself for it. 'I didn't even know.'

'Oh, come on, everybody else knew. He's a letch. Famous for it. He's had about half the women round that table. Must have thought he was on to a good thing.'

She'd tried to think back, wondering if she *had* opened the button. Had it been hot? Had she done it unconsciously? She hated that doubt even more than she hated the stammering. She wanted to explain and detested that too. She felt small and silly and weak.

'Or maybe he *knew* he was on to a good thing, eh?'

She whirled, aghast, shaking her head, suddenly needing to deny the hovering accusation even though she knew she had nothing to deny. He'd kept it up for more than an hour, swinging from disdain to hot accusation and back again. She'd felt warm tears bubble up and tried to blink them back, only to fail miserably. They tracked shiny down her cheeks, giving him another focus.

'Oh stop snivelling. If there was nothing in it, you wouldn't be crying,' he'd snorted, glaring at her in the righteous indignation of his cracked logic. She'd been too tired to fight, too hurt under his onslaught, that she'd said nothing, letting him pummel her with his words and his dark eyes and his turned down mouth, feeling her value diminish and trickle away.

The silent beatings hadn't yet started, not then. By the time he first raised his knuckles to her, her confidence had been eroded so flat it was almost expected. She kept his suits pressed and his shirt collars white and made sure his dinner was on the table and just as he liked it, when he liked it.

And she never, *ever*, put on the scoop-neck dress again. She always wore her blouses buttoned to the neck and at the wrists, not just because of the danger of his anger, but because if anyone else had seen the bruises, they'd know, and she'd have let him down again, and he would punish her again for shaming him in front of people.

Paul hadn't been a bad man, at least not at first, she told herself because it made it easier to accept the fact that she had given up her own career and subsumed herself. He just hadn't been a very good one.

Bastard.

It hissed out again, sounding like her tyres on the wet road.

When the scary travelling people had moved out of the village, so had Paul Thomson. He'd only ever come back once, and that

17

was to ruin her life for the second time. He'd come back and the clock had started ticking.

Beyond the clouds moonlight glimmered and it made her shiver. They had only days to go before the full moon, before the winter solstice would bring the longest night of the year. She had to get them back before then and she had to keep them until that day was gone.

'A child has to die as the blood of rape is spilled on the stone,' the old man with the short white beard had told her, and she hadn't believed him. 'A child must be consumed on the nameless day.'

The *Nameless Day*, conjunction of the full moon and the depths of winter. It was only days away.

In her mind's eye she saw writhing bodies on a stone and then, without warning, the dreadful dream came back to her.

The gypsy laughed from the shadows her face old and lined now, shrivelled and dry, as if she'd been drained of all humanity. The witchety thing cackled at her and pointed to the stone. The carved shapes were still writhing, little stone demons forcing their way up from the surface on which the pale shape lay trussed, arms and legs spread and a wet chasm cleaving from chin to crotch.

She'd seen Judith in the dream, trussed and bleeding, and there had been more. Much more.

Judith lying spread-eagled on the stone, the dreadful gash running from her neck to her pelvis, a great red chasm in which purple-slicked organs still writhed. Her daughter's legs twitched helplessly and her eyes stared out at her mother and the little bleating noise died away with the slowing movement.

Overhead in the storm clouds, the moon was only a glimmer. The awful foreboding pressed in on her as Patsy Havelin drove through the night with her children, knowing the gypsy would try to hunt them down.

3

Ahead of them, far off in the distance, a dull red glow reflected from low cloud. It was the kind of glimmer she'd seen on the way north when she'd passed Sheffield where the steelworks vented their fumes through vast chimneys, reflecting hot against the sky, like bleak concrete volcanoes.

Patsy had bit down on the flare of sudden terror when she'd stamped hard on the accelerator and boosted away from the groping man, but she could still feel a cold and repugnant after-touch of his hand on her skin as if he'd passed on a disease. All the what-ifs were scrambling and jumbled in her mind as her fingers clenched the wheel with enough force to make her knuckles stand out white. If she slackened her grip for an instant, she knew her hands would tremble like birds wings, so she held tight and drove on, trying not to think at all.

What if?

What if he'd pulled her from the car and onto the wet road? She saw the scenario unreel in imaginary playback, saw herself dragged through the gap of the wound-down window, screaming in fear, paralysed in horror while his fingers twisted in her hair and pulled her out and down to the wet road. She saw his hard and hairy hand reach down and rip at her jeans, hauling so hard the waistline scoured her hips with enough force to break the skin. Down on the ground and he'd have forced her legs apart and he'd have slammed himself down on her and he'd be inside her, ripping her skin while his face wavered and changed and he became something else.

Patsy gasped, throwing herself out of the imaginary picture. It hadn't happened. She'd got away.

But what if? What if he'd dragged her down to that burning wreck where the black and sickening movement twisted behind the smoke-misted window? What then? What would the others have done, the ones who warmed their hands on a funeral pyre.

And the children? She wouldn't have been able to save them and they'd be gone. Hurt and torn. Killed.

Or worse. They'd be taken back to Broadford House again as the moon swelled to fullness for the approach of the five dead days. She shuddered away from that thought, the nightmare that had brought her north to save them from the altar stone in the cellar of the house. But the visions kept returning like the foul and groping probe of an incubus, showing her the memory of what had happened, the paralysing glimpse of what could have happened.

But she'd made it. She'd got him off. Something had broken, she remembered. It had made a hard metal sound. For one nauseous moment, she thought she might have amputated his finger as the window closed to the top at the same time as the car had shot forward. Her stomach rolled again and she almost pulled her eyes away from the road in front to scan in the shadows of the foot well. Just as quickly she shook her head, trying to expel the vision, not wanting to see if a thick and hairy finger, ragged and red at the knuckle end was lying there at her feet. If she looked down there, she might see something that might make her stamp on the brakes and stop the car and get out and run and run and run. If she looked down there and saw that mangled finger, it might just move. It might point at her. It might beckon to her.

No!

She shook her head again, a brief motion of denial, making her fair hair whip at her cheeks. *Not true.* Just scared, she told herself. The man had badly frightened her. He'd have frightened any woman.

'Bloody animal,' she hissed under her breath, keeping those might-have-beens at bay. Anger was a more positive emotion and she tried to summon it, make it strong enough to overcome the fear.

He hadn't been a policeman, that was for sure. She tried to remember details of the cap, what kind of badge it had borne, but it had been too dark, the orange light held obliquely away from the face, to make out those details. When it had swung round, she had only seen the light reflected in the man's eyes, making him look like some kind of animal, and the changing shadows which made his face ripple and stretch. No matter. She'd stop at the first service station and report him. The real police could go pick him up, get him off the road. Patsy hoped that no other women were driving on the road tonight. If they were, she hoped they wouldn't stop.

Patsy looked quickly at the fuel gauge. It was half empty.

'Half *full*,' she muttered quickly to herself. The engine was running smoothly, and she had at least another two hundred miles before the needle would dip towards the red. As long as she was careful, she'd get there, get her children home. She looked over her shoulder and saw Peter leaning back, his cheek cradled in his hand. She wanted to reach and cuddle him, bring him tight to her chest, but she couldn't stop, not so soon after Broadford House. They'd be after her now. *She'd* be after them, that deranged woman, hounding them down to drag the children back.

'Are you all right?' The question was lame but it was the best she could do. He nodded.

'Hurts a bit.'

'You're a brave boy. It was good of you to try.'

'Why did he do that? I thought he was a policeman, but he hit me and he tried to take Judith.'

'I thought so too,' she said, trying to justify herself for stopping, but even then she knew that was fatuous. Anybody would have stopped for a man in uniform waving a hazard blinker.

'I think *she* sent him to stop us.'

Patsy felt a cold ripple drain through her. 'No. I think he was just a crazy. Probably escaped from an asylum. I'll report him first chance I get to stop.' She didn't want to think of all the implications of what he'd said. She'd been driving through the night, fleeing with her children, all the time expecting the danger to come from behind. If she thought they would ambush her she might just give up and that would destroy them all.

The glow in the sky flickered and flared. She knew, or assumed, that it was the lights of a city bouncing from the low cloud cover. What city it might be, she had no idea. Somewhere along the road, in this unfamiliar place, she'd taken a wrong turning. She didn't even know which direction she was headed, but it didn't

21

matter. The lights of a city, any city, meant people and shelter and safety.

'Have we got far to go, mum?' Peter murmured in the back, right on cue. 'I'm hungry.'

'Not far, tiger,' she said, risking a quick backward glance, forcing the smile onto her face. 'First chance we get, we'll stop and have a bite to eat, and something warm to drink.'

'Are we going home now?' Judith asked tiredly. It was almost the first time she'd spoken since the mad panic of Broadford House.

'That we are, sweetheart,' Patsy promised. 'Just as fast as I can get you there. Try to get some sleep now, eh? There's a good girl.'

'Where's daddy?'

'He . . .' Patsy faltered. She had to grit her teeth to bite the words back. '*He can go to hell,*' was the phrase that had sprung, sudden poison, to her lips. She swallowed quickly. Paul Thomson was headed there anyway. She remembered the scream back at the gates of Broadford House. Somebody had been hurt, badly hurt. She knew it hadn't been Carrick, for though she'd never heard her brother-in-law scream, he'd have roared like a bull, she was sure. It could have been Paul, and she hoped it was he who'd been hit and hurt and had suffered. A malignant anger inside her welled up like a hot flow of lava and despite her own nature, though the thought appalled her, she wished he was dead.

'He can't come with us,' she finally said, almost a sigh. *Not ever again, I promise you*, she added, to herself. *Not as long as I'm alive.*

'I was frightened,' Judith said.

'Me too,' Peter agreed. 'It was like *Rambo*, wasn't it? There was all this noise and then Uncle Carrick came in and lifted me straight out of my bed. Somebody fired a gun too.'

Patsy had heard the shot, though from which side of the little war the gun had been aimed, she didn't know. She wondered if Carrick had carried one, or the other two men who had come with them. She'd learned only one of their names.

'They've done this kind of thing before,' Carrick had said, by way of introduction. 'They want to help you.'

22

That was all she'd needed to know. Somebody had wanted to help her. Names hadn't been important.

Thinking back, all she felt was gratitude for her brother-in-law and for those two strangers who had fought for her and hers, and for the man with the white beard who had followed her into the darkness of the cellar where the visions had come looping out of the shadows and the nightmares had come to writhing life.

It had been an illusion, she knew, told herself anyway, but she still remembered the ripple of the carvings on the stone and the sense of overwhelming evil and the red glow in the vortex that flickered like the fire of hell, drawing her down to its depths.

That had happened only three hours ago, but already it was beginning to seem like a distant memory.

Since the gunfire and the angry shouts and the scream of a man in pain, she'd been fleeing, running for home, eyes flicking to the mirror to check for signs of the pursuit that was certain. They'd be on her tail, on her trail, sniffing her out and hounding them down. She had to keep going, driving through the storm to keep ahead, while all the time the ripple of apprehension down her spine told her the dogs were out and howling at the swollen moon, baying for blood. For the blood of her children.

'Don't worry,' she replied to Peter. 'Everything's all right now. Try to get some sleep. I'll wake you up when we get there.' Patsy pressed the switch on the heater and heard it whirr to life again, the warm draught welcome on her ankles and quickly banishing the condensation from the screen.

The glow was brighter now, as if the clouds had lowered, or maybe because she was getting closer to the city. She tried to recall the towns she'd passed by on the journey north, but after she'd crossed the border, as her fear had swelled, they had just been signposts half glimpsed on the roadside, vague names barely recalled from the news or weather reports.

'A real mess,' the madman had said, savouring the knowledge of disaster. 'A big pile-up along the road.'

The recollection of the burning car, the oily smoke and the red glow of hot and twisted metal came back to her. Maybe it *wasn't* a city, that red light in the sky.

There's blood and guts and bits of bodies all over the place.

He'd taken pleasure from telling her that, scaring the kids half to death before he'd reached in to attack them. The very fact of his enjoyment had frozen her in shock.

But he could have been right about the accident. Maybe it wasn't a city. Maybe it was that pile-up. She pictured crumpled cars, winking blue lights of fire tenders and ambulances. The screams of the hurt, the dying. Images of destruction and hurt. She didn't want to see that, didn't want the children to witness it, not after what they'd already been through.

Bits of bodies . . .

She shuddered, heart sinking.

That would mean no people, no service station with its warmth from the hot trays of sausages and beans and the familiar electronic whistle and clatter of the arcade games, a sound she'd missed since Peter had gone – *been taken* – leaving his computer screen blank and silent.

Instinctively she eased her foot on the pedal, letting the car slow, now torn between the need to put as many miles between her and Broadford House (and the foul man who had pawed at her) and the desire to avoid the wreckage and the pain that lay on the road ahead.

Just as the car slowed, a big sign flickered to life a hundred yards ahead. Weak lights below it sent a green glow over the flat surface, picking out in silver the individual drops of rain blown against the flat plane. A bent arrow indicated a left, while beside it two perpendicular lines were capped in red, showing the road was closed ahead. She leaned forward, peering at the sign, passed it by and saw another, not far beyond it, an electronic motorway director set on a slim gantry bridge over all three lanes. Again, Patsy read that the two fast lanes were blocked and that she should pull to the left. The message was augmented by a flashing red warning cross made up of winking red dots.

STAY IN LANE.

She edged to the left, skirting the red blaes gravel of the hard shoulder and feeling the tyres grind on the scattering of grit that had spread out to the smooth blacktop. Just in range of the full beam, she saw the first of the traffic cones, lined up in serried ranks, witches hats in dull red curving in from the central reservation, beginning the barrage which closed the lanes. Every fifty cones or so, one bore a winking orange lamp, each out of synch with its neighbour so that they glittered like the light that had reflected from the man's eyes as he leaned into the car.

'Oh, stop it, woman,' she told herself. The man was gone and it would do her no good to dwell on it. She leaned closer to the wheel, avoiding the strobe effect as her lights picked out the traffic cones. Peter said something and she glanced in the mirror.

And just at that moment a roar sounded in her ear, loud enough to make her hands jerk on the wheel. A small cry escaped before she knew it and the nearside tyres swerved onto the shoulder, blag-blag-blagging on the cat's-eyes.

'Jesus,' she gasped aloud as she steered back to the tarmac. Beside her, another immense truck hauled by in a judder of noise and vibration and spray, even bigger than the first that had given her just as much of a fright on the road behind her. It had a mountain of a trailer which swung and rumbled behind the cabin and another trailer attached to the first. One of the tarpaulin stays had worked loose and was whipping about viciously in the slipstream. The canvas covering had shredded and it flapped from side to side like a schooner's sail, like a giant bat's wing.

Patsy's heart leapt into her throat. Her first thought was that they'd been caught on the open road, that somehow Paul and the crazy folk from Broadford House had come sneaking up behind them.

The wheels, whirling tops almost level with her eyes, ground past. She was right on the edge of the road when she sensed the thing was too close. Her eyes darted to the left just as the tie-rope flicked in a whiplash and cracked hard against the window, just inches above Peter's head. Behind her Judith wailed again, but Patsy didn't hear that. The trailer swung, more than a foot, with a quick, snake-like motion that told her the movement was no accident.

'He'll kill us,' she hissed.

She swung the wheel and moved to the left, stabbing hard on the brake. Behind her something toppled from the seat and onto the floor and the seat-belt dug into her breast as the momentum forced her forward. The black truck jerked again, its bulk blotting out the glow in the sky and the winking hazard lights strung on the bollards. She pulled the car right off the road, feeling the tyres skid with the sudden change of direction, then the juggernaut was past her, still pulling to the left in that lethal side-swiping manoeuvre.

'*Bastard*,' she mouthed vehemently, heart kicking hard in throat. 'Tried to kill us.'

The lorry was just ahead of her, orange tail-lights blazing and the canvas flapping on both sides, in great tattered sweeps. It made it look even more like a bat, a vast night flyer trying to take to the air.

She slowed even further, letting it pull ahead of her, the immense wheels still making the road judder. The orange lights, two wide-spaced tiger-eyes blared hot then flicked out. She could still hear the crack of the ropes and the flap of the canvas, but the lorry disappeared into the haze of darkness and spray. She saw a brief outline of its bulk then a whole section of the traffic cones simply blasted apart, flying into the air in an explosion of bowling-pins and winking lights as the trailer rig swerved into the middle lane.

Some of the cones flipped out of sight, while others cannoned off each other or hit the barrier on the reservation and came flying backwards, red spikes, missile warheads tumbling towards her. Patsy yelled without even knowing she'd made a sound. One of the bollards came spearing right at her, hit the road in front and bounced off to the side. Another came rolling and her tyre crunched over its narrow point. There was a small pop and the cone flipped up right beside her, spinning like a top, clattered against the roof and was gone. She hauled the car right to the edge, swerving between two of the plastic spikes and was through, breath clenched in her throat and her whole body shaking.

'What's happening?' Peter squawked.

'Nothing,' Patsy lied, forcing the word out as flat as she could manage and hearing the quiver in her own voice. She took three long breaths. 'Everything's fine.'

'Did we hit something?'

'Just a traffic cone. The lorry knocked it over.'

And tried to kill us.

She got past the breach in the line of cones, scared to stop just in case the maniac in the lorry had pulled in somewhere ahead and was lying in wait, but it was clear the driver, the murderous *bastard* of a driver had ignored the signs and had ploughed straight ahead.

Patsy pushed forward again, picking up speed, but driving carefully, mind and body singing with tension. The barrage of hazard cones stretched on for another quarter of a mile before the next sign.

KEEP IN LANE. *YOU HAVE BEEN WARNED!* The words blared.

'Been warned all right,' she said to herself. 'Should never have come on this road.' The hot snarled words came back to her and she shied away from them. They'd been meant to slow her down, paralyse her and make her believe flight was futile. That's what she told herself, even though she had felt the power of the mad woman's curse. She gritted her teeth and drove on.

Overhead, a flyover soared in a shadowed arch. Patsy got the impression of lights travelling along on the top side, but the rain was too heavy to make anything out, and then she was underneath, crowded in by the red plastic teeth of the bollards. Lightning spat again, a knife of light that left images dancing on the back of her eyes and she was forced to slow down until it cleared. There was a break for a while and then another light, this one low on the road, winked at her, fiery orange, reminding her of the eyes of the man reaching inside the car, bringing back a memory of the lights at Broadford House.

Her mind did a backward flip and she was back in time to when the long nightmare really started.

4

The tinkers, the gypsy folk, the new age travellers, whatever way they saw themselves, had arrived in the early spring, a few weeks before the equinox.

They had come in ones or twos, strange and unfamiliar faces in the narrow streets and on the cobbled market square; odd and unkempt folk drinking on the village green on a mild afternoon. They merited a glance of curiosity, a frown of disapproval from a pair of old matrons on their way to the hairdresser, nothing more, for in any rural small town there are always passers-by, people who stay a day or two before moving on.

The first of them had parked their rusted and dented vans in a field near the prehistoric megaliths that had been called the ringstones since anyone could remember and had pitched their tents under the beech trees bordering the lea, now budding to a springtime green. There had been only a few of them, eight, a dozen, but over the next couple of weeks, they had poured in along every road and track, a tide of the unwashed and unshaven.

John Newcombe who had owned the field since his grandfather had died couldn't care less who stayed on the land. He was collecting a rent from the travelling folk and spending most of it every night at the Cupstone Inn, not half a mile from where the ranks of the tinkers were camped. The windfall meant he could get drunk every night of the week, and while not completely unaware of the mounting concern of the staid and mostly middle-class townsfolk, he didn't give much of a damn.

'Best harvest I ever got out of that land,' he boasted to the farmhands whose elbows had polished the bar to a fine aged sheen.

The travellers were shiftless folk who would stare people straight in the eye with that open-eyed challenging arrogance of the dispossessed. They were people with no roots and few manners and no possessions except the stained matresses and dented pots which they hauled from the backs of their juddering, smoke-belching vans. They had shaven heads some of them, and others, men and women, sprouted Mohican crests with tattooed scalps and declarations of love and hate on their knuckles. When they passed by on the street, they gave off the smell of woodsmoke and the harsh, animal reek of unwashed bodies and the unmistakable scent of animal sex. They looked as carefree as the hippies of a bygone generation, but somehow fiercer, as if love wasn't all they needed. They were the new agers and the opters out, but among the travelling people who came pouring in along the highways and byways were a different type of folk, olive-skinned and dark-eyed people who walked with a fluid grace as if they'd walked the land for a long time. These ones were different and for some reason she couldn't name, they looked even more dangerous than the ruffians with the Mohican crests.

'Damned nuisance,' Paul declared. 'Couldn't get out of the village for more of those bloody vans. Where they're all coming from I don't know, and why they're here is a complete mystery to everybody.'

'Something to do with the Druids,' Patsy ventured. 'They seem to think the old stones are special at this time of the year?'

'What time is that?'

'The equinox. March twenty-first. And at the Beltane festival in May.'

'Who says?' he demanded to know and she wondered if he meant who said the equinox was in March, or if he wanted to know who told her the reason for the tinkers' invasion.

'Someone mentioned it in the butchers,' she said, not quite truthfully. She'd always known about the equinox, and ever since she'd stayed in the village, she'd had an interest in the history of the Cupstone ring. 'They said there used to be an old festival at the stones in the olden days, but it was stopped by Cromwell or somebody.'

Paul looked at her askance as he loosened his tie and walked across to the drinks cabinet. He'd been almost an hour later home from the office just off Market Street, where most of the probate and housebuying for the whole area was done. Patsy had made a roast, just the way he liked it, rare in the centre, and now, because he was late, it was probably overdone. She had worked herself into a minor panic about that, preparing for

29

his disapproval. Fortunately, she'd left the Yorkshire pudding until the last moment, otherwise the meal would have been a complete disaster and he'd have gone on and on about it all night, especially after a couple of gins.

'I'm half starved,' he declared. 'Working my arse off all day, and those ne'er-do-wells do nothing but swan around and drink, and do you know who's paying for it? Me, that's who. They can go anywhere they like, every one of them as fit as a fiddle, if you don't count the fleas and lice, and none of them do a damned ounce of work. But they all get their unemployment benefit and that comes right out of my tax bill. They should all be rounded up and put to work. A spell in the army would do none of them any harm.'

Patsy didn't reply. Paul had never been in the army, though his brother Carrick had made a career of it. Patsy herself had a cousin who'd been a captain in the Wiltshires and had lost both of his legs when a helicopter had been downed by a missile. His spell in the army hadn't done him an awful lot of good, she thought, but she didn't raise the issue. Paul didn't like to be disturbed when he was on his hobby horse, whatever particular hobby horse he was riding at any given moment.

'I don't think they'll stay long,' she ventured. 'They'll probably move on at the end of the month.'

'Sooner than that, hopefully,' Paul said. 'I hear there's talk of getting them ejected. I don't know what that idiot Newcombe is thinking about, but he should know better than to let that bunch of layabouts use his field. Old Cedric Swan at the building society holds some papers on some of Newcombe's land. He'll sort something out. I think the threat of pulling the plug should get him to shift his fat backside out of the Cupstone and get those vagrants out of here.'

'He's pretty bull-headed,' Patsy said. 'And his family's had the land for centuries, so they say.'

Paul was cutting the meat on his plate, flipping the slice over, inspecting its brown interior with a frown. Any second now, he'd push the plate away and give her one of those looks which told her she'd failed again. He glanced up at her and she felt herself flinch inside.

'Maybe they have, but he'll have borrowed money for something over the years. Old Ced should find something to make him see sense.' Paul smothered the meat in the fine horseradish sauce she'd grated only an hour before, and filled his mouth with a forkful. She saw his eyes narrow as the bite of the sauce flamed on his tongue. He chewed, swallowed, took a drink of water, then dabbed at his eye with the napkin.

'Bit fierce, eh?'

Patsy felt a small sigh ease out silently.

'But if there's no lever there, then there are plenty other ways to skin a cat. We can't have those dirty vagabonds cluttering up our streets and putting decent people into a state of fear and alarm.'

Patsy could agree with that, up to a point. They *were* strange and threatening people. They came and went as they pleased, unbound by the constraints of the town dwellers. Their gardens were fields and roadside verges, uncluttered with dwarf juniper and plaster gnomes and concrete slabs. They didn't seem to have any fear for the future, or of anything else, and that's what made the townsfolk uneasy. These strangers had no ties, which meant that they lived to a different set of rules.

She looked at Paul, who was wolfing his roast despite its being overdone and had even taken an extra helping of creamed potatoes. He was still wearing his tie and his white shirt was unbuttoned at the neck.

None of the travellers wore ties, or suits, or white shirts. But none of them, she imagined, were eating so well, or would sleep so warmly on this early spring night.

Peter coughed and made a lunge for his water glass, eyes screwed up against the radish burn, and his father laughed, patting the boy heartily on the back.

'That'll toughen you up, son. Make a man of you.'

Patsy saw the irony of that. Paul had warned Peter to stay away from Newcombe's farm where there was a fallow stretch beside the thicket where the boys gathered to play football after school.

'Don't want you getting mixed up with any of those people,' he'd said. 'You could get hurt. I've seen them hanging about those trees, smoking and drinking. You keep well clear of them.'

Patsy didn't want her son playing up there near the encampment where the music of drums and guitars thudded across the valley when the wind was in the right direction, but it was the mother-fear in her that made her wary. It rekindled the fairy tales and the nursery rhymes of children stolen by gypsies, taken by faerie folk, replaced with changelings. Nonsense stories, but instinctive tales imprinted in the heart of any mother. Paul kept telling his son to keep his chin up, and his shoulder to the wheel, and to keep a stiff upper lip; all the things that would make a man of him, put hairs on his chest. He didn't want him to learn anything from these other people, the ones with the hard look and the casual toughness in the way they walked. Paul wanted his son to grow into a man like himself, successful and white-shirted and the master in his own home. Patsy just wanted him to be safe from harm.

'Yes, we don't want that sort around here,' Paul continued. 'Where they're all coming from I don't know, but if they don't move along, there's bound to be trouble.'

'You think so?'

'Bound to happen. I had to bail two of them out of the station this morning. Trading without a license, and they'd the nerve to tell me they qualified for legal aid. Showed me their welfare benefit books.'

He raised his fork and pointed it at her. 'I didn't put up too much of a case, not with old Digby on the bench. He's one of George's golfing four, and there's no point in falling out with the senior partner at this stage of the game.'

Paul had been made a partner three years before, one of three in the office just off the market square, and he made no secret, at home anyway, of his ambitions to take over when George Urquhart, a craggy but genteel Scot, retired in a couple of years time.

'No. I managed to get them to cop a plea, which got it over and done without a fuss. They got a fifty pound fine apiece.' Paul smiled darkly. 'But then I made sure somebody will give the nod to the welfare boys. If these folk are trading, they must have jobs and they shouldn't be living off my money, should they?'

Patsy shook her head, wondering if Paul had done anything unethical. She knew a solicitor should do everything in his power for a client's benefit, even if he didn't agree with the client.

'They're bad men,' Judith piped up. She had two cushions under her chair to help her reach her food, and had a ring of gravy around her mouth. 'Angela told me her mummy said they were bad men.'

'That's right, young lady,' Paul agreed. 'They're bad men and you mustn't to talk to them, understand?'

Judith nodded brightly. She was small and dark-eyed, just like her father, in contrast to her brother who favoured Patsy's corn harvest hair and blue eyes.

'She said they steal things, and they're all smelly.' The little girl wrinkled her nose, ''cause they don't wash and have baths.'

'Lucky them,' Peter said. 'And they don't have to go to school.'

'That's another thing,' Paul broke in. 'It's not just that they're all thieves and rogues, but it's the kids I feel sorry for. What chance to do they have, roaming around, feeding off the state, and ending up just as illiterate and shiftless as their parents. I shudder to think of the living conditions in some of these old vans. The child mortality rate must be enormous. Maybe I should get the environmental health office involved. At least for the children's sake, these people should be made to live in houses.'

'Maybe there just aren't enough houses,' Patsy said. It had been a number of years since she had studied politics and anthropology, too many years.

Paul glanced up from his plate.

'Ah, the old socialist argument. You'll be telling me they commit crime because they come from broken homes and because they haven't got jobs. That's hogwash. If they'd get out and get jobs, then they'd have the money to live like decent people, in decent houses.'

'But there's no jobs either,' Patsy said before she could stop herself. Paul's eyes narrowed and Patsy felt herself stiffen. She'd pushed too far.

'That's just the kind of propaganda and bunkum you get in the left-wing rags. Of course there are jobs. There's plenty of them. The country's well on the road to recovery. No, these folk just don't want to work. They want people like me to pay their way and think the world owes them a living. They didn't work themselves to a frazzle at university to get a good degree. No, they were out poncing off the state and they're still at it, and what's worse, they're thieving off everybody else as well. And their children will turn out just as bad, or worse. Up at that site, they must see everything, for there's no morals among that lot, I can tell you. Probably getting handed round to every pervert for a few pennies.'

Patsy flicked a glance at Judith, but she was too busy with a mouthful of potatoes.

'They've been given no example, these kids, so they'll turn out just as rotten as their parents.'

Paul shoved his chair back emphatically and dropped his napkin on the plate where the gravy soaked into the linen. Patsy wished he'd stop doing that because it left the napkin with stains that were hard to remove. It didn't cross her mind, hadn't for some time, to tell him so. She didn't realise how much of her own self was submerged here in the modern cottage with his BMW in the integral garage and his white shirts flapping on the line. But there had been a time when she relished a debate and a fiery argument in the pub at the end of a lecture when she'd been sharp and spirited and she'd wanted to change the world.

He came back to the table with a large brandy in a small glass and drank half of it in one gulp.

'Just makes me angry, thinking about it.' He wiped his lips. 'What's this equinox thing anyway?'

'*Beltane*, I think they call it, or maybe that's the May day,' Patsy said, glad to change the subject. 'I did a piece for the Heritage Society last year. They wanted something for the tourist brochure and I got lots of information from the library. It's when the day is just as long as night. It was thought to be a special day in Druid times, and the ringstones are supposed to have been built by the Druids.'

'All mumbo-jumbo,' Paul snorted.

'There's an old legend that Merlin was buried in a cave under the Cupstone in the centre of the ring. They used to have a festival centuries ago on the special days of the year and a big one at midsummer where people gathered from all over. The legend says when the time comes, Merlin will come back again to help save the country.'

'Well the country's safe enough, thank you very much. And it would be a lot safer without those ne'er-do-wells, believe me.'

He took another drink of his brandy, almost draining the glass. His brow furrowed for a moment, then he looked at her across the table.

'And did they put all this in the tourist brochure?'

'Yes. I showed it to you last year, remember?'

'Oh. That was clever, wasn't it?' His brows knitted and Patsy felt her body move back just a fraction, the way it always did when she knew she'd done something wrong.

'What do you mean?'

'You write a story about the myths and legends and what happens? We get flooded out by a whole army of nutcases and sky-pilots. They've never bothered with this place before, but you had to go and advertise it. As soon as they heard there were loony-tunes pagans dancing about in the woods, it must have sounded like paradise to them. Wouldn't surprise me if every one of them was into devil worshipping. You might as well have sent them a gilt-edged invitation.'

Patsy squirmed at the phrase. She'd been in primary school, only seven years old, hair flax-fair and in pigtails. Their young teacher had gone off to have a baby and her replacement had been a squat, grey-haired and evil-tempered woman who terrified the class by the power of her strident voice and the incessant haranguing of the children. She remembered being called out to the front, all eyes upon her, to answer for some mistake in punctuation. She'd gone hesitantly, afraid of the old woman.

'What's keeping you, girl? *Do you need a gilt-edged invitation*? Or should I come and fetch you?'

The thought of old Miss Clancy coming to fetch her, to drag her out, red-faced and tearful to take her medicine – another handy phrase – had frozen her to the spot. The grizzled teacher had roared at her in a voice too loud and low to be a real woman's, and when Patsy had got out to the front, standing at the heavy desk, Miss Clancy had continued her verbal attack, punctuating each word with a hard finger, stabbed just under Patsy's collar-bone. She had never shown anyone the bruise.

Now she felt just as she had then. Paul had a hoard of sarcastic phrases which he doled out with superior generosity and casual accuracy. And when he ran out of them, when his temper flared high enough to halt his speech to staccato gunshots, he'd use his hard finger to emphasise the importance of each word. It was only a small step, if he'd had enough drink, and he wished to make special emphasis, for that finger to merge into his hand, turn to knuckles to skilfully jab and hook at her arms.

'But it was the Heritage Society who asked me,' Patsy spoke up before her speech froze to a ridged glacier. 'Mrs. Urquhart suggested it.'

She cringed, knowing she had told a small lie. Mrs. Urquhart, wife of old George, senior partner, was secretary of the Heritage Society, a big-boned woman with a warm heart and a booming laugh. She hadn't come up with the idea at all, but she'd been all in favour of it. Paul put his glass down.

By now Peter and Judith were aware of the tension that had suddenly stretched between their mother and father. They sat at either end of the table, eyes sliding between Patsy and Paul.

'Oh she did?'

Patsy nodded. 'They thought it might be good for business.'

Paul considered this. Old George swung a lot of weight in the town, but it would be only a couple of years, three at the most, when he'd go off and play golf full-time instead of just most of the time.

'Well she's as senile as he is,' he finally said. 'It's about time those old duffers got their zimmers out and toddled off to a rest home.' He lifted his glass, saw it was empty. She could see his indecision and hoped he wouldn't have another, but he put it back on the table again. 'You'd think they would know better.'

Patsy didn't know whether to agree. She stayed silent.

'But next time they come up with a crackpot scheme like that, let me know.' He stood and sauntered round the corner of the table, ruffling Peter's hair as he did so. 'It might come in handy. In fact it might still come in handy. Maybe you've done me some good after all.'

He stood beside her and gave her a smile. 'Maybe I can mention this where it matters,' he said. Then he leaned towards her and ruffled Patsy's hair, as if she were a child. She felt herself flinch again and hated herself or it.

Paul went out that night to the Cupstone Inn and came back the worse for wear, but quite jolly. In the morning, he'd had a hangover and made a meal of it. Peter stayed out of his way, though Judith didn't notice. She'd one of her springtime colds and her asthma was worse than usual. Patsy debated keeping her home from the playgroup where she was just settling in. She made the decision after Paul went off in the car. Judith's temperature was up a few degrees and she couldn't finish her cornflakes. Patsy charged her inhaler and wrapped her up in a quilt on the settee where she could watch children's programmes. Peter slung his satchel over his shoulder and gave his sister a boyish but gentle nudge on the chin with his knuckles.

'Stay cool,' he told her and sauntered out, grabbing an apple from the bowl with a practised swipe. Judith saw him, noticed Patsy had missed it, and giggled. Peter winked at her from the door.

That afternoon, one of the younger women from the Heritage Society came by with a petition to get the council to act on the travelling folk.

'There's a danger to the historic site,' Jane Travers said. 'And they've blocked the right of way. I daren't let Phoebe out on the bridle path with her pony, even with the rest of the riding school.'

Jane was slim and expensively dressed, the sharp-faced wife of a stockbroker who spent most of his time in London and came home at weekends. Their house had a swimming pool and each of their three girls had a pony.

'If we get enough signatures, and I'm sure we will, at least we can get some action done.'

'But they'll be gone in a week or so,' Patsy said, reasonably. She didn't want to get involved. The travelling folk scared her a little for a reason she couldn't quite identify, but she wasn't sure she wanted to take action against them. That would, she thought, make her just like Jane, comfortable and spoiled and somehow valueless.

'Maybe so,' Jane said, 'but a week's a long time with these people around. You never know what could happen. And have you *seen* that place? That camp?'

Patsy said she hadn't, and that wasn't quite true. She'd passed by some of the tents close to the woods when she'd walked the children to school the day before, and something had made her walk closer to the encampment. Perhaps it had been the sense of wildness, the hint of danger about the travellers, she didn't

37

know. But there had been a magnetism about the camp that drew her towards it. The smell of pinewood and oak bark kindling had drifted down on a cool breeze and from the near edge of the copse, somebody had played a lone and wistful tune on a flute, the notes drifting plaintively down the slope in the warming sunlight. The melody was mournful and haunting and mystical, and though she'd never heard it before, it had tugged a chord in her, made her feel, somewhere deep, the confines and restraints of her own life. Yet there was something else in the music that was strange and alien, the kind of music that would mesmerise and cast spells like the Pied Piper of Hamelin. She'd known that was a ridiculous thought but all the same, it had given her a shiver.

'It's like an army camp from the Middle Ages,' Jane had said, 'and that raggle-taggle army could come down from the woods any night and slit our throats as we sleep.'

But there was something about the real gypsies, dark-eyed strangers that sent a shiver down Patsy's back and made her want to hug her children close.

'Oh, that's taking things a bit far,' Patsy protested despite her own sense of unease.

'Maybe it is. But if your house if the first to be broken into, then you'll wish you'd signed.'

Patsy thought about it. There were two or three hundred folk on Newcombe's five acres, all of them strangers, none with credentials. She remembered the group she'd seen on the green, just on the far side of the market square, women in leather jackets and poncho capes, drinking from cans of lager and sharing what looked like cigarettes, but had the sweet and spicy smell of something else. One of them had waved to Judith then laughed out loud and Patsy had held her daughter's hand tighter. They might not be bad people, but they were a strange people, and the other ones, the swarthy, fierce men with the flashing dark eyes and the women wearing the gold bangles, there was something alien and dangerously alive about them. She signed the petition. Later she wondered if she'd done the right thing.

Paul was late back that night, though he'd phoned to tell her not to cook him anything. He'd an important meeting which she assumed was something to do with his plans to see the travellers out of the village. Judith was still lethargic, but her asthma was less wheezy. Peter did his homework and she made them burgers and spaghetti hoops which they ate while watching television, instead of sitting formally at the table. She was asleep when Paul came home, humming to himself and he cursed quietly when he stubbed his toe on the leg of the dresser. The noise woke her up, but he said nothing further. She could hear him fumbling in the dark and then felt the sinking motion as he got into bed beside her. She smelled something unfamiliar and began to drift off to sleep, recognised the smell of woodsmoke, and under that, another, muskier scent. She dozily wondered if he'd been at a barbecue. In the night she dreamed of burning fires and shapes moving in the smoke.

The petition was the main item of news in the local paper the following day. The council's environmental health committee held a meeting and voted to serve a notice on the travellers to quit the area, the vote to be ratified at the full council meeting in two weeks time. The travellers stayed put.

On the Friday night, two days after Patsy signed the petition, a woman was raped in a car-park behind the country club. Both her eyes were blackened and her dress was ripped from neck to hem when she was found weeping and sprawled against her sports car by two women who had been playing badminton. Word spread like wildfire and within the hour, some of the young bloods – and older bulls too – from the rugby club, fired up on beer and whisky, decided the council meeting was too far away. They gathered at the south end of Newcombe's lea, where the bridle path skirted the trees, arriving in Land Rovers and an assortment of four-wheel drives, and charged in like Vikings They overturned one van, heedless of the screams of terror of the children inside as they were tumbled from panel to roof. A big, heavy-set and bearded man came racing up the footworn track, a screeching woman at his heels. He snatched up a thick branch from a pile of firewood and felled the best prop forward in the village with one blow to the forehead. Like the well-trained team that they were, the marauding pack crushed him to the ground under a press of pummeling and kicking bodies, breaking four ribs and dislocating both shoulders and leaving an imprint of a boot on the man's temple that would still show cleat marks three days later when he woke up in intensive care.

The screeching woman attacked with her fists and nails and was poleaxed by a vicious punch which smashed her nose. By this time, people were running and yelling in a mêlée of bodies, few of whom had any idea what was going on. Inside the toppled van, a fallen candle set fire to a piece of an old coat which dripped melted polyester onto a three-year-old boy and then spread the fire to a pile of newspapers stored for kindling. The child suffered agonising but not life-threatening burns on his shoulders, but as soon as the smoke began to pour from the smouldering newspapers, all four children in the van panicked and their terrified screams, though dulled behind the closed van doors, could still be heard at the other end of the camp.

The rugby scrum ploughed on, snapping guy ropes on the tents, and barging through the canvas benders and makeshift shacks, hitting at anything that moved.

Some of the men from the camp, now armed with heavy tent-pegs, smooth stones from the campfire circles and one powerful crossbow, came charging in from the opposite direction and met the locals head on. One of them, engaged in a single-handed tussle with a brute of a scrum-half who was still wearing his headband, heard the screams of the trapped children. The other man had him by the throat in such a powerful grip that if the frantic wails of the children hadn't given him the jolt of adrena-line, would have killed him. He twisted hard, breaking the grip and in one smooth movement he grabbed his assailant by the ears and drove his head forward so that his brow hit his opponent's nose with a fruity crunch. The traveller didn't wait to see the other man flop to the ground. He turned, ran for the van and jerked on the handle. Smoke billowed out, along with four small, coughing and crying children and in the sudden in-draught of air, the flames exploded into a fireball. The man hauled the kids away, dragging the two smallest by their arms, incidentally causing further damage to the terrified toddler whose skin simply peeled off in a handbreadth of agony. He rushed them to the trees just as the heat melted the fuel pipe. Oily flames simply flooded out in a tide of fire, covering the trampled grass in a searing river of heat. A nearby tent caught and went up like an instant bonfire. Somebody stumbled out of the back, hauling on a pair of jeans and raced for the trees.

A woman came running from between two vans, screaming for her babies. One of the rugby players grabbed at her and she lashed at him with a small pail she was carrying. The edge scored the man from eyebrow to chin and he roared in pain. Worse, the handle of the tea can broke with the force of it and the boiling contents drenched him from hairline to neck and the roar became a strangely high-pitched squeal. The woman didn't stop, but ran towards the burning van, now a blackened and contorted hulk in the middle of a ring of fire. She would have run into the flames if another man hadn't grabbed her by the waist, lifting her bodily off the ground and spinning her away from the inferno. 'It's all right, Meggy,' he bawled at her, voice battling against the roar of the fire. 'They're all safe. We got them out.'

The woman, her face yellowed in the light of the flames looked at him uncomprehendingly, eyes wide, mouth wider, then she collapsed into a dead faint in his arms.

Ten minutes later, the blue lights of police cars and fire engines came flashing along the bridle-path and their sirens, blaring into the night like a coven of howling witches, only added to the confusion. The leading fire tender got stuck in a mud-patch, which held up the action for another ten minutes, during which time two vans and half a dozen tents were reduced to ash and twisted metal. Three of the travellers ended up with broken bones, and four of the rugby team were laid out, one of whom had been hit so hard with a pickaxe handle that his left knee was shattered and his sporting career ended that night in John Newcombe's fallow pasture.

The battle of Cupstone Lea made the early morning news and caused an instant polarization between the shiftless and the unshiftable. Questions were asked in Parliament and the replies carried all the hallmarks of a two-tier society with statements on law and order, family values and the need to get back to basics without scrounging on the state. What seemed to have been forgotten was that people who had done no-one any harm had been attacked and savaged by people who wished them harm.

In the aftermath, statements were taken, though the police, aware of local feeling, pedalled slowly. The small boy in the van needed skin grafts on his shoulder and the puckered scar on his neck would leave him with a reminder for the rest of his life. The man with the scalded and blistered face made a show of macho bravery which was broadcast nationwide and claimed he was only out to protect women and children from rapists and murderers. His team-mate with the shattered knee whose promising international career had been abruptly ended, touched the nation's hearts as he tearfully protested at his fate at the hands of these hippies. The casualty department did a brisk trade until the following morning, during which time the press had picked up the story and descended on the scene in hordes.

The story got out about the rape at the country club and the first headlines in all but the left-wing press suggested that the rogues and vagabonds had deserved everything they got, until a young man from the rugby club, whose father was not only a leading businessman but a member of the same committee which had opted to force the travellers out, was arrested and charged with rape, battery and attempted buggery on the wife of a local architect who had decided to end their brief affair.

On the following night, Paul was working late. Patsy had let Peter stay up to watch a repeat of a space-fiction movie then sent him to bed with a cup of hot chocolate. The news came on and the Battle of Cupstone Lea, now its official journalese title, was top of the bill. The camera panned round the ashes of the tents and the tortured frames of burnt-out vans, a drizzle of rain adding to the picture of misery. Sullen, suspicious faces, looking dirty and grey in the weak daylight, stared into the lens. They did not look threatening now, these people, only stunned The cameraman skilfully focused and framed his pictures, capturing the sense of Auschwitz and the Russian gulags, people beaten down by their own society.

As it shifted from tent to tent, Patsy felt a strong pang of remorse at having signed the petition. She had wanted none of this, children hurt, men and woman injured. The camera zoomed in to a woman's face, her nose almost black and twisted to one side. One eye was completely closed over. The camera panned to the left and caught a pale, striking woman with a mass of dark curls. She stared into the lens and the light flickered in the green of her eyes.

'You'll get your reward for this,' the woman said in a soft and clear voice that was somehow loud and ferocious at the same time. Her eyes glinted and her black, arched eyebrows drew down. 'You'll see.'

Patsy felt as if the words were directed at herself and a ripple of unaccountable anxiety went through her. The woman's eyes held hers until the scene shifted back to the newscaster who briefly ran over the story for those pot-holers who might have missed it. He mentioned the rape incident which had sparked the attack and the subsequent blood-letting.

'But is there a place in today's society for these new age travellers?' he asked. 'Here to answer that question is Paul Thomson, spokesman for the gypsy encampment, a local solicitor who, some might say bravely, is the only villager prepared to fight their cause.'

Patsy jerked back in her seat. The picture flicked and there was Paul, hunkered down beside a fire, the light showing his best side to good advantage. A small, dark-haired boy was standing close and Paul had his arm around the child's shoulder.

'Somebody has to do it. To do the right thing, I mean,' he said, maybe a little unctuously. 'We have to realise what we've done here, and by we, I have to include myself for my blindness and ignorance. I want to make it up to these innocent people.'

He waved his hand in a sweeping gesture. 'Look at them. What have they done to anybody? Nothing. They only defended themselves against a vicious and brutal attack from people who should have known better. And why? Because they have no homes and because they have no money.

'All they want to do is travel in peace. They came here, not to stay forever, but only for a short while, to take part in a peaceful ceremony, one that dates back to ancient times, to celebrate the coming of spring. A harmless ceremony, one of peace and joy and hope for the future, and what did they find? No peace and no joy, and dammed little hope.'

He smiled deprecatingly. 'Sorry about the language, but I'm angry, dreadfully angry about the kind of society where people can be persecuted for their way of life. We've seen it before, in Hitler's Germany, in Stalin's Russia, and we haven't learned a thing.'

Paul turned and looked directly into the camera.

'Well, it's time somebody stood up for these harmless and peaceful people. They might not have designer clothes or fashionable haircuts, but they don't attack people in their beds and burn their children. They don't rape other people's wives. And they're going to stay here to carry out their celebration of spring. I have agreed to take their case, and I'll fight it in every court in the land, because we are a civilised nation, or at least we should be. I want to make sure that we are.'

He drew his brows down, just as the dark haired woman had done.

'Somebody has to pay for this barbarity, and people must learn that they cannot try to destroy a section of our community who are going about their lawful business. I have already made representations to the Crown Prosecution Service and if they fail to take action against those savage attackers, then I will be raising a private prosecution, plus claims for damages, against every one of them.'

He smiled, almost gloatingly, letting his words land.

'And those pillars of society needn't think that they have safety in numbers. I'm talking about the members of the county council, and in particular certain members of the Environment Committee, who made remarks and decisions deliberately calculated to incite the barbarity which was visited on this place. I have already taken out an injunction which prevents them implementing their decision, and I have started proceedings to sue them for damages on the basis of their incitement.'

The camera flipped back to the newsman.

'And the battle rages on in Cupstone Lea, but this time, the hippies and new age travellers who gathered here for the spring festival, have their own champion.'

Within a week, Paul was asked to resign from the golf club and the country club and he was told his membership of the Junior Chamber was no longer acceptable. He conceded with a shrug and a lazy, superior smile. Senior partner George Urquhart came in from the fairway, under heavy pressure from the hoar-headed pillars of the community and demanded to know what Paul was playing at. Paul showed him his contract and defied the old man to sack him. He was a better lawyer than the senior partner, but he also had his face on prime-time news.

On the night of the broadcast, he had come home, flushed and elated and with drink on his breath, but he wasn't drunk. When Patsy asked him about his change of heart he said he'd seen the light.

But he added something else.

'I can forget taking over the firm, that's for sure. But this case is going to make me big.' He gestured around the room, but the expansive wave of the hand indicated he meant the whole village. 'I've realised I don't want to be stuck in this backwater, playing jester to the zimmer brigade. There's a big world out there, and I'm having some of it.'

There was something about his manner that made Patsy look at him askance as he strutted round the room. As he passed her she smelled woodsmoke from his clothes, the warm scent of burnt pine, and over that, the other, musky fragrance that she couldn't identify, though it was familiar. He was animated now, his cheeks red and his eyes bright. It was as if he'd suddenly been converted.

The council postponed their decision. More travellers arrived in the days before the equinox and on the special night they lit huge bonfires on the edges of John Newcombe's field which lit the sky with deep red glow and sent sparks soaring into the night sky. The Chief Constable had drafted in forty extra men from outlying towns and they ringed the whole site, but mindful of the television cameras, lenses adjusted for dim light to capture the festival for the nation, they kept their distance.

Whether it was a re-enactment of the old Druid festival, no-one would ever know. Paul stayed out all night, and appeared on all the networks, including channels in the United States and on the continent which had picked up on the story.

'This is what all the fuss was about,' his voice-over broke in as a procession of white-robed men and women came slowly forward from the edge of the copse, each of them bearing a flaming torch. The flames made red and green after-images flicker ghostly on the television screens.

'A celebration of peace and prosperity, invoking more gentle days when people were at one with the earth, nurturing the land instead of despoiling it.'

Watching from her lounger, drinking a warm cup of tea, Patsy couldn't help but smile ruefully at the irony of it. Barely a month ago, he'd had nothing but contempt for the friends of the earth, the *save the lentil brigade* as he liked to call them. But now he was on television, casually but smartly dressed beside the shaven-headed crowd watching the procession. In the past few weeks she'd hardly seen anything of him. Sometimes she'd wake up when he came in. He'd lost some weight, and there was a nervous tension about him that was a complete change to the affected languor which was part of his previous image.

At their rare mealtimes together, he hardly spoke and it was as if he'd only the time to stoke up, barely tasting his food before he was gone. A strange unspoken truce existed in the village, but for some reason, Patsy seemed more aware of the travellers than she had been before. There were more of them around the place, more of the swarthy travellers, the real gypsy folk. When she passed them by, she was aware of their eyes upon her, men and women, could sense them staring at the children, but instinctively she'd known it would have been a mistake to mention it to Paul. Now he was on television as the cameras followed the procession and she was glad that it would soon be over. The gypsies would pack up and move on and the village would return to normal and maybe Paul would have some time for the children. Maybe he would have more time for her too. They hadn't had sex in almost six weeks.

On screen the dark-haired woman led the procession from the trees, walking so slowly in the long robe that she seemed to glide. The flickering torch reflected bright in her eyes and on the glossy tangles that tumbled over her shoulders and onto her breasts. She looked beautiful in the firelight, a dark goddess of the trees. Patsy recognised her immediately and sat up straight, her senses somehow alert and straining. There was something about the woman that had set off a reaction inside her. The teacup rattled in its saucer and she found her hand was shaking and her heart was thudding against her ribs.

'It's an ancient ceremony,' Paul explained as the procession reached the broad ring of stones, entered the gap between two of the monoliths and moved forward to the cupstone, a massive flat slab of rock set on three boulders, positioned right in the centre. 'The rite of spring, welcoming the true new year and a new age.'

His voice dropped to a whisper. 'For this they were beaten and bludgeoned and burned.'

On screen the cymbals shimmered sound and tambourines jangled and a voice in the centre of the ring began to chant. The words were in a language Patsy had never heard before, rising clear into the night sky, resonant and strangely powerful. All the music stopped and the camera zoomed in to catch the woman's face. She raised her head and stared into the lens and Patsy felt the eyes bore into her own.

The woman smiled, wide and feral, and then the press of bodies surrounded her. As soon as the eyes were gone, Patsy felt as if she'd been somehow released. Her heart still thudded against her ribs.

'Get a grip of yourself,' she said aloud in the empty room, yet the image stayed with her as if she'd been singled out. On screen the cowled figures were huddled over the Cupstone and everything went quiet. A small bleating noise was the only sound and for a moment Patsy thought it must have been a small child. Then music started again, drowning it out.

Patsy's teacup seemed to leap out of the saucer of its own volition. It landed on the tiled table and smashed into shards.

That night she couldn't get to sleep. Lying alone in the dark, waiting for Paul to come home, she saw those eyes glaring out, riveting her with their wild knowledge and strange anger. In the shadows of the night she saw the press of bodies and the cowled figures huddled over the Cupstone and heard the bleating sound again, and it tugged and twitched at the underside of her mind. Finally she drifted into a sleep in which she was part of the procession, walking past Paul who turned his head away from her as if he didn't recognise her. He was standing with the children, holding their hands and she tried to call out to him but the words wouldn't come. She tried to reach out, but the crowd of figures swept her along until she was in the centre of the stones, surrounded by the cloaks. The bleating noise was loud in here, in this ring of silence. One by one the circle of figures pulled back their cowls and she saw they were all dark haired and fierce eyed, men and women, all of them looking at her, smiling without humour, almost hungrily. She tried to get way, get out of the ring, but they pressed closer, forcing her backwards until she was pressed against a hard edge. She turned and the bleating sound soared to a high crescendo, and she reached down to the spring lamb shivering on the Cupstone, legs bound in golden ropes. She reached down to comfort the terrified animal and she blinked back a tear, and when her eyes cleared it was not a lamb.

Judith was lying spread-eagled on the stone, arms and legs pinioned by braided sparkling ropes and her whole body shivering violently. Patsy blinked again and saw the gash running from her neck to her pelvis, a great red chasm in which purple-slicked organs still writhed. Her daughter's legs twitched helplessly and her eyes stared out at her mother and the little bleating noise died away with the slowing movement. Patsy's mouth was opened in a frantic scream as she tried to get to her daughter, tried to reach the red and bloodied scrap on the stone. She blinked again and something leaning over the flat stone pushed itself upwards and she heard the buzzing of flies and a dreadful thing, misshapen and twisted, a grey and scaled monster raised its head and looked into her eyes and the sick orange light reflected the candles of the worshippers.

It made a sickening gulping sound and blood *her daughter's blood* dripped down from its toadlike mouth. A roiling cloud of black flies came buzzing up from the jagged rent and Patsy's heart stopped dead in her chest.

Patssseee . . . it slobbered, and she woke with a scream locked in her throat and the smell of blood thick in her nostrils and she made it to the bathroom just in time to be sick.

5

The glow in the sky was stronger now, like the flickering reflections of the bonfires in the mist that had swirled around the copse at the Cupstone, an eerie glimmer of distant heat. She could smell fumes on the air, the kind that would catch in the throat in one of the long traffic jams on the motorway closer to home. The cones flickered in peripheral vision, catching the light of the full beams as she kept to the far left, tyres blagging down on the cat's eyes flashing as green and piercing as witches' eyes. Green as Kerron Vaunche's eyes. That bitch. That *witch*.

Those eyes had haunted her for nearly three years.

Patsy drove on, glancing every now and again in the mirror, wary of another truck hauling up silently behind her, even more afraid of signs of real pursuit. The first one had been frightening enough, a black and roaring shape just beside her on the stormy road. The second one could have killed her, and she was convinced the driver had tried to. Both of them had sped on, trailing orange light. She couldn't remember seeing a number plate on either of them, but at the time she'd been so startled all she could think of was keeping the car on the road. She had even thought that there might only have been one lorry, an insane driver playing cat and mouse with her, the way it had done on that old movie about a demented trucker duelling with a terrified driver. She dismissed the notion for she'd carried on straight along the road and as far as she could recall there had been nowhere the truck could have turned and doubled back. She was sure of that.

A quarter of a mile along, the cones narrowed yet again and another signed loomed into view. The beams picked out the word. *DIVERSION*. A few yards beyond it stood a white triangle, bordered in red bearing a single bold black exclamation mark, a calligraphic jolt.

Judith whimpered behind her and Patsy heard Peter whisper again. She felt angry tears smart in her eyes.

They'd been stolen from her and now she had them back. She hadn't even had time to cuddle her daughter, hug her son. It had happened too quickly. Even though it was only a few hours in the past, the images and scenes were still jumbled in her mind. She'd been terrified the whole time, with only her desperate need battling on her side. She shoved the images away from her, trying to concentrate on the road.

Another look in the mirror, searching for headlamps and sensing the pursuit, and all the time expecting to see a convoy come racing round the bend, headlamps reaching for her, expecting the madness to start again and for the dreadful dream to become a reality. But there was nothing. She passed a black clump of trees whose straggly fronds reached out for the road, shivered by the wind. Somewhere distant, heavy thunder rolled like muffled drums. Another overpass, a narrow bridge built for pedestrians arched across the road and hope flared. A pedestrian bridge meant there were people, and people meant houses and safety. As long as she could lose herself among people, at least until she was beyond the full moon and that dreadful midwinter day, they'd be safe, safe from Paul and his madness, safe from Kerron Vaunche and her evil.

Her eyes scanned the road ahead, ignoring the poisonous flicker of the hazard lights, still searching for a telephone. She checked her mile counter. They'd travelled two miles since the first big sign and the start of the traffic cones and still there was no emergency telephone to be seen. Another clump of trees drew near and flashed past and just at the edge, something big and black, too big to be a crow, swept out of the covert and winged ponderously along the road. The beams reflected in its eye as it swerved into the path of the car, great wings flapping like the loose tarpaulin on the truck. She touched the brakes, scared to skid, hemmed in by the bollards, when the bird, whatever it was, twisted again. The offside headlamp missed it by an inch and the airshock pushed it to the side. Patsy's heart leapt again, but she kept going straight ahead. Something moved on the other side of the glass and her eyes snapped to the right. The shape was still flapping just beside the car. One wing clattered against the roof and scraped down the window. A triangular head turned and a mouth opened.

Not a bird.

She heard the words in her head. The mouth (*she couldn't see a beak*) gaped in a huge yawn. Something stabbed out, a barbed tongue, yellow and sharp. The thing screeched hoarsely. Behind her Judith yelped in fright. Patsy felt the hairs on the nape of her neck crawl. Something clawed down the side of the car and then the thing was gone.

'Jees . . .' Patsy breathed, heart thudding hard on her ribs.

'What was that, mum?' Peter asked, more in wonder than any fear. She heard the chink as he unsnapped the seat-belt catch.

'Nothing,' she lied again. 'Just sit down and get strapped in.'

'Wow, it was an eagle, I bet,' Peter cried. 'It was huge. Did you see it?' He clambered to his knees and held on to the back of the seat. She could see her son's head, just a silhouette framed by the rear window.

'It's still flying . . . I thought you'd hit it.'

Patsy glanced in the wing mirror. The black shape was still in the air, heavy wings labouring in slow swoops, not far behind. It was no eagle. The narrow head and the huge gape in the window was like no bird she'd ever seen, she knew, but she tried to tell herself it must have been some kind of bird. The rain and condensation had fogged the glass, and it was dark there. She'd only had a brief glimpse of it. She looked again in the mirror, trying to see what kind of bird it was. It had to be a bird. Nothing else as big as that could fly. The dark shape swooped along, close to the road. Something drooped from the underside, and she assumed it was legs, though it was difficult to see.

'Come on, Peter, sit down and get your belt on,' she ordered. He was still kneeling on his seat, staring out of the back.

'It's still coming,' he said, excitedly. 'Look at the size of that thing.'

Patsy took her eyes off the road ahead and glanced into the wing mirror. It was coming. It was coming fast, nearer now that it had been the last time, and she felt the hairs prickle on her neck again. She'd scared crows on the road before, scattering them in a flutter of black as they pecked at the flattened kills. They hopped or flew off, noisily protesting, but they always fled. The black shape was getting closer, shadowed wings sweeping

51

the air, almost scraping the road. The reflection of the car's tail-light reflected in an eye.

It was coming after them. As soon as she thought it, Patsy's belly clenched again and a cold ripple shuddered down the length of her spine.

What's happening to us?

It was as if she'd grabbed her children and driven into a nightmare. The red eye glinted from the mirror, just a pinprick in the darkness. Over the sound of the engine and the hiss of the tyres, she could hear the slow, measured *whoop* as the wings beat the air. The red spot never blinked off and she sensed the bird glaring at her. She couldn't pull her gaze from the wing mirror and for a second the baleful glint of light held her eyes, froze her still.

Then the offside wheel hit one of the cones. The plastic spike bent in towards the wing and the tread of the tyre flicked the bollard right up into the air with a hollow slapping sound. The noise released Patsy from the expanding red dot of light. She twisted her head just in time to see the nose of the car aim straight for the diagonal dragon's teeth barrier and instinctively she jerked on the wheel. In the back, the sudden swerve threw Peter off balance and he tumbled into the well behind the driver's seat.

'Did you see that?' he yelled, still excited.

'Oh sit down, will you?' Patsy snapped from a mouth that had gone dry. 'And get strapped in Peter, will you do that, please. Now.'

She heard the buckle snap closed.

'Nearly knocked it out of the air. That plastic thing went right up and just about killed it.'

'What?' Patsy's foot had gone to the floor and the car had accelerated, throwing them all back against their seats.

'The cone. It bounced up and nearly hit the bird. It's gone now.'

His mother jerked a look over her shoulder. Peter's eyes were wide with excitement. 'You could have killed it,' he declared.

The red glint in the eye still hovered in Patsy's mind. Whatever it was, eagle or not, she wished she *had* killed it. She wished she'd hit it the first time and knocked it fluttering to the roadside rather than have gone through that dreadful gut-fear of the unnatural. Big birds didn't fly along roads like this and big birds never chased cars.

Right on the heels of that thought came another.

Where is this place?

There was something wrong with this road, wrong with this night. Right from the moment she'd grabbed for Judith outside the gates of Broadford House, when she should have been pumped up with elation and triumph, things had started to go wrong. It was as if she herself had taken a wrong turn and got herself lost. Things were happening here and they were just not right.

The realisation came to her again, hard, like a low blow in the belly. She had taken her children out of one danger and brought them right into another. They were completely alone on this strange road, a mother and two children racing for home in the middle of the night storm, and she did not know where in the world she was.

Kerron Vaunche. That *witch*. She'd cursed them.

The lightning flickered distant and through a break in the clouds, a curve of the moon showed dull orange, as if it too was reflecting the glow of a smouldering fire. She kept her foot down on the accelerator and pushed the car up past seventy as the realisation began to grow in her. She had to get off this road, because there was something badly wrong with this place.

Half an hour later, she had passed nothing, no sign, no bridge and no telephone. The night wore on and the needle slowly edged towards the red mark on the fuel gauge.

Sometime in the night, Judith whimpered again, and Peter snorted, turning in his sleep.

'It's all right, baby,' Patsy soothed. 'Just go to sleep.'

The little girl moaned softly and then began to speak, the way children do when they're less than half awake. It was just a jumble of words, but there was something about the sound, something incomprehensible and foreign that reminded her of Kerron Vaunche, and the hot anger came welling up like heartburn.

Paul had staved off the eviction beyond the night of the equinox in March when Patsy had awoken with the horror of the dream still twisting in her vision. He'd fought the council and used his new-found television skills to their best advantage, always appearing to be the caring crusader, a gentle but strong advocate of reason. His old clients fell away, as did their friends. At school, Peter was getting a rough time, because as March gave way to April and then to the summer-warmth of May, everyone was fed up with the stalemate, with the national media focus, and most of all with the travellers themselves.

They had trickled into the village in twos and threes throughout the late spring and by June, the whole of Newcome's field was packed with tents and old buses and converted, obsolete ambulances. Farmers lost sheep and cattle, though nothing could be pinned on the hippies. By mid-June, there were more travellers than there were villagers. Children were forbidden to play near the Cupstone lea and even as the nights grew lighter, mothers still formed watch groups and drove their children from one house to another.

Paul seemed to relish the hate mail and the threatening telephone calls, as if they defined the value of what he was doing. He certainly never missed a chance to mention the price he was paying for *doing the right thing*.

Patsy felt more and more besieged. Her friends, who had mostly been the wives of Paul's friends, had stopped calling round for afternoon coffee. They would cross to the other side of the street when she went down to the shops. Their children stopped inviting Peter and Judith to birthday parties.

More and more isolated, she had tried to explain her feelings to Paul, but his work had taken precedence over everything else. He worked long and late, sometimes not coming home until the small hours, and sometimes not coming home at all. He was distant and preoccupied, and never had time to play football in the back garden with Peter, or even to read Judith a bedtime story as he always had since she was old enough to understand the words.

But he was thriving on all of it. He was more animated than he had been in quite a while, and on the rare occasions he talked about his campaign, he was like a new convert.

'This is what I've been waiting for. This is what it's all about, don't you see?' he told her when she'd explained her fears over the sick letters and the rasping telephone calls that came in the afternoons when she was home alone.

'They only persecute because they will lose, and we'll win. It's shown me the road I want to go. No more small-time conveyancing and trust deeds. Any two-bit lawyer can do that. I'm meant for better things, and by God I'll have them.'

'But I'm scared for the children too,' Patsy had protested. 'Peter's been getting such a hard time at school. People are taking it out on him.'

'That'll toughen him up. He'll learn that it's best to fight and hit back. It'll make a man of him. And what's a couple of telephone calls and loony letters? Just as long as you don't let your weakness affect them. I wouldn't like that.'

She had never mentioned it again, but in the days running up to midsummer, she rarely had the chance. In hindsight, once again wonderfully clear, she could see how Paul had changed, though she had been unable to see it then. Sometimes, she remembered, on the times when he'd actually spent time at home, he'd sit at the table with a blank, distant expression as if his mind was far away.

Peter noticed something. He wondered why his dad was never at home, why he wouldn't come and play football or go fishing. Once or twice, perceptively, he'd asked if his father was ill and Patsy had shushed him, telling him not to be silly.

She had even squashed her own instincts, shut away her fears because she thought those changes had been in herself. In the mornings she'd come awake, hauling for breath, pinioned on the spike of a nightmare in which a red and snarling moon blazed down upon her and hands reached to drag her children into the shadows. In the mornings she'd wake up, washed out and hollow and exhausted. The dreams haunted her and she couldn't shake them, and for the first time she wondered if she was having a breakdown.

One night she'd woken again, panting for air and lacquered with perspiration, and Judith had been standing beside her, tears streaming down her face. She'd pulled her daughter towards her and caught a glimpse of them both in the bedside mirror, and in the aftermath of the dream she thought she saw Judith's face ripple and turn to parchment and she felt fear that she might really be cracking up.

In the second week in June the number of travellers almost doubled. They poured into the village on every road, in their clapped out trailers and horse-drawn caravans. The trickle in the preceding months became a flood until the encampment spilled on to John Newcombe's turnip field. He'd become such a hate figure in the area that he'd moved away to a cousin's farm in Devon and continued to drink as much of the now vast rental he was getting for the use of his land. Up at the coppice at the edge of his land, the real gypsies had set up their separate encampment, away from the tattered vans and squats of the new age travellers. There were more of them now, those strange, dark people who spoke in guttural accents and walked as if they owned the whole world. There was a strange arrogance about them that unnerved Patsy. She'd be walking Judith to play-school and she'd sense something and turn to see one of them, maybe a man sitting on the stump of the old tree at the end of the road, regarding her with those black and flashing eyes, as if appraising her like a piece of livestock. Once, she was in the garden helping Judith colour in a painting book when she felt the touch again and whirled round to see a movement in the birch thicket beyond the little stream, and she knew that somebody had been watching them both. It seemed to her that everywhere she went she felt eyes upon her and upon her daughter. She tried to shuck it off, telling herself she was becoming paranoid, but the feeling persisted, growing stronger as the summer swelled. She admitted to herself that she wanted them gone.

In June, the news reports carried stories about the hippie migrations. There was another riot at Stonehenge when police banned access to within a mile of the ancient stones, but all over the country, new age travellers, gypsies and tinkers were setting up camp at other ancient sites. The insular population on Lewis appealed to the Secretary of State when thousands of the roving folk set up their tents at the standing stones of Callanish. On Scotland's west coast, the convoy of battered buses and trailers blocked the scenic Oban road for four days and almost led to warfare with haulage companies and locals alike. All over the country, hordes of the unwashed and tattered appeared as if by magic at the old Druidic sites.

On midsummer the television cameras were back at John Newcombe's field where the travellers had lit immense fires and danced and sang among the stones beneath a velvet sky on the longest day of the year. The media crews never got within a hundred yards of the ringstones, pushed back by the press of bodies which cut the view to the Cupstone. It was a hot, oppressive night, sticky and humid and tense with the expectation of thunder. The cameras caught the flickering motion as the robed figures came through the avenue of bonfires. The crowd parted just enough to let them through. It was impossible to make out individuals in the red glow. One cameraman tried to follow the procession inside but the crowd closed again and the figures vanished.

From the cottage, Patsy could hear the clash of cymbals and the steady heartbeat of Celtic *lambeg* drums. The air was thick and heavy as she lay on top of the bed, watching the scene on the little portable, drinking a cool lemonade. There was little to be seen, but there was a powerful sense of expectancy in the air. Paul was up there somewhere and she expected he'd be home late, his work for the travellers done. As before, the music stopped suddenly and a hush fell over the crowd. Through the open window she heard the voices fade, giving her an odd stereo effect.

A lone voice, a woman's voice began to chant, high and clear and musical. The words were incomprehensible, spinning notes on the still air. They continued without a break for five minutes or more and then when they stopped, the silence was so profound it was uncanny. Even the bonfires seemed to stop crackling.

A man's voice, strong and deep, somehow familiar, replied in a fast-chanted string of words.

Something bleated, like a baby goat, maybe a lamb, though it sounded weirdly human. The woman cried out. The little sound cut off again and the crowd roared like thunder. The whole night erupted in sound and fire. On screen the cameras were blinded and the new-lit torches left green and red squiggles as the sensors tried to compensate for overload.

A shiver of cold rippled through Patsy as the recollection of the dreadful nightmare of the spring festival came instantly to mind. Abruptly she raised the zapper and switched the scene off. Outside the cottage, the smell of smoke and insence came drifting down from the Cupstone Lea and on the slow eddy of air she could smell the coppery scent of blood. She closed the window and lay down in the flickering gloom and wondered what had bleated in the centre of the stones.

Sometime after midnight the thunder came rolling in, but the rain held back. Patsy fell asleep after tossing and turning until the early hours and she dreamed dreadful visions where she saw Paul come through the standing stones, dragging Judith behind him, his face rotted away like a leper. On his back, a scaly and warted thing hunched like a gargoyle, orange-eyed and toad-mouthed, and in this dream she recognised the monster from the first nightmare. Paul came stumbling out and his skin was peeling from his face, showing grey stripes of dead meat on his jawline, and as she watched she saw the contagion spread to her daughter, mottled blotches spreading down her thin arm, creeping up towards her bonny face and turning her eyes a sickly green.

Patsy woke up so dreadfully afraid that she did not stop shaking for half an hour, and she never got to sleep again that night.

In the morning, the breakfast news showed some of the scenes from around the country, focusing on the scuffles at Stonehenge mainly, but then rounding up with the events at the Cupstone Lea, rehashing some of the earlier events, and once again showing Paul as the travelling people's champion. A different camera closer to the stones had caught the procession coming towards it before the cameraman was jostled away. Despite her tiredness and the hollow numbness left by the appalling dream, Patsy watched the scene while she sipped her coffee. The robed and cowled gypsies, like ghostly monks, came down the avenue of watchers. One of them raised his head a little, giving her a glimpse of the eyes and for a moment she thought she recognised Paul. She shook her head. It must have been a trick of the light.

The dream came back to her of the awful leprous *dead* look he'd worn, stumbling between the stones, and she squirmed away from the memory.

The press of bodies excluded the television cameras from the ceremonies at the centre of the ringstones, which led to speculation that animals were being sacrificed, and garrulous newscasters, with no footage to comment on, raised the question of a return to pagan ways, to witchcraft and demon worship. Patsy listened to the commentary and thought of the dark eyes of the real travelling folk and realised she could imagine them getting involved in black ceremonies in the depths of the forest, and again she was glad that the midsummer was over. Things would settle down now. They could get back to being a family again.

That was what she hoped, but even as the thought came, something made her shiver inside. *Somebody just walked over my grave*, she thought with sudden bleakness.

That morning, as if by black magic, as if they had walked into the ring of stones and disappeared to another world, the travellers were gone. They vanished from the ancient stone circles all round Britain, leaving only the smouldering ashes of their bonfires, and vast mounds of litter, rusting cans and broken bottles.

At the Cupstone, in the early morning mist, a lone cameraman took a picture of a congealing pool of blood in the hollow in the centrestone of the round. An early fall of rain washed it away before it could be ascertained what kind of blood it might have been. There was no-one around to talk about the midsummer ceremony. The travellers had gone, men, women, children, battered carts and all.

And Paul Thomson had gone with them.

He had come home at dawn, face grimed and dusty, smelling of the woodsmoke of the bonfires. He was wearing a pair of cord trousers that were stained at the knees and there were two buttons missing from his shirt. The children were still asleep, and Patsy was still sitting at the table, eyes gritty, head in her hands. Outside a blackbird sang a shrill cascade of notes in the garden while further off, a cockerel welcomed the day.

'Where have you been?' she asked, numbly. The dream was still heavy on her and the shivery sensation of apprehension, of someone *walking over her grave*, had left her somehow off balance.

'Busy.' Paul grunted, not even looking at her. He went through to the bedroom and she followed him. In the half-light with the curtains drawn, her mind played a trick on her, overlaying the dream Paul with the real one, making the shadows on his face seem like the cracked and peeling skin of the leprous thing in her nightmare.

'What time is it?'

'Time to get started,' Paul said. 'The kids still in bed?'

She nodded, still recoiling from the scary mental conjunction. He sat heavily on the edge of the bed, making it creak. The smell of musty woodsmoke was strong, and overlaid with the scent of sweat and the green fragrance of crushed grass.

'I thought you'd have come home earlier,' she said, not forcefully, but with a hint of complaint. *I've been all alone with my nightmares and I needed someone to hold me.*

'Had things to do. People to see.'

'Were you up at the bonfires?'

This time he nodded. 'Magnificent. It's a different world out there. Full of life.'

Paul pulled his shirt off from the bottom, hauling it over his head. His back was towards her, bent as he lowered his head. The shirt dragged over the ridge of his spine, then fell free, and Patsy's mouth fell open. Across his shoulders, slanting down in parallel lines, thick red weals were risen on his skin.

Still not completely awake, the significance didn't quite register. 'What on earth happened to you?' she asked innocently. 'Have you been in a fight?'

He turned. 'Of course not. What makes you think a stupid thing like that?'

She started to point, but he saw her eyes and ran his hand underneath his armpit and over his kin. The welts were sticking out like furrows on a field.

'Must have been branches,' he said quickly, looking away from her. 'It was dark up in those trees last night. There's brambles and holly and all sorts.'

The light was just beginning to dawn on her. She sat on the bed, one sleeve in the dressing gown. Paul had stood up, turned away from the mirror, craning his neck to see the marks on his back. On the side of his neck, two unmistakable purple marks stood out like tattoos.

He turned back to face her, saw the dumbstruck hurt on her face, and instinctively went on the attack.

'Oh, what's the matter with you?' he demanded angrily.

'You've been seeing someone else,' she said, almost in a whisper.

'I've been seeing hundreds of folk. Thousands of them.'

'I mean another woman. You've been with another woman.'

'What if I have?' he said, not even pretending. 'What's it got to do with you?'

She sat back as if she'd been slapped. The purple marks on his neck were close together under his jaw, the same shape as eye sockets in a skull.

'But I'm your wife,' Patsy said, voice trembling, now suddenly nauseous. She felt her stomach swoop and clench and she swallowed hard, hearing her throat click with the effort. The thought of him with another woman, a woman who would claw at him and suck at him out in the open air was such a vast and terrible concept, it felt as if she'd been told she'd got terminal cancer, or that one of the children had a brain tumour. The force of it was like a punch in the belly. *He hasn't slept with me in months!*

'Oh really?' he said, not a question, just a statement of cold disdain.

'Yes, really,' she reacted. 'I'm your wife, damn you.' The first surge of anger swelled, not fierce, not vicious. Like the first gust in a gathering squall.

'For all the good that's done me,' he snorted, mouth turned down. 'What support have you given me, eh? When the whole village was against me, did you stand up to be counted? Even before that, were you any good for my career? Have you ever been?'

'What do you mean?'

'I mean you haven't done a damned thing to improve yourself. All you've done is stay at home and cook meals and make beds, while I've had to go out there and fight to get on.'

'But it was you who wanted me to give up my career,' she protested. He'd done it again, jinked away from the subject, made her falter.

'What career? Sociology? That's just playing at it. I should

61

never have married you in the first place. All you've ever been is a hindrance.'

'How can you say that? You loved me. We've got the children. We've got this place.'

'Loved you . . .?'

'Wait a minute,' Patsy said, holding her hand up to forestall him. Something he said had snagged in her mind. 'What do you mean time to get started?'

He looked at her, puzzled, just for a second. Sudden and real alarm was beginning to jitter in her mind.

'I mean time to get started. A new start.'

He crossed to the built-in mirrored wardrobe, dressed only in his cord trousers. As he moved the muscles on his back rippled the raised marks like stripes on a tiger. He opened the doors with a quick snatch and hauled out the bag he used when he went to the country club to play squash with the other young professionals. This he threw casually on the bed. He reached in again and brought out two of his lightweight shirts, the ones he'd worn on the odd day the previous summer when they'd taken the children on a picnic.

'A new start on what?' she asked, now suddenly scared.

'What do you think,' he replied dryly. 'A new start in my life. I'm leaving.'

Patsy froze, all except her hands which had started to tremble. Her breath backed up in her throat and the room seemed to spin around her. Her mouth opened, closed again, opened, the the word came out.

'Leaving?'

'That's what I said.'

'But you can't. What about me? What about Peter and Judith?'

'They'll be fine. I wouldn't see them starve.'

Her brain went into overdrive. Thoughts tumbled and jangled uncohesively in her mind. She tried to quiet them, tried to think.

'Is it this woman?' she blurted. 'Are you leaving me for her?'

He stood up straight and looked her in the eye, gripping his chin with the tips of his fingers as if debating.

'I'm leaving because there is more out there.' His hands trailed down his jaw, fingered the purple marks and his eyes unfocussed just enough to let her know he was remembering.

'Who is she?' she demanded.

'That's none of your business.'

'How dare you,' she almost yelled. 'It *is* my business. I'm your wife you rotten (*Leper!*) dirty *bastard*.'

'Keep your voice down,' he said slowly, between his teeth. 'You'll wake the children.'

'Oh, you'd prefer them to wake up later and find you've gone with your floozy, is that it?'

He crossed to her in three steps, dark eyes flashing. 'You've got a nerve. She's more of a woman than you've ever been. More than you'll ever be.' The words cut into her heart, but instead of making her quail, they had the opposite effect.

'And she'll give you children, will she?' The anger was beginning to swell stronger now, trying to breach all the little walls and dykes he'd built up in her over the years. She was trying to think of the woman, trying to picture her. He had hardly talked about his work since March, hardly talked about anything. She'd heard more about it on the television newscasts.

Television. The picture came back to her in a flash. It had been way back in the springtime, just after the night when he'd complained about those very travellers he'd suddenly sworn to defend. He'd gone out and stayed late and when he'd come home, there had been the same scent of woodsmoke on him. She remembered the camera panning across the group of tinkers, dirty children, sullen-eyed women. That had been the night when she'd heard Paul on television, his measured tones explaining the rights of the people who had fallen through the safety net of society. The camera had swung on and captured the tumbling cascade of black hair and the high cheekbones of the woman who stared straight into the lens without blinking. The light of the fire had glinted in her eye, making her look fierce and predatory. In that instant of recollection, Patsy knew, on an instinctive level.

He must have been sleeping with her for months.

'She was on television, I saw her,' she said, forcing the words to sound calm. She remembered the high, clear chanting and again, she knew with that certainty of perception.

He raised his eyebrows, still standing close.

'The dark haired one. That tinker woman.'

'She's not a tinker.'

'She's a cheap, dirty whore, that's what she is.'

He leaned towards her, hand automatically raising to shoulder level. On the inside of his arm, she saw a curved red line, a serpentine sliver of red, fresh, but already beginning to heal. A small drip of blood oozed out as the muscle flexed underneath.

'And you've been rolling on the ground with her like an animal.' The nausea rolled in her stomach again. 'Like rutting pigs.'

His hand flashed down, but instead of flinching, she grabbed him by the wrist. The shock of the blow shivered right up to her shoulder, but she had the strength of anger. His eyes widened in surprise. It was the first time she'd ever defended herself against him. The retaining walls were beginning to crumble under the storm of her anger.

'Don't you dare hit me ever again,' she hissed, raising herself off the bed, forcing him back. He was so astonished he stepped backwards.

'I'm not letting you leave here with that tinker whore. Not while these two children need a father.' She shoved his arm away and bent to the tote-bag, snatched it from the bed and stormed over to the wardrobe. She slung it inside and slammed the door.

'What good will that do you?' he asked.

'You can forget about leaving,' she said, hot tears now blurting from her eyes. 'You can't do it to them.'

'It's done. They'll be fine.'

'And what about me?'

'What about you?'

'I'm a woman. Can't you see that? I don't know what she's done, but she's got your mind twisted. She's nothing but an unwashed hippie tramp.'

'No, she's not,' Paul said in a very quiet voice. 'She's free, a completely free spirit. She's taught me so much and there's more to learn. She taught me that there's more to life than this, more than a small-town lawyer's job. She can achieve anything, and so can I.'

'It's just sex, isn't it?'

He laughed. It was a harsh, shocking sound.

'No, it's not just sex. It's more than that. But now that you mention it, she's taught me a few things I never knew before.'

A sharp pain twisted under Patsy's ribs, and she put her hands to her ears. 'I don't want to hear it,' she screamed.

'You asked me, and I told you,' Paul replied in feigned hurt.

'I don't want to know about you *screwing* with that bitch,' she said before she turned and stormed out of their room. At the end of the hallway, Peter's door opened and he poked his head out.

'What's wrong, mum?' he asked, hair tousled, face puzzled.

'Just go back to bed,' she snapped. The boy looked at her blankly. 'I mean *now*,' she bawled. His head ducked back inside and the door shut with a bang.

In the kitchen, she went through the motions of filling the kettle. Her hands were still shaking and she dropped a cup which landed on the table, bounced, hit the floor and shattered into small pieces, the second one gone from the set. She bent down to scrape the shards together, wondering what on earth she was doing. It was as if her whole life was falling apart and all she could think of was picking up pieces of broken crockery. Paul didn't stay long in the bedroom. He came through, now dressed in his casual jerkin, the one she'd bought him for his birthday, and a new pair of jeans. The bag bulged. He had washed his face and hands, but the smell of woodsmoke told her he hadn't bothered to shower.

'Listen, Paul,' she pleaded. 'Please.' She bit down on the anger and the hurt, forced down the shame of her blank capitulation. 'Don't do this to us.'

'I have to,' he said, dumping the bag on the table. 'It can't be stopped now.'

'But why?' she wailed.

'Because I can't be held back any more.'

'Is that what *she* told you?' Already the word had taken on capital letters in her mind. *SHE*.

He nodded, almost sympathetically. More patronisingly.

'Can't we start again? The children need you. I need you. Please don't do this to us.' She pulled him by the elbows, but he remained stiff and unyielding, almost as if she repulsed him. 'Don't you realise, I love you?'

65

He stared her straight in the eye. 'You don't even know what the word means,' he snorted, then turned, opened the door and was gone.

She slowly subsided to the wooden seat at the breakfast table, tears streaming down her face, one hand held out in silent appeal. She was still like that when Judith came padding into the kitchen in bare feet and pushed up beside her. She looked up and saw her mother's tears, and she too began to cry in uncomprehending, innocent sympathy.

6

She put her foot down, trying to clear her mind of the memories clamouring for attention and tried to concentrate on going forward.

Peter had calmed down after the excitement of the huge bird that had lunged at the car but she could sense his restlessness, though even in the mirror he was just a silhouette in the shadows of the back seat. She wished she'd brought some sweets, even a flask of soup, but in her anticipation of the encounter at the old house, she'd made no preparations at all.

The traffic cones still stuttered by in a continuous flicker, forcing the car to keep to the inside lane. Ahead, just out of the reach of the full beams, a shape began to resolve through the drizzly rain. She leaned forward again, for the tenth or fifteenth time since she'd come on this road, wiped the screen with the cuff of her sleeve, and peered out. It was a motorway sign.

Gradually the big green square drew closer and the white letters reflected the light: *JUNCTION 13.*

She let out a heavy sigh. Finally there was a ramp to get off this single lane and away from this eerie and frightening road. The sign flicked past and she edged closer to the hard shoulder. A half a mile further on, the cones narrowed in and she found she had no choice anyway for the road ahead was blocked by the bollards and she was forced to steer up the slip road. Ahead of her, tall lamps on slender poles swayed in the wind while they shed light on the junction. She reached a short level plateau and sat high in the seat to look over the crash barriers bracketing the ramp. In the distance, on the now-blocked road she'd been approaching, she could see the winking fires and the oily smoke billowing up into the night air.

Patsy shuddered, recalling the growled description. *A real mess.* In her mind she could imagine the screams of people trapped in cars while flames licked about them, blistering the paint, rolling in rivers as petrol and oil spread across the road. The low cloud over the scene was tinged a dull pink from the flames. Patsy pulled her eyes away and drove on the flat until she reached the point where the road dipped in a long curving run to merge with another main route. She slowed, looking for a place to stop, but there was no sign of a lay-by, no sign of any other traffic. She steered onto the road, this one wider than the first. Ahead, the lights reflected from the cat's-eyes which glared back at her. Behind her Judith moaned and then coughed harshly. Patsy tried to ignore it and drove on.

A mile or so further on there was another slope, curving to the right this time. The car soared upwards and she had to change down a gear to keep up speed. From the vantage point she could see other roads in the distance, a complex merger of circles and slipways, and she let out another sigh.

'Thank God for that,' Patsy whispered to herself. A real junction meant she must be close to a city. It was far ahead in the distance, but if she could see it, then it couldn't be too far, not more than an hour or so. She gunned the engine again and pressed on for another two miles on the straight, staying alert for any signs, and keeping a cautious eye on her rear-view mirror. Despite her apprehension, she saw no sign of pursuit, but the tension did not diminish. The sense of threat trailed like cold fingers up and down her spine.

After three miles she saw the telephone box, and if she'd been looking in the wing-mirror for a second she'd have missed it. As it was, it took her a hundred yards to bring the car to a stop.

'Whassat?' Peter asked groggily from behind.

'There's a phone,' Patsy told him. 'We can find out where we are.'

Inside, she could feel the hot flush of relief as she reversed the car back on the grit of the hard shoulder, twisting round on the seat to get a view of the road behind her. Peter glanced at her and looked away. Judith was snuggled in beside him, her face a pale oval in the shadows. Patsy couldn't tell whether her eyes were open or not.

The tyres crunched on the gravel when she finally stopped some distance away from the emergency phone box. It stood on a single orange post, a foot or so in from the kerb.

'Stay here. I'll be back in a minute,' she told Peter, unhitching the clasp on the seat belt.

'I need the toilet,' he said.

'In a minute, love.'

'No. I *really* need.'

'Can't it wait?'

He shook his head in mute appeal and despite herself Patsy almost laughed. 'All right. You can get out, but stay close to the car.'

She heard the chink of metal as he unbuckled himself. Judith made a small sound of surprise.

'You stay here, Jude,' Peter said.

'Where are you going?' Her voice was weak and quavery and she sounded sick. The past few hours had been traumatic, but it was the months before that concerned Patsy more. Judith had been almost hysterical when she dragged her out through the gates and she'd been acting strange ever since. The anger started to bubble up again.

'I need a quick pee,' Peter told her. 'Back in a minute.'

'And stay strapped in,' Patsy ordered. She got out of the car and stood up straight, letting the door swing shut. She stretched reflexively, feeling the ache of stiffness in her spine and shoulders. The rain had eased off to a fine smirr that was almost a mist, though the air was thick with the greasy smell of smoke and burning oil, and underneath it all was a hint of something sour and rancid. She ran her hands through her hair, lightly raking her scalp with her nails and felt some of the tension ooze away. On the other side, the door opened and Peter got out.

'Be quick, and stay close to the car,' Patsy said. Off the road the shadows were like pools of ink. 'Don't go off the road.'

Peter nodded. Even in the dusky light she could see the urgency on his face and felt the smile trying to overcome the anger.

'Oh, go on then,' she said. He nodded again and turned away from the car.

Patsy walked quickly down the edge of the road, staying close to the white line. On the outside lane she could see the black debris of truck-tyres scattered on the hard-top, ridged and curled, like pieces of shrivelled and shiny crocodile skin. Just out from the edge, something small had been flattened and squashed on the rough surface. Whatever had been inside it was spread for a foot on either side. As she passed by she could smell that hint of rot. A cloud of black flies buzzed upwards momentarily before they settled back down. Patsy shied away from the sudden memory the flies brought back.

The telephone box was paint-peeled and patches of rust showed through in brown scabs.

'Please God, let it be working,' she breathed. On the short walk she imagined reaching the phone and opening the locker door to find bare wires jutting out from the back of the box. She grasped the metal handle. Something soft and fluffy brushed her hand, but she ignored it and yanked on the grip. There was a high screech of metallic protest and the door opened a centimetre. A rusty flake of paint flickered off the top hinge. She pulled again and the metal groaned, yielding another inch. Patsy got both hands on the handle and leaned backwards, grunting with the effort. The hinges screeched again and then the hatch flew wide, almost sending her off balance and sprawling to the ground.

She reached inside, felt more of the downy stuff, felt the smooth cold plastic of the receiver and then something fast and chitinous scrabbled over her fingers.

Instant terror exploded and her squeal of fright sounded exactly like the sound of the rusty hinges. She jerked back, snatching her hand out of the little recess. Her throat had clamped shut on the scream and her heart was bouncing around crazily against her ribs. Patsy put a hand to her breast-bone, bent forward to get her breath back when she heard the scraping sound inside the box. She took another step back, eyes wide, skin crawling. The sound came again, a dry, rustling noise, amplified in the confines of the phone-hatch.

'You all right, mum?' Peter's voice came from close to the car. She tried to call back, but her breath wouldn't come.

'Mum?' Peter called again. Patsy's throat unlocked with a dry click.

'Fine,' she managed to blurt. 'I'm okay. Get back in the car.'

'Not finished yet,' he bawled back.

'Well make it quick. I'll be there in a minute.' She stood up straight again, breathing hard, and turned towards the phone-box. The sound came again, but she was far enough away so that whatever was in there couldn't leap out towards her.

'Damn fool,' she said aloud. 'Probably a mouse.'

A quick and nervous grin twisted the corners of her mouth. It probably had been a mouse, now cowering, terrified, inside its downy nest, quivering in fear of the monstrous hand that had lunged inside its sanctuary. Patsy almost reached for the phone again, then paused. It probably *was* a mouse. But it could easily be a weasel or a stoat. Though she hadn't seen one of either for years, she knew they could bite. She turned away and scanned the edge of the hard shoulder for something to poke into the shadowed recess. A few pieces of blasted tyres lay on the red grit, but they weren't long enough. She moved on to the verge where the willow and alder scrub crowded on the sloping flank, found a piece of dead wood and went back to the phone. Without a pause she pushed the stick into the shadows. There was a drag of slight resistance and a feathery ripping sound. She pulled the stick back, hoping she hadn't destroyed a mouse nest, hoping more that she wouldn't see a cataract of little pink and helpless baby mice tumble to the roadside. She began to pull the branch out, felt that papery resistance again, and saw something white fluttering at the thin end of the stick.

She leaned forward, reaching a hand out towards it, when a grating sound rasped inside the hatch. There was a blur of movement, too fast for the eye to follow, and a black shape spat out from the shadows and clamped itself to the end of the branch.

Patsy blinked in surprise, jerking her head back, mouth forming a small circle. Her hand was still outstretched, still reaching for the gauzy film. For a split second she thought a fieldmouse or maybe a vole had leapt out in a panic and clung to the stick. Then in a jolt of realisation, her brain recognised what her eyes were seeing. The shape shifted within a veil of tattered gossamer, then it clambered up and over the ragged point of the branch.

Spider.

Two hairy legs lifted up and semaphored the air, as if testing the wind. Patsy heard her own breath draw in sharply, though for a second her whole body was locked and frozen. Her hand, seen in peripheral vision, was only a foot or so from the swollen creature that was hauling itself over the piece of deadwood. She

71

could feel its weight and the vibrations of its motion in her other hand as she stood paralysed. The big distended abdomen scraped against the bark and then swung upwards into view. A piece of the gossamer snagged and tore away, showing a rounded black body, so smooth it glistened wetly and swollen so tight it seemed ready to burst. The waving front legs came down and she heard the soft *snick* as they grasped the branch. Patsy was still locked within the fear that had ballooned inside her when she saw what had come blurting out of the telephone box.

The thing jerked forward, legs scrabbling fast, then it stopped, six inches or more further along the knotted stick. Two orange eyes, perfectly round and poisonously blank glared along the shaft at her. Behind them she could see the glint of smaller eyes on top of the flat glistening head. It lifted itself up, as if breathing, then settled back down again, seeming to ponder its next move. Beneath the eyes, two curved black hooks tapped lightly on the wood.

Fangs. Oh dear God, it's got poison.

Patsy's paralysis broke and she jerked her hand back so fast it almost threw her off balance. As soon as she moved, the spider's legs blurred. Without warning it came scuttering down the branch towards her. Patsy grunted in utter loathing as she turned away, though the piece of wood was still clamped in her right hand. The sudden movement caused the thing to slip to the side, swivelling downwards. Patsy swung the branch in an instinctive lurch and the spider slipped further. Its jointed legs scraped on the bark and she jerked again. This time the bloated thing went swinging up and away trailing a white arc of webbing.

Patsy shuddered, eyes fixed on the writhing creature as the trailing line slowed its descent in the air. It floated only a yard or so from the telephone stanchion, strangely light for such a swollen thing, and the orange eyes still gleamed with a light of their own. She breathed in again, whole body shaking, when the breeze caught the web trail, billowing it towards her. Her eyes were still locked on the spider and at first she didn't feel the caress of silk until the skin on the back of her hand flared in a sudden scald. Her eyes flicked down and she saw the strands of spiderweb wrapped across her knuckles and in the same instant she saw the spider itself, only inches from the ground, strangely reverse its fall, first stopping, then rising upwards again. At first, her attention divided between the burn on her skin and the strange sticky strands of webbing, she didn't realise what was happening. Then it dawned.

It was climbing up its own web. The comprehension came on a wave of utter revulsion and dreadful fright. It was clambering up the trail of silk. She could feel its movements through the line, small jerks and tugs on the skin of her hand. The burn faded as suddenly as it had flared but to Patsy the vibrations of the thing's motion was more horrific than any pain. With appalling speed it clambered up, somehow absorbing the web as it came. In the blink of an eye, it had reached halfway. It would take only a second, maybe two, to close the distance, to get those skeletal legs onto her hand and sink those curved black hooks through the skin into her flesh. The bloated nightmare swung and the eyes glinted and the image of poison dripping from glistening fangs got Patsy through to the other side of shock. Without conscious thought she grabbed the stick in both hands and swung it as hard as she could, spinning on one foot like a baseball hitter. The branch whistled in the air as it swung in an upward curve. It missed by inches, and for an instant the spider wobbled in the slipstream turbulence.

Oh no. Oh please. The voice inside her head wailed again.

Then the branch caught on the web. It dragged the spider along with it until Patsy's swing reached the end of its arc. The momentum carried the bloated thing round in a smaller circle and it whirled around, caught on its own trail-line in a fast-spinning spiral as the web wound around the wood.

Patsy didn't wait for the little *plop* that would tell her she was back to the beginning again, that the spider, with its grossly distended body had landed on the end of the stick again. She spun again, swinging the branch with all her power, groaning with the sudden effort. The force of it sent the spider tumbling, drawing more web out from behind the bulging abdomen. It twisted again, trying to get a grip on the line, but this time Patsy was ready. She jerked the branch upwards, watched the spidery monstrosity float slowly for almost a yard on its silk parachute, then she really swung. This time there was a snap, like a pencil breaking, as she connected. A dark part of it, maybe a leg, flew off and landed on the verge. The rest of the spider went spinning straight upwards, its web broken. It came down on the far side of the telephone post and hit the road with the sound of an egg cracking. Despite her revulsion and the rising nausea burning in her throat, Patsy ran forward and as she did, the crawler flipped over, spun in a circle, and without hesitation came scuttling back towards her, legs pistoning up and down, feet making a harsh scraping noise on the gravel. Patsy's heart lurched. She almost stopped, turned and ran, but inside her a sudden anger broke through the freezing fear. She jumped forward and hit desperately at the thing, catching it a hard blow on the side. It flipped over, landed on its back, and she raised the piece of wood again, paused when it was high over her head, then slammed it down with all her strength. The spider tumbled onto the hard shoulder, eyes still glowing orange. The two long legs were waving in the air again. The big sack of abdomen was cracked right down the middle in a jagged tear which started at the thorax where all the legs – *too many for a spider, she thought dimly* – sprouted in a cluster. She raised the stick again and brought it down. The end hit the creature squarely in the middle and made a crunching, somehow wet sound. The thing exploded and liquid splattered onto the road. The legs unclenched, tensed again, then went still. The orange light of the one eye she could see faded slowly then winked out. A foul, eye-watering stench wafted upwards and stung in her nose.

Patsy staggered back, feeling as if all her strength was gone, until she reached the telephone. The hatch was still wide open and inside she could just make out the shape of the receiver, grey and dusty under a ragged sheath of dry webbing. There was no movement in there this time. Patsy leaned out past the little door to make sure the smashed spider was still there. It still lay, like an upturned and skeletal fist clenched in anger. She used the stick again to clear out the web which tore with the sound of rotten cloth, and didn't stop until there was nothing left but the receiver on its cradle.

You do not need to dial, the peeling notice on the inside of the hatch told her. *Lift the receiver and you will be connected to emergency assistance.*

Patsy gingerly gripped the phone. There was a dull click as it came free of the mounting. She held it against her ear after checking to ensure there were no holes in the corners of the hatch that could hide another spider. She shuddered again but listened. There was a short, soft burring noise which stopped after a few seconds, then an unmusical selection of notes which sounded as if someone was dialling on a crossed line or playing on a dry xylophone. The notes stopped and left a complete and echoing silence. Patsy bit her lip in frustration. She leaned her elbow on the top of the hatch and brushed her hair back from her eyes. It was damp with the rain-mist. Ahead, only fifty yards or so further along the road, she could make out the car's tail-lights, dimmed now as the mist thickened. She hadn't heard the sound of the door opening again, and wondered if Peter was back inside. She was about to hang up and call out to him when there was a harsh click on the line, loud enough to make her ear crackle.

'*You are connected to the emergency service. Please hold the line and you will be answered as soon as possible.*'

'Hello?' Patsy called out. 'Can you hear me?'

'*You are connected. . . .*' the voice started over again and Patsy realised it was a recording. This time she almost slammed the receiver back on the hook, but she caught herself in time.

'It's taken hours to find this one,' she told herself aloud. 'So just bear with it.' She hoped the emergency service wouldn't play musak into her ear on this drizzly hard shoulder. If it did, she might start to scream and not be able to stop. In her mind's eye she could still see the spider scuttling towards her on the road and her belly was making involuntary little clenching motions. She drummed her fingers on the top of the metal box, tapping her foot in time with her own rhythm. Frustration was building up, a physical pressure under her ribs.

'Come *on*,' she grated between her teeth.

'Hello,' a man's voice blurted in her ear, so unexpectedly that she almost dropped the receiver. 'Roadside Emergency Services,' he went on, each word spoken in initial capitals. 'How can I help you?'

'Yes. Oh, thank you,' Patsy heard herself gabble. 'I'm . . . I mean we're . . .'

'Yes, madam?' the voice interrupted, echoing as if he was

inside a large, enclosed space. He sounded young and efficient. 'We're here to help you, so don't worry. Take your time.'

Patsy nodded as the tension inside her broke and washed away in a flood of relief. She drew in a slow breath. 'Yes. I'm afraid I'm lost. I think I need some help.'

'Not the only one on a night like this,' the man said. 'But that's what we're here for. Now, madam, can you just tell me the kiosk number and we'll find out exactly where you are.'

'Kiosk number?' Patsy asked, confused. Shouldn't the telephone transmit a signal which pinpointed the set in use? She thought she'd read that somewhere.

'Yes, madam. On the inside of the door. And the outside of course.' The man gave a small, gritty chuckle. Patsy shrugged. She swung the door wide and rubbed her hand on the layer of grit that clung to a sticker pasted to the metal. As the dirt dropped off, two numbers began to appear in day-glo orange.

'It's fifty-two.'

'The full deck,' the calm voice said, this time a little lighter. 'That means we've got all the royals plus the court jester. Not forgetting the ace of spades.'

'Pardon?'

'Just joking, madam. Now, let's punch this up. Five and two, fifty-two.' In the background she could hear the tapping which might have been a keyboard, or just fingers drumming on a table. 'Ah, got you.' An undertone of triumph.

'You've just got on to Junction 13.'

'Yes, I saw the sign. I just don't know where it is.'

'Well, you keep on going for about three miles.'

'I need a service station.'

'I'm sure you do. That's just what I was saying. You carry on for three miles and take the first slip on the left. That takes you to . . .'

A burst of static shattered the man's voice under a blizzard of electronic sparks.

'Hello?' Patsy had to hold the receiver away from her ear. Even from half a metre she could hear the harsh crackle. It died down and she listened again. At first there was no sound on the line, except for the distant hiss of the fading static interference, like a whisper from another room.

'Hello,' she said again. 'Are you still there?'

The static ebbed and flowed, like grains of sand on a windswept beach. Her voice echoed in there and faded away.

'That takes you back again, you stupid cow.'

Patsy jerked backwards as if she'd been hit.

'What did you think? That we'd just let you go? Let you take them from us?' The voice came blaring out in a harsh rasp. 'And we know where you are. We're coming for you.'

Patsy's mouth opened and shut. No sound came out.

'We're coming for you, coming for you *now*,' the echoing voice went on. It was hard to tell whether it was man or woman, but it had to be Kerron Vaunche. 'There's no escape on the *low* road.'

'Get off. Get away,' Patsy spluttered.

'Keep looking out for us, because we'll find you and we'll rip them out of your arms. You can't hide now, for we see everything on the low road. And we're going to have to punish you now, stupid woman.'

Patsy felt her legs wobble and she almost fell. It took a gigantic effort to lock her knees and keep upright. 'Just stay away from me, you cretin,' she snarled. 'Keep away or I'll kill you, understand?'

She jerked the receiver away from her ear and slammed it down inside the box. It hit with a hard crunch and she turned away, mind whirling, trying to breathe over the sudden lurching of her heart. She was backing away from the box when she heard her own name spoken.

Patssseee.

This voice was dry as dust, grinding like millstones. It came from the shadows inside the box and Patsy stopped dead.

Patsssseee, it grated hollowly. Pa*tssseee on the road*.

'Wha . . .?' she began.

'*On the junction.*' She heard the words clearly, grinding out from the dark recess. She turned, suddenly more frightened than she had been when the spider had clambered up onto the stick. The sense of absolute threat ballooned inside her and her heart was beating so hard that her vision started to waver. She completed the turn, bending slightly and looked inside the box,

77

thinking she must have missed the cradle when she smashed the receiver down.

Two empty sockets stared out at her over a row of yellow teeth.

Oh God Jesus Help Me. Her mind whimpered.

The phone was gone. A bare skull lay on the shelf, propped up against the back of the hatch. The eye sockets were black as pitch, but the shadows in their depth wavered as she pulled back, mouth agape, giving them a flicker of impossible life. The bottom jaw stuck out from the rest of the broad skull so that the lower teeth jutted like a bulldog's. A deformed thigh-bone, short and thick, the gnarled and stunted leg-bone of a dwarf, lay across the bottom teeth, both ends turned down, looking strangely like an old-fashioned telephone receiver on its cradle.

She shook her head, denying it. It *had* been a telephone. She had lifted it and spoken into it and she'd been answered. *It had not been a skull. It had not been a bone.* Patsy stumbled backwards, mind sizzling as if her brains were frying inside her own skull.

Moon's getting bigger, Patssee. The voice was grinding out from the skull, though nothing moved there except the dark shadows in the sockets. She felt hysteria rise like black bubbles. *Look out now, for the babies are not alone.*

'Babies . . .?' she started to ask, somehow able to speak from the depth of the appalling dread when a howl, high and wavering, speared through the drizzle from further along the road where she'd parked on the hard shoulder. The fear suddenly crystallised to ice in her belly. The sound spun her away from the phone hatch. Her shoulder knocked the open door, jarring the stanchion. The skull rolled outwards, dark sockets sweeping sightlessly across her. The distorted thigh-bone tumbled out like a small club. They hit the hard surface with a strangely soft crunch and shattered into powder. The long yellow teeth scattered across the hard shoulder. Even as she turned towards the howling sound she could still hear the warning ringing in her ears.

Moon's getting high. They would make a sacrifice at the full moon.

'Peter!' She started towards the car, heart pounding so hard it felt it would wrench free. Another yowl tore the damp air again, followed by a series of yelping coughs.

'*Mum*!' Peter's yell came bouncing back tight with urgency. 'Mum. Come quick.'

Another screech jarred in Patsy's ears, then another sound, high and clear. It was Judith. She was screaming. For an instant Patsy froze, unable to make her muscles work, suddenly terrified to go forward, more afraid not to.

'Get away,' Peter bawled. 'Get you *out of here*.' There was a short snapping sound, like a branch breaking, then a howl of pain that wasn't human. The noises up ahead broke through the icy web that had encased Patsy. Something was trying to harm her children. Adrenaline kicked into her veins and the lock on her muscles snapped off. There was a singing in her ears as her whole body instantly prepared for fight or flight. The cry from up ahead, Judith's wavering fear, Peter's desperation, they made the decision for her. She was moving and bending before she was even aware of it and the horror of the dry bones inside the phone hatch was simply shunted from her mind. Three steps ahead, she snatched up the stick she had used to kill the spider and had turned it in her hands within another two strides so that she grasped the narrow end, leaving the thicker part where it had broken off from the tree swinging out like a club. She raced forward towards the winking glow of her parking lights and the mêlée of noise.

'Get back!' Peter bawled again and this time Patsy heard, not fear, but fury, though Judith was still wailing. She sped towards the car, expecting to find them both inside, but as the shape condensed out of the drizzle-mist she saw her son standing on the hard shoulder, legs apart and swinging a branch of his own like a small warrior.

'*Get away*!' He swung the branch in a fast sweep over his shoulder. Something narrow and wraithlike darted back from him. On the other side, a thin shape angled in. Peter twisted his position, moving with unconscious grace, swivelled in a complete circle and brought the piece of wood whooping down in an arc. It caught the shape a hard blow and immediately another shriek, this time an unmistakable cry of pain came ripping out.

Patsy saw the movement and ran towards the car. Judith was

inside, screaming hysterically. Peter was still swinging the branch at the small shapes that hovered just beyond the range of clear vision. Patsy reached him, grabbed him by the shoulder and he jumped a foot into the air. He whirled, face ashen, then he saw it was his mother.

'In the car,' she snapped, pulling him towards her.

'Mum, there's . . .'

'In the car, Peter. *Move it.*'

Something came lurching in from the right, skirting the wheel arch. Peter spun away from her again, holding the branch out. The shape, narrow and elongated, jerked back from him. Patsy got a glimpse of something canine, built like a small greyhound, with a pointed face and bulging pale eyes. But the way it moved, a stiff-gaited low-rumped sway, reminded her of films she'd seen of hyena packs on an African plain. The animal grunted, surprisingly low and loud for something so lightly built and opened its mouth. Slender teeth reflected the red tail-lights. Its claws scraped on the gravel as it turned away. Another one loped in from the other side and this time Patsy took two fast strides forward, swinging her own club as fast as she could. The end of it caught the creature under the jaw, not with much force, but enough to make its teeth click together like a trap. It squealed and lurched away into the darkness of the scrub. How many there were in the pack, she couldn't say. It was too dark in the shadows to make out more than a hint of movement.

She skipped back and almost knocked Peter sprawling.

'Get in the car.'

He stood there, legs still braced apart, looking past her, unwilling to move.

'Peter, Move it *now.*' Behind her she could hear Judith's harsh breathing. She had stopped whimpering, but now it sounded as if she was gasping for air. Patsy had heard the sound too often before. Judith had always been prone to severe asthma attacks when she was scared or excited. There was an inhaler tube in the glove compartment which would ease the wheezing, and even as she stood outside the car, watching the loping shadows resolve themselves into the small skinny pack of vermin, Patsy could hear her daughter's breath whistle harshly. She shoved at her son who reluctantly dropped his branch, obviously loath to leave his mother outside, but Patsy had no time to argue. When he had clambered in and closed the door, she began to move round to the driver's side. As she skirted the back of the car, something moved out fast from the scrub and darted towards her feet. It snuffled as it moved and its shoulders, higher than its rump, gave it an off-centre swagger that even for its size, made it somehow more threatening. As she turned to face it, another one came skirting round the front. The pale, goitred eyes were fixed on her. A mouth gaped and a snarling chatter stuttered. Teeth gnashed like barbed wire. She twisted left and right, trying to keep both of them in sight, still moving towards the door. She got her fingers on the handle when the second animal – it had to be a dog, but it was like no dog she'd ever seen – darted in at her feet. Without thinking she swung the branch like a golf club and this time she really clipped the beast under the chin. The jaws snapped shut and the thing spun in a backwards somersault to crash onto the middle of the road. Instantly the other animal dived for it. There was a snarl as the fallen creature tried to get up, then another snarl, this time higher and somehow fearful as it fell back down again. Its partner's head darted in at the neck. Something ripped and a squeal of pain soared. The metallic smell of blood wafted thick. Another of the skinny creatures loped in from the scrub, then another. They ignored Patsy and made straight for the fallen one which was now twisting desperately, pale eyes rolling in fear and pain. Patsy dropped the branch, snatched the door open and threw herself inside. She swung the door and heard it slam. The hungry squealing and the slobbering noises stopped immediately.

Judith was lying sprawled on the back seat, both hands up at her neck and her eyes bulging as she gasped frantically for breath. Patsy scrabbled at the glove compartment and fished out the ventilator. She twisted in her seat and grabbed her daughter by the neck of her jacket. There was a slight rip as she brought the girl forward. Judith's eyes were still staring wide and for a second they were just like the bulging eyes of the dog-like thing on the road when its companions had turned on it to rip its throat out. Patsy used thumb and forefinger to open her daughter's mouth, jammed the plastic tube between the girl's lips and triggered the jet of spray hard. The thing hissed. Judith's breath-

81

ing stopped immediately. Her eyes closed tight. Patsy held on to her, waiting for the reaction, trying to count to ten. She made it to five, as her daughter's face, already red, started to turn dark grey.

Then the girl's throat unlocked in a sudden gasp and she hauled in a vast breath of air. The darkness bled away from her face. Patsy held her while the small girl panted, lungs now working like bellows. Finally she relaxed her grip and let Judith slide back down onto the seat and waited for several moments while her daughter's breathing eased. Outside the animals were howling and snarling.

She sat, holding Judith tight until the spasms completely eased, and then the shock overload hit her. For a dreadful moment her vision started to waver, darkening in from the edges as the blood drained from her head and she felt herself sag against the small frame tucked in beside her. Desperately she gasped for air, momentarily sounding as if she too was having an attack, and her vision cleared again.

Get moving! The internal voice broke through to her. '*You can't stay here. They're coming for you.*

The urgency of it snapped her out of the paralysis. She'd stopped too long. She'd been *made* to stop for too long. The realisation came to her that she'd been baited and she'd fallen for it. Her belly clenched like a fist. She eased Judith back against the seat. The girl's dark eyes gazed blindly up at her from the pallor of her face.

'Here.' She held the inhaler out to Peter in a hand that trembled just a little. 'Take this. I've got to drive. You know what to do.'

He looked at her and nodded silently. Patsy turned in the seat, jammed the key in the ignition and started the engine.

Three miles up ahead, the voice on the phone said before everything had gone completely crazy. *But it hadn't been a phone. It had been a trick to stop her, slow her down, hadn't it*? Three miles to a service station and civilisation. *The skull and the twisted bone had been the illusion*! Patsy's mind was jittering and tumbling, trying to grasp at anything, but she still stamped down on the accelerator and the car shot forward. Out of the corner of her eye, she saw the thin creatures rolling and writhing in a huddle over a mess that gleamed wet. They were squealing and chittering like miniature jackals. As the car pulled away, she saw something else approach the ruck of animals; just a glimpse of a pale shape, low and insectile on the flat bitumen surface. She was gone before she could get a proper look at it, but there was something in the half-seen scuttling motion that made the hairs on the back of her neck dance in unison. She floored the pedal and heard the rip of gravel under the tyres and she was travelling.

Up ahead, she told herself, there was a service station. She kept that thought firmly in her mind as the needle swung over the seventy mark and the sky darkened further as night took over from the stormclouds. Behind the cloud the moon was riding high, that much she knew.

They would try to take the children before it got full.

7

The travellers had gone, men, women, children, battered vans and all. And Paul Thomson had gone with them.

Patsy gripped the wheel and tried to concentrate on the anger the memory of that day summoned. Anger was better than fear, stronger than despair. It might even bury for a while the cold core of dread. She needed her anger now on this road. She glanced in the mirror again, knowing that she'd soon see the headlights behind her as they came racing up in pursuit on this road. The *Low Road*, that's what Paul's mad whore had called it, and whatever she'd meant by that, it was a place that should only exist in nightmares. Whatever crazy witchery Kerron Vaunche had worked, Patsy knew she had to beat it. Ahead of her was home, and then escape to a place she knew where they could lie low for the next few days, for the next few weeks if necessary until the sacred days were done, until the *dead days* were gone. After that, her children would be safe, and she would see Paul and the insane bitch in hell.

Peter's tousled hair was just visible in the shadows on the back seat. There were no lights behind them for the moment, though Patsy knew she'd been fingered now, found out. They knew where she was. In front, all she could see was the unwinking stare of the cat's-eyes in the road. She squeezed down on the dread, physically clenching tight to stop the fluttering in her belly and concentrated on the anger, using its heat to keep her going on this godforsaken road.

Godforsaken. Abandoned by God. A place where the notion of goodness did not exist, where sanity was an abstract concept. She told herself she was just lost, fleeing pursuit. Beneath her consciousness, instinct knew better. *Godforsaken*. Like Kerron Vaunche and whatever it was she worshipped in the dark beneath Broadforth House. Like Paul Thomson, who had left to follow in her dark wake.

They had gone, the travelling people, leaving only the scorched circles on Newcombe's field, and the detritus of the latter-day nomad. After the midsummer ceremony, when the morning rain doused the smouldering ashes of the fires, the arguments over the tinkers' encampment simply evaporated. On the afternoon of that day when Paul had packed his sports bag and walked out, a lone, final item appeared as a tailpiece on the lunchtime news. The camera, held low for effect as it moved through the dawn ground mist, eased round one of the old pointed stones and zoomed on to the central Cupstone itself. The early rays, slanting between the pillars, cast a copper glow over everything and the red stain, still dribbling down the smooth-worn sides, glinted and sparkled like some exotic molten metal. The rain soon came and washed it clean.

Patsy had been physically sick, though not from the sight of spilled blood – if it was blood, and nobody knew for sure, though Patsy knew now – on the old stone. She had seen that on the screen through a haze of fear and despair, hardly taking in any of the news. She kept seeing those red weals on Paul's back, like tribal warrior's scars, like well-earned soldier's stripes. The eye socket bruises under his jaw came swimming back in her memory, glaring dead, overlaying the still tangible deformed after-image of the dream.

The tinkers had gone, and he had gone with them. In the wink of an eye, her whole life had foundered.

Peter had asked where his father had gone. She'd turned her head away, hiding the glisten of tears and told him Paul was at the office. The boy had shrugged. He had a football under his arm and bounced it down the hallway, opened the door, went out into the garden. Vaguely she heard the ball being kicked against the wall of the house, a normal summer-morning sunny sound which jarred against the cold in her heart. In the afternoon, trying to grapple with her own emotions, making an effort just to think clearly, she'd called her mother-in-law who lived only seven miles away in the sprawling suburbs. Peggy Thomson, Paul's mother, a stout woman who wore pearls and whose grey hair was always perfectly coiffed no matter what the time of day, arrived on the doorstep within the hour. Despite appearances, Peggy was a warm-hearted woman who had taken to Patsy on first sight. As soon as she'd dispensed hugs and lipsticky kisses to her grandchildren, she immediately shooed them outside, put on the kettle, then clamped Patsy to her expansive bosom. The whole story came out in a gush.

'Do you want him back?'

Patsy nodded automatically. 'I think he's had a brainstorm or something. I mean he's never been like this before.'

She glanced quickly at her mother-in-law. That wasn't quite the truth. He *had* been like that before, but she hadn't realised it. She'd slowly let her own interests, her own career be subsumed into the support of his, while over the years, he'd become the dominant partner, master in his own household, using his position, his ambition and his maleness to maintain the mastery. Patsy thought of the bruises on her shoulders, the grip-marks on her upper arms and the sharp knuckles in the muscles of her back, and shied away from the memory. She was still his wife. He was still the father of their children. It had been too long since she had thought only for herself, and on that afternoon, sitting on the couch, with Peggy's arm around her shoulder, she told herself she wanted him back, *needed* him back.

'Well, I suppose you'd better go and find him,' Peggy had finally said. 'Though if he's taken up with one of those footloose gypsies, I can't see why you'd want to.'

When Peggy had heard the story, she'd been appalled and her own mother-love was overcome by matriarchal indignation. 'How could he possibly leave these babies?' she'd snorted. 'When I get my hands on him, I'll give him tinkers, just you wait and see. That's his trouble, you know. His father spoiled him, always gave him his own way. Well it's about time he came down off his high horse and started thinking of other people.'

Peggy had stayed to watch Judith and Peter. Patsy got the car out of the garage and angled it through the narrow gateway at the end of the garden, looking back over her shoulder to see them at the window. The children waved as she left.

The travellers' site was empty, a wide patch of bleached and trampled grass, dotted here and there by heaps of rusted cans and bottles. A few of the black craters where the fires had been were still smouldering and as she walked among them, they began to hiss as the first drops of rain began to fall. She skirted the edge of the trees as she made her way back to the car and snagged her jeans on a curving bramble runner. Instantly she thought of the weals on Paul's back. He'd blamed the thorns at first before coming out with the truth. Patsy's stomach lurched again, and the hot bile rose high enough to give her bitter heartburn. In her mind's eye, she saw him leading the woman away from the crowd, firelight glinting on her black hair. There had been loud music, fiddles and tambourines and drums that had sounded alien and foreign in the night. *Had they come here, hand in hand?* She saw them merge with the shadows, each of them breathing hard in anticipation of the heat of the night. Patsy tried to shuck the picture out of her head, but it kept dancing there, the two of them, mouths clamped on one another, bodies pressing together, hands probing and searching and grasping.

She stumbled forward, and the thorns tugged at her again. Patsy pulled away from it, shaking her head as if the motion could dispel the image, but it wouldn't retreat. Tears sparked in her eyes and a small sob escaped her as she stumbled towards the car.

That afternoon, she quartered the side roads, steeling herself to stop and ask the drivers of the beat-up vans wherever they had parked on the verges if they had seen Paul. No-one had, though they all knew him by name. Small children watched her silently when she approached, women eyed her suspiciously, and she couldn't tell whether any of them were telling the truth. The following day, after a long and sleepless night, she drove further out, on the country roads that criss-crossed the farmland. The travelling folk were fewer the further from home, and none were any help. It was getting on to early evening when she came to a dip in the road, bounded on the slope by two scraggly hawthorn hedgerows that hadn't been cut all summer and leaned out over the by-way so that when she passed, the thorns scraped on the wheel arches with a harsh crabby squeal. On the bottom, the road took a sharp bend and narrowed further, as if she was disappearing into a green tunnel. Patsy eased on the brake in case a tractor might be coming the other way, though by the looks of the track, nothing as big had used the road in a while. The road was unfamiliar and she knew she had never travelled this way before, but that could have been said for any one of the dozens she'd scoured since daybreak.

Round the corner, the road forked left and right. A solitary signpost stood at the crotch, but both arrows were obscured and the names they indicated were completely obliterated. On impulse she hauled the wheel to the left and drove parallel to a small stream, overhung by weeping ash trees and willow, where clouds of mayflies danced in the stray pillars of sunlight angling through the thick foliage. A mile further on she found an encampment, though it was much smaller than the one that had laid siege to Newcombe's field. A pack of mangy dogs yipped and yapped at her heels when she got out of the car, but she forced herself past them and into the centre where the reception was casually aloof.

'Never saw him after the midsummer,' an old woman told her, looking up from an old pot which bubbled on the open fire. Patsy couldn't tell whether she was cooking or washing clothes. From the smell, it could have been either. The woman's face was familiar, though she couldn't place it. 'What you want him for? You from the newspapers?'

'I'm his wife,' Patsy said. The old woman raised her grizzled eyebrows, and Patsy saw a glint of what could have been amusement beneath them.

'His wife, eh? Gone amissing, has he now?'

'He's gone with one of the gyp . . . one of the travelling folk.'

'Good on him,' the woman responded. She gave a high-pitched laugh, showing two teeth on a shiny row of bottom gum. 'Only place to be is on the roads, not stuck with the *gadge*.'

'He's got children at home.'

'An' he'll be having more, mark me, now he's gone with *Cat Anna*. You'd best be forgetting about him dearie, and go back to your *sett*.'

'What do you mean, more children?' Patsy felt the clench in her stomach again, like the grip of cramp. She could feel the eyes on her, not just the few lean men who had sauntered to the fire, but the unseen eyes of the rest, watching from inside the vans, and from behind the grey sheets that had been hung out to dry on makeshift lines. She felt their sniggering contempt and forced herself to ask. 'And who is Cat Anna?'

The woman laughed again, a witchety cackle, throwing her head back. A blob of spittle landed on one of the round stones kerbing the fire and sizzled like bacon. The men took up the laughter, low, yet somehow contemptuous.

'She's our *Black Annis* is Kerron Vaunche. Didn't he tell you?'

Patsy shook her head.

'She's the *Carlin Woman*, that's who she is. Her mother and her mother's mother and their mothers before yon have been the *Catanna*, since the first time they walked the roads, since before there *were* the roads. She's Kerron Vaunche, and if your man's a'gone with her, then there's no coming back, for he's been chosen, so he has.'

'Chosen?' Patsy heard the word like a dumb echo.

'Aye, she's chosen him as her champion, and a good job she did an' all, eh? He fought for us all to stay on at the Cupstone, using the *gadge* laws against themselves, until after no-night day. She took him into the *uath* stones and put her mark on him, but he was hers long afore that. But he's bound good and proper dearie, so you'd better be going back and forgetting about him. He's hers now and she's put her mark on 'im.'

Patsy felt as if her legs would give way underneath her. She could feel the blood pounding in her ears, as though an internal pressure was building up to a dangerous level. It sounded like far-off waves on shingle. She stood there, swaying a little, and dragged for breath. The air above the fire was hot and rasping.

'I don't understand you,' she panted.

'Now there's a truth.'

'I just want to find him and bring him home.' As soon as she said it, she realised how pitiful it sounded. Patsy Thomson. Patricia Havelin as she had been, before she married, and before he gave her the pet name (*When had she become his Patsy?*), with a life in front of her and dreams of success. She'd put the dreams behind her, behind *him*. And now she was standing, swaying, while the hot woodsmoke rasped her throat, begging help from a dirty old woman with a wrinkled face and two stained teeth. She recoiled from the picture of herself, as she was right at that moment, and what she had allowed herself to become. She opened her mouth again, when something else the old woman had said snagged at her.

'An' he'll be having more, mark me, now he's gone with Cat Anna.'

89

'You said he'll be having more children.' She had asked that already, but there had been no reply. The very idea of it made her want to be sick. She had asked Paul the same question when he'd stood there in the bedroom, coldly telling her he was leaving.

'Reckon he will,' the crone said, and she chuckled to herself. Beyond the fire, someone laughed out loud. 'She's chosen him on the midsummer and she put her mark on his arm. It's the ripening time, and she'll be ripe, will Kerron Vaunche, just like the Cat Anna always has been. She's put his feet on the road and he'll follow the road with her wherever it takes them.'

Patsy took a step backwards, gathering herself in.

'That's nonsense,' she cried, stamping her foot on the hard ground for emphasis, not caring how petulant it made her look. 'He's just mixed up, don't you see?' Even though she said it, she was far from convinced and from convincing. 'He's been overworked,' she ended lamely.

'Soon will be,' one of the men said, and the rest of them sniggered.

Patsy rounded on him, a tall man with a shaggy beard and a big brass buckle at the belt on his waist.

'Oh, you find this amusing, do you? You think it's funny that a man should walk out on two children? Maybe that's the kind of people you are. Maybe you don't care much for your own children.'

'That'll be enough,' the man retorted. 'What would you know?'

The old woman raised her hand. 'Enough now.'

She looked up at Patsy, eyes squinting against the sun. 'Just because we don't live under stone don't mean we don't treasure the wee 'uns. They're more precious than houses to us. They're what we've *got*.'

'And they're what I've got too. I've got two children, and they need their father.'

'Maybes they do,' the woman agreed. 'But do *you*, missus?'

'At least let me ask him,' Patsy heard herself plead and hated herself for it. 'Please, for their sake.'

The woman looked down at the pot and gave the mixture, whatever it was, a careful stir. After a moment or two she looked up and with a quick motion, she grabbed Patsy's hand. The movement was so sudden that Patsy didn't have time to react.

She felt her hand pulled forward, felt the heat of the fire against her skin. The woman twisted her wrist roughly until it was palm up.

'Don't see the harm in it,' she finally said. The skin on Patsy's knuckles was beginning to sear, though the crone's hand was closer to the flames.

'You've a long road to travel *Gadge*-woman. A long ways to go. And you won't find what you're looking for neither, and that's a truth. Best you turn back and go back under stone, for there's a bad road ahead of you.'

Patsy pulled her hand back, rubbing the skin. The smell of scorched hair flared, then was gone in the rising heat of the fire. She started to ask but the old woman forestalled her.

'No harm in saying,' she said, but the words were directed at the circle of men who edged closer. 'You take yourself north of here. She's the *Carlin Woman*, and that's where she'll be headed.'

'Where?'

'North for the Samhain, and you'd better find her before then, for she'll be gone after the dark day and him an' all.'

'What do you mean?'

'I keep telling you, missus. She's the *Cat Anna*. She's got the power and where she goes no other folk can follow except those she chooses. You find her before she gets to the stones of Callanish, for that's where she'll be going.'

'And what will she do there?'

'She'll do many things, missus. Things you don't want to know about. It's what she'll *become* when her time's ripe.'

Beyond the fire, the group of men started muttering among themselves. Patsy could only see their wavering forms through the glimmering air above the flames. The woman shoved herself back from the heat.

'You go north and you'll maybe find them. But don't expect to be going home again except on your own. She's put her mark on him and that's bound them body and soul, and nothing can untie that knot. You get yourself north, a couple of days maybe, but don't expect no welcome from Kerron Vaunche.'

She looked directly at the younger woman and Patsy thought she saw a trace of sadness, maybe even compassion in her eyes. Patsy backed away from the fire and the old woman made a flicking motion with her hand, dismissing her. She went back to stirring the pot.

Peggy stayed over and watched the children. Peter asked again where his father was, but his grandmother told him he had to go away on business. The boy looked to his mother for confirmation and Patsy could see the hint of suspicion, but Peter never voiced it. Judith wondered why daddy wasn't here to read a story to her at night. She was still small for her age, dark eyed, dark haired, just like Paul, and with just a trace of the quick temper that her father had. She'd had another asthma attack in the early hours of the morning and Patsy kept her indoors and out of the pollen-filled air. The asthma was always bad in the summertime. Everything seemed bad this summertime.

Carrick Thomson arrived that night. He was fair like Peter, with a red beard and a big brawler's laugh to match his girth. Where Paul was dark and sallow-skinned in the summer, his brother had inherited their Scottish grandfather's frame and colouring. Carrick was big and burly and built like a bull and when Patsy answered the door, heart stuttering in false hope, her brother-in-law came barging in and smothered her in a bear-like hug, lifting her completely off the ground.

'So what's the over-achiever up to then?' he asked, after Peter and Judith had been fondly manhandled in his brawny arms and had been sent out of the kitchen with bags of sweets as bribes.

'That'll do, Carrick,' Peggy scolded her son, but he just gave a rumble of laughter.

'See what I mean?' he chuckled, leaning over to engulf Patsy once again. 'Always the favourite, while the rest of us black sheep had to work our arses off to earn a living.'

'Now that's not true,' Peggy protested.

'Only kidding, Ma,' Carrick soothed her, still laughing. 'Don't get your frillies in a flutter.'

Despite herself, Patsy couldn't help but smile. Peggy retreated to the breakfast bar and put on the kettle. Carrick took Patsy's hands in his, completely engulfing both of them. His fingers felt hard and dry and warm and the callouses on his palms scraped against the tender skin where her knuckles had been singed.

'Done a runner, has our Paul?'

Patsy nodded, eyes down on the table.

'Someone else?'

Another nod.

'Must be off his flippin' head when he's got a cracker like you.' Peggy tutted her disapproval. Patsy felt the smile try to force its way through again.

'And you've been out looking for him, on your own?'

'Yes. I think he's gone north.'

'Well, I reckon you should give him some time. He'll probably wake up with a hangover and come back with his tail between his legs.'

'No.' The word came out and landed like a weight. The kitchen went quiet for a moment.

'No?'

'No. It won't happen and I can't wait.' Patsy thought of what the old woman had said at the campfire. Most of it was just a jumble, gypsy mumbo-jumbo. But there was something about the way she had talked about the other woman, this Kerron Vaunche. She had felt it in the tone, in the reaction of the men around the fire. There was something about the dark haired woman she had seen on the television. She had sensed it then and she could feel it now.

She's chosen him. She's put her mark on him.

Paul had come home from the midsummer fires after a night in the forest with that woman. He'd had that curved line down the inside of his forearm. Had that been her mark? It had twisted like a snake, like some of the roads she'd followed to find the gypsy camp. If she had done that to him, and he'd let her, she couldn't hope that he would wake up full of regrets. And those weals, the marks of a woman's nails dug into his back, the bruise where her mouth had sucked under his chin, hands clawed in passion, hungry mouth upon him. Patsy felt the lurch of nausea again.

'No,' she said again. 'I can't wait.'

Carrick clamped her hands inside his and leaned over the table, his bulk blotting out the late-afternoon light that filtered through the frosted glass of the kitchen door.

'Okay, Paddy,' he said, voice low and reassuring. He had called her that ever since the first night they'd met, when she and Paul had been engaged and Carrick had come home on leave, big and imposing in his dress uniform and more than half drunk. No matter how many times Paul had tried to correct him, Carrick had persisted, laughing at his own joke every time he said it. Patsy hadn't minded at all. Her grandfather had called her that when she'd been small.

'But not on your own. I'll go with you and see if we can't both talk him round. I'll get him in a head-lock and you can twist his goolies. He'll probably see sense.' Peggy tutted again, making a point of rattling the teacups. Patsy's brother-in-law winked and gave her a big, conspiratorial smile.

Carrick stayed for dinner, played frisbee with the kids in the back garden until the disc got stuck in a tree and he slept on the couch with his big feet hanging over the arm. In the morning, after another fitful night where in dreams, Patsy saw the old woman's face squinting up at her before the wizened features ran and melted and changed into the darkly arrogant gypsy face of Kerron Vaunche and then crumpled into the flaking skin of her missing husband, she woke to the smell of bacon sizzling under the grill. Carrick had raided the freezer and made enough to feed a standing army. He ordered Patsy to eat and she surprised herself when she found she could. Peter and Judith sat on either side of him and burst into laughter every time he poked them in the ribs or squeezed their knees. Patsy couldn't help but compare his sunny nature with the dark and brooding side her husband had shown too often. Despite that, despite herself, she was still willing to go and find him and bring him back.

They left after breakfast in Carrick's new car. Since he'd left the army, he'd taken over his uncle's dairy farm and had made a success of it. The BMW still smelt of polish.

'Should have brought the jeep,' he said as they nosed out onto the road, missing Paul's car by a whisker. 'I just got this to impress the wankers at the bank.' He spun the wheel and they were on their way, taking the main road north out of the village. Patsy gave him a running commentary on where she'd been the day before and what had happened at the travellers' camp.

'Silly bugger,' he said. 'I should have known something was up when he took on the tinkers' case. Always got an eye on the main chance has my brother. Never did something for nothing.'

He stopped and his face went red as his beard. 'No offence, Paddy.'

'No, you're right, I suppose. But he's got responsibilities.'

'Too damn right he has, hon. Let's hope he realises what he's losing.'

They drove on the dual carriageway for ten miles or so, beyond where Patsy estimated she'd spoken to the old woman, though on the main road it was hard to tell. They kept going past a succession of small towns and villages until they came to a junction. Carrick slowed down.

'I think we should start looking on the side roads. There's no way they'll park in a lay-by. They'd just get moved on.'

They pulled off and followed a narrow road that went through a picturesque hamlet of thatched cottages and rustic oast-houses then dived in a swoop of a valley. A farmer on a tractor pulled into an opening to let them pass and fingered the peak of his cap when Carrick waved thanks. They came on two lone vans, one an ancient ambulance, parked at the edge of a field. Carrick slowed and stopped, then got out. Before he closed the door, he leaned in, opened the glove compartment and took out a battered camera case.

A man was sitting at the open door of the beat-up transit van, strumming a guitar. Beyond him, half hidden in the shade of the trees, two children were kicking a ball.

'Hello,' Carrick called out. The man nodded casually and never missed a beat.

'Maybe you can help me. I'm trying to get in touch with Paul Thomson. He was with the travellers at the Cupstone the other night.'

The man stopped strumming. 'What you want him for?'

'Just an interview. He's been in the news a lot, this past couple of weeks.'

'You one of those press folk?'

Carrick held up the camera case. 'Might even do a picture profile if he agrees.'

The man relaxed. 'If you can find him that is. He's gone north, that's all I know.' He gestured with a hand in the rough direction. 'You can interview me if you like.'

'Sure, love to,' Carrick agreed. 'But it'll have to be later. You know what editors are like.'

The man shrugged and put the guitar down. It made a hollow sound. 'Never met one.'

'But if you'll be here a couple of days, maybe I can come back.'

The stranger grinned. He had strong white teeth. 'Sure. No hurry.'

'Can you give me any clue about Mr. Thomson?'

The man shook his head. 'Just north,' he finally said. 'There was a few of the old folk, the real Romanies heading up for the border, is what I heard. He'll be with them. They won't be far, that's all I can tell you.'

Carrick nodded, waved a casual thanks, and came back to the car.

'Intrepid reporter now?'

'Needs must when the devil drives,' Carrick said. He handed her the camera case. It was empty.

He started the car and moved off, following the contours of the valley which widened as they travelled on the snaking route. They passed three more villages until a left bend took them across a shallow ford, water arcing up on either side as they plunged through and sending up rainbow wings in the sunlight, though neither of them noticed. They swung round the edge of a conifer plantation which gradually merged with a broad-leafed forest and in moments, there were trees all around them. The sunlight lanced through the canopy of battlemented chestnuts and ancient beech, spotlighting green clumps of ferns and clusters of wood anemones standing silent in the still air.

'Never been this way before,' Carrick observed. 'Should have brought a map.'

Patsy kept her eyes in front, occasionally swinging her head left and right, hoping to see a van or a tent.

The road narrowed at a stone bridge athwart tumbling stream and stayed narrow on the far side, twisting round the boles of big and old trees. A roe deer in the centre jerked its head up as they approached then bounded away in a fawn flicker. Somewhere in the trees a pigeon's wings clapped the air and another unseen bird cawed harshly.

'I reckon we'll come out the other side in a minute,' Carrick said, easing on the pedal on a tight curve. Ahead of them, the forest seemed only gloomier and thicker. Rhododendrons pressed close from the edge, rubbery leaves slapping against the headlamps, and ropes of honeysuckle vines dangled from the trees, trailing their cloying scent on the air. Down a sudden incline, up on the far side, then round another bend and into a clearing.

'There,' Patsy said, but Carrick was already slowing down. Off the road, in the dappled light of a large clearing, a semi-circle of caravans stood close by the banks of a stream. Smoke rose in a straight line from a small fire beside one of them.

'They're different,' Patsy said. She put a hand on the dashboard and leaned out of the window. There were no battered and rusted vans here, no converted transits or creaking single-deck buses. The caravans in the clearing were mostly brightly painted in gaudy colours, each heavily patterned in reds and blues and greens. Their wheels had polished wooden spokes and they all had long shafts for harnessing horses. Even as Patsy noticed that, she heard the whinny off at the far side of the clearing. A line of horses was tethered to ropes slung between the trees.

'It's like something out of a fairy tale,' she said.

'Let's hope it's got a happy ending.' Carrick opened the door and put a foot out onto the short grass. A figure moved from behind one of the ornate caravans and stood still, watching them. Patsy put a hand on Carrick's arm.

'No,' she said, stopping him mid-stride. 'Let me go.'

'But he might not be here.'

'If he is, I have to speak to him myself.'

Carrick looked at her, considered it, then shrugged. 'Any trouble and I'll be there,' he said. Patsy nodded and got out, letting the door swing half shut before she stopped it and left it open. She was reluctant to disturb the silence, even though the man beside the caravan was still watching. Her footsteps crackled in the dry leaves as she made her way to the far side of the clearing, and with every step, she could feel the tension wind up inside her. Maybe Paul wasn't here. Something inside of her knew that was wrong. *Maybe he was.* And if he was, what would she say? How would he react? In the past two days, she had

97

thought of what she might say to him when she found him, but all of her ideas, her well-chosen words, they simply evaporated on that short walk across the clearing in the forest.

She reached the line of caravans. The man stood silent, feet braced apart. His eyes, though shaded by the wide brim of an old hat, seemed to glitter. She'd seen that look in the eyes of the other gypsies who never seemed to be far from the house, always seemed to be around when she walked with the children. Patsy stopped. They eyed each other for a long moment, then finally she spoke.

'I'm looking for Paul Thomson,' she said in a rush.

'Aye,' the man replied. It was more of a question than a statement.

'Is he here?'

The man shrugged. 'Who wants to know?'

'I'm his wife.'

He shrugged again, and put his hands in the pockets of wide trousers. He was wearing a shirt that looked as if it was made of leather, cinched at the waist by braided thongs, adding to the quaint, fairytale image.

'Well? Have you seen him? Is he here?'

The man merely looked at her from under the brim, face impassive. The silence stretched out.

'What do you want here?' Paul's voice came ringing across the clearing.

Patsy whirled. He stood there, on the ornate steps of the caravan, hands on his hips, one foot resting on a higher step. The sun caught on his dark, short hair and made it shine. Behind him, the wood of the caravan gleamed, the only one not gaudily painted. Its lintel and door-frame, every panel of natural wood was carved into intricate shapes of animals and birds and other creatures which were neither. They seemed to move and ripple with a life of their own in the shards of light filtering through the tall trees.

'I . . .' Patsy started and faltered. She took a deep breath. 'I've come to talk to you.'

'So talk,' Paul said. His black brows were drawn together. He took a step down to the ground and folded his arms across his chest.

'Paul, you have to come back.'

'Why do I *have* to come back?'

'Because . . . because the children need you. I need you. We're all worried.'

He looked at her across the distance of ten yards. 'Do I look worried?'

She had no answer to that. She felt her breath quicken. 'Please Paul, we have to talk. You have to realise what you're doing.' Once she'd started, the words came out in a torrent. She told him that he needed help. That they would all support him. She told him many things, every one of them predicated on his getting into the car and coming back with them. *Back home.*

'Home?' he finally retorted when she'd run out of breath. 'I have no home, not any more. I have this,' he said, sweeping his hands out on either side, indicating the clearing, the forest, maybe the whole world.

Patsy felt her anger rise. Since he'd left she'd been drowning in a maelstrom of worry and fear and self-pity. And now he was standing there in the sunlight, handsome in a new buckskin shirt, telling her that she meant nothing to him; that the life they'd shared, that the career she'd sacrificed at the altar of his, were all worthless.

A faultline inside her cracked under the seismic pressure and the anger came brimming up to the surface. She shouted at him, voice rising higher and higher as the rage blurted out in a sudden release. She told him he was a coward, a faithless bastard, not fit to be a father. She stood there, fists clenched into tight balls and let the pent-up emotion cascade in a cataract.

Finally the words dried up and she stood there, panting like an animal, chest hitching from the effort. Then she simply burst into tears.

Paul stood there, expressionless but for a hint of a smile which got nowhere near his eyes. 'Are you quite finished?' he asked softly. In those four quiet words she could sense his own anger. She was about to reply when a noise behind him broke the silence. The caravan door swung open and the woman appeared. Patsy wiped away the hot tears and felt the cold anger tighten inside her again. The woman was slender and tall. She came slowly, gracefully down the steps, moving with an animal fluidity, taking each one deliberately, as if she had all the time in the world. She had searing green eyes which never left Patsy's for an instant. Her mass of raven hair gleamed an irridescent blue-black in the sunlight. Here, in the clearing, she was even more beautiful than she had seemed on the television. Patsy felt herself quail, knowing *this* was her rival.

The woman came gliding towards Paul, her feet making no sound at all on the grass. Her eyes did not blink, but stayed locked on Patsy's. A powerful current of energy seemed to jitter between them, an arc between opposite poles. She said nothing.

She's put her mark on him. She had cut Paul on the night of the midsummer. Sucked his skin to a bruise. She approached him now, face white as candlewax, almost translucent in the filtered light under the trees. She had cut him till he bled. *Had she licked the blood as it flowed? Had she swallowed it?* Her face was impassive now, eyes flashing emerald across the glade. For a quailing instant Patsy thought her skin looked too white to be real and on the heels of that she thought that the gypsy woman might smile, and if she did that she might show two long pointed teeth sharp and white against the sensuous red of her lips.

Kerron Vaunche did not smile, not then. She stopped beside Paul and leaned a hip against his. She stood tall, only an inch or two shorter than he did. Her gaze conveyed many things, contempt, amusement, maybe even pity, though the expression on her face could have been carved from stone.

'She wants me to leave,' Paul said. The woman remained motionless, but even so, Patsy sensed that she had heard, understood, communicated.

'You want me to give this up?' Paul asked Patsy. She nodded slowly, unable to take her eyes away from the other woman. The anger inside her was battling the despair that had swooped inside her when she recognised the uncanny, malignant perfection of Kerron Vaunche.

She has the power, the old woman at the fire had told her, and Patsy could sense that power. It was the might that all truly beautiful women possessed over men. There was nothing mystical or magic, but it was the power that had sent men to war, and made them kill and mutilate other men. *She's put her mark on him and that's bound them body and soul, and nothing can untie that knot.*

'I want you to come home,' Patsy blurted. Kerron Vaunche tilted her head and smiled. There was no malice in it, just an acknowledgement of condescending superiority. The victor's recognition of the vanquished.

Paul unfolded his arms and snaked his right hand round the woman's shoulder. He too was smiling, but there was a gleeful malevolence in it. He drew Kerron Vaunche closer to him. Patsy stood mesmerised, her stomach clenching in spasms as she watched Paul's hand pull back the ornate lace shawl from the dark haired woman's neck. It slid down to the crook of her bare arm. Without stopping he eased his fingers under the scoop neck of her bodice, sliding it down the smooth skin. It disappeared from view, but the thin material hid nothing. Patsy stood in the sunlight, mesmerised by the woman's eyes and by the fact that her own husband was standing there in front of her, deliberately kneading the woman's breast. Under the silken blouse, she could see his knuckles and fingers moving, recognised the teasing movement. Kerron Vaunche stiffened for an instant. Her eyes seemed to look into the far distance and from across the intervening space Patsy recognised the pleasure that rippled through the woman's body. Kerron Vaunche took a sharp intake of breath and then her eyes focused again.

She turned her head, freeing Patsy from the hold of her gaze, leaned in towards Paul and slowly, very sensuously bit him on the cheek. Her lipstick left a trail like blood.

Patsy felt a jagged knife of anguish twist in her belly. A helpless moan escaped her. Kerron Vaunche drew her head away and turned to fix those eyes on her again. The woman eased herself away from Paul, gently raising his hand out from the folds of her blouse. She walked away from him, eyes never leaving Patsy for an instant. All sound died; the chirruping of finches in the trees, the crackle of the fire, the whinny of the horses, they faded out as if a door had been shut, leaving Kerron Vaunche and Patsy alone in a bubble of their own reality.

The gypsy woman walked towards the fire, walked beyond it, gliding with infinite grace past the wavering air above the flames. Her image rippled, though the eyes gleamed luminous, then she was on the other side, circling Patsy who had to turn, move her feet to keep the other woman in view. Kerron Vaunche circled her, like a predator stalking prey, a female stoat closing in on a mesmerised rabbit. Patsy felt the tension sizzle, winding up taut as violin strings. She turned as the woman circled, trying to keep pace, lost in the mutual, malign orbit. The background green blurred past. Kerron Vaunche glided faster, past the fire, into the wavering turbulence of the heat. Smoke billowed suddenly, roiling out to envelop Patsy. The scent of woodsmoke, resinous pine, aromatic oak filled her. The world looped and tumbled and spun.

Patsy saw . . .

Kerron Vaunche come out from the darkness, lunging forward like a snake, a white face against the black. The deathly visage exploded into fragments that became the wings of a million black flies rising in a thick swarming mass from a shape that lay on a flat stone. Lightning sizzled, searing the stone in phosphorescence and the shape on the stone was Paul, naked and spread-eagled, arms wide. The tracery of scars snaked up the inside of his arms in whorls like the fingerprints of a giant. He was turning to face the pale shape that came gliding towards him and the whorls spun and wove and Kerron Vaunche condensed out of the swarm of flies and climbed athwart him, easing herself down onto his bucking pelvis, her hair writhing and twisting, black snakes striking out in gorgon coils. They hissed and spat while the gypsy woman's breath became a pant and then a howl and a snarl, and Paul was bellowing like a bull and shoving himself into her. Kerron Vaunche arched her back and the snakes became rats' tails and her body elongated and her eyes changed from green to orange.

Patsy saw . . .

Paul on the stone, face contorted in ecstasy, neck corded, wrists manacled to the stone where the cravings wriggled and contorted out from the surface and where the light of a baleful moon shone through the narrow leaded windows onto the altar and his skin began to peel away from his face, wrinkling and shivering while the thing upon him hunched, darkening now, foreshortening as it shrank and widened, became a squat shape, head bowed. Paul moaned a shudder of sound and the head came up and she saw it was the monster of her dreams, mouth gaping and shard-teeth dripping with poison and blood. It snuffled and grunted, fixing her with malevolent orange eyes that had no pupils. It lowered its warted head ... and the form on the stone was not Paul but Judith, slender and gracile, flopped and dead. The monstrosity snuffled again, gobbling down there in the wet mess of the chasm, and when it rose again the flies came bursting out in a fog and Judith's dead eyes fixed accusingly on her. Kerron Vaunche laughed from the shadows and Patsy turned. The woman's face was old and lined now, shrivelled and dry, as if she'd been drained of all humanity. The witchety thing cackled at her and pointed to the stone. The carved shapes were still writhing, little stone demons forcing their way up from the surface on which the pale shape lay trussed, arms and legs spread and a wet chasm cleaving from chin to crotch.

Patsy saw ...

It was not Judith on the stone. It was herself, and she was not dead. She was twisting and shuddering on the stone while a dark squat thing drew the life out of her into its orange eyes and the flies crawled over the splashes of blood. From somewhere up above, blood dripped into a round, black bowl and from the shadows a dreadful raggedy thing with a broad squashed face contorted in a demented scream came lurching on stick-like limbs. The scarecrow thing gibbered mad laughter and the dying Patsy on the stone altar opened her mouth to cry out. A red bubble swelled between her lips.

There was a small popping sound.

And Patsy was back in the clearing. The light flashing through the leaves stabbed in her eyes and Patsy staggered off-balance, gasping. A pulse was pounding in her temples and her heart squeezed like a fist inside her chest.

Kerron Vaunche had not moved. She was still standing hipshot, leaning against Paul, only now turning away from where she had drawn her white teeth down his cheek, leaving a red trail that was not lipstick, but a trickle of blood where the skin had broken. Paul's urgent fingers worked away under the silken sheen of the blouse.

Patsy took two stumbling steps backwards, still in the after shock of the preposterous vision that had exploded in her mind.

That had been blasted into her mind, her brain corrected. Kerron Vaunche fixed her with those green eyes. Her lips parted in a slow smile that was absolutely chilling. Her canine teeth were smeared with red.

Patsy turned and ran. A sob blurted out from her and tears blinded her eyes as she came scrambling across the clearing. She banged her thigh on the headlamp, stumbled, made it to the door and clambered inside.

'Get me out of here,' she cried.

'Wait a minute,' Carrick said. It sounded as if he was speaking through gritted teeth, but Patsy was wiping the tears from her eyes. She didn't want to look at him, did not want to see pity in his eyes too. 'I'm going to have words with that bloody fool.'

'No,' Patsy yelled, hearing her own voice screech. 'No please, Carrick. Just take me out of here.' The power of the vision was still hunting inside her, and instinctively she knew that the woman had mesmerised her, put the foul hallucination into her mind. She wanted to be as far away from her as possible, and as far away as she could get from the gut-wrenching sight of Paul fumbling at the woman's breast. *Bucking on the stone.* Bleeding from her bite.

'No way is he getting away with that,' Carrick growled back, obviously unaware of the strange and terrifying mental encounter. He had clicked the door open and had one foot out on the grass. 'That was the rottenest thing I've ever seen. What a little shit.'

'No, Carrick. Leave him,' Patsy cried, grabbing the big man's arm. 'Just leave it. I can't take him back now. Not ever.'

She closed her eyes tight shut, straining to keep the tears inside, and clenched her hands into fists pressed on her knees. The vision came loping back at her and she shrank from it in dread. A sudden foreboding closed in on her like an eclipse. She felt the car reverse, jolt forward and then they were going back the way they had come along the twisting forest road.

Up in the trees a bird chattered raucously. Patsy imagined the sound of the woman's gleeful laughter and she wondered, shuddering, if the gypsy had put that too into her head.

8

She couldn't stop shaking. Small earthquakes, little seismic tremors would make her knees jerk, or her shoulders twitch and Patsy had to hang on to the wheel tight enough to make the knuckles stand out white again. She heard Judith snuffle miserably. Peter whispered to her and Patsy's heart ached for both of them. They were scared, all three of them, though Peter had shown that he'd enough guts for them all.

'Nine years old,' Patsy whispered to herself.

Nine, and he'd stood out there on the hard shoulder, legs braced, preparing to take on the pack of scavengers. There had been no time for explanations, but he had resisted when she'd ordered him back to the car. Without looking at him, she'd sensed his resolve to be the *man*. He'd wanted to protect his mother and his sister. She felt a surge of pride which went a long way to calming the internal tremors, but she was still scared, still desperate and still filled with a creeping dread.

Worse, Patsy felt the heavy squeeze of guilt. Wherever they were (*and God alone knew where* that *was*), she had brought them here. They hadn't been given a choice. Peter and Judith had been bundled into the car and driven off into the night and now they were stuck on this misbegotten road where nothing at all seemed normal, and everything seemed to be completely *wrong*. She felt as if she'd stumbled out of one nightmare and into another.

She drove steadily, watching out for the sign that would tell her the service station was only a mile or so further ahead. To the left, high above the red glow in the distance, the thick clouds parted, blown apart by some turbulence of the storm and Patsy got a glimpse of the moon. Another shudder, another set of footsteps on her grave, rippled through her when she saw it was almost full. Another day or two and it would be complete, and the time would be ripe.

Get them out before the midwinter. The girl had taken her

hands and looked in her eyes and pleaded with her. *Come the full moon and she'll take them.*

Patsy hadn't believed, not completely, not then. She knew better now as the moonlight glowed through the gap in the clouds, glowing a dull and dirty orange, shading to red. The clouds knitted themselves together again, cutting off the light. Patsy glanced again and the moon was gone, but there was an after-image dancing in her eyes. She tried to focus on it, but it faded away. She couldn't be sure, but she thought that in the brief glimpse of the lady's face worked in the canyons and plains of the lunar surface, it had reminded her of someone. And – though again she couldn't be sure of this – the face had been glaring down at her. She shook her head, dismissing the notion.

'Getting paranoid,' she told herself. Things were bad enough on this bleak road without conjuring up fantasies. *You've a long road to travel* Gadge-woman. The old woman had held her hand over the heat of the fire. *A long ways to go. Best you turn back and go back under stone, for there's a bad road ahead of you.* She'd been right about that, sure enough. A long road it had been and a bad road now.

The man with the beard, Crandall Gilfeather, he'd warned her, told her of the *Ley Road*, the Low Road. *He claims the souls who travel the low road, but that is his right.* That's what he'd said about the dark force. It had all been mumbo-jumbo, stuff and nonsense. Then.

She drove on, trying not to think of what he'd said, following the highway as it curved to the left, banking up an incline. She reached the crest and started down the far slope, seeing the sky lightening in the distance, layering bands of luminescence above the far horizon in greasy streaks of turquoise and mauve. Way off to the right, she could make out the enormous curve of another motorway riding high on concrete pillars. There seemed to be movement there, though it was too far away to make out. Certainly she could hear the rumbling sound of distant traffic and the air still carried that oily, clogged scent of road fumes and mould.

'Is it morning yet?' Peter piped up.

'Just about that time, honey.'

'I'm really hungry. I could eat a scabby horse.'

106

'That's disgusting,' Patsy retorted, laughing despite herself. 'Tell you what. If they have scabby horse on the menu at this pit stop, then I'll order you two. And you'll have to eat both of them.'

Judith made a small shuddery sound in her sleep and Patsy reached behind her to take her daughter's hand. It was clammy and hot and under the skin the nerves were shivering with some sort of tension. It didn't feel right and Patsy knew she would have to get Judith off the road, into somewhere warm and dry. She let the hand drop listlessly to Judith's lap, knowing she'd done the right thing in taking them from Paul yet still castigating herself for it bringing them both into danger.

The road swung downhill now, a long, smooth slope and in the early light of dawn Patsy was able to see beyond the scrub alder and willow that had densely colonised the verges. She reached the bend and onto the straight which still descended to a flat plain. Beyond the scrub and the low wooden fence that marked the motorway boundary she saw the first building since Broadford House. In the distance, silhouetted in the wan light, an old derelict church stood alone, the roof swaybacked and nailsick. Most of the slates were gone and the little pointed steeple stood askew, almost beyond its centre of gravity. It looked as though it would tumble and crash through the roof of the nave at any moment. Beside the church there was an old graveyard surrounded by a tumbled dry-stone wall. The headstones were aslant and listing, grey as worn-down teeth as they sank into the ground. The church and graveyard looked gaunt and forbidding, standing alone on a bleak moor. It did not look like the kind of place where a traveller would stop and seek comfort. To Patsy it did not look like the kind of place a traveller would *ever* visit. It had a haunted look, an aspect of decay and rot, and beneath that, something more sinister. The narrow gothic windows held black shadows in their depths, like scoured eye sockets on long-dead bone, yet there seemed to be *life* of a sort encapsulated in the crumbling ruin. *Not a house of God*, Patsy thought. Not any more, no matter what it had been in the past. The dismal little church, now sliding out of vision offered no welcome at all, but it had a strange, chilling magnetism, like the atmosphere of Broadford House where bad things had happened again and again over a long time. Patsy felt it draw her eyes back towards the dank and mouldering stone, and in an instant she was certain that there was something, some unknown *entity* inside the old church, some being that sensed her passing and turned over in a long and restless slumber and dreamed hungry thoughts. She recoiled from the image, but it lingered with her like the cold touch of disease. She dragged her eyes away, fighting against the strange and coldly flaccid contact. Deep in the primitive centre of her brain where all instinct lies, she felt a mental wrench and the sensation was gone. She moved on, fingers of apprehension trailing up and down her spine.

A few hundred yards downslope, closer to the road than the church, a single tree stood out against the skyline, barren and as gaunt as the derelict church had been, its twigless branches bare and peeling, and covered in a hoary moss. It looked as if it had sucked poison up from the moorland soil and died of it. Again there was a sensation of a *wrongness*, something dead but still alive with dark and foetid malignancy waiting to burgeon in some unholy springtime. Patsy recoiled from the notion, wondering where these weird – *and scary* – ideas were coming from. She looked away, but a fluttering movement drew her eyes back to the tree.

Birds were roosting on the empty boughs, big black carrion birds, crows or ravens or rooks, though she couldn't tell at the distance. They sat still, beaks pointing into the wind, black eyes fixed on the car as it moved past. They looked too heavy and ponderous to be crows, and she immediately thought of the bird in the night that had almost flown into the path of the car. They sat there, heads now turning to follow the motion, black and hunched. They looked like vultures waiting for something to die, funeral birds dressed in the sombre suits of the wake. Patsy looked away, but she felt those eyes on her and she wished she was anywhere else but here. She wondered if perhaps she'd missed a turn-off (*assuming the first voice on the emergency telephone had been telling the truth*) but she couldn't recall passing a ramp.

That didn't mean there hadn't been one, for she'd been driving on her nerves, on her last reserves. And she'd missed so many turn-offs in the past, taken enough wrong roads ever since Paul

Thomson had stood there in the forest with that Vaunche woman and had looked in Patsy's eyes while he broke her heart. She'd come a long way since Kerron Vaunche had glided round her in a circle, staring into her soul.

She had left the forest clearing that day, tears blurring her vision, running down her cheeks, salt on her lips. They were the hot tears of dread and rage, hurt and loss, and no matter how she tried to blink them back, they flooded out until she had to ask Carrick to stop. He drove on another four miles on the narrow road until they reached a small village. He stopped in the square and put an arm around her shoulders, pulled her in towards him. She buried her face in the hollow of his shoulder and let the sobs judder through her until they exhausted themselves. Finally she pulled away and dabbed at her eyes with a handkerchief, feeling sick and weak and scared.

'I don't know what to do,' she said, voice quavering with the force of her tears. The image of Paul's leprous face kept swinging back up to the forefront of her mind, jostling with the memory of the cold, contemptuous look in his eye as he groped at the woman.

'You should have let me kick the crap out of that little shit,' Carrick said. 'He might be my brother, but by God he deserves to have his legs done for that.'

'It's too late for that. I just don't know what to do now. It's all happened so fast. I thought we were happy.'

Carrick sat back and looked down at her. 'Did you? You mean there was no clue?'

She sat still for a moment, then shook her head. 'No. I'm wrong. There were plenty of clues, but I didn't see them because I wasn't looking. I never thought, really. You don't, do you?'

'Can't say,' Carrick shrugged, trying to make light of it. 'Never been married yet.'

'Well, if you do, don't let her change you. It's the biggest mistake you can make. I know that now.'

'Let's rustle up a coffee,' he suggested. 'You look as if you could use it.' They got out of the car and he put his arm around her shoulder, pointed to a tea shop on the far side of the square and angled her towards it. She felt tiny next to him. Despite what his brother had done, with Carrick, Patsy felt safe, and for some reason, that thought dismayed her. Already she knew she had to change back to what she had been before, instead of feeling weak and helpless and feminine. If she had learnt anything, it was that she could no longer be dependent. Not now, not ever.

The coffee was strong and black and bitter and just exactly what she needed. The image of Paul in the forest hovered in her memory and she had to force herself to push it to a mental arm's length.

'It's my fault, really,' she had told Carrick. 'I changed too much. I just wanted us to be happy and it didn't happen.'

'I don't get you,' he said, looking at her over the rim of the cup. He had a big, craggy face and weather crinkles on either side of his friendly blue eyes. His broken nose, slightly kinked to one side, should have made him look tougher, but gave the opposite impression. He was like a rumpled bear of a man, but comfortable and easy. He seemed to have none of the tension that had made Paul so tightly energetic.

'You should be what you want to be, not what somebody else wants you to be,' she started. 'I didn't realise until now how much I've let myself down, so it's my fault for letting Paul change me.'

'I don't see much of a change. You don't look more than a couple of years older.'

She shook her head and a smile came unbidden from some rosier depth. 'Big smoothie, but that's not what I meant. I remember when I first met Paul. We were both at university. He was in law and I was doing geophysics with a sideswipe at anthropology. God, I was *good*. Everybody said so, but more than that, I knew it myself. Not in a boasting way, you understand. I mean, I had to work for it like everybody else, but I had a *grasp* of things. I was on the debating team and I had a brown belt in Shotokan and I was on the second fencing team. I mean, it was the best time of my life, and look where it's all gone.'

She looked up at the big man. 'I threw it all away on a man who would rather live in a caravan and feel a gypsy woman's tits,' she blurted. Two tables away, three old women with blue hair and tea-cosy hats turned to stare. One of them tut-tutted loudly in disapproval. Even Carrick looked surprised.

110

'You've got the kids,' he ventured.

'Sure I've got them, and at the end of the day, they're all that matters. I mean that bastard doesn't care, does he? He's got a little girl and a son of nine and he's out there in the woods *screwing*, for heaven's sake.'

The elderly tutter did it again and Carrick laughed aloud. He turned and looked at the old women, worked his face into a glare and they all hastily went back to their gossiping.

'But it's not that. It's not even him. It's *me*. It's my fault, because I let him do it to me. I don't know when it started or how he managed it, but he made me change, and I want to change back again. I want to be myself again.'

'I still don't get you.'

'It's simple. I used to be Patricia Havelin, bright young thing, over-achiever. I was fit and healthy and popular and then I met a guy who was all of these things, at least so I believed, but I was wrong, because I was better than he thought I was, and he was less than he believed himself to be.'

Carrick simply looked puzzled.

'I could have done anything,' Patsy went on, 'but I didn't. We got engaged after we graduated and Paul took his indentures with George Urquhart. I'd been headhunted by plenty of firms, probably they were intrigued by the fact that I had an anthropology degree plus a decent pair of legs, but I thought I'd give myself some time, so I went on a trip to Olduvai to help with a dig that was going on. Anthropology was my real love anyway. I stayed for nine months and when I came back, we got married. Paul was doing well, then I got pregnant, and somehow it was agreed that there was no point in me getting a job, starting a career. I don't remember it being discussed at the time, but it just sort of happened. I stopped being Patricia, stopped being Trish. Paul called me Patsy and that's what I became. His *patsy*.'

She stopped and her eyes unfocussed as she looked back in time. 'That's the way it was. I was setting the pattern for things *just happening*. Peter came along and Paul had his associate's position and a promise of a partnership and he was mixing with the county *mafia*. He'd forgotten the old me, and I had forgotten the old me because I was wrapped up in little Pete at the time, and we had long since stopped talking about me and it was

111

all him. He had a career and plans and ambitions and I let mine unravel, and at the end of it I was just a decoration at the faculty dinners. It just happened because Paul didn't want me to be bright or assertive or ambitious, and it has taken me until now to realise what it was all about. He was jealous. I was a bloody threat. So he took that threat away by smothering me in domestic bliss and after that he started wearing me down, and I let him erode my own self without even realising I had lost my identity.'

She stopped, drew her brows down.

'So I'm going to get it back. No offence, Carrick, but I'm dropping the Thomson, and I'll do the same for the children too. I want to be Patsy Havelin again.'

'Did he beat you?' Carrick asked, ignoring the statement with a shrug.

'Oh, he slapped me once or twice. I got the odd dig in the ribs and the knuckles on my arms, but nothing you could call brutal. No broken bones. But the real brutality was what was going on here.' She tapped her forehead. 'He stole the *me* to make him feel better, and I won't forgive him for that. It's going to be hard enough to forgive myself for letting it happen, but I'll work on it. Today I saw him for what he really is and I shed my tears and I won't shed any more. He can stay in those trees for ever as far as I'm concerned, and I hope he freezes in the winter. I hope his *balls* freeze off.'

One of the old women looked round again, glanced at Carrick, and hastily turned away. He leaned over, reached his hands across the table and engulfed hers.

'Good girl,' he said and gave her a straight wink.

Back in the car he drove through the square and out of the village, heading away from the trees. Patsy did her best to shuck the memory from her mind. By the time he stopped at the bungalow, she was already planning the future.

'Thanks for everything,' she told her brother-in-law, stretching up to kiss him on the cheek.

'Oh, any time,' he said, putting his arm around her shoulder and pulling her towards him so strongly she felt her ribs crack. 'And I meant that,' he said, looking down at her, his expression grave. 'Because I love you.'

Patsy froze. She looked up and he was looking back and she felt her face redden.

'Oh, Carrick, that's the last thing I need to hear right now,' she snapped, awkwardly trying to pull away from him.

At first he drew his head back, eyes as puzzled as they had been in the coffee shop, then without warning he burst out laughing. He still held Patsy close and she could feel his body shake with the force of the laughter.

'No! Silly bugger,' he said, spluttering. 'I don't mean *in* love. That's reserved for a very pretty major in the Royal Fusiliers, who you'll probably meet pretty soon. You'll like her. Lots of freckles, great legs.'

He laughed again and Patsy felt her blush deepen. 'Listen, when I say I love you, that's exactly what I mean. It's not a pass. It means that any time you need help, you only have to ask. Somebody in the Thomson clan has to be on your side.'

She had filed for divorce within weeks, though Paul's mother had pleaded with her not to be hasty, to think of the children. Patsy had thought of the children and had then contacted another lawyer who started the proceedings, but a start was all it had amounted to because after the shattering confrontation in the forest, Paul had simply vanished which meant the initial papers couldn't be served. Patsy hired a detective who earned a heavy fee for the week's work he claimed he'd done – plus expenses – but came up with nothing. Big Carrick had offered his help. He'd put the word around with his former forces friends, but Paul still stayed unfound. It was as if Kerron Vaunche had woven a gypsy spell and made him disappear. More than a year dragged by. The children had been fretful at first. Peter took to walking in his sleep for a few weeks, asked a few awkward questions, and then went back to playing football. Judith was still too young to be seriously affected. Her asthma was still a year or so away from becoming a serious problem. Patsy began getting over the trauma. She picked herself up, got in touch with a few people from the old university days who opened a few doors for her which got her some consultancy work with a couple of conglomerates and one very large oil exploration firm which was enough to pay the bills and allowed her to do most of the work using a computer link from the spare room.

She was getting over it. She was Patsy Havelin again and the two worry furrows between her eyebrows gradually smoothed themselves out and a couple of laughter lines began to work themselves on either side of her lips and she was making it, though on some nights she still dreamed of the woman stalking round in a circle and the vision that had come through the billowing smoke of the campfire, and in the dream she saw those mocking green eyes and Paul's hand working away under the sheen of the blouse and some nights she woke up crying out in anger.

Almost two years after that cataclysmic meeting in the forest clearing, on a high summer's day, Patsy had been in the garden behind the cottage pottering in the borders, cutting some of the fragrant tea roses for the vase she kept by the kitchen window. The children had been playing on the swing Carrick had fixed on the looping branch of the old weeping ash tree. There were two blue braided ropes securely fixed to the bough and each end was attached to an old car tyre which was big enough to take two small backsides. Patsy had watched Peter push his sister who was so small she kept slipping through centre of the tyre, much to his amusement. Judith was squealing with delight as her brother swung her higher and higher until her feet almost disappeared amongst the heavy leaves on the lower branches. Patsy had snipped some roses and put them in water and then she'd gone back through the kitchen to the vegetable plot to pick a lettuce for the salad she planned for dinner. She cut a tight iceberg ball and then winkled out a handful of baby carrots.

A deadly silence impinged on her consciousness.

She lowered the basket to the ground and stood up slowly. The silence was almost complete. Save for the murmur of slow water in the brook that skirted the garden, there was no sound. The warm breeze had died completely. It was as if a sleepy summer spell had been cast over the garden. The birds had all stopped singing, even the robin who pugnaciously proclaimed his territory from a quartz stone in the rockery in the corner. The drone of the bees over the wild poppy border had faded to silence and the hum of the insects in the tall lime tree which shaded the lawn had hushed. It was if something had come into the garden that the small creatures could somehow sense and

114

they had frozen in fear. It was as if Patsy was in a warm capsule of her own, where time stood still. She raised her face and felt the sun on her eyelids, unaware on any conscious level of anything wrong.

Except. Something inside of her sensed it and gripped at her belly.

There was no laughter, no squeals of delight. *Her heart started to pound under her ribs.*

There were no high-pitched demands from Judith to be pushed higher and higher. *And her blood seemed to freeze to slush in her veins.*

There was a dead silence all around her and an empty place in her soul where she could always sense the presence of her own children. *And while she knew none of these things on a conscious level, the* mother *in her felt it like an echo of the pain of childbirth and the alarm bells were clanging in her mind and a voice in her head was babbling and yelling and telling her something was wrong, that something was awfully and dreadfully* wrong.

Patsy stood up slowly and turned, trying to be completely normal. A cool eddy of wind came from nowhere and shivered the tips of the birch trees. For an instant the sunlight faded and then it came back, as if a shadow, a *presence* had somehow swirled into the garden and then gone. Gradually the sounds came back as she crossed from the vegetable plot to the corner of the house. The bees started droning in the border. The robin warbled its piccolo notes and was answered by a wren, even more liquid by the moss bank at the brook. The insects hummed in the tall lime tree. But there was no sound of children at play.

'They've gone into the house,' she told herself, speaking out loud. *Of course they'd gone into the house*, her brain told her heart and her heart bawled: *Fool!*

Patsy made it to the corner, breath beginning to back up in her lungs where a valve in her windpipe had clamped shut. She turned, skirted the clematis blossoms, crossed the flagstone path onto the short grass of the lawn next to the weeping tree. The old tyre swung lazily at the end of the ropes. She opened her mouth to call out to Peter and Judith while the cold hand crept up to her heart and squeezed. She tried to think, tried to recall when the silence had started. Had she heard the slam of a car door? Had she. *Had she?*

A bright yellow ribbon lay curled where it had fallen under the swing. The children were gone.

Patsy Havelin didn't see them again for more than a year.

In the frantic hours and days that followed, Patsy worked herself to a state of near collapse. She had called in the police but Paul had got there ahead of her. Her divorce had never been finalised and the question of custody had never been determined, and in the end they shook their heads and told her there was nothing they could do. Paul had disappeared again and this time he had taken her son and daughter, and for six months her whole life was focused on finding them and getting them back again.

It was Carrick who found Broadford House, more than three hundred miles north, across the border in Scotland. How Carrick had traced his brother, Patsy never found out and he did not tell her. All she knew was that Paul was involved in some kind of religious organisation. She had travelled north, but had never got past the front gates. Paul had stood there, hands on his hips, his black hair now long and braided at the back. He'd lost weight and his eyes were dark and hard and cold. The woman had been there too; Kerron Vaunche, standing close to him, eyes glinting with smug mockery. Paul had come up to the gate and stared at her through the peeling iron bars.

'There's nothing here for you,' he'd said flatly, unblinking. 'You should have saved yourself a journey.'

'I want to see Peter and Judith.' The words came tumbling out in a rush. She could hear the panic in her own voice.

'They're safe now. They're with me and that's where they'll stay.'

'I have to see them now.'

Paul had pushed himself back from the wrought iron. 'Time you were on your way. We're busy here, and my children are happy. They don't want to see you.'

She recalled screaming something at him as he walked away, braided hair swinging across his shoulder-blades. Kerron Vaunche had stared at her and then she'd grinned a cold rictus that was chillingly grotesque on the chiselled perfection of her face.

Despite Patsy's pleas, the police had refused to get involved

116

in what was obviously a domestic issue which they said should be resolved in a court. Patsy had gone home and filed for divorce, claiming custody of Peter and Judith. Paul counter-filed, spinning out her anguish, and the legal papers went back and forth for months.

Then Carrick came over to the cottage with the new woman in his life, the pretty major from the Royal Fusiliers who did have freckles and great legs. Her name was Connie and she knew someone who knew someone else who helped operate an organisation which rescued cult members, and who had told her what went on behind the big gates at the front of Broadford House. Patsy only ever knew him as McGregor, and whether that was his real name or not, she never discovered. He was small and wiry and had staring, fanatical eyes, and when Patsy met him she thought he looked as crazy as the kind of people he seemed determined to wipe out. McGregor brought two people to speak to Patsy.

Lisa Prosser had been the first.

'Get them out of there, missus, for there's something bad going to happen at the midwinter, I know that for sure.'

Lisa had been whip-thin with her brown hair caught back in a pony tail and great wide eyes that flicked from Patsy to Carrick, nervous as a roe deer. She looked as if she hadn't eaten in weeks and ate that way too, head down on the plate, one arm crooked around it to barricade her territory. Patsy and Carrick had sat in silence, watching fascinated as Lisa's working hand shovelled sausage, egg and bacon away as if her life depended on it, pausing only to take a man-sized swallow of tea, then bending to the task again. She'd the soft West Country burr of a farm-girl and looked as if a fresh breeze would tumble her down; but when she finished her meal, sitting with elbow pressed down on the old pine table in the kitchen, her eyes had hardened.

'Sure, I seen your lad,' she'd told her. 'And the little one, the girl. That's the one you should be worrying about because the *Catanna*, she'd got her most of the time, got her dressed the same and learning all the chants, stuff we never got taught.'

She took a big drink of tea which must have been scalding, but seemed to have no effect.

'But if I was you, I'd be getting them out of there quick as

117

you like. It was bad enough when Kenyon was running things, though I never saw that at the time, but now with them two, your husband and the woman, beggin' your pardon Mrs Thomson.'

'Havelin,' she corrected automatically. 'My own name.'

'Sure,' Lisa said, shrugging her shoulders. 'Ever since they came, it's got weirder still. Old John Kenyon, he was out to make himself bit o' money and bed most of the women, I realise that now, though I thought he was God at the time, but he weren't a *bad* fella, so to speak. Not really *evil*. But things began to change after they arrived.'

'In what way?' Patsy wasn't really sure what this was all about. Carrick had told her to take McGregor's advice and just listen to the girl and to the elderly man with the neat white beard who sat quietly at the far end of the table with his eyes half closed.

'John Kenyon had our heads all full of rubbish,' Lisa went on. 'Like we was hypnotised. Must've been something like that because I thought he was God. George, that was my boyfriend, he wanted out of there and I told him he could go any time. He stayed on a while, even after I went to bed with John Kenyon, but by then I'd have slit my wrists if they'd asked me to. It got so you couldn't think for yourself and you had to tell them everything and when I said George had wanted to take me away, they said he was a sinner and he'd go to hell.'

I'll see you in hell first. Patsy got a sensation of *déjà vu*. She saw Kerron Vaunche's flashing eyes and imagined how it had been with Lisa. Not as scary maybe, but every bit as vicious.

'George stayed on and after a while, he got just like the rest of us, and he didn't seem to mind what happened to me. I think his family were giving money in, so they'd worked on him pretty good. At the time I didn't care. Kenyon was doin' the rounds with me and every other girl and he said it was holy. Every time he lay on top of me it was like a sacrament and I just wanted to die and go to heaven. Shows you how weird it was, eh?'

Lisa gave a sad little smile and shrugged her thin shoulders.

'I can't remember when it really changed,' she said, eyes unfocussed as she searched her memory. 'They came at the tail end of the year. Old John Kenyon was raking in thousands from collections and donations. He saw himself as a messiah and he could save us all and we all believed him. George and me had been squatting in London and we were hungry. He had tuberculosis and I was popping anything I could get my hands on, speed, acid, you name it. Then these folk started coming round and giving us food and saying what a better world they were making, and they got George into hospital and fixed him up. Never charged a penny and when he got out they got us to come along with them. They were smart all right, for George came from money. His family had plenty of it and he'd never asked for any before, but there was money there and the New Dawn Brethren knew about it. They had a centre in the East End, just an old church, but it was clean and warm and everybody was so happy and smiling that it was like going to heaven. All we had to do was believe in John Kenyon and that wasn't hard to do. He'd a way of talking to you and a way of looking at you that made it okay, know what I mean?'

Patsy knew what she meant. She'd only realised how much she'd sublimated her own personality after Paul had walked out.

'I can't say how long it took, but I'd have done anything for him. He said we could all be free and happy. All we had to do was believe in him. Everybody did, and it was fine until then. Weird, but fine. He said sex was okay, better than okay, but only as a sacrifice and only once you'd reached the plateau of grace. Guess who was the only one on the plateau? Right.'

Lisa Prosser reached for a cigarette and lit it, inhaling in one long drag. 'But it didn't seem to matter. It just seemed right at the time. Looking back he was so chock-full of grace he couldn't have had time to sleep. But then Paul Thomson, your man came along, and the woman with him, that Kerron. I never saw it at the time, but they were like a couple of wolves finding a flock of sheep. They just came in and it was like they'd always been there. At first they mixed in, but it was clear right from the start that they were different. Just how different, nobody had any idea.

'Looking back, John Kenyon wanted her pretty bad. You ever see a stallion in a stall next to a mare in season? That's what old John was like. His eyes would follow her around and you could even hear his breath wheezing, the way it did when he was having me. He lost interest in all of us and I remember being pretty cut up about it because of all the grace I was missing. I get embarrassed telling you about it Mrs Thomson, but they said I was to tell you everything.

' 'John Kenyon thought the sun shone out of her backside. His second in command was a woman called Angela. I think she was one of the first. A couple of months after they arrived, she jumped off the roof and broke her neck. There was some whispers about it, but not much. You see we didn't do that much thinking for ourselves. John, or one of the others would tell us what to do and we'd do it and think it was fine.

'But then things started to change, and it was easy to see, looking back, who was behind it. John never seemed to get over Angela's accident, though now I don't think it was an accident. Paul and Kerron were always with him. I don't know what happened behind that door, but she must have been working on him. He just seemed to get older every day and while that was happening, what they were telling us started to change.

'It was about that time they opened up the bottom basement that nobody even knew existed and started clearing out all the rubble that was piled in there. They found the stone table there, right under the tower, and it was like Kerron knew it had been there all along. Things started to change pretty quick, but to us, somehow it seemed kind of normal.

'The New Dawn Brethren, I know how it was all a con, but then it was about enlightenment. We had to improve ourselves all the time and reach a higher plane. But it changed when Kerron started to organise things, and that was when they started having the ceremonies down in the basement or out at the standing stones that go all round the grounds.

'We hardly ever saw John any more, except at the ceremonies which were mostly chanting at first and invoking – that's what they called it – a lot of names that nobody knew at first. It was fun at the start, because they said it was from the old times, from the Druids, and that the personal fulfilment could be stronger with the help of the earth forces. We had Beltane and Samhain and other special days, and it was around this time that John stopped coming out and Kerron and Paul were running things and she said she was the *Catanna* which is a kind of go-between. That was when the sacrifices began. Easy at first, just fruit and things from the garden and then other offerings, but it didn't take long until they were cutting the heads off chickens. At Beltane, that's in the spring, they killed a goat and its blood was smeared all over the stone and over our foreheads, and the Catanna said that we were getting close to the power of the great princes. After that, Kerron had the women giving drops of their blood. By this time old John had a stroke and they wheeled him about and all he did was dribble down his chin, but they said his mind was still sharp as a tack. They would, wouldn't they?

'I never noticed really how weird things had got. Kerron told us the world was in pretty bad shape because of all the pollution and the ozone layer and stuff, and she said the old ones were beginning to wake up and take notice. We were the only people who could save the world, like the chosen few. She told us there would be a disaster and the old ones, the old gods, would rise up again, but we'd be saved, and that was fine by me. I really believed it. She said they were the princes of power and they would listen to us as long as we made the offerings on the stone. She told us this was the hub of all the ley lines and all the power would flow through them and into us and we'd all be saved.

'It was after this that George came to me in the garden and pulled me down among the trees. He said he had to get away from the place and he was all scared and jumpy, looking over his shoulder all the time like somebody was following him. I said not to be daft, but then he showed me a book with pictures in it. It was just like the big stone down in the basement, but the picture showed women tied on it with their throats cut and all the blood running down the sides of the stone. It was all in a funny language, but he said he could make sense of it. It was some sort of thing that was to happen on the midwinter, which is a big important day. But George said it was witchcraft and these princes Kerron was talking about weren't gods, but devils. He said he had to get away because he thought they were going to start really cutting people's throats, and he said Kerron would curse him and send flies after him; you know, really mixed-up stuff?

'Again I tells him not to be such an idiot, but he was really scared and said he was getting out of there. He made me promise not to tell and I said I wouldn't tell, but I had to, you know? I told Paul and he said I done the right thing, and the next thing

121

I know there's a doctor in and he says George was sick and had to go away for a rest. I thought that was good of them, considering what he'd been saying, and I never thought much about it until my uncle came one afternoon with some men when I was out in the field and dragged me into the car. I fought and screamed, because I thought they were wrong to take me away. Looking back, I know they weren't, and I don't believe George was sick, neither. Looking back, I reckon he was right, because there were one or two things happening that I never noticed particular. I reckon now that they *were* going to do bad things to the girls, maybe still are, and I think you should get your little girl out of there. I heard a couple of the men talking about their own girls and how they were pleased Paul had taken a shine to them and what an honour it was. I think there's something really bad going to happen and you want to get your kids away quick.'

Get them out before the midwinter. The young woman, hardly more than a girl, had looked up at Patsy, her eyes brown and glistening and it was clear from the way she held Patsy's eyes that she meant everything she said. *Come the full moon and she'll take them . . .*

Patsy could still see those eyes, dark and earnest. Lisa had believed that the crazy folk at Broadford House had somehow flipped into madness and Patsy could believe that. She had felt the power of Kerron Vaunche in the forest when the gypsy had stalked around her. The vision she had experienced then had been as shattering as the sight of Paul groping the woman's breast. Even now she was unsure of just what had happened in that strange and bewildering moment.

But a sudden chill gripped her when she recalled the grotesque thing on the altar of stone hunched over the bloody slit on the small, pale body and the impact of the girl's words began to ricochet around in her head.

She'd had a premonition of sacrifice on a carved stone. She'd seen it happen in the vision.

For a dizzying moment a seismic tremor of panic rippled through her.

The elderly man with the neat white beard who had sat quietly at the far end of the table with his eyes half closed now opened them and looked directly at Patsy. He smiled without humour and nodded, telling Patsy in that simple movement, that she should believe everything she had heard. The chill squeezed her heart in a fist of ice.

9

She was thinking of Kerron Vaunche and how she'd beaten her in the cellar, when the lights of the service station twinkled in the distance.

'Okay, kiddies,' she said. 'I told you we'd find somewhere.'

She thumbed the nearside indicator to pull in on the inside as the relief drained some of the tension away. The lights were winking ahead and that meant they were safe. Patsy told herself they *had* to be safe as she eased off the throttle, instinctively looking in the mirror yet again. Paul and his witch hadn't come yet. There was no sign of lights on the road behind.

Maybe they won't, came the forlorn voice of hope and she smothered it before it could grow and fester. If she thought that, she might believe it and if she believed it she'd drop her guard. Right up at the forefront of her mind she had it emblazoned: *They're coming for the children before the full of the moon.*

It was the only certainty on this nightmare road. Even pulling in to the pit stop was a risk, but she had to get them food and drink and something to take Judith's temperature down. She could smell her daughter's breath now, sickly sweet, like the breath of the diabetic, but worse than that. It smelled as if she was rotting from the inside. Patsy had to shy away from the memory of hallucination where the contagion spread from Paul to her daughter, crawling in mottled corruption.

Only half an hour before, Peter had leaned forward and held on to the back of the driver's seat. Patsy turned her head just enough to see his face.

'You okay?'

'Just hungry now,' he said. 'I was a bit scared before.'

'The dogs?'

'No. Well yes, I was a bit scared, but not that much. I was more scared when Uncle Carrick came in and pulled me out. I didn't know what was happening, but I'm glad he came and I'm glad you were there. I didn't like that place. I don't like *her*.'

'Me neither. Did she hurt you?'

'No, not really, not like hitting or anything. But mum, she really scared me. Worse than anything. There's something wrong with her.'

Peter's voice was strangely different as he spoke. It had tightened and lowered, like the voice of an adult who's had a shock or a narrow escape. To Patsy it was a dreadful thing to hear such strain in her son.

'She was always with Judy, talking that funny stuff all the time. Dad didn't notice and I couldn't talk to him. He was always in at meetings and things. He's different from before.'

Not that different, I'll bet, Patsy thought to herself.

'I wanted him just to come home, but he said I didn't understand. I don't know what it was I was supposed to understand.'

'You don't have to worry about it now. All you have to understand is that we're going home.'

'Will I see dad again?'

Patsy flicked another glance at her son, trying to gauge his question. 'Let's take it a day at a time. I haven't seen you for ages. Haven't even had the chance to get a decent cuddle from my main man.'

Peter groaned and knuckled her shoulder. There was a silence for a moment, then he started again. 'I don't want to see *her* again, not ever. She's really creepy. I think she's made dad a bit crazy, you know? And I think she was trying to make Judy crazy too.'

Patsy bit down on her bottom lip, keeping her emotions on a simmer rather than the boil. She could handle all this later. There was a silence for a few moments. In the shadows, Judy whimpered again, quite loudly. Peter tapped his mother's shoulder again.

'Mum, are we lost?'

'Course not,' she retorted, a little too fast. Mothers can lie, but always quickly. 'You can't get lost on a motorway. They always end up somewhere.' She risked another glance and even in the dim light she could see the scepticism on his face, trying to push away the memory of what Kerron Vaunche had screamed at her as she fought her off.

All of it, what Lisa Prosser had told her, what Crawford Gilfeather, the man with the neat white beard had told her, it all gelled

125

together. If she hadn't believed before, she believed now. Kerron Vaunche had the power and she had used it.

You've a long road to travel Gadge-*woman.* The old Gypsy woman had made a prophesy and it had come true. *Best you turn back, for there's a bad road ahead of you.*

It was a bad road now. She had to get off it as soon as she could.

'All right,' she told Peter. 'I don't know *exactly* where we are. This is only the second time I've been to Scotland and I think I might have taken a wrong turning somewhere, but I told you, nobody gets lost on a motorway, and once we find out where we are, we'll know exactly where we're going.'

'I don't like this road,' Peter said softly. 'It's weird. It doesn't feel right. It's like *her*.'

'Just empty, and unfamiliar,' Patsy said, ignoring the reference. Kerron Vaunche had disturbed Peter, and she'd had control of Judith. She'd hear all about that soon even though the prospect of listening made her quail. The anger bubbled and she squelched it down again. 'I think maybe it's a new road that hasn't been opened for long.'

'But there's nobody else on it,' Peter said in a small voice, 'except for those trucks. I haven't seen anything for ages. That big bird was weird, and those dog things, they were really creepy. Did you see their eyes? Anyway, it's like we're the only people.'

'It's late, or early,' Patsy said, trying to put the assuring tone into her voice, hoping it would assure herself too. 'Maybe it's just not a busy road at the best of times.'

And in the worst of times? The skin puckered on the back of her neck. *Was there really a spider? Had she imagined the skull?*

Peter nudged her shoulder again. 'I think we should get off it as quick as we can, mum. There's something funny, funny peculiar I mean. It gives me the creeps.'

Me too, big boy, she said to herself. Out loud she said: 'Look, I told you. We'll be fine.'

The lights of the service station were closer and they passed the first of the exit warnings. Patsy began to pull off, touched the brakes to slow and reached the sloping ramp.

HAVOCK SERVICES:

The sign reflected back at them. It was as paint-peeled and

126

rusted as the hatch on the roadside emergency phone, but the
metal plate bore a punctuation of .22 dents and holes. Patsy
eased the car onto the access slope and gave the pedal just
enough to pull off the motorway. She slowed at the top of the
incline where it levelled to the flat asphalt of a parking lot.
Beyond the lot a brick-and-steel petrol station filled a corner
and further on, another brick building flashed a roadhouse restaurant sign in gaudy neon. ELCOME AVERN. The first letters of
each word had blanked out and every couple of seconds they
would blip and stutter spasmodically, as if trying to squeeze
enough power to make complete words, but never quite achieving it. ELCOME AVERN it remained. Somehow it was weird enough
to fit the place.

Patsy glanced at the fuel gauge and saw the needle was hovering on the red border. The direction signs separated cars and
trucks. She took the right, followed the white lines and made it
to the first of the pumps.

'Two minutes and then we get something to eat,' she said,
easing herself out onto the tarmac. 'And believe me, you can eat
as much as you like, ice cream, cola, the works.'

The air smelt of spilt petrol and old oil. Way over in the other
parking area, she could make out a dark line of trucks, hunched
together against a stand of tall trees. There was no sign of any
movement over there. Patsy reached for the nozzle, unshipped
it while using her free hand to unscrew the petrol cap. A dull
whine and a bubbling sound swelled, as if there was an airlock
in the hose. The whine rose higher, sounding rougher and at first
Patsy thought the pump was dry. She was about to draw it back
out when a rumble shivered the ground under her feet and a
vibration in the hose shuddered into her hand and the nozzle
coughed loudly. For an instant she imagined that instead of fuel,
slimy mud would glop out of the end. The nozzle coughed again,
belched loudly, then petrol spat into the tank, back-foamed a
froth which dribbled at her feet and then started to gurgle in
a steady stream. Patsy breathed out again, only now aware that
she had been holding her breath for probably the tenth time since
Broadford House. At least she was getting fuel. She squeezed the
trigger until the tank backed up again and clicked the flow off.
On an impulse, she drew the nozzle out slowly and kept pouring

until the petrol started to drip from the filler onto the ground. The tank was full and she could travel across the country on that.

She holstered the gun and walked between the pumps towards the cashpoint. It was the usual motorway pit stop, window festooned with furry things for fools to hang from rear-view mirrors and name sheets for drivers to identify themselves and their idiocy on front screens. Patsy pushed the door. It squeaked a loud protest as it opened, as if it hadn't been used in a long dry while, and swung slowly inwards against a shelf bearing a dozen cans of WD40 lubricant. She smiled at that (while inside the wary, instinctive part of her mind tried to fathom out how a motorway pit stop door would screech from lack of use) thinking one squirt would silence the door.

She pushed inside. Two of the overhead light tubes were flickering badly, jittery as the restaurant sign, throwing strobe shadows on the floor and walls. Patsy raised a hand over her eyes to cut out the worst of it and reached the cash desk. Behind the glass, a figure moved, though in the flashing light which reflected harshly from the screen, she couldn't make out whether it was male or female. The base-tray slid open and she put her Visa card down. It slid away out of sight. A printer rattled and buzzed, the tray slid back with the card and a receipt. She ran an eye down the figures, not really taking them in, signed at the bottom and passed it back through. She would have paid virtually any price for a full tank. The cashier on the other side hadn't said a word.

Patsy slipped her card back in the folder, and the receipt in the back pocket of her jeans, half turned to go, then looked through the glass of the partition.

She stopped in the act of turning. The atmosphere made a strange *twist* and in that split second she knew something was wrong. The feeling came up from the pit of her stomach.

Overhead, the lights flickered jerkily and emitted a high-pitched buzz of electricity, like a swarm of flies hatched inside a tin can. Even inside the shop there was a scent of decay and long-dried oil. She peered beyond her reflection which stuttered on the glass in time with the flashes from the faulty tubes.

There was no-one behind the counter.

Patsy stepped forward, heart beginning to beat out of step, raising her hand again to cut out the light, and leaned right up against the glass, killing the reflection. There was a cash-till, one of the old hand-driven ones with a pull lever at the side and antique typewriter money-keys on the front.

Hadn't she heard the electronic buzz of a credit printer? She was sure she had. She must have done, for she had folded the receipt and put it in her hip pocket.

She leaned forward even further. A doorway stood closed on the wall on the far side. She hadn't heard it open, hadn't heard it close. Patsy glanced back at the till. The drawer was open and a small spider was spinning a web on the corner. She froze. The little spider swung on its thread and dangled from the cash-tray.

The hairs on the back of her neck started to crawl.

She hadn't heard the jangle of the till drawer. There had been no sound at all except the electronic corncrake scrape as her card slid through the slot.

What slot? She leaned forward, hands on the formica edge. There was no computer link, no rolls of printout receipt. Behind her, something skittered on the floor and she whirled, all tense and tight now. *Something was different.* She glanced around, heard the squeak of something small behind a burlap sack of potatoes against the near wall and she let her breath out. Only a mouse, and she wasn't scared of mice. They were cute, and soft and harmless. She started to turn back towards the counter, still aware of the lights flickering on the wall, completed the turn and froze again. Her heart vaulted inside her ribs and stuck, quivering violently, at the back of her throat. A pulse started beating heavy and liquid just behind her ear.

The lights were on the wall.

The lights were on the wall and not the ceiling. Her hand groped and found the counter edge again. Her vision blurred just a little as she gasped for the breath that was suddenly hard to draw. A splinter of wood from the flat surface pricked her finger and she dimly felt the small point of pain.

Through the metal grille she could see the old set of scales and the skillfully crafted set of brass weights, golden chess pieces in diminishing sizes down to tiny pawns which must have weighed mere grams. On the wall, an old-fashioned mirror bore the legend

Havock Way-Station, done in a fancy pedantic script which reminded her of saloons in old westerns. The borders of the mirror were etched in fancy, writhing patterns.

Underneath it, the advert cajoled: *Last chance before the junction!*

And below the mirror there was an old set of telegraph keys, made in shiny brass, with a black kick-handle.

Patsy held onto the counter, breath panting shallow, eyes now wide.

The lights were on the wall and not the ceiling.

The sudden panicky fear of the inexplicable gripped tight in her belly.

The glass partition was gone. There was no reflection from the metal grille which stretched from counter to ceiling.

'Oh, please,' she heard her voice, distantly, appealing to any power that would listen.

In the mirror, she could see herself, face so pale she might have been made of porcelain. Behind her reflection gas-mantle lamps flickered on the wall. The cloying smell of oil and rust and old rotted wood came thick on the dusty air, thickening with every shallow breath. She turned away from the counter, saw the row of sacks along the wall, and beyond that the stand of barrels each with a different symbol branded on the curved oak staves. The musty smell clotted, gagging and dank, like fungus on a rotten tree stump. Something twittered again from under a low shelf where steel traps with teeth like carnivorous dinosaurs lay in a clenched tangle. Beside them coils of rope lay turned around wooden capstans. In the shadows of the shelf something moved and for an instant Patsy thought the rope had slithered off its bobbin like some braided, blind snake. There was another squeak, louder and more rasping than the first. A dark thing scuttled out and Patsy jerked back, expecting another spider, but it was only a rat. It scampered out onto the wooden floorboards and hunched there, pinpointing her with a tiny orange eye. It lifted something to its mouth in two delicate forepaws and she heard the crunch of something dry. She drew her eyes away, back to the mirror, saw herself pallid and bloodless and then behind her own reflection, a shadow that expanded to blot out the rest of the room.

Her vision blurred, began to fade out. A feathery touch caressed her on the back of the neck and she squealed aloud, her whole body vibrating with fright, turning to face the shadow looming behind her.

There was nothing there. A fluttery shape swung silently past her face, a big moth flying on powdery wings, flip-flipping towards the cobwebs in the ceiling. The lamps flickered on their brackets, catching the motes of dust spinning on the thick air. Her locked lungs released themselves and stale breath whooshed out.

The whole place had changed. It was as if she'd been abruptly thrown back in time to some travellers store of a century past. For a bewildering second, she thought she heard the whinny of a horse outside.

'Oh Jesus,' she gasped. Was it different out there too? Had it *changed?* She stumbled forward, towards the door, angling down the narrow alley between the barrels and the hardware shelves. Behind her the telegraph key started chattering morse and she was too terrified to turn around to see what kind of hand was making it move. She got halfway down the passage when her knee cracked on something solid and she stumbled forward. Her hands reached out and clattered in mid-air against hard metal corners. She squealed, more in surprise than pain and for one dizzying instant the whole room spun and tumbled. A flash of light burned in her vision and in the sudden glare the old barrels and burlap sacks winked out of existence. She was sprawling into a shelf stacked with cans of oil and bubble packs of windscreen wipers. Her knuckle grazed the corner of a box of spark-plugs, blared fire for an instant, and she reflexively grabbed the shelf to prevent a headlong tumble among the cans.

Overhead the lights flickered their stroboscopic rhythm. Patsy hauled herself to her feet. The service station was just what it had been before. Even the smell of the air changed, though it was still greasy and damp, and still bore that neglected, mouldering scent of age. She turned, completely bewildered, saw her reflection again on the glass partition. A dark shape moved behind the glass, unclear in the flickering light. It swelled silently and Patsy backed away, unwilling to see what was on the other side. Outside, she heard the rumble of a truck engine and tried to turn. The shape in the glass rippled as if the glass itself had shuddered and she saw again her reflection staring back at her, hair caught back in two pony-bobs, mouth agape.

The swipe-machine rasped its corncrake scrape and the receipt wheel started to spin, streaming out a twisting tape of paper. In the glass Patsy's image wavered, swelled and contorted. It held her eyes mesmerically and in those seconds she saw her own face change. The skin shrivelled down and the mouth widened in a gape and the eyes darkened, became sockets and she saw herself as a screaming skull in the reflection. Inside her the disgust and horror bubbled upwards.

'Not true,' she blurted. It was all in her mind. She backed against the door, eyes still fixed on the writhing, desiccated thing that was her own reflection, shaking her head in denial. The skull-mouth was opening and closing, mouthing silent words. For an instant she thought she heard the wheeze of dry air. She reached behind her, found the handle, turned quickly against the powerful draw of the vision in the glass and pulled hard. The door opened without a sound. She stumbled out and headed towards the car. Peter and Judith were pale smudges against the window. She stopped, chest heaving, mind whirling.

What's happening to me? The thought blared at her. She whirled to face the door again, and it was just as it had been when she first went inside after filling the tank. Yet it had changed somehow when she was in there. She had walked into another place, another dimension. (*Haunted . . . it's haunted*, her mind babbled) It had metamorphosed in the blink of an eye.

Or had it? The voice in her head demanded to know. Had it changed? Had she seen herself in the mirror? Or was she just beginning to crack under the strain of the past few days, the incredible tension of the wait outside Broadford House, the sheer panic of the mêlée which ensued. *Or was Kerron Vaunche reaching into her mind again?* She tried to hold her thoughts together, wondering if she was having complete nervous breakdown, and hard on the heels of that conjecture came the real fear. If she cracked up here, the children would be left on their own. Patsy put a hand out and leaned on the metal top of the railing, physically trying to draw herself together, attempting to ease her breathing.

'I imagined all of that,' she told herself, out loud. Over in the car, Peter and Judith were watching her curiously. 'I imagined that, because I was scared and I'm tired and I'm confused.'

And it's got nothing to do with that bitch!

She clenched her fists and dug the nails into the palms, not hard enough to break the skin, but with enough force to make it hurt. She gritted her teeth and hissed at herself: 'You are not insane. You are *not* freaking out. We are going to get home today.' This last came out like a prayer.

What has she done to us?

Patsy took a deep breath and walked towards the car. Despite her admonitions, she could still see in her mind's eye, the old, flickering gas lamps from a bygone time and the billowing shadow that had crowded in on her degenerating reflection in the mirror. She tried to shuck the vision away, but it clung to her tenaciously, and behind it all she saw the twisted face of Kerron Vaunche.

The man in the uniform waving the orange crash-lamp: had she imagined him? Dreamed up his hand scraping and squeezing inside her jacket? Had she really seen the burning car and the lurching shape behind the glass? Had she fought off the bloated spider? The dogs, thin-faced and bulging eyes and strangely mis-shapen, they were real, but that could have happened (*surely it could!*) on any lonely road. There were plenty of foxes living in towns now, and maybe they *had* been foxes.

But the filling station's transformation from brick and steel beams to old wood and crumbling stone, that had been in her mind, no matter what the gypsy had told her. It must have been. *It had to have been*. She shook her head angrily, telling herself to get a grip. When she reached the car, she yanked the door open and got in quickly, still unable to smooth out the jerkiness in her muscles.

'My stomach's rumbling. Can we go and eat now?' Peter asked, so straightforward and natural that a hot surge of love for her son washed through her.

'As much as you can tuck away,' Patsy told him, forcing a smile to her face, hoping she could keep herself intact, stop her mind from fragmenting, and get all of them home. The arrows on the asphalt guided them out through the pumps and along a lane bordered by small conifers then past the truckers' park. The line of big dark rigs still hunched, dark and powerful, against the taller trees, hidden in the shadow, a pride of black beasts resting until daylight. They were as massive as the rumbling monster that had almost flipped her off the road with a swipe of the tow-trailer and she wondered if that truck was among them. There was no sign of movement along the black rank.

The restaurant was part of a little mall, built of red brick and sporting a quaint yellow-tiled roof, like a cottage from a children's fairy tale, though on its walls, the sign still flickered: ELCOME AVERN. A name from middle earth. Peter pushed the door open and the smell of roadhouse food came wafting greasily, the easy-eat mixture of beans and burgers, skinny french fries, fatty donuts, the universal olfactory signal for hungry travellers the world over. Patsy felt her tongue contract in anticipation.

'I could murder a coffee,' she told them, taking Judith by the hand. The girl came listlessly, but without protest. Her hand was still hot and clammy and she still had that tired, faraway look, as if she was coming down with a cold, or measles. A slight rash was reddening on her hairline.

'Need some aspirin,' Patsy told herself, trying to get her mind down to a level of calmness in which she could operate.

From one of the side-units, the unmistakable electronic whistle and crash of an amusement arcade reeled Peter in and Patsy had to grab him by the collar, steering him away from the gaping Aladdin's cave of flashing lights, walking him past the door of the small self-service market. He grinned, boyish honest and blatant. 'Later,' Patsy conceded. She hadn't seen him for months, had prayed and anguished and agonized over getting him back, and now in that grin it felt like he'd never been away.

Peter winked at her, grabbed Judith's other hand, and all three of them pushed through the doors of the canteen. The smell of cooking food was thick on the air, but the place was empty. Normally there would have been a couple of travelling salesmen over by the window, hurriedly drinking coffee and smoking cigarettes. There would be an old couple sitting close to the warmth of the hotplates, hoarding their tea and not looking at one another. Even at this time of the morning, there would always be somebody stopped on the road. Beyond the counter there was a swing door – and again Patsy was reminded of an old saloon in an old western – leading on to a truckers' section where the rig-drivers would gather in their dungarees and over-alls, playing darts and pool and getting the kinks of the road out of their backsides. There was some noise filtering through the doorway, the sound of men talking and laughing. She couldn't tell if it was coming from a television set, or whether the only folk in the way-station were truck drivers.

She picked a seat by the window (where the salesmen would have sat) and got Judith settled down. Her eyes were puffy from tiredness and her face was pale. Under the skin beneath her eyes, dark half-moon cradles swelled. Her black hair was tousled and looked as if it could do with a shampoo. Time for that later, Patsy assured herself. Plenty of time. She sat Judith in a corner seat, propped against the wall and Peter came with her to the counter. On the wall beyond the hot bins the regular fare was advertised on glossy too-good-to-be-true posters which boasted huge portions of perfectly crinkled bacon, godly-golden fries.

'Scabby horse?' she asked, trying to raise her own spirits.

'Chips first. Beans, sausage, fried eggs. And a cola. Haven't had one of them for ages.'

Beyond the portholed doors on the wall a familiar kitchen-clang of pots rang out. Patsy rattled a coin on the glass top and a few moments later the door swung open and a thin girl backed out, pulling a trolley. She turned and pushed it past the food and unloaded plates onto a sprung stacker. Finally she tilted her face and acknowledged their presence. Her hair was stringy, rat's tails trailing down from under a greasy cap which had probably been white some time in the distant past. Her eyes were the palest green Patsy had ever seen, like watery jade and the left one was squinted inwards in a violent strabismus which gave the unfortunate girl a look of complete idiocy. It was difficult not to look at that inward-pointing eye with its green half-moon. Peter started to say something but Patsy dunted him on the arm and he stopped. She kept her own eyes on the menu on the wall and repeated what Peter had asked for. 'Three of them. A pot of coffee.'

'Can we get custard and rhubarb pie?'

Patsy nodded. The girl took a pencil from behind her ear and bent close to a small flimsy pad, sticking her tongue out to one side as she wrote the order laboriously. She didn't nod, though there was a twitch of acquiescence as she turned to the hotplate and broke open three eggs. They sizzled tantalisingly. Patsy told Peter to go back and join his sister and she took the opportunity of going to the bathroom. In the mirror she looked drawn and disheveled, but the water was warm enough to wash some of the grit from her eyes. On an impulse she went into the self-service shop – here too, no-one was shopping and no girl sat at the single cashpoint. She filled a wire basket, not stopping to think of what she was buying, but loading it with packets of soup, tins of beans, corned beef. For some reason, it just seemed the right thing to do. She searched until she found aspirin and Brufen tablets and then left the basket at the door, confident that there would be some early morning cashier ready to take her money after they had eaten. She went back inside the canteen. The three plates were on two trays on the counter. The coffee smelt bitter, but strong. The girl with the imbecilic squint was gone.

Patsy cut Judith's sausage into small portions, suspecting that her daughter was too tired to eat much. Judith stirred dozily, shook her head when Patsy offered her a piece of sausage, but her mother insisted and finally got a piece between her lips. Judith began to chew. Peter wolfed his food, hardly pausing for a breath, then started demolishing the pile of toast. Patsy managed her egg and a few fries while still force-feeding Judith, punctuating each morsel with a drink to help wash it down. Judith ate slowly, as if she was sleepwalking.

'Can I go play a game?'

Patsy came out of a daydream, blinking back a vision of Kerron Vaunche leaning into the car and making a grab for Judith. She had deliberately held back from asking either of them about Broadford House. It was too soon, plenty of time, she told herself. She wasn't sure yet that she really wanted to know. Peter was looking up at her, still chewing. He finished his Coke in a long swallow, smacked his lips and wiped them with the back of his hand. He had grown an inch or two since she had last seen him, but he was surprisingly *normal*. He had that boyish nonchalance that made him look as if he'd been away for a long weekend instead of months.

'One of the arcade games,' he prompted, interpreting her blank expression. Patsy managed a smile, delved into her purse and gave him some change. Peter slid off the seat and angled past the counter. When he pushed the swing door, she could hear the clatter and whistle of the computer games across the way. She turned to Judith who was sitting back, dark eyes staring up at her mother.

'Can't you eat any more?'

Judith shook her head slowly. 'Not hungry,' she said plaintively.

Patsy gave her a tablet which she hoped would lower her temperature. Judith swallowed with difficulty. She had some egg on her cheek and a patch of marmalade on her chin. Patsy wiped them with a napkin. Back at the cashdesk, the girl with green eyes was nowhere to be seen. In the shop, no-one had turned up yet, so Patsy filled another basket with biscuits, crisps and barley sugar sweets. She calculated the total and left the money beside the till. In the arcade, Peter was engrossed in a flashing, blaring shoot-'em-up game, eyes fixed on the screen, his body tense in the heat of the moment. Patsy judged it safe to leave him to it and led Judith out to the car, lugging the wire baskets in each hand. Outside, the sky was lighter, though the grey clouds were rolling and tumbling up there, tinged an odd green, sweeping across the sky on the brunt of raw strong winds. The line of black trucks were facing into the breeze, tarpaulins flapping noisily. Patsy couldn't see through the glossy black of the windscreens, but for an instant she felt exposed, and just as quickly she was sure she was being observed from the dark rank of trucks. Eyes were fixed upon her, looking her up and down. She could feel their contact. Patsy turned away quickly and loaded the provisions in the boot. She was about to put Judith into the back seat and go back for Peter when she halted. The unseen eyes were still caressing her hungrily. Patsy picked her daughter up and took her back inside.

Peter was on another machine this time, staring fixedly at the moving images on the screen, but now hauling a steering wheel left and right, making the racing-car image bob and weave on the track.

'Just going to finish my coffee,' Patsy called out to him. He risked a flicker of a glance before the motion on the screen demanded his full attention. Back in the restaurant, the greasy plates were still on the table, but the coffee-pot was still warm. She poured half a cup, stirred in two spoons of sugar and drank it down quickly. It was a strong, almost instant hit of caffeine.

'Right, darling, let's get going.' She zipped up the jacket she'd brought for Judith, a little red jerkin with a hood. It was a neat fit, even a shade on the small side, but better than nothing. Patsy had bundled a change of clothing into the car before she'd come north with her brother-in-law and the others, which had turned out to be a good idea. When she'd come running and stumbling Judith was still in her nightdress and Peter had been wearing only a pair of jeans, training shoes and an old shirt.

Patsy went back to the counter and rapped on the glass again. From behind the swing doors, the sound of water draining from a sink was unmistakable, but no voices spoke.

'Hello?' Patsy called out. 'Is there anybody there?'

The draining sound went on for a few moments, followed by the glugging of an air-blocked pipe. Beyond the other swing door, the heavy thump of bass pounded out from a juke box, overlaying the gravely tones of a singer Patsy thought she recognised. She heard the snatch of lyrics, something about roads in Texas.

'*There's miles and miles of road out there,*' the singer growled. Patsy suppressed a wry smile. *Not only Texas*, she observed silently. No-one replied when she called out again. The water stopped running and the blocked drain belched strongly, much as the fuel-hose had done, then gulped, rattled and fell silent. The singer with the voice like a cinder-track grunted his road-movie song in a twelve-bar boogie riff and somebody in the other room laughed boomingly. Patsy stopped, unsure of her next move. In the room, the truckers' room, a man had laughed. She turned to face the swing door. The emptiness of the place was unnerving. It was like any other motorway station, except that apart from the unseen rig drivers and the strange almost sightless face of the serving girl, there was no-one else.

Go now. Get out of here. Instinct exhorted in alarm.

Places like these were normally bustling oases twenty-four hours a day. Judy coughed wheezingly and Patsy squeezed her hand. She'd picked up another ventilator refill from the rack in the mini-store, not pausing to think or question. After the night's drive, she was running on instinct and wasn't prepared to fight it.

'They're coming now,' Judith said. Patsy turned, surprised, one hand on the swing door. She paused with the door half open. Beyond there was the hard click of cannoning pool-balls. A chair scraped back on a floor with a juddery squeal. A man laughed, low and rumbling and somehow dangerous.

Patsy swung the door open and pushed herself through, pulling Judith behind her. The music on the juke-box faded away at that moment and the low, rumbling laugh died. A silence descended on the room. Two big men in denims, over by the pool table stopped moving. One had a huge belly and a massive beard which came down in straggly kinks to scrape against his chest. The other was taller, but whip-thin, long spindly arms covered in thick black hair. His adam's apple bobbed in his scrawny neck as if he'd swallowed the eight-ball. A spider's web tattoo on his neck quivered and stretched with the motion.

Patsy stood looking at the men and they stood looking back. A flat silence settled and stretched out for several moments before there was a jarring crack from the old juke box in the corner, a series of dull beats from the speakers and then the growling voice was back on with a different song.

Something wrong, the panicky internal voice urged. Judith tugged insistently at her hand. Over at the window, a man with a peaked cap and hoary mutton-chop sideburns was hunched over a heaped plate, grunting to himself as he used a fork in each hand to shovel food into his mouth, hardly pausing to chew, not pausing for breath. She couldn't see his eyes under the peak but she could feel them on her the way she had felt the palpable inspection outside and her throat tightened of its own accord. There were other men in the far corner, several of them sitting around a table playing some game. Their heads swivelled towards the woman and the little girl.

Get out of here, the instinctive, primitive part of her brain ordered urgently. *Don't wait. Don't stop.*

Get a grip of yourself, the rational side objected. They needed directions, had to find out exactly where they were.

One of the men at the table mumbled something and the others sniggered. Patsy could feel their eyes on her. Mental alarm

139

bells were jarring. Judith was pulling at her hand. One of the men at the pool table stood up straight, slung the cue over his shoulder and advanced slowly. He got halfway across the room when she saw his eyes, as blindly pale green as the girl who had served the food, alien and almost animal. He grinned, the stubble on his cheeks bristling with the moment, and for an instant she thought he was the man in uniform on the dark road.

'Bad,' Judith said. She could feel the girl's fingers squirm in the cup of her grip, trying to wriggle free. 'Bad men.'

The approaching man grinned wider and she could see his teeth, long and stained, too many in that wide mouth for they were snaggled and crooked. Over at the table, somebody laughed aloud, but there was no humour in the sound. Over the beast of the music, the laugh echoed in an odd counterpoint. Patsy backed away from the man. His hands were gripped on the cue, hairy knuckles calloused and dry-cracked. He stopped and looked Patsy up and down, his pallid gaze crawling on her, lingering at her crotch.

'Lost, eh?'

She nodded, still backing away.

'Lost on the junction, this lady is,' he said, turning his head just a fraction so that he was speaking to the other men. He took another step forward.

'Shouldn't be here, lady,' he said, voice so deep it was almost a growl. 'Should never travel the junction by yourself. Some bad things happen on this byway.'

Another step. Judith whimpered. The man's smile widened further and his tongue slid over his lower lip. The bristles whiskered out making him look hungry and canine. 'Better be on your way before something bad happens,' he rumbled. Patsy could hear the sound of grindstones. 'Be dark soon and the moon's gettin' fat.'

'I need to find my way . . .' Patsy said. The moon was getting fat and that was bad. Come the full moon and Kerron Vaunche would put Judith on the stone and . . .

'Dat ole debil moon,' the thin man with the spider's web on his neck crooned back, off-key enough to sound retarded.

'Moon's gettin' fat and everything changes,' the man with the stubble went on. He had a leather hat, like an old-time flyer's

140

helmet pulled down until it leaned on an eyebrow. 'Better you stay here, lady. No place to go anyway.'

'No,' Patsy said. 'I've got to go home.'

The green eyes blinked sickly, the colour of shallow rip-tide waves. 'Lady, nothing moves out of the way-station. Whoever comes in here stays here.' He leaned back, grinning widely and turned to face behind him.

'Am I right boys, or what?'

He brought the cue up, swinging it in a leisurely arc. She saw his hand, big and wide and somehow paw-like. *Was it hairier now?* The tip loomed in front of her eyes. She flinched back, pushing Judith behind her. Over at the table, another man growled something and somebody howled in a laugh that sounded more like a hound baying.

The nearest man took two steps forward. 'Can't go, lady. Gotta stay here.'

He reached out a hand, big spatulate fingers spread. The boar-bristle hair stood up from gnarled knuckles.

Without warning Judith let out a howl. The man stopped. His green eyes swung towards the girl. Judith pointed up at him and the eyes widened in consternation. Judith muttered a string of sounds, full of fricative consonants and hissing sibilants.

'Little Red Riding Hood,' he mumbled. 'Spoken for, eh? Got somebody else's brand on her.' He stepped back, muscles working under the skin of his face. The green eyes blinked again and Patsy saw the ridge of bristly hairs poking out from under the leather.

Changing, a part of her observed distantly.

'Better be out of here before they come,' the man said, his voice deepening to a rumbling bass. For a moment Patsy didn't have a clue what he was talking about. Neither did she care. She reached the door, dragged Judith behind her and then squeezed out through the narrow gap. The door swung back on its hinges. The rubber edges whumped together several times as mother and daughter backed away. She expected both door wings to slam open and a big shadow to come pouncing out, the shadow of a truck driver who had seemed to become something *else* in this way-station. A soft touch rapped on the door. She could hear a rasping scratch on the paintwork on the other side and

141

then, unbelievably, the animal sound of panting. Wild panic exploded and she turned and ran, knocking over one of the plastic chairs, snatching Judith into her arms, nerves in her back cringing with the expectation of some long hand – *some long hand with claws on it* – reaching out to snatch her backwards and haul her back into the truckers' room. She straight-armed the door to the mall, feeling the jar punch into her shoulder. Judith was jabbering incomprehensibly. The door hit against the stop, bounced and slammed shut behind her.

'Peter!' The arcade was filled with blinding pulses of light and shuddering to a jangled cacophony of shrill sound. Without a pause, Patsy went straight inside, calling out to her son. He was just turning towards her, both hands on the lever of a game with fast-moving images of fighter spacecraft tumbling on a big high-resolution screen.

'Come on, Peter, come quick,' she said, trying to keep the panic out of her voice. 'Just a min . . .' he started to say when the screen flashed brilliant white, went blank, then flickered back on. Patsy was reaching for him with her free hand as he was turning away from the game, and then she saw
herself.

At first she assumed it was a reflection, blinked, and the picture sprang into tight focus, pin-sharp on the screen. It was a close-up of her face, eyes wide, mouth wider, skin bleached white. The image shrunk down, showed her shoulders, then the viewpoint pulled back to show her whole body. She was running. On either side, unmistakable in the fine-grained resolution of the game machine, Peter and Judith were running alongside her, each holding one of her hands. They were running on a flat road, haring along the centre-line.

Patsy stopped in her tracks, hand still stretched out towards Peter who yelped something which she didn't hear.

On the screen the point of view swooped down, right to the road level, pulling back from the approaching figures. The black road narrowed into the far distance and the broken white centre-line lanced like tracer fire. And behind the three running images, way back in the distance, something moved, far enough away to be just a glimmer. The music in the speaker stopped and for a second complete silence fell. All the other machines

142

in the arcade winked out. Then from the one remaining screen came the distant sound of howling. Peter jerked back, both hands flying from the joysticks. The game machine chirruped electronically, cross-hair sight decals whizzed uncontrolled and unaimed in looping patterns across the surface. Behind the tall cabinet a coughing sound became a crackling of electric sparks. Inside the gaudy casing a rending noise screeched and the screen went blank.

Patsy's hand completed the motion, grabbed Peter by the shoulder and yanked him away, turning as she pulled. Peter yelped again, in surprise and possibly in pain as her fingers dug into the skin at his collarbone.

'Come *on!*' Patsy almost screamed. She swung him round in front of her and pushed him through the gaping entrance to the arcade. He stumbled, almost fell and the instant they crossed the threshold a dizzy plummeting sensation lurched through them. A snapping sound burst inside Patsy's ear and in the flick of an eye, the mall *changed*.

Just in front of them, the wall rippled as if a tremor had riven through the ground. Beside the door to the restaurant, the brickwork bulged. Under their feet the red and yellow square tiles merged into a muddy brown, became grainy and pebbled, the texture of hardpack. The air instantly thickened and it bore the unmistakable smell of dust and woodsmoke and slaughtered meat. Patsy turned away from the swing door. The glass centre-panel was rippling in time to the movement on the walls in a smooth pulsating rhythm. Through the glass she saw the girl with the strabismic eye who had served behind the food counter, only the counter wasn't there any more. It was just a glimpse, but the glimpse was enough. An old wooden plank spanned two uprights. On it lay a blackened and charred thing that might have been an animal, stumpy bent limbs pointing at the ceiling. The serving girl was leaning over the counter, like a menial wench at a medieval banquet, slicing a curved knife down the length of one of the thick limbs. The glimpse was enough. The girl looked up and Patsy saw that her face had altered. The abysmal squint was still there, but the expression was different. Now it was no longer blank, almost idiotic. The girl grinned, just like the hairy man with the pool cue had done and the eyes glared

143

with a strange, hungry mirth. A slice of blackened meat came peeling off the charred thing on the board and the girl held it up, dangling it tauntingly before she crammed it into her mouth, forcing the long strip between her teeth, pushing it down, stuffing it in until her cheeks bulged. Nausea rolled inside Patsy and the image came back to her of the burning car down in the scrub beside the road. Something had moved behind the glass while the shapes hung around, warming their hands by the heat of the flames. Something had moved inside the smoke and flames, something dark and shadowed and gaping in desperate pain. Patsy looked away before fright and horror made her sick.

It's an animal. Her mental defences went on the attack. *It's a piece of cooked meat.* She whirled and went down the wide mall centre with Judith still in one arm, held tight against her shoulder, Peter still gripped by the collar. Their feet thumped and thudded on rough wooden boards that gave and sank under their weight.

Patsy felt that mental *flick* again as the texture of the atmosphere changed without warning and the walls simply leaned out towards her. The boards transformed into rough cobbles and the air thickened to a soupy smog, rank with burning smoke and fermenting refuse. Behind them, where the canteen had been, she heard a crunching sound she knew was bones being crushed, and the nausea rolled again. To the right, an animal squealed loudly and a flare of bright orange blasted out of a rugged entrance along with a stench of burning hair and charcoal. She ran, shoving Peter ahead, feeling Judith's fingers dig into the skin of her neck. Ahead of them, where the entrance had been, there was only the mouth of an alley. A ragged figure squatted at the corner and she did not want to see what it was. There was no pause. A hand reached out from the tattered shape and by luck her shin batted it away. They came skittering out of the narrow alley onto mud. Patsy felt her foot slip from under her, swung her body, regained balance and kept going.

'Where's the car'?' Peter bawled.

They were in a tight square, bounded in by rickety cottages and narrow buildings. On the far side, close to the belt of trees – tall trees with scraggly twisted and looping branches, trunks festooned with creeping ivy – a line of huge black coaches stood in a row. Between the yokes gaunt horses stood, heads bowed, nuzzling for the straggled, dust-covered weeds.

'Just move,' Patsy bawled back.

They were trucks. *Not wagons. Jesus, what's happening to us?*

She knew this was all wrong; she told herself that this was *not real*. All she had to do was think, just concentrate. She had to beat back this crazy hallucination.

Behind them a hoarse roar of hunger or anger came rolling down the alley and from across the way, a wavering howl replied. As one, the horses lifted their heads, and Patsy could see the bones of their jaws and the lines of their ribs. One of them whinnied and shook its head, sending its harness jangling, and flicking a spray of frothy saliva in an arc. The animal was like a tethered black skeleton, emaciated and wasted, like something from a children's nightmare. A green eye rolled wildly in a socket and ribs like slats on a washboard heaved and settled. The trucks had become wagons and that was just crazy. Instinctively she turned away from them, gauging the distance from memory. This was all a mental thing, some sort of breakdown, she knew. *It had to be.* Patsy pushed Peter faster, angling away from the trucks, heading for an open space between two crumbling buildings which leaned precariously towards each other. A dark thing leaned out of a window and drooled, a gargoyle face caught in peripheral vision. Patsy swerved past it and crashed with stunning force into an invisible barrier blocking her path. Peter yelped, went spinning out of her grasp and Patsy flipped up and over in a near-perfect somersault. Her hands reflexively grabbed Judith tight as she went spinning through the air, the whole ghastly scene looping dizzily in front of her eyes. She landed with a thump on her backside, hard enough to make her teeth click together and send a vibration rattling into her skull. She scrambled to her feet, turning just in time to see Peter spinning, arms raised, gathering his balance.

And the car was there. It had materialised from nowhere, just as the shelves in the gas-station had appeared. She had hit it with her hip and gone tumbling over in front of the windscreen. The sky blazed in her vision, went dark again. Little twinkling lights orbited just in front of her eyes for a few moments before the world came back into focus. She was sitting on the hard asphalt of the car park. Judith was whimpering again, fingers still clenching her mother's skin. Peter stopped spinning and reached them in three strides.

'Into the car,' Patsy gasped, trying to ignore the pain in her hip and pelvis. Peter didn't reply. He just grabbed the handle, opened the door and piled in. Patsy had to peel Judith off, hating the way she had to unclamp the tiny fingers and bundle the girl roughly into the back seat. She got into the front, almost hyperventilating with panic. Just as the door shut, she heard the rumbling growl of a diesel engine and before she could prevent it, her eyes flicked across to the edge of the trees, even as her hands fumbled to shove the key into the ignition. The wagons were trucks again, big and powerful in the shade of the trees. A cloud of dirty black exhaust belched from the high chimney stack and the nearest truck shuddered like an angry beast. Air brakes sneezed in a cat-spit. Patsy turned the key, made the engine start, slammed in the gear and felt the wheels spin on the flat surface. The car fish-tailed as she angled for the exit, not daring to look right or left. She reached the ramp and swooped down it, hitting sixty before she got to the merger. By the time she reached the motorway she was doing eighty and her hands were clenched on the wheel so tightly she would have muscle cramps for days.

She drove for three miles in complete silence, mind a whirl, trying to concentrate only on getting as much distance between her and the service station at the junction as she possibly could in the shortest time. Finally, behind her, Peter spoke up.

'What happened, mum?'

Your mother's freaking out.

'It's all right. I just got scared,' Patsy said. 'It's my fault. I've just been a bit upset for a while, but we'll be all right.'

'No, I mean back there,' Peter persisted. 'I saw the game change. I saw you and me and Judy in the machine, running on the road. That shouldn't have happened.'

'Just imagination,' she said, trying to convince herself more than him. *Had he seen that too? Was this a group hallucination?*

'It shouldn't have happened. And the building changed. They *morphed* into different shapes. I saw them do it. When we got out, there was no car park, and the trucks were gone. The buildings looked like something out of Robin Hood. All those

146

horses and carts. And the horses didn't even look real. They looked like zombie-horses.'

Jesus, had he seen all of that? Patsy took a breath. It had been *her* imagination. Her hallucination. Hadn't it?

'Look, we're all tired,' she insisted. 'All we need is to get home and get a good night's sleep and everything will be different, you'll see.' She drove on, still shaking, unable to disguise the tremor in her voice. She could feel Peter's eyes on her, sensed his intensity.

The boy was staring at her, wondering what was wrong with his mother. Had she seen what he'd seen? She couldn't have missed it. There was no confusion in Peter's mind. Children do not think madness is a reality, that hallucinations exist. They see what they see and accept it as truth. In the clarity of his mind, Peter looked at his mother and felt the real stirrings of anxiety. If she hadn't seen it, there was something wrong with her, then they were all in trouble.

'Mum?' he said after a few moments.

'What is it, tiger?' Patsy said, trying her hardest to keep her voice light.

'I think there's something bad going on,' her son said flatly. 'I really think we should get off this road.'

10

'So what do we do?' Patsy had asked. She had that disoriented sensation as if she'd just woken up from a nightmare and found that it hadn't been a dream.

'We're going to get them out, of course,' Carrick said. 'We've some people who have promised to help.'

The elderly man with the neat white beard who had sat quietly at the far end of the table with his eyes half closed while Lisa Prosser told her tale had gone now.

His name was Crandall Gilfeather. He had opened his eyes and looked directly at Patsy. He had smiled without humour and nodded, telling her in that simple movement, that she should believe everything the girl had said.

Crandall Gilfeather started talking after McGregor had taken Lisa away into the dreary night. Carrick had sat close and covered Patsy's hand with his own. The older man leaned back in the seat, pressing his two hands down in the flat polished wood of the table on either side of a glass of wine which gleamed like a magic potion in the overhead light. Patsy could still recall the moment. Hard scrapes of spindrift from the ice-hoared trees rasped the window-pane and a cold wind moaned under the eaves.

'You must believe what she says,' Gilfeather began. 'And get your children away from that place.'

He had a slight accent which she couldn't place. Maybe Scots, maybe Irish, a kind of lilt that gentled his words. His grey eyes caught the flicker from the stove and reflected it merrily, but there was no humour in his expression.

'Where to begin, eh? Best if I tell you that I know of Kerron Vaunche, as I knew of John Kenyon, who was an idiot and not worth bothering about. I also know Broadford House and its history and I know that history is the reason that Kerron Vaunche has taken up residence there.'

'I'm not interested in history.' Patsy interjected, pulling her

148

hand from under the warmth of Carrick's. 'I just want my children back.'

'Understandable, commendable, and in my opinion very urgent.' This time Crawford Gilfeather did smile. His neatly cropped beard gave him a gnomish look. 'I urge you, however, to proceed with caution and hear just what you will be up against.'

'All this mumbo-jumbo is nonsense. They can worship fairies at the bottom of the garden for all I care.'

'If that were all, then there would be no cause for concern, but I can assure you, there is great concern, and time is short.' He lifted his glass and took a sip and nodded. 'Good wine. Beats the chill.'

He turned to Patsy. 'But even though time is precious, I must ask you to indulge me just a little while more. Then you can make your decisions. So long as you make them quickly and take advice from Mr McGregor who is a good man.'

He leaned forward and snagged her with his eyes. 'You'll have heard about Druids?'

'They built the standing stones, didn't they? What have they got to do with this?'

Gilfeather chuckled. 'Quite a lot, actually. To a certain extent, I'm, how shall I put it? A . . . student of their ways. You could say that I'm one of their number, though we don't call ourselves Druids and we don't dress up in white robes, if we can help it. I'm more an explorer of the old ways, and if that sounds a little eccentric, then that's fine too.'

'I don't understand . . .' Patsy began, but the elderly man held up his hand.

'You see, there's two sides to everything. If there's white, there's black. Good and bad, that kind of contrast. There's always a converse, right from the beginning when there was light and darkness. Still is, I'm afraid, and that's half the fun. Hate to think of heaven as pure white with everybody playing harps and thinking holy thoughts. Would drive you to drink so it would.'

He grinned infectiously. Carrick caught it but Patsy was still immune.

'As you might have gathered, our friend Kerron Vaunche is

149

on the other side. The opposition, if you like. And that's what makes her dangerous.'

'She's just a gypsy who stole my children,' Patsy grated.

'Oh, she's taken the babies, that's for sure. But gypsy? That's only half right. Our Kerron is one of a long line going back to a time when people here wore skins and made tools from mammoth's bones and the antlers of the great elk. Her people were shamans, the magicians who passed their knowledge down from mother to daughter in an unbroken lineage. Always they've been linked with the dark side. She's what her folk call the Carlin woman, though she's had many names, like Catanna, and Black Annis. They all mean the same thing, that she is the embodiment of the *Cailleach*.'

'And what's that?'

'Well,' Gilfeather began, rubbing his hands together. 'She's the earthly counterpart of the underworld powers. Like a sorceress, so to speak. And she's dangerous.'

'More mumbo-jumbo?'

'Sure,' Gilfeather said agreeably. 'Plenty of it. Kerron Vaunche is a master of it. Mistress of it is more appropriate, because she's the hag in all her forms. But just because it sounds like gobbledegook doesn't mean it has no power. The Carlin woman, the *Cailleach*, she has power all right, and she'll use it. That's what she's been doing these past few years and that's why she's in Broadford House now. It used to be the home of Sir Angus Kilbrade, who was the mentor and guiding light of Aleister Crowley who called himself The Beast. Crowley was one of the leading exponents of black magic, but before him Kilbrade had attempted to raise underworld powers on a stone altar under Broadford House. Kilbrade disappeared in 1897, in the *winter* of that year, and that's significant.'

The ice crystals hissed on the window-pane again and a hard breeze crackled the leafless branches of the birches close to the house.

'As far as I understand the story, Kilbrade tried to open up the gateway to the dead lands using the stone altar at the crux of the ley lines. He was never seen again. Now, if you bear with me, I'll show you some similarities in what has happened recently.

Kerron Vaunche was involved in the spring and summer ceremonies at the Cupstone here before she left with your husband.'

Patsy nodded, wondering where this was leading.

'From there, she went to Callanish on the Island of Lewis for the Autumn Equinox in September and Samhain Festival on All Hallows Eve. In the winter she was in Linnvale, the other ley line hub and the following spring she conducted the ceremonies at the Rowldritch Stones near Oxford, then down at the Merry Maidens megalithic circle at Land's End. In the summer she was seen again in Cashel Aenghus, wrongly known as the house of the love god, in Ireland. It's the centre of the most westerly ley line complex. All *mumbo-jumbo*, I concede, but very important to the Carlin woman.

'You see, it's all a build-up, slow and sure, the way it was done in the old days, and I believe Kerron Vaunche knows the old days well because it's my true belief that Kerron Vaunche is old, older than any of you would believe. All of the ceremonies are recorded in the Druid histories, all of them, each one more powerful than the last. They all culminate on the Nameless Day.'

The way he said it gave the word capital letters. Patsy's raised eyebrows were enough of a question.

'In the Celtic calendar, there are five seasons, thirteen months, and a period in midwinter known as the Five Dead Days when the forces of darkness gather close and the earth power is at its weakest. Within that time, in exceptional circumstances, comes the Nameless Day, when the conjunction of the planets and the arrival of the full moon coincides with the winter solstice, the longest night of the year.

'That, according to the ancient legends, is when the *Cailleach* makes the sacrifice to the *Fasgadh*, Dark Lord, the guardian of all the ways. And that is the moment of greatest danger for your son and daughter.'

'I don't understand you,' Patsy admitted. Crandall Gilfeather gave a little shrug and took the opportunity to take another drink of the wine.

'I told you the *Cailleach* is old. Older than any of us. I can't say just how long she has lived, though looking at her it's hard to believe she's a day over twenty-three. What you have to understand is that the Dead Days, the five *dark* days are a time

151

of death and rebirth. To keep her beauty, to keep her youth and to maintain her enormous power, the Carlin Woman must commune with the Lord of Death, the Prince of Shadows, and he will demand his price ... the soul of innocence, the seed of life. That's what this is all about, and here's where it gets complex.

'The *Cailleach* will use the flesh of her consort. It is the most powerful, most terrible ceremony of them all. Every great sin must be committed on the altar, every one. The *Fasgadh* demands the price.'

'Every great sin? How many are there?' Carrick asked.

'You can work it out for yourself. She needs the flesh of the consort to make the sacrifice of his own. A child has to die as the blood of rape is spilled on the stone. A child must be consumed while the Carlin and her consort consummate their evil. The price is absolute corruption, but there must be a feast at which the Prince of Shadows will feed.

'And you believe all this rubbish?' Patsy said, though a cold slithery sensation was worming its way under her skin. In her mind's eye she saw writhing bodies on a stone and then, without warning, the dreadful dream came exploding up to the surface.

Kerron Vaunche laughed from the shadows and Patsy turned. The woman's face was old and lined now, shrivelled and dry, as if she'd been drained of all humanity. The witchety thing cackled at her and pointed to the stone. The carved shapes were still writhing, little stone demons forcing their way up from the surface on which the pale shape lay trussed, arms and legs spread and a wet chasm cleaving from chin to crotch.

She'd seen Judith in the dream, trussed and bleeding, and there had been more. Much more.

Judith lying spread-eagled on the stone, arms and legs pinioned by braided sparkling ropes and her whole body shivering violently. The dreadful gash running from her neck to her pelvis, a great red chasm in which purple-slicked organs still writhed. Her daughter's legs twitched helplessly and her eyes stared out at her mother and the little bleating noise died away with the slowing movement.

The ultimate sin?

Paul on the stone, face contorted in ecstasy, neck corded, while the thing upon him hunched, darkening now, foreshortening as it shrank and widened, became a squat shape, head bowed. It lowered its warted head . . . and the form on the stone was not Paul but Judith, slender and fragile, flopped and dead. The monstrosity snuffled again, gobbling down there in the wet mess of the chasm, and when it rose again the flies came bursting out in a fog and Judith's dead eyes fixed accusingly on her.

The sound of the buzzing cloud of black flies came back to her and she shook violently, casting the memory away from her as if it were a diseased blanket. Her heart was thumping painfully in her chest. What Crandall Gilfeather had said was so close to that awful dream that a shiver of paralysing fear gripped her for a moment.

'As a matter of fact, I *do* believe all this rubbish,' he said, quite gently, keeping his eyes on hers, aware of the sudden change. 'Think on it as a battery charger, except she'll be plugging in to a terrible source of power.

'I believe it, but that's by the by. It's not necessary for you to share my belief, but it is imperative, it is absolutely urgent that you understand Kerron Vaunche believes. Your faith is not important, except your faith in what I tell you will happen. She believes it, and I am utterly convinced that she now plans the ceremony of renewal. She will not get another chance for a long time. You wouldn't believe how long, so I won't tell you. She needs to take the opportunity *now*.'

'But why?' Patsy's voice was small and shaky.

'Because she wants power and she wants life. She always has and she always will unless you stop her. There are different faiths, but each are interlinked and have common bases, roots that go back to the beginning, whether it is in the transition of the soul to heaven, or the transference of reincarnation. Both are true, both are possible. Then there is the dark transference of the renewal. In the ceremony, souls are lost, but the *life* is transferred and the bargain is made. She needs the flesh of his flesh to make the bargain.'

Crandall Gilfeather leaned forward and took Patsy's free hand. 'It is her chance now, and she will take it, and I'm afraid she will take what is yours.'

'What's in this for you?' Patsy asked, feeling a sudden anger towards the elder man. A nerve behind her knee was kicking erratically.

'I don't want to see two innocents lost, and that's the truth. But more than that, even if you don't believe, I do. If the *Cailleach* makes the sacrifice on the Broadford Stone, then she'll have more power than ever before, and that kind of darkness in the hands of Kerron Vaunche could set country against country and open up the dead paths of the *Ley* roads. She could bring forces through from that side that would turn the world into a hell on earth. We can't let her do it.'

Crandall Gilfeather leaned back again, keeping his eyes fixed on Patsy. They were mirrors of his sudden intensity.

'Why does she need *my* children?' Patsy asked, aware that in that instant she had accepted at least some of what Gilfeather had said.

'Because she has chosen your husband. It's as simple as that. She's chosen him for some quality only she knows, whether it be his birth date, or a resemblance to someone from the far past, or even a reincarnation.'

Hadn't the old tinker in the forest told her that? *She took him into the* uath *stones and put her mark on him, but he was hers long afore that.* The guttural accent came back along with the memory of the smell of singed hairs.

'That's neither here nor there,' Gilfeather was saying. 'But because she has put her mark on him, then he's bound to her, body and soul, heart and mind, and his children, well, they're hers too.'

'Over my dead body.'

'If necessary, that's how she'll see it too. She will bind the girl to herself with the hand of glory, with a grip of death, so that they will never be parted and in that way she will make the connection through which the transference is possible.

Patsy understood none of that. Her mind was still concentrating on more mundane matters. 'But can't we call the police?'

Crandall Gilfeather shook his head. 'The police have been to Broadford House once or twice in the past few years. But they will only investigate if they have good reason, and so far, there has been no good reason. Nobody has complained, at least, not about any crime. Anyway, to forewarn Kerron Vaunche is to forearm her. If she thought you had any inkling of what she intends, then she will simply disappear, and so will your children, and I'm afraid that would be the end of everything, and I will have failed.'

Patsy shook her head violently. 'This is all madness. I mean, I've never heard of any of this before. *Ley Lines?* What on earth are they supposed to be? And the Prince of Shadows. It's like something out of a fantasy novel.'

'True. Many of those books are based on racial memory of the old rituals, if somewhat distorted. *Ley Lines* are connections of force, joining one centre of power, of magic if you like, to another. Where they join, at the hubs, are like the centres of vortices where the power is strongest, and the membrane, the partition between the world and the underworld, the *Ley World* is thinnest.

'All the ceremonies since the Cupstone have been building up, drawing the power from each axis, sending it along the lines to where it is concentrated. I imagine Broadford Stone is fairly sizzling with it now.'

In the dream, in her vision, had there been fuzzy arcs of phosphorescence jittering out from the stone?

'Now the hubs, axis points, they are like gateways, through which the powerful – and the protected – can travel beyond and *between* – down the *Ley Roads* where time is different, where the whole *world* is altered beyond your imagination. But that doesn't concern us, not for the moment.' He gave a little encouraging smile as if to say he'd get back to that shortly.

'The Prince of Shadows, well, it's simple. You know him as the Devil, Satan, Baal, whatever. He's the bad guy, the Lord of Death. Highfalutin' name for such a horrible beast, and his names are many. They will use the names to summon him.

This time Carrick sat upright. 'The *real* Devil?' His big, ruddy face was a picture of disbelief.

'The very same. Now, as I said, all faiths, all religions, have their roots in the oldest, most primitive of human cultures, from a time when whatever walked on two legs was not even human yet. Even the Neanderthals knew of the contrast of light and dark, of night and day, of life and death. They buried their dead

155

and they left offerings for a safe passage.' He paused and looked at them both.

'Shouldn't let me deviate, you know. I could talk all night. Anyway, if there is a good, and there is, I can assure you – though generally it's a pretty unfocussed type of good and doesn't like to interfere – then there's a bad, and it really *does* interfere, because it has no lofty ideals, only a hunger and a hatred and a need to corrupt. Whatever its name, from whichever culture, Skratta, Set, Asmodeus, Taimat, it is the same, though His names are legion. He claims the souls of the dead who travel the low road, but that is his right as the Lord of Death.

'It is when he claims the soul of an innocent in life that the balance changes, and everything changes with it, and that is why you must get ready to move.'

'Why?' Patsy asked flatly. Her mind was whirling, all the thoughts jumbled and tumbling so fast she couldn't grab one to hold down and examine. Too many of the things Crandall Gilfeather had said sparked off reactions within her, memories of other things. *Put her mark on him.* The old gypsy had told her that. And she had mentioned the stones at Callanish. *It's what she'll become*, the crone had said, speaking of Kerron Vaunche.

'As I said,' Gilfeather responded, 'even if you don't believe any of the *mumbo-jumbo*, you must concede that Kerron Vaunche is a very strange lady. No lady in fact, but someone with remarkable power. What she intends to do will come on the *Nameless Day*, when all conjunctions are in place and the full moon rises. That can only happen on one of the five days devoted to the *Fasgadh*, the shadowed one.'

'And when is that?'

'The Winter Solstice, the longest night of the year, when the partition is thin and the year is dead,' Gilfeather said slowly. 'December twenty-first.'

'That's less than two weeks away,' Carrick said.

The older man nodded. 'That's why you must get ready to move. I wish you had come to me sooner.'

156

11

They drove thirty miles in the early light, heading south-east, so Patsy estimated from the glow in the sky, and that was fine enough. South and east meant homewards if you were travelling from the north and west. She told herself that, muttering it to herself like a mantra, but in all those thirty miles heading in the right direction they never saw another car. The far-off murmur of traffic was still a lazy hum, barely audible, but definite. Every now and again, Patsy would look in her mirror and scan the road behind. She could sense them following, though how far away they were, she didn't know. She could visualise them snuffling along behind her, imagined them baying like hounds. That Kerron Vaunche and the followers who had put up such a fight would be on their trail, she had no doubt. Every time she looked in the mirror, she expected to see them on the road behind, beetling along fast, gaining on them. When they did finally appear round the long, slow bend, she did not know what she would do. For the first time in her life, she wished she had a gun.

But there was more than Kerron Vaunche to worry about after the dreadful scare at the service station.

What Peter had said was right. They should get off this road, wherever it was. Something had happened at the service station, something that her mind could not rationalise at all. The shop had changed in front of her eyes, rippling and wavering and mutating until it had become some *other* place. Peter had got the word right, something straight out of his computer simulation games. It had *morphed*. It had altered from one thing, melted and run to become another. The girl behind the counter, the silent, imbecilic creature with the turned-in eye the colour of mould, she had become something else in the space of seconds. And in the car park, when they'd burst out, away from the howling sounds and the charred meat on the counter, fleeing from their own images running down a wide road on the crazy game-screen, the asphalt had become mud and cobbles. She tried

157

to shake the picture of the horse that had raised its head, peeled skin with bones showing through and a phosphorescent eye glaring in a wide socket. It had been a dead horse, harnessed and ready to run, brought to life by some dreadful alteration in her own mind, or so she had thought, until Peter had told her he'd seen it too.

When he'd said that, she'd felt that dreadful fear well up. All her life she'd been sickly frightened by the idea of mental illness, of *madness*. The thought of cracking up, freaking out, breaking down, losing control of her own *self*, was one of her own secret phobias, something that had scared her even as a child. It was a worry that had come back to her strongly when she'd analysed the extent of how she'd been manipulated by her husband, how she'd changed to suit him. If that could happen over the years without her even noticing it, then worse could happen when she faced real stress, serious tension.

What could happen was that she might imagine things, like the filling station shop changing into something else, an old and musty shack infested with vermin. She could conjure up bloated spiders inside phone-boxes, great loathsome things with curved fangs which dripped poison. She could make up images of herself and the kids fleeing on a computer screen highway, conjecture a policeman with a coarse face and long horse-like teeth and scaly hands fumbling and groping at her breast. Someone suffering from stress could imagine that everything was out to get her, the police, truck-drivers on lonely roads whose only desire was to swing their trailers and flip her off the road and into the side of a flyover pillar. Someone whose mind was beginning to crack under the strain would imagine a charred and smoking body trying to get out of a burning car, would see threat in everything.

But would Peter have seen it too?

Patsy had always been scared of having something wrong with her brain, having a lesion inside her skull, a tumour growing among the convolutions of her cortex that would somehow change her character, her very self. But after Peter had told her he'd seen the three of them fleeing down that road with a computer-generated menace looming behind them, an even worse fear began to burgeon and swell.

If he had seen it, if he could tell her that the junction filling station had changed out of all recognition, then either they were all mad, or, as her son had succinctly put it, there was something really *wrong* with this place.

All in your mind, the rational voice said, but the other part, the primitive part where all fears are born, knew that was a lie. It had *changed*. Some of it might have been illusion, something shoved into her mind by whatever awful power existed here, but it had riven her with fear. If she looked in the mirror and saw those mouldering horses heaving on the traces, galloping round long curves with a sinister, clattering nighthawk looming up behind her, she just didn't know what she'd do. If she saw that great truck, exhaust stack belching fumes, hammering up along that road like a charging beast, she thought she might lose control of herself and the car and maybe run them all off the road.

She kept her foot down on the accelerator, counting the tenths of a mile as they steadily rolled up, keeping a grip on the wheel and staring straight ahead except for the times she risked a glance in the rear-view mirror (*Still nothing in front, nothing behind, we're all-clear and we're going places, Patsy girl*) and wished she would wake up and find herself home with her children tucked up in their beds, clean and fed and safe.

But somewhere along the line, somewhere between the havoc at Broadford House and the terrifying changes at Havock way-station, she'd taken a wrong turning and found herself on a road that had swooped into a nightmare.

'We're lost, aren't we?' Peter said. Judith was looking up at him, dark eyes wide in her pale face. The half-moon smudges were spreading and her cheeks had taken on a waxy sheen. The rash at her hairline was risen and angry looking.

'Let's say I'm not sure exactly where we are at the moment.'

'We could try the radio. See if there's a traffic programme,' he suggested.

'Good idea.' Patsy reached for the knob. She could have kicked herself for not thinking of the radio. At least she had a chance of picking up a station, some connection to reality. The radio clicked on and she twisted the tuner control, listening to the burps and coughs of static as the needle ran up the scale. There was a silence after one whining burst of interference, then suddenly a voice boomed out from the speakers so loudly it was just a jarring blast of noise and the whole car shuddered. Patsy twisted the volume and brought it down to a bearable level. The voice tailed off in the slide of a high guitar chord. There was something familiar about it. She reached towards the tuner again when it started up once more. Her hand snatched back immediately as if something had bitten her fingers. The nerves in her spine seemed to contract and freeze.

It was the voice she'd heard on the juke box in the service station before it had become someplace *else*.

The gravelly tones ground out, rolling like boulders on a riptide beach, deep and echoing. She heard the lyrics again, the *miles and miles of roads out there.* The boogie-riff came thumping on behind the voice, taking over from the singer. She'd heard this song before now, heard it on her own radio at home, but now it sounded different. Those twelve-bar roadhouse chords had been up-beat and hot. Now they were off-key, jangling and discordant, playing too slow. Behind the chords, there was a rumbling that was not the singer and not drums. It sounded like the vibration of the big rigs roaring past on an empty road. Patsy reached again to turn the radio off when the music simply faded and died.

Hey travellers, that's one for all those folks out on the big blacktop, another voice crackled out, fast and street-smart. *As the man says, there's miles and miles of roads out there and we're here for all you listeners on the move. Just keep your eyes on the road and your ears on rambling radio, the station that keeps you right on going down that ol' road, and on and on and on. If you're tuned to us, then you're on the road all right, rolling along on Route six-six-six.'*

The mid-Atlantic dee-jay jive rapped along.

Now our eye on the roads tells us there's trouble up ahead for some travelling folks, so you be careful out there, y'hear? We've got jams and tailbacks at junction 11, near to gridlock, so we hear. We're talking bumper to bumper, good people, swear to that as I live and breath, cross my throat and hope to die. That's all down to a big pile-up in the rain on the long stretch between exit eleven and the run-up to the junction. There's a lot of activity down that way and we hear there's been a lot of damage. We'll get back to that later, but you can believe it's a real mess, that's for certain.'

Patsy's head snapped back as if she'd been slapped. She'd heard that phrase before. Instantly, the policeman's face flushed in her memory. *Too late for those down there*, he'd said, nodding his head towards the flickering flames of the car down the slope in the scrub. He'd been talking about a multiple car-smash up ahead on the road, warning her to take the left exit to avoid it. *It's a real mess*, was how he'd described it.

Another cold wave of foreboding washed through her. On the radio the jockey was talking again.

'*It's a real mess all right, so our roadrunners tell us, but that's just what happens when you take your eye off the road, ha ha ha.*' His voice broke up into raucous laughter and tailed into a fit of coughing. They heard the unmistakable sound of water being gulped fast, and the cocky, almost frantic broadcaster was back on the air. '*But there's worse ways to go, am I right or am I right? You travelling folk know what I'm talking about now, don't you? Sure you do.*'

He laughed again, manic, almost hysterical.

'*And for those of you who've just joined us, take care on the junction. It's a real mess, I can tell you . . .*'

The voice changed pitch, deepened out, thickened to gruffness.

'*It's a real mess,*' it growled, rumbling now almost as deep and rough as the singer. '*There's blood and guts and bits of bodies all over the place. It's a slaughterhouse.*'

The car swung hard to the left as Patsy jerked on the wheel. She could sense Peter and Judith being thrown sideways. She overcompensated, felt the back wheels slip just a fraction, drove into it and straightened up again. Her heart was kicking at her ribs, beating too fast. A quiver of dizziness blurred her vision for a disoriented moment.

'Oh no,' she heard herself moan, though whether to herself or out loud, she couldn't tell.

'It's the policeman,' Peter yelped. 'That policeman's on the radio.'

She reached out again to turn the thing off and everything seemed to go in slow motion. She saw her hand soar away from her, pale fingers moving at snail's speed. Peter was saying something else, but his voice dopplered away to infinity. Her whole attention was riveted on the sound coming from the set.

Having a good trip, Patsy?

The coarse voice ground out from the radio, speaking directly to her. The skin between her shoulder-blades puckered tightly. A drip of sweat trickled down her spine.

Think you can get away? Underneath the gritty words she could hear the slow wail of a siren. Peter's voice had faded to silence. It was as if everything had stopped, even the car engine, while she kept going at the same speed, linked in time to the dreadful voice now spilling out from the radio. '*It's a long, long way on the junction, heh heh, a real long way.*'

A cold dread. clammy as the sweat trickling down her backbone, rippled through her. Was this the true madness? Was she in the grip of a nightmare? She turned her head, feeling her muscles creak in protest, and saw Peter's face, mouth open, blue eyes fixed on her, frozen in time. Suddenly, in a burst of instant clarity, she knew she was not going mad, had not cracked up. The realisation came from some part deep within her mind where her true sense of self burgeoned. She was not going mad, not falling apart. She was sane and rational. It was everything else that was wrong.

'*You're getting there baby,*' the grindstone voice rumbled, right on cue. '*And keep looking in your mirror. You've got something she wants, and she'll be coming to get it . . .*'

'Who?' she heard herself ask.

'*She's taken from you already and she's coming for more. You can run, little Patsy, but you can't ever get off this road.*'

'Don't kid yourself,' she grated, her own voice sounding almost as hoarse as the words came out through clenched teeth. 'Whoever you are, you bastard.'

'*Just so you know, here's a word from our sponsor . . .*'

The rumbling distorted DJ's voice rolled away like a stone across a wide floor and behind the sound another sound hissed like static interference then soared in a gabble of mad hysteria. Whatever laughed at her, it was not human. The cackling went on for a long time and she could do nothing about it except bear the dreadful brunt of its unearthly lunacy. Finally it began to trail away. It faded out, leaving an echoing ambience, a hollow silence that held an eerie and ominous throat.

'*Listen now, Uanan, my lamb.*'

162

The words hissed out without warning. Instantly a chill colder than ice stabbed through Patsy. Her hand was still stretched towards the radio, but she couldn't make it move any further.

'Catanna,' Judith shrilled. It was the first time she'd really spoken with any enthusiasm since the mêlée at Broadford House. Patsy had recognised the voice. So had Judith.

'*I am with you now.*'

'And for always,' Judith responded, almost in a sing-song. Her voice sounded distant, somehow dreamy.

'*On the darkest path,*' Kerron Vaunche's words came hissing.

'And the deepest night,' the girl answered.

'*In the valley of the shadow of death wherein you dwell. On that nameless day.*'

'There and then I will offer . . .'

The cold sweat evaporated on Patsy's back and a sudden wave of real anger swept up, hot and fiery, swamping the dread. The bubble of no-time burst with an almost audible pop.

'. . . the radio, mum. Switch it off!' Peter's voice had started low, like a warning klaxon, quickly warming up to normal speed. Patsy's floating hand reached the switch and her finger stabbed out and the rumbling laugh died instantly. Judith shrieked once and then burst into tears.

'It *was* that bad man,' Peter insisted, sounding breathless. 'And then I heard Kerron.'

Patsy nodded, feeling the heat of fury sizzle through her.

You've got something she wants, and she'll be coming to get it . . .' There was only one possibility there. That bitch Kerron Vaunche. What Crandall Gilfeather had said came back to her. She hadn't believed him then, but she believed him now. It had to be Kerron Vaunche. She'd stolen her husband, and she had stolen her children, and she was at the root of all of this madness.

'*I see* you *there*, gadge *woman.*' The woman had spat at her. '*I see you on the low road, and you go there* first.' And then she'd really spat, sliming Patsy with her spittle. '*I set your feet on that road forever.*'

Patsy's foot was on the brake, slowing the car down from the high velocity, while at the same time she was trying to slow her thoughts down. Peter said something else, but Patsy was holding on to the memory of the woman's words. She slowed further and pulled over to the hard shoulder, her whole body buzzing with a strange excitement. The car stopped a hundred yards before the first sign she'd seen in a while.

NO STOPPING! The sign flashed out over each lane. Patsy ignored it.

'Why are we stopping, mummy?' Peter asked. Judith was sobbing softly.

'Just for a minute, honey,' Patsy mumbled, still holding on to the recollection.

She'd told Kerron Vaunche she'd see her in hell and the woman had cursed her. The damned bitch had *cursed* her in that guttural language. It dawned on Patsy in an instant of wonderful clarity.

The bitch had done it.

How she'd done it Patsy could not begin to fathom. But for some reason, the *Cat Anna*, the *Cailleach* had done something to the fabric of Patsy's world. She closed her eyes and concentrated further, recalling what Crandall Gilfeather had told her. The *Cailleach* could use the standing stones to walk the Ley Lines, take the low, magical routes at the thin places where worlds merged.

'*She's the earthly counterpart of the underworld powers*,' Gilfeather had said. '*Like a sorceress, so to speak. And she's dangerous. She's the hag in all her forms and she will use her power.*'

The witch had used her power all right. Patsy could still hear the scrapey voice on the radio, speaking directly to Judith, making her respond. It had been like a litany. The dark path, the Nameless Day.

'*That is when the* Cailleach *makes the sacrifice to the* Fasgadh, *the guardian of all the ways. And that is the moment of greatest danger for your son and daughter.*'

Horror and a strange sense of relief battled with each other inside her mind, while up ahead the gantry sign flashed its orders at her. The relief at the knowledge that she was not going mad was countered by the realisation that this was no dream. It was real. Kerron Vaunche had made a curse and Patsy *had* taken a wrong turning and got herself and her children onto this road where the laws of her world did not begin to apply. Down on the Ley Roads the whole world is altered beyond your imagination, so Gilfeather had said. And this place was different. The service way-station had altered beyond her imagination. Beyond belief.

'I don't think we should stop here,' Peter said. 'This is a bad place.'

'You're right, son,' Patsy admitted to him. 'But we'll try to find a way out of it.' She turned round in her seat and cupped his cheek in her hand, feeling the boy-smooth skin, feigning a confidence she did not feel. Judith was slumped against the back of the seat, her face a pale oval under the tumble of black hair. She was snuffling quietly. Patsy touched her hand, felt it stiffen just a little in response. It was still hot and clammy. Kerron Vaunche had reached out to them and touched them again. She had touched Judith and made her respond, reciting ingrained phrases. Patsy didn't know whether the heat in her daughter's skin was a result of what the gypsy had done, or whether Judith was really ill. She let the small hand drop. 'I'll get you home,' she whispered to both of them. 'Trust me, okay?'

'But I think we should go now,' Peter said, nodding. He raised a thumb and indicated behind him. 'There's something coming on the road.'

Patsy whirled round in her seat. She stared out at the long curve of road behind them. It dwindled in the distance, into a far haze where the parallax made all the lines converge. Way back there, something black, no more than a dot, was coming towards them.

She stared at it for a moment, torn between the idea of waiting – that her new-found belief was completely wrong and that it was a friendly fellow traveller who could offer her directions on how to get off this blasted road – and the sudden urgent necessity to get moving and to keep moving and to out-distance the black shape coming up on the road. The instinctive part of her mind, the part that had opened up and shown her the clear picture was clamouring urgently now. She listened to the inner voice, turned the key again, put her foot down and felt the shove in her back as the car leapt forward.

They were coming for her. The certainty of that was suddenly so strong it was like a siren wail inside her head. She accelerated, following the curve of the road until the black shape far behind had dropped out of sight. Up ahead a signpost at the side told her there was another junction. When she reached it, she had a choice of keeping to the main road or following an exit ramp. The sign, rusted and pitted, only showed a diagram of the route itself, white against a scabbed blue background. The names of the destinations had flaked away to oblivion. The new instinct told her to get off the road. She swung the wheel, soared up the slip, felt the route curve to the left, reach a crest then drop down again. From the height, off in the far distance, she could see another immense junction, a great conglomeration of interwoven roads soaring in majestic curves, diving in underpasses. She pulled her visor down against the odd glare of the livid sky and peered ahead. The road dived, still pulling to the left and just before she reached the flat, she looked out of the passenger window. There in a field silhouetted in the strangely pearlescent light, stood the old derelict church.

She felt her knuckles tighten on the wheel. 'Damn it to hell,' she grated.

'We've been here before,' Peter said. There was a slight tremor in his voice. 'I saw that old church.'

Patsy nodded. 'Must have come in a circle,' she said, though none of the road they travelled since they'd fled that junction roadhouse had been familiar. 'We'll find another way.'

She glanced at the church, looked away and then snapped back. It was even more derelict than before. The roof was still swaybacked and nail-sick, but there were gaping holes now where slates and shingles had been. The ancient bell tower was even further askew, leaning right over the nave, and now a hoary snarl of ivy had the narrow steeple in a withering stranglehold. Again she could perceive the complete and utter lack of warmth or welcome in that tumbledown church, and, even more strongly than before, she sensed the presence within the crumbling walls and knew that something reached out dark tendrils of thought that groped and slithered over anything alive. An awful perception of bleak and blind hunger made her shudder in revulsion.

'I don't believe this,' Patsy said aloud.

'It's different, isn't it?' Peter asked. Judith unshipped her belt and knelt up on her seat.

166

'I see a man in the field,' she observed dreamily. 'We have to go to the church.'

'No, silly,' Peter told her. 'It's a scarecrow.'

And that wasn't there before, either, Patsy said to herself. The scarecrow was tall and gaunt, standing alone on spindle-stick legs, the wind ruffling a raggedy coat. One arm was straight out at the shoulder, the other pointing in front, right at the car. Even in the distance they could see the hollows where the eyes had been carved from something, maybe a turnip for a head. It stood just beyond the wall of the churchyard where the snaggled gravestones leaned and tumbled and Patsy felt that twisting sense of hunger again. It was coming from the fluttering figure which stood in the field as if it had emerged, scrawny and tattered, from the shadows inside the church. She shuddered, recoiling. She dragged her eyes away and drove down the hill while in her imagination – she hoped it was her imagination – she could hear something whisper her name like a scrape on the inside of her skull.

'Look at that!' Peter pointed out across the verge. She slowed the car, staying away from the hard shoulder. The old oak tree was still there, but this time there was only one crow in the brittle spread of dead branches, a great dark shape, hunched like a vulture, though its sickle beak was clearly visible, jutting in an obsidian curve. Off to the side of the tree lay the twisted remains of a crashed vehicle. As soon as Patsy saw it, the smell of rot hit her as if she'd driven into an open grave. Instantly she recalled the picnic she'd had with Peter and Judith only a couple of years back when they'd explored the dales. She'd crossed a stile at a hillside dyke, clambering backwards down the rustic wooden steps and, still walking backwards while helping Judith to climb down, she'd stepped in something which gave liquidly under her boot. The smell of the dead sheep had been overpowering and she'd felt herself gag chokingly. But the stench that came from the tangled wreckage – and she could now see through watering eyes it was a coach of some kind – was infinitely worse than the foetid stink of the carcass on the hill.

'Ugh,' Peter gurgled just behind her. 'I'm going to be sick.'

'Try to hold it in,' she barked, though her own throat was going into spasms as the dreadful nausea welled up. She gunned

167

the engine and the car sped forward and in a few seconds they were out of the wind-trail blowing from the wreckage. She was now almost level with the twisted mass of metal and risked another glance. There was not much to be seen, except for the crows, bigger than any crow she had ever seen. One of them, only fifty yards from the verge, was pecking at something on the ground, the great black scimitar digging down in a series of jerking stabs. The others were all in a fluttering pack right on top of the crashed coach. She thought she could see something that looked like an arm hanging from a broken window and looked away quickly when she saw one of the immense birds open its beak, snap it closed on the pale object, and twist its head back, trying to rip a piece for a meal.

'Don't look,' she ordered. 'Sit down, Judith. You too, Peter. And get her strapped in.' Patsy heard a seat belt click home. She stepped on the pedal, forced herself to concentrate on the road ahead while in her peripheral vision she was aware of the black flutterings of the big birds as they fought and squabbled. Even over the road-noise and through the closed windows, she could hear their vicious, raucous cawing. The road eased on to the flat and they zoomed along it until the church and the crows and the wreckage and the smell were far behind them. They kept on for more than ten miles, until Patsy felt it was safe enough to stop. She looked in the mirror, peering behind her again, straining to catch sight of any movement. No black shape appeared in the distance, where the lines on the road converged. She pulled in again and stopped the engine.

'We should keep going,' Peter stated.

'Maybe we should,' Patsy agreed. 'But I just want to stop for a moment and have a think. Can you give me a few minutes for that?'

'Okay,' Peter said, and slowly sat back against the seat. Patsy crossed her arms on the wheel and stared out through the windscreen, wondering what the hell she was going to do next. The little tremors had started again under her skin, but not as violent as before. For some reason she felt more in control to herself, as if the huge mental leap that took her from absolute panic in the face of the unacceptable to the strangely numb acceptance of the unbelievable, had numbed the shock receptors in her mind.

The little tremors began to ease away and flatten out as a strange calm overtook her.

Patsy took a long, deep breath, while she mentally counted off what she knew.

Point one: She and her children were stuck on this road where the reality she had always known did not exist.

Point two: Kerron Vaunche had done this to them. She had cursed them, put a spell on them (*and only now was Patsy able to consider that as a serious option*) that had kicked them through whatever barrier existed between their own world and this blasted place.

Point three: If there was a way in, there had to be a way out. One of these roads had to lead back to where she had come from, and she had to find that road and get them out of this nightmare, get them home.

She inhaled again, filling her lungs. There was only one real option. They had to keep going. Patsy knew they had passed the crows on the bare oak tree the previous time just before she had come up to the service station. She knew she had to avoid that place, for if the old church had changed, become more decayed and derelict, then the junction roadhouse would have changed too. She tried to remember if the main road had been blocked, or whether she had the choice to avoid the way-station, but just couldn't remember.

'Right you two,' she finally said, 'We've got a bit of a problem, but nothing we can't handle.'

'No probs,' Peter said lightly, nudging Judith in the ribs. 'It's a holiday, isn't it. Like a mystery tour.'

'Exactly,' Patsy agreed, loving him for that. 'Just like a treasure hunt. So when I start the car, we're just going to keep going until silly old mum finds us the right road, and then we'll be fine. Everybody okay with that?'

Peter nodded, keeping his eyes fixed on hers. They were open and honest and she could see the odd mixture of fear and resolution in them. Her son was nine years old and she hadn't seen him for so long. In that time he'd grown a little, but there was something else about him. It was as if he'd grown up a little. He was still the same Peter, still had the easy nonchalance and the look of mischief about him, but there was something more,

169

something deeper, and she wondered what had happened in the past year to put that change in him.

'I put some stuff in the back,' she said, breaking the thread. 'Split the back seat and reach in. There's some sweets and things.'

He unhooked the back of the seat, easing his sister to the side and swung it down to open the trunk. Patsy turned to face forwards again, started the engine, and they began to move. The tyres ground on the red grit of the hard shoulder then went silent as they found the blacktop. Behind her she heard the rattle of the usual junk she kept in the boot then a grunt from Peter.

'Got it,' he said, voice muffled enough to let her know he'd crawled halfway through the hatch. A rustle and clank followed and he emerged, dragging one of the plastic bags.

'Plenty here,' he said. It had only been an hour or so since he'd eaten last, but his appetite hadn't changed. 'Can I have crisps?'

At least whatever she'd bought at the junction hadn't turned into something else, Patsy realised with some relief. She'd accepted as a fact that things *had* changed in the roadhouse, and that it hadn't been her imagination, some crack in her mind where crazy visions lurked.

'Sure you can. Take a can of Coke to wash them down, but just one between two.' She'd bundled half a dozen Cokes into the first basket, acting on that new-found instinct before she'd even understood what was happening. Some part of her brain, some sixth sense must have been operating for her while the rest of her mind was busy having hysterics, taking the 'screaming meemies' and rejecting everything her eyes told her must be true. She smiled grimly at that. Maybe Kerron Vaunche did have some sort of power, maybe she was the apotheosis of mother earth, but Patsy Havelin, Thomson *as was*, she had power too. She was a real mother, and her mother's instinct had been working just fine and dandy, obeying all the rules: protect the kids, feed the kids, keep them safe from harm.

I'll do my best, she silently promised them. *Trust me, Peter, trust me Judy. I'll get you out of this.*

Already the instinct was working on her. It had been less than a day since she'd fled, shaking with anger and fear, from the gates of Broadford House, less than twenty-four hours since she'd looked at that shadow inside the burning car. There were cans of juice in the basket, enough for a couple of days if necessary, but down in that deep part of her *self* where that new instinct was getting stronger, the calculations were being made. Consciously she knew she was in trouble, but she expected to get out of that trouble in just a little while. She'd plenty of fuel and the car had been serviced only a month before and she'd keep going until she found the right road that would take her off this junction and set her on the way home. It was only a matter of hours, maybe half a day at the most, so her rational mind told her, while underneath all of that, the silent voice was urging her to prepare.

Behind her Peter popped a can and a fine spray hissed out. Judith muttered softly and Patsy heard her slurp the bubbles of Coke while her brother opened the crisps. The scent of cheese and onion filled the car, overpowering the dead smell of stale oil and fumes.

The sign was not long in coming, the big white square, pock-marked and paint-flaked. HAVOCK SERVICES. She read the black words again and ignored the tense clench of her knuckles. She drove faster, just in case some hypnotic magnetism would make her pull up that slip road again and on to the flat asphalt where the big line of black trucks growled in the corner and where the rig-drivers would turn round and stare at her with blind-green devil eyes and their faces would ripple and change and melt until they were something less than human. The merger signs followed, counting off the yards before the cut-off. She drove faster, pushing her foot down, feeling again the surge as the seat pushed against her back, and even as she did so, she was aware of the drag of the station on the junction, the dreadful pull of fearful fascination that makes a deer stand wide-eyed in the glare of the approaching headlamps, that makes a rabbit freeze while the stoat does its dance of death. Patsy could feel the black magnetism of the place in the big nerves running down her spine. Her inner ears felt the sudden drop of pressure as if the atmosphere right there at the junction merger had somehow *twisted* out of shape and become charged with energy. The metal fillings on the two wisdom teeth at the back of her jaw begin to tingle, as they always did whenever the barometer plummeted.

She could feel the vibration singing in an itch along her bones. The entrance was tugging at her, attempting to lure her like a stupid fish, reel her in. Patsy kept her eyes fixed on the wide road ahead. She forced her hands to grip the wheel and set her shoulders, pulling out away from the entrance, rather than towards it. The wheels blatted the cat's eyes again and she was past. Immediately the sense of foreboding drained away and she let out a whoosh of breath, unaware that she had been holding it in.

The entrance vanished behind her and in a minute or so she pulled back into the slow lane again and let her speed ease off. She was unaware that Peter had moved up behind her, kneeling on the back seat to lean on the back of hers, until he spoke into her ear. The sound startled her so much she almost drove them all up the steep verge.

'We got past it, didn't we?' he asked. Patsy had to wait until her heart calmed down before she could answer.

''Course we did.'

'It's a bad place,' he said, keeping his voice down, keeping this between his mother and himself, the way their previous eye contact had dictated. 'I didn't know at first, but now I do. It smelled like where daddy took us to.'

She gave him a quick glance. He was wrinkling up his nose as if something had died.

'Broadford House? Where you were yesterday?'

'Yes. I wanted to come home, but he said we'd get used to it. He said that *she* was our new mummy now.'

Patsy felt the instant clench of anger and bit it back. She wanted to hear this.

'Is that right?'

'Uh-huh. That's what he said, but I said we already had one and we didn't need another one, especially somebody that had made you cry.'

'And what did he say to that?' Patsy was surprised. She'd always thought she'd kept the tears to herself, kept them from flooding her children with her own torn emotions.

'He got a bit annoyed. He said I was to be more respectful and I would understand anyway. In time.' Peter leaned right between the two front seats, holding on to the head rest so that his face was right next to his mother's. 'But I just wanted to come home. I didn't like that place and I didn't like *her* and the way she smelled and the way she looked at Judith like she wanted to eat her up or something.'

The cold fingers clenched around Patsy's heart again at the thought of it. Kerron Vaunche had had a predatory look, but there was something more in what Peter was saying. He had sensed something, some ambition or some purpose. There was no time now, not while they were moving on this road, to find out everything, but she was determined that when they did get off this godforsaken road – *godforsaken, that was* exactly *how she sensed this roadway* – she would find out what really had been going on between Kerron Vaunche and her children. She would haul that woman, earth mother, earth *witch* or not, through every court in the land and she would drag him with her if it meant keeping them away from Judith and Peter forever. The cold evaporated in yet another blaze of anger and Patsy knew that she could kill that woman if she needed to protect her own. She turned her head quickly and gave him a kiss on the cheek, smacking her lips loudly.

'Love you, hon,' she said, and she meant it more than ever before.

'Aw mum,' he said, grinning sheepishly, knuckling the kiss away. Judith burped as the Coke bubbles forced their way out and for a precious second the three of them were in an oasis of normality as the scrub alder and brambles beyond the hard shoulder whizzed by. Peter sat down again and Patsy went back to concentrating on the road. The children finished their crisps and the can they shared and Peter crushed the packets and put them and the empty can into a plastic bag which he tucked back into the cubby hole.

Overhead, the bruised sky darkened as clouds rolled in to drop a smattering of rain on the windscreen. In a matter of seconds, the squall thickened, driving in fast and furious, rocking the car with the force of the wind which swept down on them on the straight stretch of road and now pelting it with hailstones which hit so hard it was like being inside a snare drum, and for a moment Patsy was concerned that the toughened glass might not be tough enough to cope. She drove on, through the deafening hail, wipers at full thrash, slowing just enough for safety, but not too much in case some other traveller just might be driving in the same direction. The storm lasted only five minutes or so and ended as abruptly as it started. Patsy got out from under the black cloud and back into the banal grey of the overcast that had dominated since the morning. The road curved round to the right, through a channel that had obviously been blasted out of old volcanic basalt, and as she drove between the towering walls of gouged rock, she wondered just *how* it had been blasted. That she was still on the flip side of this journey, still on the wrong side of the partition, she could tell by the colour of the sky and the smell of the air and the sensation of wrongness that tingled in her nerves. Did they have road workers here? Engineers? That new-found part of her self whispered to her that whoever had built this road had not used drills and diggers and blasting charges. Whoever – *or* what-*ever* – had used other forces to gnaw through the bedrock.

The curve carried on for more than a mile and then the road ahead slanted up in a gradual incline. Patsy maintained her speed up the straight until she reached the short plateau at the top and as soon as the car breasted the rise her mouth fell open at the same time as her foot shifted to the brake.

There, in the distance, she could see the interwoven motorway junction, a clover-leaf merger that looked like clover *field*.

She slowed her speed to a crawl, then brought the car to a complete halt, staring wide-eyed, mouth still agape at the scene beyond the crash barrier. Way off, so far it was shrouded in a haze, was a nightmare tangle of concrete, looping and soaring and twisting back on itself. It was as if every road in the world had been joined there in a serpentine mass of slip-roads and ramps, freeways and junctions. Her eyes scanned from left to right, sweeping across the far horizon.

The road network was colossal. It filled the entire scope of her vision. It looked as if it filled the entire world.

The gravely rough-core voice came back to her again, the lyrics fresh in her memory.

. . . there's miles and miles of roads out there . . .

There were miles and miles. Hundreds of miles, *thousands* of miles of roads filling the world in front of her. They seemed to arch and loop and curve around each other in a tangled knot of concrete. Way out to the right she saw an immense flyover soar over a road which curved above another in a stacked layer of highways that seemed to have no end. It was like Los Angeles and Spaghetti Junction and the Paris périphérique connected to every other bypass and loop route. To the left of the conglomeration she could see the orange glow of street lights strung across an overpass which dived under a viaduct, throwing a hazy glare on immense concrete pillars holding up the weight of the six-lane road.

The sight took her breath away while those lyrics rolled around in her head. Miles and miles and miles of roads out there, and they went on *forever*.

Patsy rolled down the window, almost absently because it was nearly impossible to drag her eyes away from the incredible junction. Immediately the hum of distant traffic, that far-off growl of trucks and cars and lorries came in waves, like the buzzing of angry insects, though she could see nothing moving on any of the routes. The air here was thick, redolent of diesel and carbon monoxide, burning rubber and the baked fumes from turbochargers. Here the air smelled of *roads*. It stank of internal combustion and heavy transport. Somewhere in the distance a horn blared and another beeped in response. A trailer-rig air horn *whonked*, a Jurassic blast in this monstrous park of flyovers and underpasses, closer than the others, and the sound rolled out on the cloy air.

'Wow!' Peter said. Patsy eased herself round in her seat and saw him kneeling up at the window on the other side of the car, staring out at the vast road network that stretched from horizon to horizon.

'It's just like *Termight*,' he said, voice agog with wonder.

'Like what?' Patsy asked, though her attention was nailed on the vast network of concrete and asphalt which stretched into the distance.

'It's in a comic I used to get. It's a place where all the roads come together in the biggest city in the world. It's science fiction. There was a wizard who had to destroy it to save everybody.'

'And did he?'

'I dunno. Dad came and took us away before I got to the good bit.'

Patsy couldn't tear her eyes away from the colossal interchange. She had no words to describe it, nothing to compare it to in reality. Very slowly, she opened the door and stepped out.

'Where are you going?' Peter asked quickly.

'Nowhere,' Patsy said, almost absently. Her senses were still reeling from the immensity of the panorama and her new-found determination seemed to diminish as her own insignificance dawned on her. She got out of the car, gently closed the door, and looked around her. The roads stretched as far as her eyes could see. There was no respite at all from the agglomeration of motorways and flyovers. It was a gigantic web of highways, waiting to trap whatever moved . . . A wind, coming on broadside to the car, moaned through the hawsers that formed a crash barrier on the central reservation, adding to the sensation.

Very slowly, Patsy walked to the front of the car and got onto the narrow breakdown lane, foot pressing down on one of the cat's eye studs. It gave under her weight with a crumbly rasp. She reached the nearside barrier, put a hand on the cold metal surface and leaned over.

Instant vertigo looped inside her and her fingers clamped on the metal in a desperate grip as the whole world spun out of focus. The road was on a bridge which arched fifty, maybe even a hundred feet above a six-lane highway. Patsy almost staggered back, frantically recalling the last few moments of travel. She'd been driving up the incline, just coming on to the plateau, and there had been no suggestion, no warning sign, that she was on a bridge. She turned away and looked back in the direction she'd come. It was a flyover, sure enough, she could see that now. Somehow, in the run up the slope, the road had altered. Way back in the distance, she could see the looping arch of another junction, though she knew with certainty that she hadn't passed that. She'd been travelling on a three-lane autoroute through flat country that had only been broken by clumps of scrub alder and low, bleak hills in the distance. She looked around her. Peter and Judith were watching her from the car.

The red grit of the hard shoulder was worn in places and the substrate cracked in others. Weeds were sprouting, what looked like coarse grass and wiry bindweed, through the cracks and in the dust-clamps in the lee of the crash barrier uprights. There was even some straggly clover and dandelions growing close to the line of cat's eyes and on the central reservation, some of the scrubby brambles and rhododendrons were stretching out onto the road. Just beside the front wheel of the car a budding fern frond, coiled like a tentacle, was beginning to unfurl, pallid and weak. A thin, scraggled ivy crawled up a stanchion.

Wherever she was, this road hadn't been used much. It looked as if it hadn't been travelled in a long time.

She turned back to the metal fence and put both hands on the surface. It vibrated under her fingers, as if the whole bridge was trembling, shivering in slow pulses. Down below, the wide road stretched, arrow straight into the distance, where, in the haze, she could see another set of circular junctions, too far away to make out clearly. But the road itself was deserted. Nothing moved down there and the moaning of the wind made the scene even more eerily empty. Underneath where she stood, she could see the faint shadow of one of the narrow pillars supporting the span where she'd stopped and then the dark curve of the flyover crossing the road below like a dismal rainbow. Right on the shadow curve, maybe thirty yards beyond the hard shoulder where the red gravel merged with the red dirt and dry bracken, she saw the heap of twisted metal. The rear end of a station wagon angled up, boot open and twisted awry. Its nose was buried under what looked like a small van which was hardly recognisable as a vehicle, and both were overshadowed by the tortured, rusting remains of a mini-coach. A hundred yards along, two cars were just edged off the road, one in front of the other, as if they had been parked. The front doors were open on both cars, stiff stubby wings. From where she stood, she couldn't tell if there was anybody in them, but from the streaks of rust, it was hardly likely. It looked as if the drivers had pulled in at the side of the empty road, got out and abandoned their cars.

As soon as she recognised one car, her eyes picked out others. Some were tumbled and wrecked, while others looked as if they had just been driven off into the scrub or onto the verges. There were cars and vans littered along the edge of the highway for as far as she could see.

177

'It's like a graveyard,' she said, and the wind plucked her words and faded them away.

Of any of the drivers of the cars down below, there was no sign.

12

They had less than a week, four days of twitching anxiety before the crisp winter morning dawned. Patsy had been unable to do more than doze, waiting for Carrick and the others to arrive just after sunrise. She'd pulled on her jeans and a good pair of walking shoes before bundling a few essentials into a rucksack. Connie wasn't with Carrick when he turned up with the others. Patsy had met the man she only knew as McGregor, though whether it was a nickname or a code or even his real surname, she never discovered. Carrick had told her he was involved in rescuing brainwashed youngsters from cults all over the country and he had a hard-eyed, almost fanatical air about him, as if he lived on the edge of anger the whole time. The other man was a stranger. Carrick did not introduce him and he said nothing, even when Patsy poured them large mugs of coffee. He wasn't tall and looked almost skinny under the old camouflage fatigues, but he moved with a graceful fluid motion that reminded Patsy of a cat and something inside her sensed the danger under the placid surface of this man. There were violent depths in there that she could probably never fathom.

Crandell Gilfeather was dressed in a heavy duffel coat and he wore an old deerstalker hat. His eyes were slate grey in the cold of the morning. For some reason, Patsy was pleased that he had come along.

She had driven north, trailing the old grey transit van that McGregor had brought, travelling first on motorway, then on smaller roads once they'd crossed the border, where the weather had changed from a sharp frost to a freezing drizzle lashed by occasional hail. It was close to dusk when they passed Levenford, the last substantial town, took the narrow route over the moor and along the edge of the loch and finally pulled in at a bank of trees. McGregor drove the van under the reaching branches and Patsy followed. She sat still, lights switched off. The van door opened and the two men got out. Carrick joined them, taller than the others by almost a head. He'd pulled on a black hat which rolled down into a balaclava. The other two wore similar masks. It made them look more like terrorists than men on a rescue mission.

'Very theatrical,' Crandall Gilfeather had commented, chuckling aloud, though Patsy sensed he was trying to lighten the tension for her. 'On their own private *jihad*. Quite appropriate for our little holy war, don't you think?'

Patsy shrugged, more to move against the trembling in her shoulders. It was less than two weeks before Christmas, but as Gilfeather had told her, in a religion that made Christianity seem like a new-fangled cult, it was only six days before the Nameless Day.

'Now, don't worry,' he had told her, patting her hand paternally. 'We've got right on our side, and she is not omnipotent, not yet, and with our help, she never will be. But she will try to keep them, and she might play a few tricks ... I can see that ahead of us, but you follow your instincts. It will be frightening, so you'll have to be strong, for the sake of the wee ones.'

'I'll try,' Patsy said. Her voice was shuddering, both from the sudden chill and from the twisting anxiety. Carrick came over to the car and leaned his head in.

'If this goes according to plan, we'll be out in less than ten minutes.'

'And if not?' Patsy asked, feeling the tension wind up inside her.

'Then we'll be a bit longer,' the big man said with a confident chuckle. 'Don't you worry. These guys are good. Turn the car around and have it facing the way we came and keep the engine running. There might be a lot of noise, but don't worry about that. We'll be coming out very fast and the kids will be upset. We've gone over this before, but best be safe than sorry. No matter what happens, Peter and Judy go in the car and you take off like a bat out of hell. You don't hang about waiting for us. We've all done this kind of thing before, one way and another.'

'No,' Crandall Gilfeather said. The word came out soft, but it had enough force to stop Carrick dead.

'She must be with you. Kerron Vaunche has had months to

180

work on the girl and the time is close. She will need her mother to find her and bring her out. It is the only way.'

The thin man shook his head. He started to say something but Patsy held up her hand.

'I want to do what he says,' she told them. Carrick looked from one to the other.

'It is the only way,' Gilfeather said. McGregor shrugged.

'Right,' Carrick said briskly. 'We'll have to get in first and open the gate.' Patsy looked in her mirror to begin reversing the car and when she glanced back at the van, all three of them were gone. She moved the car back under the trees and waited. The green figures on the clock on the dashboard counted out the seconds, but moved so slowly that the luminous figures seemed to take forever to progress. The first minute seemed to take an hour. Patsy felt the nerves begin to twitch behind her knees and inside she was tortured with the agony of worry and hope and underneath that, a clammy prescience of danger. Somewhere in the trees an owl hooted. Further up on the moor, a curlew piped a ghostly sound.

A faint screeching noise ground out and then a shape appeared at the window. Carrick beckoned and she got out of the car. Gilfeather joined her.

'We're in, and it's all quiet.' Lightning flickered off to the east sending pulses of luminescence through the clouds. Patsy's heart was high in her chest, beating so hard it threatened to cut off her breath.

'Don't worry,' Crandall Gilfeather told her. 'I'll be there.'

'And me,' Carrick whispered in her ear, putting a big arm around her shoulder. The shadow that was McGregor moved at the gate. They followed its silent progress. Patsy's feet snicked on gravel and they moved onto grass. The back of Broadford House was in complete darkness. High on the wall, an overflow pipe dripped. There was a cold smell of dampness overlaying the odour of a stale drain. A door opened with the merest hint of a creak and they were inside.

Here the dark was so thick it had weight. The air bore a musty essence, dry and fusted. Motes of dust caught in the throat. A narrow corridor – and Patsy only knew it was narrow because she sensed the sides closing in on her – led to a stairway. Off to the left, a leaky washer made a tap hiss. Down to the right something scuttled softly. High upstairs, echoing down from wall to wall, a child cried in its sleep.

Carrick leaned to whisper in Patsy's ear. 'Going up for little Pete. He's upstairs. You go with the old feller and McGregor. I'll be down before you know it.'

Gilfeather took her by the crook of her arm. Carrick and the other man flitted away up the stairs, making not the slightest sound. Patsy was led along another narrow corridor. She could hear her heart beating inside her ears, a hard pulse that she was sure must be loud in the dark. The corridor widened. A flicker of lightning stuttered and lit the passage. A small set of wooden stairs spiralled downwards to another passage. Here McGregor stopped. He leaned up against a door and slowly turned the handle. She though he'd ease it open slowly but instead he jerked the door inwards quickly, killing any squeal an old hinge might have made. He raised his hand and the slim maglight torch threw a beam onto a small bed in the corner.

It was empty.

The man swept the beam around the small room. The bed was made up. There was a set of drawers and a chair. Clearly the room had not been used.

'She's supposed to be here,' McGregor whispered.

'For heaven's sake,' Patsy said, voice rising in panic. 'Where is she?'

'Stay calm,' Gilfeather butted in gently. 'We'll find her. *You* will find her. She must be close, down at this level. The *Cailleach* will have her near the altar. I can feel it's power here.'

'What do you mean?'

'I mean close your eyes and *reach*,' the man said. 'She's your child, still a part of you. Feel for the sense of her.'

For some reason Patsy did as she was told. There was something about Gilfeather that had impinged upon her on the journey up through the valleys and thundery glens. She closed her eyes and the darkness swirled around her. For an instant she was lost in it, completely alone, as if she had climbed into a drain and pulled the hatch closed. It was abysmal, complete, infinite.

An echoing emptiness became perceptible as a sound. In the

dark she reached with her hands out before her. There was a *twist*, an odd jar within her.

And her mind reached too. The darkness roiled and rolled and she felt her touch force outwards. She took a step forward. Two. She moved on. A door loomed and she sensed it before her hand touched it. The handle turned. Beyond there were three doors.

Something feathered on her heart and a tremendous joy punched into her. In that brief instant she had felt her daughter.

'There,' she said, pointing at the right-hand door. McGregor opened it as quickly as before. The light flashed. Patsy's heart flopped. Judith's tangle of black hair was tumbled on the pillow. Her pale face seemed to glow in the circle of light thrown by the beam. Her thumb was jammed innocently in her mouth.

'Make it quick,' McGregor said. Patsy moved to the bed, lowered herself down and cradled Judith's cheek. Her daughter moaned dozily.

'Come on, Judy, wake up now.'

Judith snorted. Her eyes opened, closed again. Patsy spoke again. Judith pushed herself upright. She turned, looked into her mother's eyes.

And she shrank back as if she'd seen a snake. Her hand went to her neck. Patsy got a glimpse of a twisted little dark shape on a string, some kind of talisman. Judith's fingers closed over it.

'Come on, Judy. Hurry now. It's mummy.'

The girl shook her head slowly, mouth agape. Just at that moment, a loud noise, the sound of a door slamming hard came reverberating from upstairs. Somebody shouted.

'Hurry now,' McGregor said. 'Get her out the way you came.' He disappeared through the doorway towards the sound.

Judith opened her mouth, as if she was about to scream. Crandall Gilfeather reached forward and clamped his hand over the gape.

'Sorry, my dear. She's just confused, but we need to be quiet.'

Patsy reached and pulled her daughter towards her. *What's wrong? What's the matter with her?* The futile question was ricocheting inside her head. Judith squirmed, tried to pull away. Patsy hugged the small form into her side and lifted her bodily off the bed. She backed out of the door, along the corridor with

Gilfeather on her heels. High up in the building, a man's voice yelled.

They got to the small spiral stair. Patsy got one foot on the tread when Judith pulled back, got her mouth free and screeched like a cat.

They were just at the turn. The stair spiralled upwards while below them it circled down to a cellar. Lightning flickered through a spiderwebbed window. A shape came rushing up from below, moving so fast it was like a rippling shadow. Patsy turned as it came launching towards her. A pale hand reached out and made a grab for her.

'Stop,' Crandall Gilfeather cried. He raised a hand and the black shape slammed into it. A pulse of light sparked in the air. Gilfeather went reeling backwards, but so too did the shape. Patsy went up the stairs, too scared to do anything else. Judith shrieked again and Patsy grabbed her tight, clamping her face in against her own neck to silence her. She reached the top of the stairs. Gilfeather came behind her, panting for breath. They got to the corridor. At the far end, a light had come on, throwing enough illumination to make out shapes. They started along it.

Kerron Vaunche came up behind them and snatched for Judith.

Patsy twisted away. She screamed incoherent denial. Judith shrieked even louder.

'Give her to me!' the woman spat. She was dressed all in black, or so it seemed in the dimness of the passageway. She reached forward. Patsy was so scared she couldn't speak. Gilfeather reached again and grabbed the woman's arm. The strange crackle sparked again, as if two electrodes had connected. The smell of singed hair billowed out.

'Leave her, *Carlin-wife*,' Gilfeather shouted. 'She is claimed now.'

Vaunche turned to the older man. 'Claimed for another, old man, and too late for you and your simpering prayers.' She raised her hands, two white spiders in the dimness. Immediately the far-end light dimmed to nothing.

'*Achor, Dabbat, Skratta*,' Kerron Vaunche snarled.

'Too late to call his names,' Gilfeather cried, drowning the woman's voice.

184

'*Taimat the footless, Erebus, Be-elzebub,*' the woman jabbered on.

The dark closed around Patsy like a fist and for an instant she had no sense of reference. In her arms Judith suddenly quivered, arching her back as if she'd taken a fit.

A shape came looming out of the darkness, a dreadful gargoyle head with glaring eyes and a vast mouth. A tongue drooled slime.

'*Give up the Uanan,*' it slobbered. Patsy's panic erupted.

'Ignore it,' Gilfeather shouted again. 'It's nothing at all.'

Kerron Vaunche yammered another staccato chant. The ghastly form wavered in the air, rippled, altered, became a long, thin shape with a lobster-red face, so slender it was almost like a beak. It giggled insanely and she heard the laughter inside her head. An impossibly long, articulated arm reached out to her. Patsy squirmed away from it. As she passed it, she pushed *through* the reaching fingers, as if they were made of smoke, but even then she felt a dreadful, numbing cold lance through her shoulder where the red thing had touched.

'Deny it,' Gilfeather ordered again. 'They are only illusions. They can't harm you.' He spun towards Kerron Vaunche and called out in a language Patsy did not understand. The gypsy woman snarled something equally incoherent but more malevolent.

Patsy stumbled forward. The red shape winked out of existence. For an instant the darkness went solid and then, miraculously, she saw the outlines of a door in front of her. A light behind it worked through between the door and the jamb. In the dimness she saw the heavy, interwoven carvings. A large bronze handle stuck out and she reached for it. As soon as her hand touched the metal, a shudder of dread twisted inside her.

The door swung open and the light died. A dreadful stench of rot filled her nostrils and made her gag.

A grating sound rumbled to her right. High on a corner, a light flickered several times and then blipped on. Another joined it, circled round, a third flickered to life and then all three came whirling down from a vaulted ceiling trailing powdery luminescence. For a second Patsy thought they were floating eyes and her breath started to back up, but one zoomed closer and she saw it was a moth of some sort, shining like a glow-worm.

Right in front of her, a broad stone circle straddled three yard-wide columns.

The Broadford Stone. The words took on capitals in her mind. The jarring sensation rippled through her again and . . .

Judith was lying spread-eagled on the stone, arms and legs pinioned by braided sparkling ropes and her whole body shivering violently. The dreadful gash running from her neck to her pelvis, a great red chasm in which purple-slicked organs still writhed. Her daughter's legs twitched helplessly and her eyes stared out at her mother and the little bleating noise died away with the slowing movement

An illusion, her mind screeched. Judith was in her arms. She squeezed tight, feeling for the warmth of her daughter's body. Something inside her seemed to rupture. Her arms were tight round her own ribs. Her daughter was gone. Patsy whirled. The glow-worm moths trailed their bale light and Patsy saw . . .

Paul on the stone, face contorted in ecstasy, neck corded, while the thing upon him hunched, darkening now, foreshortening as it shrank and widened, became a squat shape, head bowed. It lowered its warted head . . . and the form on the stone was not Paul but Judith, slender and fragile, flopped and dead. The monstrosity snuffed again, gobbling down there in the wet mess of the chasm, and when it rose again the flies came bursting out in a fog and Judith's dead eyes fixed accusingly on her.

Patsy shook her head.

'Hallucination,' she grunted. 'All a trick.'

The scene winked out. Judith's warmth flooded into her. The girl's body was thrumming like a taut wire. Some kind of power reached out from the stone and touched the girl and her skin and bones and muscles resonated with the force. Patsy turned. The stone shuddered. The carvings rippled and writhed and she dragged her eyes away from them. In the centre of the stone, a dark vortex started to spin, like clouds in the centre of a tornado. The dark hole expanded and down in its depths a red glow flickered, like the fires of hell. She felt the gleam pull her and she dragged back from it.

'Please God, help us,' she cried. The glow shrank down. A

crack razored on the surface of the stone. Behind her, it seemed like some distance away, Kerron Vaunche shrieked. The door clanged hard against the wall and Patsy threw herself out and into the corridor.

'Go on, girl,' Gilfeather cried, urging Patsy away. Judith howled. Patsy turned and ran. Her daughter wriggled and struggled, but she ignored it, got to the far end of the corridor and shouldered her way through. Carrick was thundering down the stairway with Peter in his arms. Behind him, the slim man came whirling down one flight, turned and aimed a blow at a moving shape. There was a low grunt and a body flopped.

'Where's Gilfeather?' Carrick demanded. Peter's eyes were bright with excitement. They lit on his mother and widened further. She saw his instant smile and her heart did another flopping somersault.

'Down there,' was all she could say, nodding her head back in the direction she'd fled. Carrick pointed. McGregor went through the doorway. With hardly a pause, the big man spun Patsy around and hustled her along the narrow corridor. The walls closed in on them. She could hear Peter's breathing. Judith had stopped quivering and was now lying limp in her arms. They ran for the door.

It slammed shut when they were halfway down and the darkness came back.

In the depths of the shadows, squirming shapes writhed and floated. Patsy ignored them. *All in the mind, just an illusion.*

Carrick bulled past her. She felt Peter's touch as he rubbed against her, made the *mother*-connection that was unfathomable and as old as time. Carrick reached the door. He pulled at it and she heard the handle rattle.

'Back,' he said. She obeyed. There was a crash like thunder and the door flew off its hinges. Carrick had simply lifted a massive foot and kicked it out. He told her to move and she moved. Carrick veered to the left but Patsy went scampering out through the gates. She reached the car, opened it, bundled Judith inside.

Then the dusk erupted in flashes of light, crashes of noise.

Patsy automatically reached to switch on the headlamps then remembered Carrick had told her to keep the car hidden for as long as possible. She drew back, nerves singing with tense apprehension, her whole body drumskin-tight. Beyond the edge of the trees somebody shouted hoarsely, a loud animal sound of anger which changed pitch very suddenly to become a yelp of surprise or pain. Glass smashed in a crystalline explosion and then a loud metallic clang tolled from the shadows beyond the wall. Patsy could do nothing but sit, bottom lip clenched between her teeth, praying that her children were not hurt.

She rolled the window down halfway just as something crashed through the undergrowth close to the car, and she jerked back as a shadow loomed close. A dark hand reached for the handle on the passenger door behind her and she whirled, hand raised to hit the lock button when she saw McGregor running towards the back of the car.

Outside, beyond the trees and close to where the big gate stood, there was another explosion of noise. A hoarse shout tore the air and this time she recognised Carrick's voice bellowing. A second later he came tearing round the corner, using one hand to spin himself around a tree. The force of the motion almost whipped Peter off his feet but Carrick didn't stop. He reached the van in about ten strides, pulling the boy along with him.

'Quick, get in the car.' The thin, nameless man was behind them. He snatched the door open and Carrick almost threw Peter inside. He spun away towards the house. All Patsy could see was his tousle of fair hair next to where she'd strapped Judith in. Her children were just blurs in the dark. Hot tears sparked up in her eyes and she heard herself babble, drowning out the girl's low whimpers. She twisted on her seat and was now kneeling to reach into the back of the car. Her fingers found Judith's narrow shoulders, grabbed Peter by the arm and pulled them both towards her, swamped in the mother-need to embrace her daughter. She felt the small body tremble against hers; felt Judith's fright, and an unbidden flush of hatred for Paul Thomson and his whore surged inside her like a poison heartburn.

'You're all right now, Judith,' she murmured into her daughter's ear, smoothing the dark hair down with one hand, rhythmically patting the child's back with the other. Judith was whimpering non-stop, a high, juddery sound that was close to hysterics. Patsy cuddled her close and held her tight, willing the girl's fear away.

'Go now,' Carrick bawled.

Patsy was reaching for Peter, hardly able to breathe in the sudden paralysis of emotional overload, but Carrick reached in and slapped her hand down.

'Come on, girl. Plenty of time for that. Get this car going and get a bloody *move* on.' His voice, so loud in the confines of the car made her start back. Judith squealed in fright, but Peter got an arm round her.

'Hey, come on, Judy. It's mum and Uncle Carrick. We're out of here.'

He turned to look up at the big man who was pulling himself back out of the car. 'That was great, better than *Predator*.' Even in the dark, Peter's face was visibly flushed with excitement.

'Get moving, Patsy,' Carrick ordered. She loosened her grip on Judith and swivelled round in the seat. The engine had cut out and she turned the key, stabbing her foot down on the pedal. The engine coughed and died and instant alarm welled up inside her. She tried again just as a shape came running out along the path. A light came blazing on at the gates and Patsy saw Paul sprinting towards the car, his face contorted in fury. He was shouting something hoarse and incoherent and in the blaze of white light she could see the tendons stand out on his neck, giving him a cadaverous, ghostly look.

A smaller shape flowed out from the shadow and hit Paul on the side, hard enough to make the running man stumble and fall. He bounced on the grass verge, rolled and came back to his feet again, still moving fast. He reached the car and snatched the door open, roaring with anger. He reached past Peter and grabbed Judith by both arms and started to drag her out. The girl was screaming now, a shivery cry which resonated the windows and seemed to vibrate inside Patsy's skull. Peter shouted something and even as Patsy turned round to push her husband away, the boy had launched himself at his father, beating at Paul's arms with his fists. Paul reacted instinctively. One hand whipped away from Judith's shoulder and lashed out to smack Peter's cheek, knuckles foremost. The boy yelped and was thrown back against the far door. Patsy screamed in anger and then a shadow

189

loomed over the scenario. Carrick reached in and one big hand clamped around his brother's neck. He dragged Paul out in one easy motion, twisting as he moved and slung him to the ground.

'Get going *now*,' he yelled again.

'Yeah, come on, mum. Let's get away from here,' Peter piped up from the back seat. 'I want to go home.' She could hear the grit of pain in his voice. She thumbed the key again just as the nearside door clicked open and a dark shape leaned in towards Judith. Patsy's blood seemed to crystallise in her veins.

Kerron Vaunche was inside the car.

She had moved silent and fast from the shadow of the trees and as soon as she leaned inside, Patsy could sense her presence like the scrape of nails on her bones. The engine revved as the clutch came out and the car lurched forward and stalled in a grind of protesting metal. Patsy was out of the car before she even had time to think. Peter was yelling furiously, but his mother's mind was fixed on the woman, her real rival. The gypsy was leaning right inside and even in the cacophony and turmoil all around, Patsy heard her speaking low and fast and guttural to her daughter in that strange language she'd used inside the house.

Without hesitation, Patsy launched herself at the woman and dragged her away. Vaunche held on to the edge of the door, still jabbering away at Judith. She was agile and strong, but in the sudden swoop of fear and anger Patsy was stronger. She braced her feet on the ground, screeching incoherently, managed to get an arm around the woman's neck and simply heaved backwards. Kerron Vaunche peeled away from the car and the two women landed on a heap on the short grass at the side of the road.

'Get away from them,' Patsy screeched. The other woman twisted in her grip, tried to get clawed fingers into Patsy's eyes but she blocked it with a bat of her left hand and hit out with her other. Sharp pain knifed up to her elbow, but there was a satisfying meaty smack as her knuckles connected with Kerron Vaunche's cheek.

The woman shrieked like an alley cat on the rut and pulled away, lurching towards the car. She shouted out again, high and urgent, in that odd harsh language. From inside the car Judith replied in the same tongue. Patsy couldn't understand any of it, but she knew the tone of compliance in her daughter's voice and a powerful wave of dread rolled through her.

What had they done to her? What were they doing to her?

Judith started to get out of the car. Peter reached and clamped both hands on his sister's elbows, hauling her back. The girl squirmed, her face just a pale blur. Kerron Vaunche shouted something else. She reached into the car again and batted Peter away, grasping Judith by the shoulder. Patsy came up behind her and got two hands in the woman's cascading hair and leaned back with all her weight. If Kerron Vaunche had screamed like a cat before, now she howled like a wolf bitch as Patsy hauled her backwards, ripping hair out of the woman's scalp. She twisted and turned and Patsy could feel the hair coming out in handfuls. Around them, the night was filled with noise and the sound of men shouting and women screaming, but Patsy was in a little microcosm of her own, a little bubble of reality where she was fighting for her children.

Vaunche squirmed round, hooked her nails under Patsy's neck and squeezed, but not hard enough to do damage. Patsy shouldered her back against the car and managed to get an accidental elbow under the woman's ribs. She heard the grunt of pain and a savage joy blossomed inside her.

'Give me the girl,' Vaunche gasped. 'You won't have her.'

'I'll see you in hell first,' Patsy screamed at her. 'I'll see you in hell you fucking *witch*!'

The other woman lunged towards the car when the man called McGregor came in from Patsy's left and swung Vaunche away in a neat body tackle.

'You'd better move it, girl,' he grunted. 'This is going to get heavy.'

Patsy spun away. Judith was halfway out of the car, her eyes wide and blank. Peter hauled her back inside and slammed the door. Patsy slid into the driver's seat.

'Strap her in,' she told Peter while turning the ignition key again. This time the engine roared into life immediately. She slammed it into gear just as Kerron Vaunche came reeling up into the window.

'See me in hell?' she snarled, eyes flashing in the darkness, teeth pure white and wide apart. The woman's face was contorted

191

like an attack dog and her hair seemed to be standing on end like hackles. Carrick's friend tried to pull her away but she struggled, looming up close to the half-opened window.

'I see *you* there, *gadge* woman.' She raised a hand up and held her fingers out. 'I see you on the low road, and you go there *first*.' The fingers curled into hooks and she turned her wrist, holding the hand palm up.

'I send you there, from where there is no return. Go down the dead road, *gadge* woman, and I will be at your back until we take her again.'

Again she said something fast and guttural in the harsh tongue and spat into her hand. Her arm jerked and the fingers uncurled in a flick. The gob of saliva flew out and smacked against Patsy's cheek. She pulled back quickly. Vaunche laughed aloud, a strange and shrill cackle. 'I set your feet on that road forever,' she rasped, 'and I'll be coming for her. Watch the moon.'

Patsy gunned the engine, nausea rolling in her belly at the thought of the woman's slavver on her skin. She spun the wheel and Kerron Vaunche reached out again.

'Walk the dead road, *chattel-woman* and walk in the shadow of death.' She hooked her nails on the paintwork just in front of the windscreen. Patsy heard the tear as the car pulled forward and hoped the woman's nails had ripped out at the quick. She raised the clutch and the car jolted forward, ramming through the stand of bushes and onto the road just as the big iron gates swung completely open and a shadowed group of people came spilling out. In the mirror she saw a glint of metal. Somebody screamed. Two black shapes swung into the side of the car. A face pressed up against the window, only inches from hers. In the back seat, Judith was screaming hysterically, while Peter was urging her to get out, to get going.

She got right onto the road, stamped her foot down, and the figures went reeling away. A loud crack like gunfire boomed and she prayed that Carrick was safe, but she couldn't stop. The car roared down the track and the tyres fishtailed on the tight turn that took her onto the lochside route, and she was on the road and gone.

In her mind's eye she saw the contorted face of Kerron Vaunche and the spittle flying from her hand to lacquer Patsy's cheek, and the mad look in her flashing eyes when she spoke in that strange coarse tongue.

She was thinking about what Kerron Vaunche had done, from stealing her husband (though that mattered little now) to stealing her daughter and son. The woman was crazy, but there was a power about her. The old gypsy had called her the *Cat Anna*, and to Patsy she was just like a cat, feral and fierce, and somehow haughtily lethal.

I see you there ... on the low road.

Now she knew it had been a curse. Patsy drew her lips back from clamped teeth. She might have been tough and wild and she might have been powerful, but she hadn't been able to keep Judith and Peter from her. She tried to ignore everything else that had happened on this road, tried to hold on to that feeling of victory and nurse it tight to keep its heat. Above her the sky was the colour of an old bruise.

13

She had stood looking down at the scene of desolation for several minutes, trying to squeeze down the swelling despondency that had swamped her fragile confidence.

This was nowhere at all.

Down below, beyond the shadow of the bridge, dozens of dead cars, hundreds maybe, lay mouldering and rusting in the watery light, scoured by the wind that rasped the roadside grit over paintwork and chrome.

'It's like a graveyard,' she had said, and the wind plucked her words and faded them away.

It was like a graveyard for the internal combustion engine. A cemetery of road traffic. There were crashed cars and abandoned cars and rusting cars so old the rubber had rotted from the tyres and they slumped down on their axles. But though she could see for five, maybe seven miles down that straight road, she saw no movement at all, save the occasional fluttering of a black wing as one of the crows strutted in prospect among the tangled wrecks. There was no other sign of life.

It had just been a road. Just one road. The wrong road, maybe, a *bad* road, but only one. Kerron Vaunche had spat and cursed and done something with her fingers and Patsy had got lost and found herself on a road to nowhere under a glowering, infernal sky. That she could swallow, given the time, given the spider in the phone-hatch and the skinny dogs with their bulging eyes and the truckers who had started to turn into other things in the roadhouse that had become someplace else. One road and you could get off somewhere along the track. There would be a turn-off, a roundabout maybe. There would be a ramp and a slip-road somewhere. There would finally be other cars, vans and trucks, sleek sedans and rustbucket saloons.

But this was different. Down below her there was *another* road, and there had been other travellers. Had she cursed all those other people, this Kerron Vaunche, or was this even bigger than the gypsy woman's power?

The valley of the shadow of death. The thoughts sparked inside her head and she felt herself begin to hyperventilate at the sheer enormity of it all. *The dead road.* Her hands had gripped the angle-iron of the barrier so hard that one of her nails broke backwards in a little searing tear of the quick. For a moment the panic flooded through her and she felt herself racked by a spasm of hysteria so violent that her whole body shivered like a tuning fork.

Stop it! Get a grip *woman!* The voice inside her head ordered sharply and with enough force to batten down the fear. The shivery moment passed and Patsy felt her breath ease back down to near normal.

That's better. It was her own mind, she knew, but it almost sounded like someone else, like her own mother telling her to grow up and behave. Behind her, the door clicked open and she whirled round.

'Get back in the car.'

'Are you all right . . .?' Peter started to ask.

'Back in the car, right now,' Patsy bawled. Peter stood frozen, half out of the car, one foot on the red grit. 'I mean right *now*.'

He looked at her, bruised by her tone. She ran towards him and his eyes widened in alarm as if she was about to attack him. Patsy reached the door, swung it open and grabbed him into her arms. She hugged him tight enough to hear his ribs creak.

'Oh, I'm sorry,' she wailed, and then the tears bubbled up and over. She felt his arms around her, fingers digging in close to her spine, not enough to hurt but enough to make her realise it was the first time she'd really embraced her son in such a long time, and the ache in her soul was just too much. Beside Peter, Judith burst into tears and Patsy reached for her, clawing the girl in so that all three were squeezed in a desperate embrace. The tears rolled down her cheeks and the sobs racked her and she held her children for a long time.

The bridge was behind them now. They had driven over it slowly, avoiding the cracks and the shallow potholes where the surface had crumbled. The wind had picked up and was thrumming in the hawsers, making them vibrate like giant bass strings, merging with the distant sound of unseen traffic and the subsonic seismic pulse under the surface. Something was moving on this mass of roads, but while the air carried the grumbling murmur of far-off vehicles and bore the stale scent of exhaust fumes, there was no visible motion. At the far side of the flyover the road dipped down and the scrubby brambles which reached thorny runners over the galvanised brackets on the overgrown verge were thicker, sending their tendrils out into the overtaking lane and almost as far as the next. She drove past a place where the brambles and ivy looked as if they were reaching for each other across the lanes and she had to steer for the centre-line to get through. As she passed the narrow space a movement flickered in the corner of her eye, a slow, flopping motion, but when she turned to look, the ivy was still, though she had the jarring impression that the creeper had twisted and reached a little further towards the car. She shook her head quickly, forcing the notion away from her.

Down the slope and up the far side, this time on a road running between low slopes where tangled birch and gorse competed for the crowded space. She speeded up and drove on, aware of the cat's-eye reflectors, counting off the poles and furlongs and miles. Some time later, Judith, who had fallen asleep again, awoke and asked for something to eat. Her voice sounded nearly normal. Patsy slowed again on a straight stretch which was elevated above the surrounding countryside. From here, the rest of the road network was all but invisible, though a vast arch, crenellated with stubby lights was just visible in the far distance. She stopped again on the hard shoulder, looking in her mirror first, ensuring that nothing was coming up behind her and there was no threat on the road ahead. The dark shadows were still like heavy bruises under Judith's eyes, but she didn't look as ill as she had. Patsy felt her hand. It seemed a little cooler.

'I'm starving too,' Peter volunteered. Some things couldn't change. 'Is it dinner-time yet?'

'It's always dinner time for you, isn't it?'

He grinned, favouring her with a mischievous wink. She glanced at the clock which said it was eight thirty. It must have stopped. She brought her wrist up to check her watch, tilted the dial and halted. The second hand, a fine copper needle, was travelling backwards on the face.

'Is there nothing right about this place?' she breathed. How long she'd been travelling she couldn't tell, but it didn't seem more than an hour or so since the service station, yet already, though the sun was still hidden by the grainy, fast-moving clouds, the sky was darkening ahead of her in the direction she took to be east.

'A quick bite now, then we've really got to get moving,' she conceded. Peter split the rear seat again and crawled into the luggage space. She heard him rummage and he came backing out with one of the supermarket bags. He hauled it to the seat and went back in again, his skinny backside protruding comically. When he re-emerged he pulled a sizeable plastic box behind him.

'Are we going for a picnic?' Judith asked. She seemed really to be coming back to normal, but the rash was still spreading on her cheeks and the skin of her hands was dry and tight, showing her knuckles.

'No. That's been there since the last one.' The picnic box had been lying in the car for more than a year, since exactly three days before Paul had come and snatched his children from the garden. The three of them had gone out on a sunny morning for a trip to the countryside, only a few miles from home, but far enough off the beaten track to make it seem like wilderness. It had been the last really good day Patsy had enjoyed with her family.

The box rattled as Peter sprung the clips on the top. He pulled out the blackened pot and the little camping gas stove they'd used to brew tea on the green sward next to the stream. The old family flask which held nearly two pints was down at the bottom of the box along with the aluminium knives and forks. Patsy had forgotten all about the box in the past months, but now, for some reason she was glad it had come along for the ride. That odd intuition tingled inside her as she rummaged inside the plastic case. These were emergency things, flask and cooker. She planned not to need them before the night was over because she planned not to spend another night on this road or any other road. The intuition tingled at the back of her head, like a trickle of electricity and the internal voice whispered: *just in case . . .*

She allowed Peter to pop another can of Coke, though she could have killed for a cup of tea. A screw-top jar at the bottom of the box was stuffed with tea bags and those little foil sachets of coffee that are always lying around in hotel rooms – they must have been years old, back from the days when Paul was on the glad-handing trail – but there was no water, unless she used the small bottle of aerated stuff she'd thrown into the basket with the rest of the gear, and she was reluctant to waste a good cup of tea with that. She searched among the goods she'd bought and found the packets of powdered soup. If the worst came to the worst – and she said a fervent and silent prayer that the worst would pass them by – she could use the mineral water for soup for them all. She settled for a share of the Coke and a packet of crisps which she wolfed quickly, only just then aware that she was very hungry. She reached for another packet when the tingle of insight rippled again.

Just in case.

She wished the voice would go away, but she obeyed it just the same.

She waited until Judith had finished her own packet before asking Peter to crawl back into the compartment again to fetch the travelling blanket. It was an old tartan thing which smelt musty, as if it hadn't been in fresh air for a long time, which was the truth. Patsy got out of the car and shook the spread, shaking off last year's dried grass and the fine sand from the edge of the stream, wishing the three of them could be back there, back *then*. She tucked Judith up snugly before she began to drive again. In a few minutes, her daughter was fast asleep and breathing evenly.

Patsy turned in her seat and gave Peter her best smile. 'Climb into the front with me,' she said. He unsnapped his belt and came gingerly between the two seats, making sure he avoided Judith's small foot which stuck out from under the rug. The sound of the starter made Judith turn over but her eyes stayed shut. Patsy pulled onto the blacktop and they were rolling again.

'Are we going to get home?'

'Sure we are,' Patsy said, keeping her voice light and confident, waiting for his response.

'It's a weird place,' he said eventually, looking up at her, eyes wide and honest.

'You're telling me. But we can find our way back.'

'Was it her?'

Patsy stiffened. Was he telepathic? Had he read her mind, or was he just smarter than the average kid?

'Who?'

'Her. Catanna.'

'I thought her name was Vaunche.'

His eyes went blank for a second. 'That's a funny name.'

'Didn't they call her that?'

'No. Everybody called her Catanna. That's a funny name too.'

'Funny ha-ha, or funny peculiar?'

He grinned. 'Just stupid, really. Everybody had stupid names. Like Birchleaf and Foxglove.'

'So why do you ask if this has anything to do with her?'

'Because she's weird. She was always talking about magic and spells and all that kind of rubbish, but it wasn't really rubbish. She said she could put a spell on people and I think they were all scared of her. Everybody except dad. They were all scared of him, too. I could feel it.'

I'll bet they were, Patsy thought. She remembered how much of her own personality had changed, been subjugated to his, without her being aware of the metamorphosis, but he was an amateur compared to the gypsy. The dreadful images in the dark of Broadford House loomed under the surface of her thoughts.

'You believe she could do something like this?'

He had been fiddling with the knob on the radio as he spoke, but when she asked that question, he drew his hand away and looked up at his mother.

'She didn't see me. I was up in the apple tree at the corner of the orchard. She was arguing with one of the women. I couldn't hear what they were arguing about, but Catanna got angry. She started speaking loud, not shouting but loud enough to hear and it made me really shivery, the way she was speaking. I could see her and she had her hands out, just the way she had when you came to get us, and she flicked the spittle at the women. Her name was Willow and she was pretty okay to me and Judy. She used to bake cakes and she'd give us hot ones if there was no-one about. But when Catanna put the spit on her she said: 'You're going to choke on it. Or something like that.'

Peter's voice trailed away and Patsy put out her hand to take his. She could feel the tension in him. She squeezed encouragingly. He was silent for a minute or more before he started again, his voice lower, almost dreamlike.

'We were in the refectory. That's what they called the dinner hall. Dad always sat at the top and she sat at the bottom. Judy was always with her and I never liked that. Anyway, we were all eating after the big prayer, which isn't like the prayers we said at school. It's about people with foreign names and they're all the prince of some place or other and they'll get your enemies and the unbelievers and do terrible things to them. And I was always scared they'd get me because I didn't really believe, except I was still scared of them even if I didn't believe. Know what I mean?'

Patsy smiled at this, despite the cold that had seeped into her veins. She hadn't known what to believe either until the internal voice had given her a mental slap and ordered her to wake up and accept what she was seeing, even if it was a complete and utter impossibility. She had kept her eyes on the road most of the time, but she turned round to look at him. His brow was furrowed in concentration, as if the memory was costing him.

'Anyway, we were eating. It was fish and some greens which I didn't like and Catanna stands up and makes a speech. It's either her or dad who make the speeches, 'cos they were sort of the bosses and everybody else did what they told them. She was saying something, but I wasn't listening, but the place was dead quiet; you know, the way it happens if somebody laughs really loud and everybody stops talking? She started talking fast and then she went into that funny language, like Welsh or something. I was sitting near dad and Willow was opposite me. Catanna kept talking and I saw Willow's face go white. Her eyes were turning around all scared looking and then she started to cough. She put her hands up to her neck and she stood up. Catanna kept talking the whole time and she was looking at Willow, but she was looking at me at the same time and I got a really scary feeling right inside me.'

Peter was holding tight to her hand and Patsy slowed down a little, though the road was still straight as an arrow and all three lanes were completely clear. The sky was growing darker ahead as if another thunderstorm was rolling in on them.

'Willow got up and she really was choking. Her face had gone a really horrible colour and her mouth was open and her eyes were still going round and round, all stary, like they were falling out. Dad never said anything. *Nobody* said anything, because it was like it wasn't happening for them. They just couldn't *see it*. Catanna just looked at her and I saw something came out of her, honest I did. It was like a shadow. It came out and went across to Willow and took hold of her. Willow looked at me and then she looked at dad and I thought I was going to be sick. Her face went purple and then she fell to the ground and she started to shiver. Her heels were banging on the floor and everybody just sat there. I started to get up but dad put his hand on my shoulder and I couldn't move. She was lying there and her mouth was open and I knew she'd choked on a fish bone. Her back was coming up off the floor and then banging back down again and she made this horrible noise . . .'

He squeezed her hand really tight and she heard his voice crack a little.

'. . . her head turned round and she looked at me and I could see something inside her mouth. It wasn't a fish bone. I could see something that was all black and it was moving and I didn't know what it was at first but Willow's head came right down and hit the floor and her mouth opened even more and – oh, mum – it was flies. Big black flies. They came crawling out and flew around her head.

She could hear the horror of the memory tearing at his voice.

'I could see it, but nobody else was looking. Catanna just stood there and dad didn't even help her. I was really, really scared then because I knew she had done it. She had told Willow she was going to choke and she magicked those flies right into her mouth and then she made her choke on them. Somebody put a napkin over Willow's face and they told all the kids to go out, and most of them were crying and so was I. I was really scared and I kept seeing her every time I closed my eyes and I thought *She* had prayed to one of the princes and made him do something terrible to one of her enemies. And the next day, when I was sitting on the steps waiting for Judith to come out of her lesson, Catanna came up to me and gave me an apple. I didn't want to take it in case I touched her fingers, but she made me take it and then she said it was one of the apples from the tree and I should have picked it yesterday.'

The grip on Patsy's hand was now fierce. She could feel her own pulse in her fingers, and over that, the beat of blood in her son's hand.

'After that, I never said anything, but I wanted to come home. She must have known I was in the tree and heard her arguing with Willow. She just laughed and gave me a look and I went all cold inside. I pretended not to be worried or anything but I was nearly sick again.'

He released her hand slowly and she felt the warmth as the circulation returned to her fingers. Patsy's heart ached. Whatever happened in Broadford House, it was powerful enough to make you see things that didn't exist. The dreadful images had been forced into her mind when she'd fought with Kerron Vaunche in the dark of the passageway. If that could happen to her, it could easily happen to an impressionable boy.

'And yesterday,' Peter began again, 'I heard her speaking in that funny way and she flicked the spittle at you and I heard her say she was putting you on the low roads. I knew she was doing the magic because I'd seen it before and I know what the low roads are. It was in the prayers.'

'And what are the low roads?'

'They're the *ley* ways. It's the way the old people used the travel. Where the *Fasgadh* lives. He's some sort of special god, like Odin or something.'

Bet they never travelled on roads like this, Patsy said to herself.

'I wanted to come home,' Peter said. The sharp and brittle edge was easing out of his voice as if he'd put something difficult behind him. 'But I didn't know where to go. There was always somebody watching the gates and once one of the women ran away and they brought her back again, but we never saw her after that. I didn't like her and dad had gone awful funny peculiar. He never played at football or went anywhere. He was always in the big room talking to folk and doing all that chanting stuff. They hardly ever let me play with Judy and Catanna was always with her, teaching her those weird words.'

'Why did she want her to learn that?'

'I dunno, but Brian, he's fourteen, he told me all the girls had to do something on a special day. Brian was really weird. He was always trying to touch me in the showers, you know? And he used to get his sister to lift up her skirt. He said it was all right. It was holy when you did it with sisters, because his dad had told him, but I said it was dirty. He told me there was a big special night when everybody took their clothes off and they picked girls and took their clothes off and the men came in and did something, but I don't know what it was.'

Patsy shuddered. She'd listened to Lisa Prosser, who'd escaped from Broadford House. She'd spent six months in rehabilitation before they finally broke down the conditioning, before she began to speak about what was going on behind the high wall and the wrought iron gates. She'd told of the midnight rituals in the old ballroom of the house, and the naked worship at the flat stone in the deep basement where they invoked the names of the ancient gods; of *Baal*, and *Be-elzebub*, of *Thanatos*, and *Set*.

She tried not to think about it, shied her mind away from what plans her crazy husband and his mad woman had for her children. Crandall Gilfeather had only told her some of it and that had been enough. The dreadful images in her dreams, in the hallucinations, they were enough now. Patsy reached an arm out and brought Peter in towards her until his head was against her ribs. Whatever Peter has seen, it had scared him rigid. The image of flies coming from the woman's mouth, like blowflies on a corpse, tugged at her memory. Lisa Prosser had talked about the worship in the cellar and the black flies buzzing from the ventilators. *Be-elzebub*. The prince of corruption, the Lord of the Flies.

'We'll be fine,' she said, though inside she was shuddering.

'But can we get home?'

'Of course we can,' Patsy said positively, hoping she sounded convincing. 'Where there's a will, there's a way.'

In front, the sky darkened and off to the right, the red glow began to shimmer against the cloudbase.

'It's going to be night soon,' Peter said.

'No. Must be another storm coming up,' Patsy contradicted. 'It can't be night yet.'

She drove on, keeping her speed to a steady seventy and the darkness grew heavier until she had to switch her lights on. Immediately the beady eyes of the reflectors lit up the lane markings on the road. She checked the fuel gauge and saw the needle hovering not far down from the full mark.

'It can't be night yet. We've only done a hundred miles or so.'

'But it's getting darker,' Peter said, and she could not deny that. Way off to the right, way beyond the fiery glow, green lightning flickered briefly in the sky and half a minute later a low rumble, just loud enough to be heard over the noise of the engine, came rolling through the air. Not far ahead a white sign threw back the light of a road sign and she switched the headlamps on to full beam.

It was another analogue direction plate, showing the divergence of two roads, but again there were no printed names of towns. The distance markers to the exit followed, but she stayed on the main route. The sign had been like the previous one which had led her up to the service station and she didn't want to arrive in a place like that as darkness was falling. She kept on the straight until it curved round a low hillock, followed the road as it rose, turning to the left, reached the flat at the top then followed the bend on the downslope, headlamps still on full beam.

Something moved, some distance away on the nearside, just within reach of the beams. It caught her eye and she turned her head.

The scarecrow waved its arm.

Patsy's heart thumped so hard it was like a hammer-blow on the chest.

The wind had plucked at the tattered sleeve on the pointing arm of the scarecrow in the field. The halogen beam swept across the round turnip head and made the shadows move on the hollow sockets. The arm was still pointing out and the spindlestick legs cast long shadows on the barren ground of the field.

It was closer.

The first time it had not been there at all and the last time it had been standing just outside the wall of the old church. Now it was halfway to the road, one gnarled branch of a leg straddled right out in front, as if it had hauled it from the ground and staggered forward. Her foot touched the brake and the car slowed. The church was just a black silhouette against an indigo sky and the hoary ivy fuzzed the outline of the crooked little steeple.

But there was a light on in there. Not bright, just enough to be seen in the hollows of the decrepit windows. It was a pale orange light that moved just enough, like the flicker of a poor candle carried from one side of the nave to the other, forming shadows and then dissolving them to make room for others. That light jolted Patsy's heart even more than the sight of the scarecrow had. Peter was still snuggled in against her ribs, not looking out of the window and she hoped he'd dozed off. There was a light in that creepy little church and that meant there was something moving in there, and suddenly Patsy wanted to be far away from that place. How she'd arrived back on that slope she did not know, but the fact that she'd driven down the same curve three times was shocking enough. But there was something in that church and it was moving, casting a sickly orange light out through the crumbling socket-windows, and the awful sensation of threat she'd felt in the daylight came back with astonishing force. A sense of hunger, cold and mindlessly evil, came reaching out of that twisted little church, like a malignant shadow. It brushed across her consciousness in a damp, diseased stroke, and then was gone. The skin puckered behind her ears as her scalp crawled. She dragged her eyes away, found the car had drifted onto the breakdown lane as if it had been drawn towards that barren field. She over-compensated and felt herself jolted to the side. Peter made a noise as if he had just woken up. Patsy got the car back on line and accelerated down the slope.

At the far end of the field, the old oak tree was just a twisted shade, but she sensed the crows hunched there, waiting for the morning light – or maybe waiting for the dark of night – watching her with black and beady eyes, clicking those sabre beaks. She put her foot hard down when she reached the level and sped on to the next straight part. She drove for another three miles and night crawled over the sky, dragging a black cloak behind it. Patsy glanced at the clock on the dashboard. The illuminated display told her it was seven forty-five, but while her eyes were still on the little square display, the figure five became a four. A minute later, it became a three and she realised the clock was now going backwards. She checked her watch, holding it up close to catch some of the light from the dashboard illumination, expecting to see the second hand slowly ticking counter-clockwise on the mother-of-pearl face.

The little needle was stock still, pointing straight at the hour. The minute hand was pointing at the six. But the hour hand, that was visibly crawling round the face. It was the only hand that moved. 'Shit,' she whispered. She drove on for another hour, watching the cat's-eyes blur by until the last of the light began to fade from the sky. The fuel gauge was dropping down from full, heading slow, but very sure, towards the half-way mark and she wondered what she was going to do when ahead, another sign appeared out of the darkness.

HAVOCK SERVICES: 15 miles.

The words jumped out, harsh black against the reflective surface, punching into her consciousness and instantly her intestines felt as though they had turned to a cold sludge. She was back there again and that was worse, somehow, than having gone in a big circle and found herself on the downslope beside the old church, though that was surely bad enough. Her foot hit the brake, almost automatically and the car slewed to a crawl. Patsy steered towards the edge of the road, unsure of whether to stop or carry on in the hope there would be another exit she could take before she came close to the roadhouse. She didn't want to get close to that way-station, not ever again, but especially not at night. She was convinced if she found herself going up that ramp to the car park where the array of black trucks hunched in the lee of the trees, she might start to scream and not be able to stop. It took five minutes, maybe more to cover the next mile, easing carefully along beside the tasselled remnants of the willow-herb and stringy bindweed. A half a mile beyond that, the headlamps picked out a black path pulling in on the red of the harsh shoulder and just beyond that, a small sign telling her it was a police lookout post which was taboo to ordinary drivers. The sky overhead was pitch-black, unrelieved by moon or stars. Just as the car was nosing past the low ascent to the traffic-cop's lookout, Patsy made an instant decision. She twisted the wheel sharply, gave the pedal a kick and let the car cruise to the top of the rise. There was enough space there to reverse backwards so that she faced on to the road and could see in either direction. She pulled on the handbrake and killed the engine, though she left the lights on for the time being. The twin beams coned out across the central reservation and got lost in a hazy ground mist on the other side of the road. Far off, the greasy lightning flickered behind thick clouds.

'Why have we stopped?' Peter asked, surprising her. She'd thought he was asleep.

'Seems the best thing to do.'

'Shouldn't we keep going?' He turned to look up at her, his pale face catching the muted glow from the dashboard lights. Patsy reached out and pulled him against her again.

'Oh, I don't know. I was getting a bit tired and I don't like driving this road at night. Maybe it's best that we sit tight until morning. I don't want to miss a turn-off in the dark.'

'I think it would be best if we kept going,' Peter said earnestly. 'I don't like these roads.'

'Nor me, believe me,' she said, letting the words come out between her teeth in a sigh of exasperation.

'Will we really get home?' It was the second time he'd asked that.

'Yes. We will. That's a promise.'

Peter went quiet for a while. Patsy could hear Judith's breathing, low and not as laboured as she might expect. She turned the headlights off, leaving them with only the faint illumination from the dashboard, but the glow in the far sky seemed brighter though already a few specks of rain were beginning to spatter the windscreen. Patsy checked the odometer. The little figures on the trip counter showed she'd done only two hundred miles since the early hours of the morning when she'd pressed the button which resets the digits to zero. She remembered she'd done another eighty miles or thereabouts, maybe just a little less, which meant she'd come a hundred and twenty since the service station.

'Can't be right,' she said to herself. Travelling from morning until now, maintaining a steady seventy with no stops except for the pause on the bridge and a break for the Coke and crisps – and that seemed less than an hour ago – she should have covered a lot more than that by nightfall.

The clock on the dashboard had stopped again, though her own watch had started up and all the hands appeared to be moving in the same direction as far as she could tell, but she had no idea what time it was. The sky outside, apart from the blast furnace glow on the clouds way in the distance, was pure black, night-black. Something else was wrong. She remembered thinking it was early for the sky to be darkening in the east, though she'd kept on driving, but that wasn't long enough ago for night to have fallen. There was either a fault in the trip-meter, or her speedometer or her own sense of time. She knew the clocks were not working properly but inside of her, her own body clock told her it shouldn't be night.

'I need the bathroom,' Peter said, interrupting her thoughts.

'Can't it wait?'

'No. I'm really . . . I have to go.' Even in the faint light of the dashboard screen, his face was an earnestly comic picture. Patsy smiled and ruffled his hair.

'Right, but be quick, and stay close to the car.' She herself felt the pressure of the Coke they'd had earlier, but thought she could wait until morning. Squatting beside a wheel arch on a patrol lookout in the middle of the night had no appeal. To that extent, she thought ruefully, men, even men-to-be like her son, had the best of it. She levered the handle to open the door, pushed it and began to swing her legs out as the greasy damp air eddied inside.

'Come on then,' she beckoned, deciding she needed to stand and stretch and force the kinks out of her back. Peter began to clamber past the gear lever and onto her side of the car. Patsy put a foot on the ground, began to ease herself out when an enormous terror jolted through her like a powerful electric shock. She was turning her head away from Peter when it happened and he saw his mother freeze. The powerful black fear

208

washed over her, a complete and comprehensive sensation of utter dread.

A few yards away, down the small tarmac incline that led up to the lookout post, something moved in the darkness. It was just a small movement, only a rustle, a scrape on the stone, but for some reason, for *no* reason that she could identify, that little sound wormed its way into that deep and primitive part of the underbrain where all survival instincts lie and the sense of foreboding swelled in a black tide. The feeling of utter menace was so powerful that she felt the muscles in her leg, the one which was bearing her weight, loosen and fail, as if her strength was draining away. She felt herself slide downwards, realised she was about to faint and an even more absolute fear exploded inside her at the thought of falling out of the car, lying down on the asphalt surface, while something that crawled and made that unearthly little scrabbling sound was still creeping in the shadows.

She felt a sudden scream begin to wind up in her throat. Peter said something behind her, something about being really bursting, and Patsy's throat clamped shut. Suddenly the strength came punching back into her muscles. Her leg jerked, throwing her backwards into the car, knocking Peter back onto his own seat. She hauled her leg inside, while at the same time she heaved on the door handle and swung it shut, almost catching her toes. She sat there panting like a dog, waiting for the pounding of her heart to settle down. It was hammering away there, beating so fast that little dots of light were dancing in front of her eyes.

'What's wrong?' Peter asked.

She tried to speak, but the words got stuck between her throat and her mouth and nothing came out except a little click. She reached and grasped his hand, trying to communicate with him, letting him know he should be still for a moment. He looked at her, eyes puzzled and wide again with concern, but he waited until the panting stopped and until the dreadful pallor faded away from his mother's face.

Finally she got her voice back.

'We have to stay inside.'

'But I need to go,' he protested. She held her hand up and stopped him.

'I know. I do, really. But we have to stay in the car.'

To emphasise the point, she reached quickly beyond him and hit the lock on the passenger door, twisted in her seat and did the same on both rear doors. Judith stirred in her sleep as the locks snapped on, but she did not awake.

'You'll have to go in here,' she said. 'Do you still have that Coke can?'

He nodded dumbly.

'Well, you're a boy. You can use that.'

'Aw mum . . .' he began, but she held her hand up again.

'No argument, Peter. I know it's embarrassing, but you can't get out of the car. Understand?'

'But why?'

'I don't know why,' she retorted, voice rising. 'I just *know*. I'm sorry, Peter, but you either use the can or you keep it in, but there's no way any of us are getting outside of the car tonight.'

She took both his shoulders in her hands and turned him towards her, leaning right down until her nose was only a couple of inches from his: 'You understand me, Peter? I love you to bits, I really do, but you've got to listen to me, even if sometimes I sound like I'm just an old flake. And you've got to do exactly what I tell you. Mums sometimes know these things, and I know something now. We have to stay in the car. Got me?'

He nodded slowly. 'What's out there?'

'Nothing. I don't know.' Patsy hunted for the proper reply. 'Something. But nothing can harm us if we stay tight in here.' She ducked her hand behind her seat and found the empty can, held it up to him and tried to muster a smile.

'Now try to aim right, okay?'

He took it sheepishly and turned away, half kneeling on the seat. He fumbled with the front of his jeans, hunched over and made a hollow noise as he relieved himself. She could feel his embarrassment, but there was nothing else she could do about it. He finished and put the can down on the floor well.

'Might as well get some sleep,' Patsy said, trying to keep her voice even, though the prospect of any sleep seemed remote. She hustled Peter into the back and followed him through, clambering awkwardly between the seats. Judith moaned dozily, snuffled, and turned over. Patsy sat in the middle, spread the rug

210

over all three of them and snuggled down. In the distance, lightning stabbed across the sky and a crack of thunder startled Peter. The noise rolled across the darkness for a long time. The light rain spattered the windows and worked up to a steady drone on the roof. Outside she could sense whatever it was that had drilled her with the utter sense of dread. Things were moving in the dark, snuffling and hunting for them.

Peter tried to sleep, but now he'd dredged up the memory of Willow, a memory that had been so numbingly scary he'd bundled it up and hidden it away where it would be hard to find. Staying at Broadford House, he'd seen Kerron Vaunche, the Catanna, every day and at first the visual image of that awful episode would come surging up in a rip-tide. He'd had to learn how to side-step the memory, like a skilful bullfighter, letting it pass him before it could impale him. It was either that, or be driven crazy by the mental recollection.

Now it was out of its box, sprung by the need to tell his mother. The memory was out and it was rattling around inside his head and he would have to wait until he grew so tired that he would not be able to support it any more.

Willow's face swam in front of him, her eyes wide and rolling wildly, while her hands were up at her throat fluttering uselessly. Her mouth was wide open, so wide he could see all of her teeth and the flapping pink palate at the back. The choking, gagging sound emanating from there had made his blood freeze in his veins, while all the time the Catanna had kept talking and he had realised in a snap of horrific comprehension that only three people in the entire refectory were aware of what was happening. The rest of them were listening to the words, and even a part of Peter's mind was aware of what she was saying, but the central part of his consciousness was fixed on those rolling eyes and the gaping mouth and the rasping sound that came from deep inside the choking woman.

He hadn't told his mother everything, because the recollection had come in flickering bites, stuttering snatches that he kept shying away from, but now they were out of their hiding place and they had come looking for him and there was nothing he could do about it.

Willow's eyes rolled, protruding from the sockets as if they might fall out onto her cheeks and immediately Peter had thought of the mare that had tried to leap the hawthorn hedge at the far end of the paddock and had slipped and broken its neck. That had been sickening enough, a terrible and tragic little accident witnessed by some small children, but what Peter had seen in the refectory was between him and Willow and the Catanna. It had not been until later, when the scene had tumbled around in his head hour after sickening hour, that the little side details had come back to him, as if, in that appalling treacle-slow perception that had surrounded the three of them to the exclusion of everybody else, all of his senses had become supernaturally sharp.

Over by the ornately carved door, somebody dropped a fork which had bounced on the polished floor, making a strangely low metallic clatter that had gone on and on as if Peter had been transported into some slow motion time scale. At the adjacent table, a child had coughed and the sound had come rumbling over in a sonorous grunt.

The Catanna had kept talking and one part of him was aware of what she was saying, about the forces of the outside who were arrayed in their legions against those who followed the true path, while in front of him Willow was dying.

He'd tried to call out, to get somebody to help her, but he was frozen in his own slow time warp. He heard the muscles in his neck creak, like ancient and rusty hinges as he turned to look up at his father, hearing the blood pound like the distant surf in the depths of his ears. Dad had been like a statue. His hand was halfway down towards the table and his eyelids were halfway up from a blink, moving imperceptibly, his eyes glassily fixed on the dark haired woman whose voice rumbled in real-time and in Peter's slow time, without interference.

One of the rolling eyes had fixed on him and had drilled him with the mute appeal and terrified despair. Willow had got to her feet, the chair scraping backwards and tumbling away slowly. Peter had swivelled, starting forward, but moving through molasses, eyes swinging around, trying to get someone, anyone, to realise what was happening, and then the Catanna's eyes, green as emeralds, had locked on his and a cold twist of understanding had drilled him.

Willow tumbled backwards, hands still clawing at her neck, and the Catanna kept talking her double-speak and the noise of the dropped fork started to fade away.

The Catanna turned her head, keeping those glittering eyes fixed on him and for a moment Peter saw her in two places at once. She had turned towards him and her face had been calm, though he could sense her vast contempt, but at the same time, as if part of her had split away, she was facing down the length of the refectory to where Willow was writhing. The other image of the Catanna peeled away, leaned over the table, and every muscle on her face was twisted into a mask of sheer animal ferocity. Her arms were reaching out towards the other woman, long and thin and pallid, and for an instant, they looked like the arms of a skeleton. The mouth had opened, lips pulling back on skin that was now wrinkled and ragged and he could see the twisted teeth crowded together, too many for a normal mouth, too sharp for a normal mouth. The other-image, almost translucent, like a double exposure on a photographic film, had started talking, though it sounded like the growl of an animal, while the serene and haughty figure had continued addressing the people at the tables, her eyes still lancing through Peter's soul.

He had watched aghast as the two images separated further. The twisted shadow, grey and ragged and somehow preposterously evil, had pulled away and come scrabbling towards Willow. A part of Peter's mind saw this witchy thing come *through* the heavy table as if there was no obstacle in its path and scuttle forward, arms elongating impossibly while her face lengthened and the mouth widened until the thing that darted towards the choking woman had become something so hideous and diseased, it did not even look animal. To Peter it resembled one of the gargoyles on the high gutterings of Broadford House.

The shadow Catanna streaked down the centre of the room, hideous arms outstretched and snatched at Willow's head, spinning round so that it was looking directly into the other woman's eyes. Peter saw the instant comprehension and utter fear in them and his own unnatural dread ballooned.

Nobody else moved. Willow fell to the floor with a low thump while the grotesque and shadowy half-image, the thing that was ragged and darkly transparent, like the discarded skin of a dragonfly larva, settled over the dying woman. One long and bony hand reached out and clamped on Willow's cheeks and the other moved very quickly, stabbing forward into the woman's mouth. Willow bucked on the floor. The thing that had peeled away from the Catanna scuttled backwards, moving with mantis-like speed. Its head swivelled on a scrawny neck and pale, sickly-orange eyes had fixed themselves for a poisonous second on Peter. The mouth had widened and a black tongue had drooled and then the thing was back at the table, moving again through the flat surface. There was a weird, uncanny *snap* of tension which Peter felt, rather than heard, and the ghastly thing merged again with the Catanna. She gave a little shiver, slowly turned, eyes still fixed on Peter. She smiled and then let him go. It was as if she had cut a cord between them. Peter slumped against the back of his seat as if he'd been pushed, bounced forward, half rose to his feet. Willow was on the floor, twisting as though she had just fallen from her chair which went tumbling away slowly. Somebody coughed close by and it was almost a normal cough, quickening out of slow motion. Willow's mouth opened and something black and shiny had come scrambling up inside her throat and he had seen the fly. Its head turned, swollen eyes staring blankly. The front legs rasped against each other and then it took off, wings buzzing loud in the hollow of the open mouth. Another followed and another, until the mouth was filled with them. They came swarming out and crawled over the woman's face, great shiny flies with papery wings and rasping legs. For a long moment, Willow's face was just a mass of crawling insects and then, all at once, they took off with an angry buzzing. The cloud tightened into a ball, then streaked for the corner and disappeared into the shadows. The buzzing went on for a long time, but the flies simply flew into the shadows and disappeared.

Willow made a harsh gagging sound and a dreadful nausea looped inside Peter, so violent he thought he was going to be sick. He made it to his feet, began to yell. His father's hand came down on his shoulder. Somebody turned round. The Catanna stopped talking. Willow gagged and her face went blue. She rolled on the floor and one of the women got to her and lifted her head up, but it was too late. Peter could see it in her eyes. They just rolled up and whatever the shape that had been part of the Catanna had put in her mouth, did something inside her and she died right there on the floor. Her body gave two big twitches and then was still. He remembered drawing his mesmerised eyes away, looking up and finding that green gaze still fixed upon him and a dreadful sense of peril shuddered through him.

He'd seen it happen, but had it been real? Had he imagined it?

It had seemed all too real in a dreadfully *unreal* way. There had been a connection between him and both women, but for a while he was never sure whether it had actually happened the way he had seen it, though his nightmares were riven by that darkly diaphanous and emaciated shape which had split from the woman, as twisted and decayed and grotesque as the Catanna was tall and strong and blackly exquisite. The alter-entity came at him from the shadows of his dreams and chased him through a forest of hoary trees, rustling behind him, growling and grunting at his heels while he scrambled up muddy slopes, feet slipping backwards as paralysing terror tried to freeze him still, and in his dreams he knew the thing that scuttled like a dragonfly nymph would catch him and put flies down his throat and they would wriggle and twist inside him until he burst.

Peter would wake up in the little room he had to himself at the far end of the west wing of Broadford House, a scream stuck in his throat and cold sweat soaking his sheet. He had tried to believe he had imagined what had happened to Willow, told himself that it had been unreal.

But the Catanna had come and given him an apple, like a beautiful Eve revealing a mystery to him, and she had smiled at him in that compassionless way and had let him know she had *known* and that they now shared a secret that no-one else knew.

Instinctively, he had understood that he couldn't speak to his father. Even at the age of nine, he could see that Paul was gone, lost to the woman, and that if he said anything, it would just increase the danger. He was scared for himself and just as concerned for Judith because she spent so much time with that woman.

215

Was it his imagination, or was his sister developing that glassy stare?

He didn't know what happened behind the big green door where the woman and the girls went in the early evenings. He had heard the faint sound of chanting, but the words had been incomprehensible.

Peter missed his mother and worried about his sister and at night he ran and ran and ran from a hideous gargoyle. Now, in the back seat of the car, free of Broadford House but lost on an improbable road, the dream had come back to haunt him, though as he twitched and jerked under the travelling rug, he was not running through a forest of old and hoary trees. He was fleeing down a long, eroded road while the thing reached for him and his mother and his sister.

It was a while before Patsy got to sleep and even then it was more of a fitful doze. The engine clicked and pinged as the metal cooled and contracted and condensation fogged the windows, blocking out the night. Judith was tucked in against her side, a bundle of warmth, snoring very quietly, while Peter's breathing was slowly beginning to even out. He'd mumbled something in his sleep and she had gently stroked his brow until he'd quietened, but there was no-one to stroke her own brow and chase away the night demons.

Every time she closed her eyes she saw again the running, melting face of the big trucker with the pool cue, knuckles twisting and buckling and becoming more than just fingers, his face broadening and changing into something less than human. She was torn with regret at bringing her children here, though a deeper, more central part knew that was wrong. They were in danger here, an awful, incomprehensible danger, but she was confident she would get them out of it. It was only a matter of time and finding the right way.

At Broadford House, they had been in worse, and that was something she knew on the intuitive level. Young Lisa Prosser had needed six months of mental decontamination after her time at Broadford House, but her boyfriend had never come out. She remembered the young girl's thousand yard stare into her own memory as she recounted how he had held her hands tight as

216

she lay on the stone altar while John Kenyon, who had run the commune until eighteen months ago, had taken her. Kenyon was gone, so Carrick and McGregor had told her. Paul Thomson and Kerron Vaunche had arrived at the place and had quickly worked their way into Kenyon's confidence and then they had broken him. According to Crandall Gilfeather, the organisation Kenyon had run had been a small-time cult for sexual deviants on a power trip. But with Kenyon out of the way, the followers had been led in a different direction. Lisa Prosser had told her of the nights of chanting and the prayers to different gods and the promise of dark powers. She had also confirmed something Peter had said earlier.

It had been all right to do it with sisters. With mothers. With daughters.

And Patsy knew that if she had not got there to Broadford House with her brother-in-law and the two men, something dreadful would have happened to her daughter. Even if Gilfeather hadn't spelled it out, she'd have known. Her instincts told her that Paul had not just wanted to have his children with him. There had been some dreadful *need* to have them close at hand.

She shook the repugnant thought away from her and tried to think of Carrick. Patsy remembered hearing the screams and the angry shouts and the crack of gunfire, and she could only hope that Carrick and the others had escaped from the mêlée in front of the iron gates. The followers of Paul's organisation at Broadford House had come spilling out like a demented pack of animals, screaming and shouting and ready to kill.

It seemed so long ago since she'd sped down that narrow, winding road and along the main route, heading south. Somewhere along the way she'd found herself on a wide three-lane road with a thunderstorm stirring the sky and sheets of rain sweeping across the hard-top and she'd driven out of her own reality and into a place where nightmares lived.

Patsy snuggled further under the blanket, aware of the chill creeping into the car and the dampness oozing into her joints. She knew she'd be stiff and sore in the morning and already she felt dirty and unwashed. She closed her eyes, held tight to Judith and tried to get to sleep.

Some time later she woke with a start.

Outside the car, something screeched, high and rasping, like a bird of prey, and in the distance another thing hooted in response. There was a silence for a few moments while Patsy sat, holding her breath, listening intently, when just outside the car she heard the sound of scuttling across the loose gravel. She moved to the window and slicked a curve of condensation from the nearest window. Outside it was dark. She leaned close to the glass, and as she did so, something low and black scrabbled past, a liquid shadow that had no definition. It darted from front to rear and disappeared into the patch of scrub behind the car. The silence descended again for five minutes, while she sat still, every nerve wound tight.

Then only a few yards away, down at the roadside, a beast howled and she almost screamed aloud. The noise came from close in, loud enough to be heard clearly, a high and despairing wail of pain that was not quite animal and not quite human. Patsy almost reached to wipe the condensation from the other window and look out but she snatched her hand back before it touched the glass. She didn't want to see what was out there, sounding not animal and not human, but in terrible pain. She did not want to see, but even more than that, she did not want to clear away the condensation on the glass and see whatever had done something terrible to cause that scream come leaning forward, a black and grotesque ogre, staring in through the window only inches from her own face.

Patsy sat very silent, forcing her breath to slow down. Peter mumbled again and she stroked his head, willing him to be quiet. Beyond the car the scrape of footsteps rasped, just heavy enough to be heard, then more silence that went on for a while. Despite her fear, Patsy dozed off again, dreaming dreams of things with long vulpine faces and gaping mouths lunging over her daughter who lay spread-eagled on a stone altar while clouds of black flies darkened the room. In her dreams she cried futile tears and pleaded with them to let her go, and they looked at her with contempt and they laughed in her face.

'Go back to sleep, Patsy,' the nearest of them slobbered at her and she saw it was Paul, but somehow changed, twisted and darkened until he looked like a grotesque caricature of himself. 'We have what we need here.'

218

Outside the car, down on the road sometime in the night, a monstrous vehicle went roaring past, fast and massive enough to make the car rock on its springs. Its horn blared and Patsy awoke, eyes wide and staring, hauling for breath, with the image of her own husband lunging into Judith still dancing before her eyes.

Down on the road, something crunched and the sound of the truck faded away in the distance. Much further off, the thunder rolled sonorously.

Tucked in beside her mother, Judith had been sleeping and dreaming. In her dreams she walked down the pathway through the copse of trees beyond the gardens at Broadford House. She was with Kerron, holding her hand as they strolled in the gloaming of early evening. Kerron had been speaking to her, talking in the new *secret* way that she'd been teaching Judith, showing her the tracks of the rabbits and the other secret paths between the trees. It had got darker here in the trees, but she felt safe and sure with Kerron, despite the small voice inside her that told her that this was not right. In her dream, Kerron was speaking fast and insistently, and the power of her words overwhelmed the doubts and she walked in the shadows until she heard the voice calling for her. She looked up at Kerron but the woman had not looked back. She had tugged at Judith's hand and started to walk quickly along the track and the shadows grew darker and Kerron walked quickly, so quickly that it felt they were flying and now they were in a tunnel formed by the trees, or was it a real tunnel and they were really flying forward while behind her somebody was calling her name and it sounded like her mother and she wanted to go back awhile, she wanted to go forward because she knew her father was up there ahead of them at the end of the tunnel, at the end of the low road and she could join him but she wanted her mother and the need for both of them was tearing her apart and she was scared, so scared that she couldn't breathe and . . .

She awoke in the darkness and she couldn't breathe. The dream was fragmenting, although she still felt as if she was flying through the darkness and those green, blazing eyes were drawing her onwards, but she was awake and her lungs were almost locked shut and the air was just a whistle in her throat. A warm weight pushed against her right side and she twisted against it,

219

the sense of suffocation clamping in on her. The weight gave a little but did not move and then real panic erupted inside her. She tried to cry but there was no air in her lungs. She twisted desperately, mouth agape, eyes now wide while in the dark little orange globes flickered across her vision, slowly turning to purple in the first stages of oxygen starvation.

Judith twisted again, crushed beneath the warm weight, dying for air. Her knee jerked in a spasm and hit against a yielding surface. Above her, a low groan broke the silence.

'What?' her mother asked.

Judith couldn't reply. Beside her, Patsy moved, turning slowly, still half dozing. The girl desperately tried to draw a breath and she could feel the muscles of her diaphragm expand and contract so violently they must surely tear and rip apart. Her hand came up, jerking involuntarily and caught her mother just under the breast.

Patsy yelped, turned, came completely awake and heard the little choking sound in the darkness.

Instantly she knew what was happening. Her hand came down on Judith's back and she could feel the spasms as the little girl's whole body was wracked by the demand for oxygen.

'Hold on,' she ordered, though it sounded more like a plea. Beside her, Judith was thrashing frantically, completely silent except for the hiss of air rasping through the tightness of her throat. Patsy threw herself forward. Beside and behind her Peter said: 'Whassamatter'. She reached for the glove compartment, not bothering even to switch on the courtesy light, flipped the opening down and grabbed inside. Without hesitation her fingers closed on the smooth cylinder of Judith's inhaler. She grabbed it, pulled herself back – and twisted a muscle in her hip which would cause her pain for more than a day – turned the ventilator right-way up, grabbed Judith by the back of the head and jammed the tube into her daughter's mouth while her thumb depressed the plunger that would force the spray into the back of the girl's mouth.

Judith jerked, her whole body arching off the seat. She shivered and then went completely flaccid. Patsy triggered the inhaler again, giving her a double doze and then pulled the thing out. There was a silence for three seconds and then Judith's breath whooped inwards with the sound of a wound-up klaxon horn. Patsy heard the air being sucked deeply into her daughter's lungs as if it would never stop. Finally it did and then it all came out again in a rush and Judith hauled in another giant breath. Patsy held her daughter tight, feeling the great inward breaths subside gradually until it was something close to normal, and only then did she reach forward and press the little roof light.

Judith's black hair was tangled and rat-tailed with sweat and her face was still pale. Patsy held her close, though not tight enough to affect her breathing, and she could feel Judith's heart, fast as a bird's, fluttering against her ribs.

'It's all right now, baby,' she soothed. Judith was still unable to speak, but she looked up at her mother. Even in the faint yellow glow of the courtesy light, Patsy could see the two blood-shot halfmoons underneath the black irises of her daughter's eyes. It had been a close-run thing. She held the inhaler up and gave it a shake. It was almost full and Patsy said a prayer of thanks for that.

Beside her Judith had quietened down and her mother could feel the tension ebb slowly away. After half an hour or so, Judith was breathing easily, deep and slow. Outside the night wore on and sometime just before dawn something else mewled plain-tively outside, but by this time Patsy was so exhausted that she was asleep and she heard nothing until Peter woke her an hour later, with a dirty orange sun glowing through the mist which floated over the moorland far off to the left.

14

The sky in the east had a spectrum somehow shifted towards the green and the orange. Dawn was breaking, a strange, unnatural sunrise which threw a pallid aurora into the low sky, painting it in gradual layers of sickly colour. To Patsy it looked as if she was viewing through tinted glass. Peter had nudged her awake and for a moment she was completely disoriented, caught in that half-world between dreaming and waking, trying to throw off the uneasy visions of sleep, unwilling to face the unreal reality of the day.

'Come on, mum,' he insisted. 'We have to get going.' He was pushing her shoulder, rocking her gently back and forth. In the odd, pre-awake seconds, while she tried to shake off the dream images of her husband and her daughter, she was only marginally aware of the events of the day before and they too seemed fuzzy and distant. As she fumbled and clawed her way through the surface membrane of sleep, she dozily agreed with herself that this too had been a dream.

Peter pushed at her again and everything came back to her in a snap of unwelcome clarity. She jolted to complete wakefulness and instantly the muscles low down on her spine protested in a jagged squeal of pain. She was stiff from the neck to her backside and that part of her was numbed from sitting through the night. With the movement, the numbness was immediately replaced by the stinging creep of pins and needles.

Outside, the strange bleached-green colours of the dawn told her yesterday had not been a dream.

'We have to go now,' Peter said, still nudging insistently.

'Yes,' she finally answered. 'I'm with you. Just give me a moment.' A big yawn was winding itself up and she gave in to it, stretching her hands out in front of her and feeling the clench of stiffness burn away. Beside her, Judith was fast asleep with her thumb jammed in her mouth, the way she had been when Patsy first saw her in the halo of the flashlight beam. Without thinking, Patsy reached out and felt her daughter's forehead. It was warm and slightly clammy again, though Patsy couldn't tell if she was running a fever.

'Did you sleep?' she asked Peter, turning towards him while her free hand started to roll back the blanket.

'A bit, but not much, I don't think. There was too much noise.'

'I heard some of it,' she agreed.

'What was it?'

'Hedgehogs probably, maybe rabbits. I don't know what kind of rabbits they have in Scotland.'

But it's not Scotland, her inner voice whispered at her and she knew it was right. *This is nowhere at all.*

'I think it was those dogs again,' Peter said matter of factly. 'There was something scratching outside the door and I could hear it breathing. I didn't want to look.'

Me neither. Her heart went out to her son. She'd thought he'd missed the noises last night, hoped he'd gone to sleep before those strange scurryings had scratched the darkness. He was too young to be so frightened that he didn't want to look out of the car window. A sudden burning hatred for Kerron Vaunche came bubbling up within her and she knew that if she had seen the woman at that moment she would have picked up a rock and smashed her to the roadside.

'No. I think it was hedgehogs,' she said, deliberately lying. The bestial howl of something not quite human came back to her. 'I had a look, and I didn't see any dogs.'

It was a white lie, but worth it. She couldn't let him know how petrified she had been of her own mental interpretations in the dark hours. She'd been scared to wipe away the sheen of condensation just in case something from her own nightmares had glared in through the glass and made her scream uncontrollably.

'We should get moving again,' Peter repeated. 'We can find a way in the daylight.'

'Sure we can,' Patsy agreed.

'And I'm hungry again.'

That bought a hint of a smile and she worked at it until it was almost a real one. ''Course you are. That's in the contract when you're a boy. You're my own personal waste disposal.'

223

'Can we find somewhere to eat?'

Patsy nodded, trying to show confidence. 'If only to get you off my back, tiger.'

She folded the rug right back and clambered into the front of the car. In the glove compartment beside the spare inhaler, she found the little box of wet wipes and used one to smear the sleep from her eyes. She rubbed the cool cloth against her temples and on the back of her neck, feeling the moisture evaporate coolly on her skin. The medicated scent covered the stale smell that had accumulated inside the sealed car overnight. She unlocked the door and opened it. Peter said nothing, though she could sense his immediate alarm.

'Just a minute while I get the old body working,' she said, pushing the door open. Immediately the wet-wipe scent was overpowered by a sulphurous odour and the heavy smell of burning rubber. Woven into that strange *mélange* of smells was a warm, almost metallic underlay that was reminiscent of continental butcher shops on hot summer days, a smell she associated with clouds of buzzing flies and meat just turning over. She put her foot on the surface outside, and while a tingling unease stirred inside her, it was only a pale echo of the paralysing dread that had shivered within her in the gloaming of the previous evening. Patsy pushed down against the road surface, like a skater testing the ice, eased herself out and stood up, ignoring the creaking protest down her spine.

The greasy scents on the air caught in the back of her throat, but it was the only air available and she breathed it in. The rain had stopped and she couldn't yet tell whether the sky was cloudy. Above her it glowered, the colour of a stormy sea while to her right, all the way to the horizon it was still a deep, sombre purple. Beyond the car where the sky was brightest, she could just make out the globe of the sun pushing its way through a thick mist which floated over the low moorland in the distance. It looked pale and weak and somehow tainted, as if its light had no strength to warm the world. An uneven row of dark spots smudged its surface and a thin skein of pale gas seemed to be arcing out from the top curve. The light made her eyes smart with tears and she turned away, blinking them back. The car was pointing at right angles to the road, sitting on the patrolman's lookout ramp about two metres back from the carriageway and maybe five feet above it. Left and right it seemed to stretch on forever, straight in both directions, narrowing with the distance until it was lost on each side in the early morning mist. From Patsy's vantage point, it could have been an isolated section of road, ending on each horizon, a piece of hard-top complete with central reservation and white lane-lines cut from an inter-city route and laid in the middle of a barren moor.

From her vantage point it would have been the only piece of road in the world ... if she did not look straight ahead, where the land dipped between two bare and pock-marked swellings and she could see beyond the moor to where the great curve of a motorway overpass arched above the ground mist, swooping on spider-thin legs above another convoluted stretch of roadway. She went round to the back of the car and popped the lid, letting it swing up. Just inside the trunk was the big travelling bag she'd packed for the trip with spare clothes for Judith and Peter, just an overnight selection, along with their toothbrushes and a little black and white stuffed badger that Judith had slept with since she was a baby until the day she'd disappeared from the garden. She lifted the cuddly toy out while surveying the rest of the clutter. The golf umbrella with its dirty aluminium spike was jammed in the corner beside the old fishing basket Carrick had given Peter and another cardboard box with more picnic stuff. She'd had better things to do than clear out the mess in the past months, but now she was glad it had come along, though she could not have said why.

Patsy came back round the side and sat on the driver's seat, her feet on the bitumen surface. Close by, the earth looked infertile and gritty, though thistles and hairy coltsfoot had managed to shove themselves through the surface and eke a meagre living from the impoverished soil. The small ramp led down to the hard shoulder and she could just make out the impressions of tyres from the night before. Beyond the hard shoulder, out on the flat surface of the road, there were pieces of cast-off tyres in a straggled line to the centre lane and closer in, some wet stains that could have been hedgehogs and rabbits or toads which had been flattened into the surface. She vaguely remembered the thunder of something big, some great trailer rumbling past in the darkness, horn blaring into the night, and she wondered if there had been other vehicles moving while she slept. *Had they come hunting for her and passed her by?* The greasy red and viscid spots looked fresh.

Behind her Judith mewled softly and began to stir. Patsy got back in the car and closed the door. Peter leaned over and looked at her anxiously.

'Can we go now?'

'In a minute,' Patsy told him. Judith's eyes were open, but they had that glazed, bewildered look that said she was still half asleep. Patsy leaned further and tucked the rug tightly around her. Judith's forehead was hot and damp and it did feel as if she might have a temperature. Patsy smoothed the tousles on the little girl's hair and gently pushed her down against the seat.

'Try to get some rest,' she said soothingly. Judith's eyes cleared. She blinked, looked around her, and jammed her thumb back in her mouth. Patsy held the toy badger up, saw the instant recognition in Judith's eyes and tucked it in against her daughter's neck. The little girl's eyes crinkled sleepily, but in obvious pleasure, and that alone rewarded Patsy with a warm tingle. She started the engine, let off the brake and let the car ease down the ramp towards the road, heading in the direction of the pale sunrise.

Down on the flat, she negotiated between the clumps of tyre fragments. Something crunched under the wheels and in the mirror, a ridged black and rubbery crescent rolled slowly and went still. Patsy pulled out further, automatically scanning the road behind in the overtaking mirror and the fragment of alligator-skin tyre rolled over on the road again.

She jerked her eyes away from the slithery motion, shaking her head quickly, denying that she had seen anything. The road stretched ahead of her into the far distance and she speeded away from the ramp, ignoring the sudden magnetism the wing mirror had developed as it tried to draw her eyes back again to look behind her. If that piece of heavy-tread that had peeled off a six-wheel trailer had actually moved of its own volition, she did not want to know about it. She drove out into the centre lane, picking up speed.

The sun rose quickly over the low hills, a pale, bloated orb crowned by that flaring corona, and the rolling mist began to burn away slowly. Judith snuffled quietly then coughed and Patsy checked the passenger seat for the inhaler just in case. In less than ten minutes, the road began to curve and rise steeply enough to drag a rasp of protest from the engine and she had to drop a gear. At the crest of the hill the dual carriageway squeezed through a narrow gully that had been blasted through black rock and was shaded from the direct sun. A wide lay-by beckoned here, empty but for a rusted wheel lying against a tumbled boulder and a wastebasket in which something bulky and black overflowed the rim. She had planned to stop somewhere along the road to give the kids something to eat, even if it was just another packet of crisps and a can of Coke, but there was no chance of stopping here in the lay-by, when the road ahead and the road behind was completely cut off from view. She drove on with the noise of the engine reverberating from the vertical face in a clatter of sound and then they were through the gap and on the downside.

Ahead of them the road swooped away down the curve of a wide valley and seemed to disappear in the distance, but beyond that, miles ahead, the vast interchange rose up from the haze. From the vantage point on the hill she could see it now, an enormous web of highway looping and arching, soaring and diving, the mother of all junctions.

Again the hum of distant traffic came wafting on the air, telling her that *something* was moving out there. But apart from the noise of the engine and the whisper of the wheels on the road, there was no other sound, no normal sounds of seagulls in the air, blackbirds and chaffinches quarrelling in the undergrowth of the verges, not even – though she did not truly want to hear it – the gruff staccato brawling of the crows. The murmur of moving traffic was as constant as the sound of water in a far-off stream, but there were no counterpoints. It sounded all too unnatural. It sounded somehow lifeless.

Walk the dead road, chattel-*woman, and walk in the shadow of death*.

Down the hill, keeping at a steady sixty, and along the straight as the morning swelled and the green-tinged lamination of colour lightened to a pearly brightness. Patsy could feel the sun on her

227

face through the windscreen and though the rays were hot, her skin immediately felt dry, as if the light was drawing the moisture from her. She pulled down the visor so that the direct light was cut off from all but her chin and kept going east. The swoop of the downslope evened out and the road followed the contour of the next low hill, swerved to the right and she found herself on another straight stretch which followed the border of what looked like a conifer plantation covering the ground in a thick blanket, edging to within fifty feet of the road.

The tall tree-trunks stuttered by in her peripheral vision and tried to draw her eyes towards them. Patsy felt her attention tugged and started to turn her head, realised what she was doing, and snapped her eyes back on the road. She'd only had a glimpse of the shadows between the trees and nothing had moved, but again that inner alarm system was clanging away and the fine hairs on her neck were beginning to crawl to attention. The blackness between the trees was infinite and while nothing had moved in there, the sudden and absolute sense of presence, of alien menace, had come reaching out from the depths of the trees and she had known, just as she had known that the old crumbling church had not been completely deserted, that in the shadow behind the tall trunks and under the spiky green canopy of the conifers, something lurked and looked out at the road with a strange hunger.

'*Fasgadh*,' Judith blurted. Her face was pressed up against the glass, eyes fixed on the trees.

'Yes, mum. Go quick,' Peter urged. He leaned across through the space between the seats. 'Can't we go faster?'

'Why, what's wrong . . .?' she began to say, and the stopped. He was leaning forward, but his face was turned not towards her. His eyes were fixed on the thick belt of trees which had come to fifty feet from the road but now, though she had seen no movement at all, were pushing right up to the hard shoulder. This time she could not resist the mental lure and turned her head. The depths were filled with shadows so deep they seemed to writhe and coil around themselves, as if the very darkness itself were alive. She slowed, involuntarily and Peter almost screeched in alarm.

'No, mum,' he bawled, voice high on the sharp edge of panic. 'Don't stop.'

Twenty yards on, the hard shoulder disappeared into the forest. It was as if the leading edge of the trees had crawled out to occupy the red grit. The sensation of threat inflated within her. Her eyes caught the tangled roots looped through the barrier which was now twisted and bent out of line. Just beyond that, the galvanised railing was torn apart and Patsy got a glimpse, not more than that, of the back of a car which was angled up and canted sideways. She was dragging her attention back to the road again, not wanting to see the car at all because her mind had done an instant calculation and had seen there was no way it could have got between the tightly backed trees that stood between it and the road. Her eyes were swivelling back on course when she saw the small movement on the grit of the blacktop where a root, just a small, scraggly surface root had lifted up from the tarmac and quested, like a thin whip snake, a mere inch or two above the road.

Patsy's mouth opened in a perfect circle, but no sound came out. The sight of that little root moving on its own was enough to shock her to complete silence. She gulped, trying to swallow in a throat that had gone dry as bleach. Behind her Judith was muttering something.

It was just then that Patsy realised the car had drifted closer to the edge of the trees. She had been in the centre lane when they had come abreast of the first of the trees, but now they had crossed to the inside, right up against the line of hoary old trunks. It was as if the unearthly attraction which tugged at her attention was luring her in towards the woods. A branch, or maybe a root crackled under the nearside wheel and immediately the scent of fresh resin filled the car. A long dangling branch bearing a thick frond of dark green needles smacked the windscreen and scraped along the side.

'Don't stop!' Peter yelled, throwing Patsy out of the frozen immobility. Her hands jerked on the wheel, hauling the car out from the edge just as a long green frond came reaching lazily out of the depths. What looked like scrawny branch fingers opened, just a blur in the corner of her eye but clear enough to convey even more strongly, the sense of utter menace. It hap-

229

pened so quickly that she had no time to do more than shove herself away from the motion, jamming herself reflexively against the door while her foot kicked down on the pedal. The branch raked the paintwork with the sound that Kerron Vaunche's nails had made, sharp enough to send a shiver down the length of her spine, and then they were past the edge of the trees. Beyond, the road swerved to the right, pulling away from the dark belt of the plantation. Patsy kept her eyes firmly on it, despite the eerie insistence of the dark shadows.

'It's alive,' Peter said. 'The trees can *move*.'

'That's enough,' Patsy said quickly. 'It's just the wind.'

'But mum, I saw . . .'

'No you didn't,' Patsy almost shrieked. 'Do you hear me?'

She shot a glance in the mirror and saw him, still wedged between the seats, eyes wide with agitation.

'But mum,' he started, but she cut him off. She had seen something move out of the corner of her eye, something that had moved with an awful slow deliberation. He had seen it too, but Patsy was not yet ready to accept it. If she cast it off and didn't mention it, then the image might go away and maybe she could convince herself that it had merely been a blur in her peripheral vision, that it *had* been the breeze.

'I said that's enough,' she hissed at him and he looked at her, puzzled. She glared back, giving him the look that told him to go no further. Peter blinked twice and dropped his gaze, now looking more confused than scared. Judith was mumbling now, face still pressed against the glass. Her eyes were shut.

'Get her to sit down,' Patsy barked. 'And strap her in.' The muttering continued. 'And stop that, Judith. Please.'

The forest tailed away behind them and the road took a dog-leg, twisting between two low conical hills. Patsy still kept her eyes firmly on the road, unwilling to look back just in case she saw any more movement in the dense thicket. In moments the car was round the curve, following the white marker-line and then on to a straight section on a slight downward incline. The wheels rattled hollowly, letting her know she was on a bridge again. On either side the land fell away abruptly in a narrow gorge and in the few seconds it took to cross over, she fancied she heard the sound of running water far below.

230

Beyond the gorge, the motorway arrowed straight and level on a broad flat plain. By now, the sun was much higher in the sky, a bloated and weak orb seen behind veils of cloud. The clock on the dashboard had stopped again, but Patsy knew she would have to stop somewhere so the children could eat. Her eyes felt gritty and raw and she had a hollow, nagging sensation in the pit of her stomach that she took for hunger pangs. Below that, less hollow and much sharper, was the early warning drag of cramp. She drove along the straight section, now checking in her mirror to see the road narrow in the distance until it was lost in the distant haze. Behind her, she could sense something moving, though she could see nothing. Ahead of her, the highway tapered to infinity. Nothing moved behind or in front despite the insistent trickle of unease that told her she was being followed. She slowed the car down, let it drift again onto the hard shoulder and coasted for half a mile before she stopped at a place where the verge was flat. Beyond the barrier, the land stretched on for miles, covered by bracken and heather and low, stunted bushes, and dotted here and there with clumps of tangled witch-hazel.

She let Peter and Judith out of the car after she herself had walked to the edge of the road to have another look back at the road she'd travelled. Here she only felt the persistent sense of unease, which she could handle, for it was nothing compared with the appalling and overwhelming sense of dread she'd had to endure the night before. Whatever instinct, whatever pre-science she had suddenly developed, she told herself, it had either gone or else it was working just fine. If it had gone, though, she thought she might have been aware of its absence. The unease fluttered like a warning flag, but there was nothing she could do about it.

Judith sat on a smooth boulder near the fence, cuddling the toy badger. She was still pale and her hair was tousled, lacklustre and dull. Dark and puffy crescents scooped under her eyes, making her look sick and bloodless. Her eyes were glazed as if she needed sleep.

Peter helped Patsy get the gear out of the boxes and onto the short grass on the margin. The old cool-box with the picnic supplies was stout enough to sit on and after Patsy had made a real inventory, she shoved it across to Judith's rock, pulled Peter down beside her and put an arm around each of them.

'Hungry?'

'Starving,' Peter said, unsurprisingly. Judith gave a listless nod. She was shivering a little, though the air was not cold.

'We've got some Coke and crisps, but that'll rot your teeth out. On the other hand, we've a tin of corned beef and some beans which we can heat up on the camping stove.'

Peter suddenly became very animated, and even Judith managed a half smile. Patsy got the little gas stove out and let Peter open the beans while she managed to peel the corned beef tin without damaging herself. The beans took less than five minutes to heat and she scooped them into the small plastic plates beside the slices of cold meat. The smell of the simple meal was tantalising and she watched them eat, Peter wolfing the food down like a hungry puppy. Judith nibbling as if the food were tasteless.

While they ate, Patsy wandered to the edge of the road, ignoring the ripples of unease. Beyond the crash barrier, a trickle of water flowed down a narrow drain runnel. There was enough to fill the kettle and the old flask, more than enough for a coffee. It took precious minutes to boil, but the coffee was like nectar. There was enough warm water left when she'd done to soak a handkerchief and give them all a brief wash, though she felt she could have killed for a long hot bath. While Peter repacked the picnic gear, Patsy went back to the stream to fill the kettle and the family-size flask *just in case*.

She was determined to find a way off the road before nightfall, but the voice of instinct had reawoken and had begun to chatter insistently. The warm beans had brought some colour back to Judith's face and she had stopped shivering. Patsy checked the inhaler by weight, making sure there was plenty in there to last the day, though there was a spare one in the glove compartment. By then she was hustling them back into the car, the sun almost directly overhead, though it seemed to have risen only an hour before. The day was brighter, but still strangely discoloured, lending the grass and the heather a pallid, bleached tone.

She started the car, pulled out again and drove on. A mile or so along the straight, Peter let out an enormous belch that sent him into an uncontrollable fit of laughter, and even Patsy couldn't stop herself smiling. For a moment, but for the fact that an infected sun was almost hidden by bloated, lowering clouds and there was a smell of corruption hanging on the air, she could have imagined the three of them were out on picnic.

15

The needle on the petrol gauge was dipping down to the halfway mark and the smile was long gone when they came across the wreckage at the side of the road. She had seen the shape in the distance and at first her heart had leapt in the natural hope that there would be someone to help, then it had thudded hard at the thought that if might really be someone else on the road, and she realised the danger of that. As she approached, she slowed warily, dropping a gear, ready to accelerate and speed away if she had to.

The old car lay at an angle, canted down the ditch that ran alongside the road. The paint was long gone and the tyres were just mouldy skins round the wheels. A running board ran from the wheel arch to the rear door, like the kind of car she'd seen in the old black and white gangster films. It looked as if it had been sitting there, back raised askew, for decades.

A hundred yards along the road, two cars, both more modern than the first lay together in a metallic embrace, merged inextricably by the force of a powerful head-on impact. It was difficult to work out how it had happened because the opposite track, beyond the galvanised barrier running the length of the central reservation, was completely cut off. Both cars were twisted and blackened, as if they'd crashed and then burned. She drove past slowly, skirting the wreckage and broken glass that spilled across two of the three lanes, and scanned the road ahead.

For as far as the eye could see, it was littered with the hulks of cars. She kept moving, weaving her way between the wrecks, skirting an abandoned coach up against the barrier, tangled weeds braided through the gaping rust-holes in its flanks. Just ahead of it, an electric blue Porsche lay on its roof, gently rocking in the wind. Beneath it, a black stain on the road could have been oil or petrol or anything. Patsy quickly averted her eyes. The Porsche was clean and still unrusted but the stubby little roadster had flipped over and sent jewelled fragments of toughened glass scattering right across the road. It looked as if it could have happened yesterday, maybe even today. She did not want to look at the crumpled compartment underneath the alloy wheels just in case the stain on the road was not oil or petrol, but blood which had leaked out from whoever had been driving the car and made it somersault here in this automobile graveyard.

Whether this was the stretch of road she has seen from the bridge, it was hard to say. In front and behind, there was no sign of a span across the highway.

'Wow, look at that!' Peter exclaimed, and for a bleak second she thought he might have seen what she had tried not to see, but he was upon his seat again, leaning over, facing the nearside, pointing much further ahead. As soon as she slowly swerved around the rocking sports car she could see the reason for his excitement. The road took a slight dip, giving them a panoramic view of the entire stretch and in front of them was a whole necropolis of cars that went on and on and on. The road and the roadside, the verge and the hard shoulder were littered with wrecks, new and old, large and small.

Peter asked her own unvoiced question. 'Where did they all come from?'

'I don't know.'

'It's like the elephants graveyard, only for cars,' Peter said, alive with wonder. 'Look. There's a Jag. And there. It's a Rolls-Royce.'

Patsy eased between the front bumpers of a van and a station wagon that faced each other like nervous dogs. At first she thought the van's windscreen was shattered by the impact of a stone, sending concentric cracks from the point of collision radiating across the surface. She eased forward through the narrow gap and just at the point where there was an inch between her wing mirror and the van's crumpled headlamp, a small movement in the corner of her eye caused her to turn and she saw that it wasn't a series of concentric cracks. Stretched across the gaping void in front of the twisted steering wheel was a spider's web, thick and ropey and grey with dust. Right at its hub something bottle-green and shiny sat hunched, completely still but for the slow, gently stroking movements of two long and jointed legs testing the tension of the guy-lines. Patsy's stomach clenched as she recalled the thing that had lurked inside the phone box and had come clambering up the stick towards her hand. The spider, even bigger than the fat and bloated thing that she had split open on the roadside, froze just as she passed by. She couldn't draw her eyes from it although reason told her that if it had spun a web, it must be after insects and it would not, could not, have any purpose in attacking anything as large as a human.

Inside her the voice that had nothing to do with reason told her to drive on, drive *fast*.

The car eased through the gap, but because her eyes were glued on the swollen shadow and the two raised forelegs, she had drifted inches to the right. That was just enough to let her wing mirror scrape against the rusted headlamp socket. The web shivered, almost imperceptibly. She saw the forelegs tense on their wires and then, in the wink of an eye, the thing came rocketing out from the centre of the web. It was twice the size of the other spider, a monstrous beast with legs thick as twigs and a distended abdomen of bluebottle green, dotted with little poisonous orange globules.

Patsy froze in fright, but only for an instant. The spider came scuttling down the line, faster than anything that size had a right to move, angling straight towards the point of connection, unerringly sensing where the van had been touched. Even in that split second she could see the head come up and the pale light reflect in pinpoints on those flat eyes. Underneath it she saw the two curved needles of the fangs. The legs were moving so fast they were just a blur. It came skittering down the guy ropes radiating from inside the cab, expanding in her vision.

'And there's a stagecoach,' Peter yelled, bringing her out of her frozen trance. Her foot pushed down and the car jolted forward. Judith squawked in surprise and Peter's yell was cut off instantly as they were thrown backwards and down into the well behind the front seats. The other wing mirror cracked against the stalled wreck and flipped back against the glass as the car lurched through the gap. Patsy was half turned in her seat, unable to think of anything but getting away from that spider. She saw a dark shape come flying off the front end of the van and land on the road and then she was away, hauling the wheel to avoid a transporter angled across the road, a big gaunt bridge of steel beams at the top of which sat one small and forlorn little car. She missed the transporter by six inches at the most, veered around its sagging back wheels and straightened up. Nothing on legs came skittering round on the road behind her. Her eyes stayed too long on the mirror as the car hurtled forward. Peter was clambering back up again. A shadow loomed in front of her.

'*Look out, mum!*' he bawled in her ear, just in time. Her hands moved on the wheel, operating on pure reflex and a jolt of adrenaline socked into her veins. The wooden wheel of the old coach, almost five feet high and tangled in bindweed, clipped the edge of the rubber bumper, hard enough to send a jolt through the car and a loud splintering crack into the air.

'It's a stagecoach,' she heard herself say stupidly. It was a stagecoach all right. The front end of the car had glanced off an old black coach. It lurched under the impact and a puff of grainy dust billowed off the bundle roped to the back board. It rolled forward a foot or so and ground to a halt. Patsy came round the far side as the thing was rocking stiffly on what might have been springs. The nearest wheel was missing several spokes and the ones left looked as if they were ready to crumble to powder. It could have come from the back lot of a film studio or a scene from an old western.

'It's from *Back to the Future*,' Peter cried. 'Look. It's a real stagecoach.'

She was slowing down now, shaken by the jolt of the near disaster, just skirting the old and tattered carriage.

The nearest door was hanging agape, leaning outwards from one leathery hinge and swinging slowly. The front wheel had almost all of its spokes, but the wood must have shrunk enough to let the iron girding ring slide off. It leaned against the side of the coach in a big rusting circle. As she passed by the open door, she saw a long tattered shape lying sprawled half out of the doorway but she was past too quickly to see what it was. Beyond the front wheel the driver's ledge trailed two braided pairs of long traces which swung as slowly as the door, stretching out towards the four grey mounds in front of the carriage.

Patsy glanced at them, looked back to the road and did a double take which almost cricked her neck.

The mounds were horses. The bones showed clearly through

237

the grey and flaking hides which stretched over them in a dirty membrane of shrink-wrapped skin. They were crumpled between the shafts, lying where they would have stood when the coach ground to a halt for the last time. Black eye sockets stared at the sky and the brown teeth looked as if they still ground together in death. The nearest horse was lying on its side, legs outstretched, mere bones covered in traces of old rotted skin. Patsy turned her head and got half a glimpse of another shape up on the driver's board and decided she didn't want to see that either.

'What do you think killed them?' Peter asked.

'Probably ran out of feed,' Patsy told him, snatching the first reply that came to mind.

She hadn't had time to look at the corpse horses, so she couldn't tell whether they'd been shot where they stood or whether they had just crumpled and died. The long shape lying half out of the coach, slanted across the little courtesy step. and the other shadow up there on the driver's post, they were trying to insinuate themselves into her mind, taking on significant human form and she backed away from it.

Out here on this appalling road, where dead and twisted cars and trucks littered the highway for mile after mile, stood an old stagecoach which had stopped here and been left to moulder. Her imagination saw the carriage come clattering slowly down the road, harnesses jangling, horses hooves clopping on the road metal and sending up the occasional spark from an exposed piece of whinstone hardcore. In her mind she heard the neighing of horses, panicked by the strangeness of a road which could not possibly exist. Would the teamster have been as scared as she was now, as numbly bewildered? Would the passengers have realised what was happening to them?

The coach looked as if it had been crumbling at the side of the road for a hundred years. When she thought of that, the other questions came jostling for answers.

How had it got there? Had some old witch woman made a curse and sent them galloping down a dusty trail that somehow led onto a three-lane blacktop at an interchange that swallowed highway and byway into an infernal maze? She couldn't tell whether the coach was really an American stage or not, though it looked that way. Had the passengers – maybe those half-glimpsed and tattered shapes – looked out and seen the distant arch of the overpass and though they'd been transported into some hellish turnpike or (and this was even worse) had the horses, lathered in sweat and panting with exhaustion stopped on the grass beside an old dusty trail and simply died, while the wide carriageway grew up around them over the years?

Again Patsy resisted the urge to look around and see the shapeless heap slumped on the buckboard. Whatever sat there had sat alone for a long, long time and she did not want to see that, because if she looked too closely and saw it was a man who had stopped to rest on this road and died here, she might entertain the possibility that it could happen to Peter and it could happen to Judith, and such a thought was unacceptable. The idea that somebody might come edging along this vast road that was lined and dotted with the dead remnants of cars and trucks and delivery vans, slowly steering past the rusting wreck of this car and averting their eyes from the sightless sockets of two children and a dreadful, mummified thing that sat there clenching the steering wheel, that was a thought that would ricochet around in the mind and drive a woman crazy.

She sneaked a glance at Peter and was grateful that his attention was riveted on the mounds of bones lying in the road between the shafts.

'Look at them,' he was telling Judith. 'That's horse bones. You can see the teeth.'

'Dead now,' Judith said flatly. She was holding tight to the little badger.

'How d'you think they got here?'

'Probably took a wrong turning.'

'But all these cars. They go on for miles. I never saw anything like this, not *ever*.'

'Always a first time for everything,' Patsy said, keeping it light, though the impact of the miles and miles of crashed and twisted and abandoned vehicles was only now beginning to dawn on her.

Somehow, and for some reason, each car and truck and coach had arrived on this road. Whether it was yesterday or last year or a century ago, they had all found their way onto this infernal highway and they'd stayed here. They had stopped or crashed or swerved off the hard shoulder and taken a dive down into the

239

narrow storm ditch. It was only now that she realised she had not looked in through the windscreens of any of the cars she'd passed, and that had not been a conscious decision. She'd seen the horrible and bloated spider come scrambling out of the web, like an amputated hand; that had been bad enough, a moment of phobic nightmare, but for some reason, it was *acceptable*. She had looked at a spider that was bigger than any arachnid that could possible exist and it had come racing down the web to attack her and her brain had rationalised it and gone along with it (though her heart had almost punched a hole in her ribs at the same time.)

But she had not looked in through the smashed and starred windscreens or the lolling and gaping doors and tailgates because her mind had been unwilling to take in anything that could not be rationalised away, not after the overload it had suffered in the past forty-eight hours.

Only two days?

She had side-stepped any notion that the people in these cars and buses and soft-top roadsters had not stepped out of them, whether they were crashed and crumpled or burned. Her need to believe that they had got out and walked away and found their way home was paramount in her own subconscious because that was what enabled her to drive on. Her own sense of survival had been suddenly honed to razor sharpness, but even that was blunt in comparison to the utter imperative compulsion that was her maternal instinct. She was not yet ready to believe that these drivers had not walked away from the road and found a way home because if they had not, then her children, now her whole reason for existing might falter and die on this abominable road.

'They're like those horses we saw at the station,' Peter was telling Judith. 'They were all skinny and hungry and you could see their bones. What are they doing here?' He turned to Patsy. 'Can we stop and have a look?'

'No. We have to keep going,' she said. His curiosity had obviously overcome his previous alarm.

'There's millions of cars here. Thousands of them at least. Its like . . . it's like . . .' his descriptive abilities deserted him. 'It's just stupendous!'

Judith muttered something under her breath. The road continued straight and the verge was flat, stretching a good fifty feet out beyond the breakdown lane and covered in sparse, ground-hugging plants with leathery leaves and thick stems. Beyond that, the storm-drain cut a shallow and tapering line running parallel to the road.

'Look, Judy. That's like a Ferrari.' Patsy couldn't help glancing over to where he pointed. It was a long and sleek thing, more nose than seat-space, still retaining most of a coat of bright racing red, but it hunkered down on the straggly plants on tyres that had long since perished. One door hung open like a wing. The car was obviously empty. Again it gave the impression – and the little unspoken plea of hope – that the driver had stepped out and gone walking. Only yards away, a big bull-nosed truck that looked like a wartime army transporter was angled down into the ditch, its green battledress tarpaulin ripped and tattered, showing the curved rib-struts that had held it in place. One of its rear lights had fallen out and dangled by black cable only inches above the ground cover. A green helmet lay on a bare patch, like the shell of a basking tortoise. For two yards to the right the ground was shaded by a wide oil-spill where nothing grew. A small breeze fluttered the tattered pennants of the camouflage cover giving the slanted truck an impression of creepily festive dereliction.

A long twiggy thing hung from the open window on what might have been the driver's side – if they were still in Scotland that was and already Patsy knew she was not – and her eyes flicked away from it. She had to twist the wheel again to avoid an old Skoda that looked as if it *should* have been in a transport cemetery in any case and she was relieved that the children had said nothing. Peter would be interested in shiny cars or old stagecoaches. A mouldering army truck would not hold this attention, and she was grateful for that. It could have been a piece of cloth. It might have been a braided and scrawny honeysuckle creeper growing up the side of the door.

But it could have been something else. Like an arm.

She eased round the unfortunate little Czech car and saw the road ahead was clear. A monster of an old sawmill lorry was lying right on its side on the far side, making a rust-wreck bridge over the drainage culvert, its smoke-stack broken off and stuck in the bracken beyond the ditch. It was a bright ochre of corrosion and flaked paint and its pulley-drum had broken away, casting off a tangle of braided hawsers that resembled a nest of red adders. The rig must have been fairly hammering along when it had veered off the road. Twin channels were gouged in the earthen wake behind it, though the furrows had long grown over, but it was the load that told the whole story. It had been carrying its stack of big trunks when it came off and it had shed them in a cascade which had tumbled the timbers in an avalanche that had rolled them for near-on a hundred yards. One of them had speared through the boiler-cylinder of an ancient tractor and pinned it to the ground, and the rest were lying in a jumbled heap. But even then, they were hardly recognisable as logs. They had almost completely decomposed under the blanket of moss and glistening fungus that was rotting them back to ground level.

Patsy had seen enough. Her mind was reeling with all the visual information and her head felt hot enough to explode. There were too many questions and a surfeit of answers she could dream up but didn't even want to consciously consider. Instead she shied away from them and tried to get away from all of this, pressing the ball of her foot down on the pedal and forcing the car down the straight. Rusted hulks and mouldering wrecks whizzed by as the needle swung fast above sixty, continued beyond seventy and only slowed when she was nudging eighty. She realised she was going too fast, but kept up speed for more than ten minutes, keeping her eyes firmly ahead. Eventually, just before the wide road began to veer slowly to the right, rising on the flank of a low incline, the jumble of wreckage began to thin out and Patsy eased up on the accelerator.

On the side of the road the land was slowly sweeping away as the highway ascended. Down on the curve there was an upturned wreck with its wheels in the air. On the other side, close to the central reservation, and old flatbed trailer stood forlorn, with no sign of the powered cab that had brought it here.

That was the last of them, so Patsy thought.

The curve in the road was long and deceptive, rising almost imperceptibly while the plain below dropped ever more steeply. She followed the route, hugging the flank of the hill as the road zigzagged around heaps of old glacial moraine which sprouted ancient and gnarled conifers like warts on a gigantic face. Up here the air smelt cleaner, if only marginally. She had to slow down again at a tight turn on the curve of a stone embankment, come along a straight stretch and was almost past the lay-by before she saw it.

The car screeched to a halt as Patsy's foot stamped on the brake.

A single motorbike stood in the centre of the lay-by, hauled back on its kickstand. She pulled in, drawing level with the bike. It was only then that she saw the sign lying on the side of the road as if it had been ripped off and discarded by vandals. It showed a steep descent ahead, stated that this was a checkpoint and suggested that heavy goods vehicles should test their brakes.

The bike was a big maroon roadster. Two long aerials curved out like fly-rods from the pillion, shivering like antennae in an eddy of wind. It was still burnished, though it had a layer of road dust on the cowling and the wheels as if it had travelled a long way.

Patsy sat and looked at it for a moment. It could have been parked there an hour ago. There was no sign of any rust and she could even see the grooved wheel-tracks in the grit. She stopped and pondered, debating what to do next. The land rose steeply beside the checkpoint, mounded with boulders and those craggy pines with gnarled branches all leaning in the same direction as if huddled against the winds that were constantly trying to push them over. She rolled the window down, listening for any sound at all, but there was nothing except the soughing of the breeze through the patchy foliage.

'It's a Honda,' Peter volunteered. 'It can do a hundred and forty.'

Patsy said nothing. Her eyes were scanning the hillside, while she considered her next move.

'Do you think the driver's still here?'

'I don't know, Peter. Maybe.'

'He might be able to help us. Show us the way home.'

He might, Patsy thought. There were all sorts of possibilities.

'Let's see,' she said, and pressed the heel of her hand on the horn. It blared a high flat note that rebounded from the high

243

boulders and came echoing back in a broken stutter. They all sat listening. There was no reply, no halloo from the high rocks. She tried again, repeating the sound several times, but there was no response at all.

'Stay here,' she told them both as she got out of the car. On an impulse, she took the key from the ignition and locked the car from the outside before she warily went round the back towards the bike.

It was indeed a Honda. A big and squat Goldwing with two panniers hanging like saddlebags over the rear wheel. The front tyre was suspended an inch above the ground and it gave the impression that it had been parked there only moments before and was just awaiting the return of its driver to roar into life and go haring round the bend. She reached out and touched the seat. It was cold. There was no clicking sound from the engine that would have told her it was cooling down after a long trip. She bent and rubbed the muffler. This too was cold.

It was a dead bike. As forlorn and useless as the vast array of dead vehicles she'd passed by on the straight road. Her feelings were mixed, though, because if at that moment someone in a helmet and leathers had come striding out from behind one of the big boulders, there was a good chance that she might just drop to the road in a dead faint. She walked warily round to the front of the bike, alert for any sound or movement in the trees on the slope when she saw the fluttering movement on the screen of the cowling. At first it looked like a parking ticket in a plastic bag jammed down between the windscreen and the fairing. She drew it out and opened the bag. Inside there was a single piece of paper which she quickly unfolded.

Four days. The words were written in block capitals in red ink. *Can't get off this road. Last of the food yesterday, no petrol now. Where in Christ's name is this place? If anybody finds this, me and Sally have gone on ahead. If we can find a garage we'll come back for the bike. If not, God help us. Anybody reads this, stay off the road at night and don't go near the dead cars after sundown.*

The note was signed: *Billy Walker.*

There was no date and nothing at all to tell Patsy when Billy Walker had run out of fuel on this hillside road and set out with his Sally on foot. On the low curved windscreen someone had used a finger to scrawl initials in the dust. *SB & WW.* Or the ampersand could have been an *L.* Sally B and William Walker. Sally B *Loves* William Walker.

Patsy tried to visualise them. Teenagers in love? Not Hell's Angels, because the bike was clean and it was expensive. Maybe not even teenagers, they could even be friends, touring together on the big bike, finding themselves on the road that went to nowhere. She could visualise Billy Walker, hunched over, eyes flickering to the fuel gauge as hers had done, watching the indicator drop inexorably towards the red, wondering where on earth this road was heading.

The fact that there was another woman here changed things for her and the hope swelled again. The finger scrawl in the dust on the screen was still clear and unblurred. It could have been done only hours ago. Sally B could have written her initials that very day.

They had gone ahead on foot, according to his note. Maybe they were just around the corner. They could be down at the bottom of the hill beyond, waiting for some passer-by to give them a lift to the nearest filling station. If someone else had got onto this road then there must be another exit. The hope swelled stronger. Patsy spun quickly and trotted back to the car, clenching Billy Walker's note in her hand. She pulled the handle, paused bewildered for several seconds before she realised she'd locked herself out, then Peter flipped the lock and she scrambled inside.

'We could be in luck,' she told them as she started the car again. 'There's a boy and a girl. They've left a note saying they've run out of petrol and have started walking to find a filling station.'

'Do you think we'll catch them up?'

'We can try.'

For some reason it was important to catch up with Billy Walker and Sally B. If she could find them, even if they were still lost on this road, she wouldn't be a lone adult with her two children. There would at least be safety in numbers, more protection for Peter and Judith. She pulled out of the lay-by, gunned the engine to get her up the sharp incline, rolled over the crest and down the far side. The rise on the road after the graveyard of the cars had been deceptive, but it must have been considerable for now they were a thousand feet, maybe more, above the rest of the land. As they turned down the hill she could see yet another vast plain ahead of them. The road swooped down towards it and cut straight across a broad valley. In the distance she could see, faint but definite, the vast tangle of roads jutting up above the land. It was like seeing a city in the distance, except there were no buildings, no towers pointing at the pale sky. Up on the height, even though the air was cold and quite sharp, she could smell the underlay of exhaust fumes and spent oil. Very faintly the sounds of massed road transport came grumbling on the breeze. Far in the distance, she realised, arching and curving in an enormous complex of road junctions and connections, was a city, not of people, but of cars and trucks. It was a city of roads that stretched forever, seen through a haze of road fog. Now it seemed closer than before, as if they were travelling inexorably towards the maze of roadways.

The highway seemed to angle straight towards it. The thought gave her a deep, cold shiver. Behind them, somewhere on the road, Kerron Vaunche would be searching for her as she had promised. Ahead of them, the complex connection of roads beckoned ominously.

But Patsy had no choice but to drive onwards.

16

Night fell like a dead weight, shuttering the world in darkness with startling and unheralded suddenness. There was hardly a twilight, no gloaming dusk, just the rapid subtraction of light.

Patsy watched the sun sink, a great oblate orb of pustulous yellow-green, punctuated by dark blotches, as if the sun itself had a cancer. It dropped towards the horizon with breathtaking swiftness, dipping through the colour-matted prism of sky, sucking the hues away as quickly as it had painted them in the morning. The dreary purples and greys dopplered down ever darker until there was no colour left but a baneful glimmer, matching the hot furnace-glow radiance thrown against the clouds far to the south.

They had come two hundred miles since the lay-by on the rocky outcrop. Patsy had reset the counter as she drove away and left the black bike on its kickstand, unable to trust the clock on the dashboard which had at least got all the hands to move in the same direction, albeit the wrong one, and her own watch which had stopped with the hour, minute and second hands all pointing to the bottom of the face.

'Six, six, six,' she'd said absently, almost in superstition. A small chill went through her.

'His number,' Judith said, startlingly loud.

'Eighteen,' Peter countered. 'That's if you're adding them. It'll take me longer if I'm multiplying. Want me to try?'

'Sure, why not. Then we can have a game of I-spy,' Patsy said, trying pretend she hadn't heard what Judith had said. She knew the number of the beast. They'd talk later, when they got home, and she'd find out everything about Broadford House and what her husband was doing there and most of all, what Kerron Vaunche had been doing with Judith. That would have to wait. For now, her job was to stay awake and stay alert and get them there.

Peter started mumbling to himself, doing the mental arithmetic, while Judith took up the refrain. 'Six, six, six,' she said, repeating the three figures over and over again, almost like a mantra. Patsy told her to stop, feeling again the superstitious twitch of foreboding, and the anger bubbling up again. She asked Judith to sing a song, but the girl just went silent. The road had zigzagged around the clusters of big rocks and then dived out into a steep glide on a straight track plunging almost a thousand feet before it levelled off again on another plain. When the car reached the flat, the sun was almost directly ahead, high in sky the colour of clotted cream. Here the land was different and to Patsy it seemed as though they'd travelled to another continent. On either side of the road, the ground was baked dry. There was no other way to describe it. In the previous valley, the one with all the dead cars, it had been damp and cold, the kind of weather she'd zipped her heavy jerkin against in Scotland. Up on the heights, they could have been in the Rocky Mountains, or maybe even the French Alps, driving past the hard outcrops of grey stone on which gnarled pines, blown into slanted curves by the prevailing wind, eked a living.

Down from the rise, she could have been in Arizona and in an instant, the air was blistering hot, as if an oven door had opened. Immediate sweat came rolling down the sides of her ribs and trickling down the length of her back.

'Two hundred and sixteen, and can you turn the heater down?'

'What's that?' Patsy asked.

'Six times six times six. Two hundred and sixteen. I did it in my head.'

'Good for you. That's really good for nine.'

'I can do harder ones than that. But can you turn the heat off, mum. It's really boiling in here.'

'Hot, hot, hot.' Judith started up a different chant.

Patsy flipped the indicator on the vents to let cooler air in, but if anything, the breeze blowing through the ducts was hotter still, searing and dry with the sulphurous scent of volcanic sand. Judith coughed harshly, gagged for breath in a high whoop.

'Heat of burning fire, there to suffer . . .' she managed to squeeze out before another fit of coughing racked her.

'Open the back windows, Peter,' Patsy said, winding hers down as she spoke. The blast-furnace breath of desert air came whipping through the openings but the speed of the car gave it enough wind-chill to make it bearable. She told Peter to open the bottle of mineral water. He twisted the cap and passed the drink to Judith. She shook her head, but he insisted, forcing the rim against her mouth until she drank. The cough eased away. They all drank, though Patsy insisted that they leave half the water for later.

The road cut straight across a flat land that seemed to have been baked under a malignant sun. The terrain at first was rocky, the colour of fire-bricks and in the depressions, pools of silty sand gathered against the lee of the rocks. Odd-shaped trees with grey flaky bark cowered under thick thorned branches, huddling from the merciless heat. Here and there, patches of rubbery succulents formed virulent, almost luminous green tapestries. Every time she passed one of the weedy strips she could smell a faint sickly-sweet scent that somehow gave her the impression of rot, as if something had died in the clumps. She drove on, while her shirt stuck to her back and Judith whined in drowsy complaint. The heat seemed to have stolen Peter's energy too, for he'd gone quiet, leaving Patsy cocooned in her own thoughts as she sped along the outlandish road.

In a matter of miles, the rocky, blistered landscape gradually changed, as if she was passing through a quarry land where the surface had been graded, crushed and graded again. The boulders became brick-sized rocks, then fist-sized stones, then ochre pebbles then shale until she was driving on a black ribbon through a desert of sand.

On both sides of the highway, oceans of desert stretched out endlessly. Great combers of powdery dunes, washed almost white in the blinding dazzle, went rolling in a dry, silent tide. Every now and then, her eye would catch a sudden movement in her peripheral vision and she would turn towards it, most of the time missing the source of motion, but occasionally catching the topmost crest of a dune crumble and avalanche into a trough. It was like watching a sea storm in slow motion. Here and there, the marching waves had impinged upon the road, crawling over the black surface, in places almost covering the bitumen and she had to weave her way through, tyres crunching on the fine grains of sand and blowing up a slipstream of powdery dust that rose into the air behind her and floated in ochre contrails.

As the quarryscape changed, the heat rose further until the reflections on the dunes were so glaringly bright it felt like needles in her eyes. She fumbled in the glove box, found a pair of old reading glasses which she slung back again, then hunted by touch until she located the little plastic wallet with her sun-glasses. She slipped them on and almost wept with relief. The searing brilliance faded to a just-bearable brightness. A big tear rolled down her cheek and dried before it reached her chin. The sulphur smell now mingled with the throaty scent of hot tar and the tyres started hissing on the soft road surface. In the mirror, when she looked she could see the tumbling dust-cloud of her wake and the jet-black tyre trails where they'd scraped away the molten tar.

'Thirsty land, burning hand,' Judith mewled, almost inco-herent.

'I know, honeybun, it's too hot. We'll stop soon.'

She knew she was pretending to herself, mishearing Judith's words. Whatever foul things Kerron Vaunche had been teaching her daughter must be coming back to her now. Patsy just did not know what to do about it. She wanted to stop soon, but she didn't dare stop here. Already she could sense that little sub-audial hiss of an engine overheating, despite the fact that there was no warning on the dials. If she stopped the car here, she might never get it started again, and that was not something she wanted to dwell too long upon.

'Drink now of the chalice,' Judith murmured. Then she seemed to come awake. 'Need a drink.'

'No. We have to keep it for later.'

'I'm thirsty *now*.'

'Me too,' Peter chimed in. 'All that last drink came out of my skin. Even my hair's wet.'

A sudden burn of anger flared inside her and she almost screamed at both of them to stay quiet and let her drive and get them all home and just give her a break. She stamped down on it hard. It was not her fault and it was not their fault, but the last thing any of them needed was for her to crack.

'All right,' she finally said. 'But just a sip. Okay? Peter, you make sure it's just one sip. We can't afford any more.'

He reached for the bottle and she told him to hold it up where she could see it. The water inside reached to the top of the label and it looked like the best drink in the world. He took the top off again and she craned to look in the mirror. Peter held the bottle to Judith's lips and let her have two swallows. The little girl drank them down with her eyes closed. Peter drank next and then passed it between the seats to his mother. Patsy put the rim of the bottle to her lips and she actually *smelled* the water. The inside of her mouth seemed to pucker and stretch towards it. She canted the bottle up and let the merest dribble wet her lips, brought it down again and passed it back to Peter. He took it from her and when she heard the cap screw back on again, she felt like crying.

She drove on for another ten miles while the sun beat down mercilessly.

The counter was just at the halfway mark, edging up to the figure eleven, when she saw the black shape lying by the side of the road. She took her foot off the pedal and slowed and as she did so the wind-chill of the turbulence diminished in inverse proportion to the sudden unbelievable rise in temperature. The air was so thick it felt glutinous and turbid. Judith began to whoop in distress.

She slowed further as she approached the black shape. Ordinarily she would have missed it, but it was the only real contrast on the unbroken burned beige of the sand. She eased to a crawl and pulled the car over to the edge. The whistling, high-pressure hiss from the radiator was just within hearing range now and that, combined with Judith's laboured panting, told her she couldn't slow for long, shouldn't slow at all. But the dark blotch drew her like a magnet.

It was a glove.

It was a leather gauntlet, lying by the side of the road, fingers clenched as the unbelievable heat shrivelled the hide and contracted the glove into a fist. It looked like a dead spider lying on its back and for one shivery instant she thought it might turn over in a quick groping twist and come scuttering towards her.

The gauntlet did not move. It lay twisted and desiccated, a

251

biker's glove abandoned on the ochre dust at the side of the highway. A few yards further off, hidden until now by a hummock of bare sand, its mate lay palm down. Two metal studs gleamed like insect eyes just behind the knuckles.

Billy Walker. The biker had gone walking with the woman. They'd come in this direction, heading up the slope to the crest of the promontory and then down the zigzags and tight bends on the serpentine road and then onto the flat where the land had changed and become a desert. She could visualise them tramping along the road, panting for breath, shedding their clothes piece by piece as the sun rose higher, blasting them with its virulence. But no. That picture jarred. She'd come speeding along on their trail, trying to catch them up. There had been no sign of them at the side of the road, no biker's leather jerkin, no leggings. Behind her Judith was panting like a dog and hot sweat was trickling down under Patsy's arms in a steady stream that had a dull, stale smell that reminded her she hadn't had a decent wash in more than two days. She turned in her seat. Peter was looking at her with tired eyes, but he winked and managed a smile. She opened the door and his eyes widened, but she held one finger up, indicating she'd only be one moment, let the engine idle and stepped out of the car.

Her shadow disappeared underneath her feet, and the heat was ferocious. Even with the glasses on, the ochre and beige of the shifting sand had squeezed up to a dazzling silica whiteness. Not a breath of air stirred. She walked towards the edge of the road while the sun, directly overhead, felt like a hot pressing weight on her skull. She picked up the gauntlet by a finger, shaking it just in case there was anything out here that might have crawled inside for shelter. A few grains of sand poured out, nothing more. The gauntlet was light and papery, completely denuded of any moisture. It had the look of a piece of leather that had been lying in the open for months, rather than days, though from the letters scrawled on the cowling of the bike, it couldn't have been more than a couple of days at most. She turned the glove over, peeling back the flap at the wrist. The letters WW had been inked in ball-point on the lining.

Billy Walker had been here Somehow he'd made it down the hill and across the desert. She scanned the road ahead, but the heat-haze was so strong she couldn't see more than a quarter of a mile before the land broke up into wavering liquid. If he'd come across this road, and if the gauntlets were the first he'd shed since setting out from the cool of the hills, then he must have come at night, or in the early morning before the sun became so malignant.

She went back to the car, still clutching the glove, a link with other humans. The heat on the top of her skull made her feel that her hair was on fire and that it was burning through into her brain. She reached the door, turned to ease herself inside, and a sudden pain lanced up her calf, almost tumbling her to the road. A cry almost escaped, quickly bitten back and she looked down. Her shoe was stuck in the melted bitumen. When she'd turned, her foot had remained where it was, twisting her leg as she'd moved. Very slowly she eased it up and out, pulling up toffee-like strands of tar that smelt oily and somehow prehistoric. The twisting pain eased off and she gingerly eased herself onto the seat.

'What is it?'

'A glove. The people on the bike came this way.'

'If they're walking, they're in trouble, unless they had some water,' he said, quite astutely. 'If we find them do you think they'll help us?'

'I hope so. Maybe we can help each other.' She got the car moving again, eyes scanning the road ahead.

'That looks like water on the road, but it's just a merger ... I mean a mirage. Our teacher told us that.'

'That's right. It's because the air gets all hot and twisted. It's like looking in a fairground mirror. Everything gets all shimmery.'

'It makes me want another drink,' he said wistfully, but she could tell he wasn't really asking. Peter didn't have that level of dishonesty. If he wanted a drink, he'd come out and ask, but she'd seen him give Judith a drink and take less for himself. He wouldn't ask at all unless he was desperate.

'It should get better,' she told him, more in hope than expectation, although on this road, things changed so quickly that the desert might end a mile or so further on. On the other hand, the niggle of pessimism whispered, it could go on forever. It was a possibility, though not one she really believed, though the arid

253

and bleached wasteland could go on for hundreds of miles. On either side, stretching to each horizon, the great waves of the sand dunes rolled on forever while ahead, the road cut a swathe through them and disappeared into the whorls of tortured heat-spun shimmers. But above the low mirage sparkles she could see the faint outline of the far-off interchange, ghostly in the haze, almost insubstantial, but solid enough to know that it was still in front of her. For some reason, she felt as if the vast road network was pulling her inexorably towards it.

At least the desert must end there, she told herself, though the thought held no comfort.

The hiss from the engine was louder now, a protest of over-heated water in the radiator leaking out through a faulty seal. It was not bad yet, but worrying enough. She stepped on the gas a little and pushed onwards. The big dunes were now getting progressively smaller, but the sand was more powdery here and the waves were creeping further out across the road surface, forcing her to weave past them again and a couple of times there was enough sand on the road for her to feel the back wheels spin as they slipped on the powdery surface, making her heart leap in anguish at the thought of breaking down. She forced the car on by power of concentration more than anything else and the dunes subsided, gradually levelling out, now talcum-soft mounds. The wheels no longer rasped across gritty sand; they whispered along, muffled by the deadening of the dust, making it seem as if they were floating. Behind them the billowing tawny contrail rolled high into the still air. Patsy steered round one narrow part of the road where a hillock of sand had crept over the surface, the motion stirring up a whirlwind of powder and then she was through the gap. Just ahead, the highway took the first bend in miles of straight and she followed the curve until she emerged between two sandy hummocks onto flat land again.

The scene ahead defied imagination. Miles in the distance, though how far she could not tell in the warped and turbulent air, the desert ended in red hills. She could see the russet spires and pillars of the heights standing against the sickly pearl glare of the sky. They were fragile and eroded, she could see that, even at the distance. To one side, the arches of the interchange wavered and danced, enticing her on, but the intervening distance they had to travel to reach the shelter of the hills was a burning wasteland that challenged comprehension. Ahead of her stretched the plane of Death Valley, of the Namib, of the Atacama Desert. It was completely flat, so level that it appeared concave, a vast plate of desert, an enormous pan in which the searing heat of the malignant sun was trapped and focused. It was almost featureless, apart from fingers of sand-polished rock which pointed out of the ground, the extremities of buried stone giants clawing their way to the surface. The sun must have moved, because there were shadows at the bases of the standing stones, so dark in contrast to the searing silica-white that they looked like black holes.

Patsy's heart quailed. The road cut straight across the pan, a black thread that stretched towards the mountains but disappeared into the haze after only a mile or so. Even through the sunglasses the sky seemed to be writhing in its own heat, as if the very air was trying to get away and find some shade. In seconds, the heat almost doubled. Sweat poured out of every pore and she could feel it collecting behind her heel, precious fluid with her vital body salts. She didn't know if she could make it to the mountains, but she knew she had to try. The needle on the gauge told her she had less than half a tank, but more than enough to get there. The hiss from the radiator was louder, but there was no sign of steam coming up through the grille.

Judith moaned, a quiet, pitiful sound. She shook her head from side to side.

'Give her a drink,' she told Peter. 'And take one yourself.'

He didn't say anything and she wondered if he had fallen asleep. She was about to turn round to check on him (praying he was just asleep and not unconscious) when his hand reached slowly between the seats and took the bottle.

'Good boy,' she said. 'Take a good drink, but not too much.'

The metal scraped on glass. Patsy heard him cajole his sister, urging her not to spill any, then heard him take a drink himself.

'It's warm,' he said. 'But it's still good.'

The inside of her mouth was doing that little crawling dance of anticipation again. He passed the bottle through to her and this time she knew she would have to take some liquid. She could not risk fainting on this stretch of the road. The water was warm and it had lost all of its fizz, but it went down her dry throat like the sweetest balm.

'We can shade in the hills,' Peter said.

'That's what I'm aiming for. And we should get a drink there too.'

'It gets cooler up high, so it won't be so warm.'

'Get that in school?'

'No. But there's always snow up on the top of mountains, so it must be colder.'

'Anywhere's colder than here.'

'Do you know where we are?'

Patsy thought about her reply. Peter wasn't stupid. She opted for the truth. 'Haven't a clue.'

'It's a weird place. Everything's different,' he said, and she could hear the heat exhaustion in his voice. 'She shouldn't have done it.'

No need to ask this time. 'No. She shouldn't. But we'll beat her.'

'You were angry. I heard you use that word. The one you say I'm not to say.'

She was too hot, and too anxious to be embarrassed. 'And you're still not to say it either. That's for big people and emergencies only.'

Behind her he grinned and part of her felt it. That mutinous smile tried again and almost made it. He leaned over and nuzzled her cheek. His skin was hot and child-soft. In front of them the mountains shimmered.

'I spy with my little eye something beginning with M.'

'Mountains,' she guessed.

'No. That's too obvious.'

'More sand?'

'No, silly.'

'Mummy grinding her teeth impatiently?'

This time he laughed out loud and it was as much a tonic as the drink of water had been. 'No. Give in?'

'Okay. I give in. Tell me.'

'Mirages again.' Peter leaned over and pointed ahead of them, sweeping his hand to the right.

Ahead of them the road disappeared into a lake of shimmering

256

light and on either side the mirage sparkled and coruscated like waves of molten silver. The heat rose perceptibly, making the air almost unbreathable. Patsy put her arm out into the slipstream and felt hardly any difference as the air buffeted her skin. It was like a cauldron of heat. The sun seared her skin as if it had painted her with caustic bleach. The malignant radiance of the sun, even seen from the heights, had made it look sick and diseased and instantly her mind had associated it with contamination. At home, the depleted ozone layer was bad enough, threatening skin cancer to sun worshippers. That was back home. Here, that bloated orb might infect her with devastating melanoma, disfiguring and gnawing carcinoma. She drew her arm back in again quickly as her skin began to pucker.

Ahead and to the side of them the mirages danced, a chorus of dazzling translucent shapes, twisting and writhing just above the surface of sand or road. Tiny dust devils, whirlwinds of heat, spiralled upwards, pirouetting in little helixes of urgent motion as the unbearable heat drew the air into swirling updraughts.

Judith whined, high and keening. Peter turned towards her.

'Is she all right?'

'I think so. She's just hot. She's all sweaty.'

All of a sudden, the girl screamed, and Patsy swerved off the road and onto the sand.

'Come now,' she cried aloud. 'Dabbat, Achor, Loki.' The strange words came out in a tumble.

'Oh God, she's delirious,' Patsy blurted.

'Burn forever in searing fire,' Judith screeched. She was lying back, eyes screwed shut, hands pushing out in front of her. She opened her mouth wide just as Patsy turned in her seat, but instead of a scream, out came a babble of guttural sounds and fricative rasping. At first it sounded as if she was choking, but then Patsy realised she was speaking in another language. An appalling sense of dread shivered through her. She'd heard the sound before, the rasping, throaty consonants, almost hissing.

Kerron Vaunche had flung her spittle at her and then she'd made a sign and babbled at her in that same brutal way of speaking, and they'd found themselves on this appalling road.

'Stop it,' she cried. 'Peter, make her stop.' The sound of the words had sent a superstitious dread right through her.

'Come on, Judy. Wake up,' Peter urged. He grabbed his sister under the armpits and lifted her up to a seated position. The girl's head lolled and her pigtail stuck out at an angle that would have been comical, but wasn't. The rasping monologue continued, a high-pitched jabber. Peter shook Judith quite violently and the girl's eyes fluttered open. It was as if she'd been slapped. She jerked back, face red with heat and internal pressure and her mouth drooped open. Peter let her go and moved back. Judith scrambled up to her knees, grasped the back of the seat. Her eyes widened further, big and luminous in her suffused face. She pointed ahead.

'Look now.'

They looked.

The dust-devils and the mirages had merged into a writhing phalanx of shapes, like a tightly focused series of small sand-storms that whirled and twisted in what seemed like a solid barrier in front of them.

'*Patseee . . .!*'

A whispering voice scraped on the inside of her skull.

'*Patseeee . . .!*' It was the dry sound of trickling sand, thousands of grains rubbing against each other, forming a word. The sense of abject dread ballooned.

Judith began to jabber again.

'*Ssso sssweeet, ssso sssoft.*'

The barrier of whirling dust and twinkling reflection coalesced, solidified, became a throng of individual shapes writhing and contorting. Little tendrils of sand, little *tentacles* of sand reached out sinuously from the mass, licking towards the car. For a second she was frozen, unable to react, paralysed by an almost incandescent surge of terror.

Behind her Judith was screaming at the top of her lungs, both hands clamped against her ears while her whole body arched up from the seat, rigid and quivering with tension. Peter had his arms around her and was shouting fit to burst, telling her not to be scared.

'It's not *true*,' he bellowed furiously. 'It's only pretend stuff.'

The car was hurtling towards the semi-circle of dust-shapes. Inside her head the scaly, slithery-dry voices were scratching at her mind, leeching her away. It was like being sucked dry. It was like a mental rape and she could do nothing about it. Everything was happening at once, every sense was searingly open and unprotected. She could hear Judith screeching and Peter shouting her down and the slither of dusty thoughts inside her own.

The writhing shapes were dead ahead, a semi-circle of twisting desert shadows. She could see the hollows of eyes and the caverns of wide mouths as one form melded with another, swelled and contorted and became something else. It was a swarm of reaching, clawing contorted ghosts, solid yet insubstantial, roiling towards her, ready to swallow them all up.

She couldn't move. Her hands were clenched in a death-grip on the wheel and her foot was frozen on the pedal. Inside her head the invasion of voices were squabbling and chaffing.

'*Come to usss, Patsssseee. Ssstay with usss. Give up the offering.*'

A shape coalesced and she saw a face, dark hollows for eyes, deep hollows under cheek-bones. The sand roiled above and around them, like tumbling hair, and she saw the face of Kerron Vaunche drawn in the fine grains and she heard among the scrabbling whispers of enticement, the scrape of the witch's voice.

Beside the moving shape, another one fused and rolled, became a skull with grinning clenched teeth and eerie bony shoulders. Behind the witch-shape she saw the face of the roadside policeman, long and lugubrious, grinning vacuously.

Terror and anger catalysed in an incandescent eruption within her. Her foot was just about to come off the accelerator and stamp on the brake when something else made her kick down on the pedal. Peter yelled out in surprise and tumbled off his seat. The car lurched forward, heading straight towards the seething mass of sand-shapes, sand-*demons*.

'*Ssssuck you dry, Patseee. We thirsssst!*'

The sand-grain voices clamoured louder, jostling and gnawing for her attention.

Something reached out from the mass, a long tenuous arm and swiped at the car. She heard the sussuration of sand rasping on the paintwork, like the hissing of a desert snake. She howled something completely inarticulate and aimed for the centre of the shapes.

In a second the car was completely engulfed. Judith screeched so high and clear the sound had the texture of fine glass.

'*Ssscorch you. Dry you up.*'

'Get out of my head!' Her mind bellowed at them.

'*Sssuck you dry, Patssee.*'

'Get you out of my mind. Damn you to hell.' It was a scream, a screech, an explosion from deep inside her. The car shot into the sand-crowd and the world went dark.

Everything moved in slow motion. Long dry fingers poked and prodded at her. A withered palm cupped her chin and she could feel the moisture of her sweat draining from her. Grainy fingers raked, surprisingly gently but foully repugnant, through her hair. Grains of sand rasped against her sunglasses, abraded her throat and scraped on the lining inside her nose. Grit sandblasted under the rims and scraped on her eyelids. Sand was in her ears, pouring into her and the voices like distant shingle on an ebb tide clamoured and bleated in sibilant appeal.

'Get you GONE!'

A grindstone screech raked the car, gaining in intensity until it was a jet-engine scream. Tears smarted in Patsy's eyes and her teeth ground together as pain ballooned in her ears. The unearthly voices scored the inside of her head and then, so abruptly it felt as if her eardrums had burst, they were gone. The sand-demons, whatever the writhing grain shapes had been were gone. She was beyond them, hurtling on a clear road across a flat pan towards the mountains looming before her.

Judith coughed, began to splutter. Peter clapped her on the back and his sister hauled in a clean breath.

'Hear people,' she said, gasping. 'In my head. Hear Catanna.'

'No, it was just pretend things,' Peter said.

'Gone now,' Judith insisted, but her voice trailed away. Patsy's eyes swung to the rear-view mirror. Behind them she could see the billowing cloud thrown up by the speed of their passing. Beyond that she could see nothing. It was as if she had imagined the whole thing.

But you didn't, the internal voice whispered insistently. Judith had heard them. Even Peter had heard something. She had seen Kerron Vaunche in a twist of wind-whirled sand and she had heard her dry rustle of laughter and she had known that witch had been leering at her.

'Witch,' she said to herself. 'Gone now.'

But they'll be back, her inside self warned. She shivered.

The road ran straight for the hills, now suddenly and miraculously close. It was as if the distance, like the twinkling tortured air that looked like pools of water, had been a mirage. The desert sand changed as quickly as it had transformed after she'd come down from the heights. In moments the powder on the road changed to fine sand and then a coarse red grit and finally it cleared from the surface altogether. On either side – and now the road was no longer a dual carriageway; now it was a two-way stretch of wilderness throughway – the grit became shale, became shingle. The shingle turned into jagged boulders and the boulders to tumbled rocks. Imperceptibly the land began to rise. She drove up an incline and down the lee in a small scooped gully. Beside the road, the red rock bore the odd blankets of greasy succulents clinging low to the surface. Here and there, out of the corner of her eye, she'd catch a blink-quick motion that could have been a lizard and might have been something else. The sun had swung way to the right (*hadn't it been overhead just moments ago?*) and was now casting longer shadows. The buttes, great staggering pillars of stones, like piles of balanced copper pennies of different ages, towered supernaturally slender, stretching for the sky.

Monument Valley, she thought. That's what it's like.

'I've seen this place before,' Peter said, echoing her thought with uncanny precision. 'In that book on the wonders of the world. Remember? It's in America.'

'I remember,' Patsy said. It wasn't Monument Valley. Here the wind-eroded bluffs and palisades craned in a huddle, like the trunks of colossal trees rubbing stony shoulders with each other. They were more slender than the craggy old men of the Badlands.

Badlands. The thought almost brought a peal of hysterical laughter. These were badlands indeed. Evil lands. Wicked lands. These were lands which should never have existed in all of creation.

'Are we in America then?' Peter asked, irrepressible.

'I don't think so.'

'That's a shame,' he went on. 'We could go to Disney World. Dad said we could go there sometime, but he wouldn't even go fishing.'

261

Unbelievably, despite the unalloyed psychotic terror that had paralysed her only moments before, Patsy actually grinned. She risked a quick turn to look at her son, heart almost bursting with gratitude for bringing a touch of childlike normality back to them. She had driven through a nightmare and come out the other side and all Peter wanted to do was go see Mickey Mouse. She could have grabbed him and hugged him until his ribs creaked. He looked back at her, wide-eyed and bare-faced and wondered why his mother was laughing.

'Believe me, I'll take you both to Disney World. It's a promise.'

'Cubs honour?'

'Cross my heart,' she said, and actually did so, and as soon as she made that little cruciform motion on her breastbone, a sunny lightness flamed in her heart, as if she'd been granted a wish.

'And we'll all go fishing,' she said. 'Your rod's still in the box. We'll go fishing on our first picnic.'

They crossed the first shadow of the mountains and the heat of the desert died.

'Bet there's Apaches here,' Peter observed, though Patsy thought he was too young to have heard of them.

The road swung due north and then south, snaking between the monstrous stacks. The pillars of stone loomed precariously, blotting out the sky. A wind moaned through the crevasses between them, a miraculously cool breeze. Here and there, at the foot of the bluffs, scrawny grasses and cacti like giant spiny hands, arthritically knobbled, clenched the air. There were holes in the rock, dark eyes of stone and Patsy could feel eyes upon her, though the internal sense, like a mental radar, told her the watchers, whatever they were, were too far away to be harmful. Every now and then, out of sight, perhaps high overhead, a bird would caw harshly and the rasping cry would reverberate from bluff to pillar to stack until the whole of the stand of pillars and scarps vibrated with the cacophony.

The shade deepened, but was never truly dark. Now and again a pebble, sometimes a larger stone, would come tumbling down from on high, dislodging a small avalanche of russet sandstone. Once or twice a single stone would drop from an overhang and smash itself to powder on the surface, but none of the debris hit the car.

'I'm hungry,' Peter said. 'My stomach's talking to me.'

'What's it saying?' Patsy asked, leaning forward to watch the road and scan as high up on the crags as she could, just in case.

'Feed me, Peter,' he said, voice dropping down an octave, giving her a hint of how her son would sound when he was a man. It was remarkably like his Uncle Carrick. 'Feed me *NOW!*'

As soon as he said it his belly rumbled quite loudly and he burst into peals of helpless laughter.

'We'll find a place soon, but I don't want to stop in these shadows.'

'Better than in all that sand. That was creepy. I didn't like the way the sand blew about. It looked like people, and when it scraped on the car, it sounded like whispering.'

'And it was hot,' Patsy said, forcing her mind away from the image of moving, shape-shifting sand.

'Sweltering,' he said. 'Can we really stop and eat?'

'Soon as we find a clear space,' she promised.

But it took them another hour to get through the shadows of the mountains, though nothing happened on the twisting road. The end of the stacks came as abruptly as the desert had ambushed them. One minute they were weaving between the scarps and next they were out in the light again. The road dropped through the moraine of scree where thorn bushes clung for a precarious living. As they headed downslope something moved close to the road and Patsy saw a huge goat atop a flat rock. It turned its head to look at the car as it passed, a powerful, shaggy beast with a beard that trailed towards the ground. The horns were massive and ridged, great tightening spirals that curved under each eye and knifed out from the cheeks. The whole body turned to follow the motion and it shook its head. There was something about the creature that gave Patsy a shiver, but it was not until she was halfway down the hill that her conscious mind sorted out the information she'd taken in at one brief glance and the sudden knowledge made her stomach shrivel to a tight ball.

The goat on the rock had turned on its thick legs, but it hadn't moved on hooves. The shaggy forelegs had not ended on cloven hooves at all. A pair of wide and spatulate human hands had been gripping the stone.

By the time she had retrieved the memory, they were easing to the bottom of the hill and the needle was falling below the halfway mark. The scree ended and the land sloped away, gradually flattening to a series of low hills. At first Patsy thought she was heading into desert again, because at first there was no vegetation on the verges. Three miles further along the road, she saw the first car in a long time. It was well off the road. She wouldn't have seen it until she was past if it hadn't been for the deep parallel tracks gouged into the dirt on the edge.

The car had gone swerving off. Not a car, she saw now as she approached. It was more like a tow-truck. A heavy rusted hook, big enough to catch a killer whale, dangled from the gantry at the back and the truck itself had ploughed its way down to the axles in the ground.

A movement caught her eye and for a moment she thought someone was coming out of the driver's door. But it was only the wind fluttering the leaves of a plant that had grown up around the car and was using it to climb towards the light. The sun was now halfway down the sky, painting the horizontal layers of atmosphere with a bizarre spectrum of purples and greens, and in that light she saw the emerald of the succulent plant woven and interwoven around the cabin of the half-submerged truck. The stems were thick and ropy, snakelike and somehow wet. All around the truck there was no plant life on the rocky soil, yet somehow this creeper had found a place to feed. An image of lampreys with sucking mouths, of leeches bloating on blood came fleeting to mind and she recoiled from it. She dragged her eyes away just as she caught another movement. For suddenly she was not sure whether it *had* been the wind plucking at a leaf, or whether the plant had moved by itself. It might have moved. It might indeed have shifted position.

Patsy just didn't want to see that.

She kept the car straight on the road, reached the flat and more fertile plain where a tangle of greenery now crowded up against the roadside and she was back on a dual carriageway again. The road had changed from single to double in the blink of an eye before she even noticed it. She got as far as she could from the scree until she found a flat and level place where the road was straight and pulled in to the side. Peter woke Judith

264

and then got the camping stove out. There was enough water in the kettle for some soup and a plate of instant potatoes which could have done with some salt. Judith ate slowly, sitting with her head cocked to the side, as if her mind was far away. Patsy wanted to speak to her, but held back. Her daughter was still sickly and there was a strangeness about her that scared her mother. She just watched, worried. Peter wolfed his food.

Back on the road Patsy drove for another half an hour. The sun plummeted towards the horizon and night fell like a dead weight.

265

17

A disturbingly mottled aurora flickered in veils of orange and purple smearing the sky to the east in layers of somehow virulent hues. The unwholesome light show lasted for five minutes or so and then flicked out, drenching the sky with darkness. Patsy switched on the lights. Far in the distance they picked out the square of a sign and threw the beams back at her and the flicker of hope stirred. A few seconds later she passed it by, leaning over the wheel to make out what it said, but it was completely illegible. Some of the letters had either fallen off, or the roadside painter hadn't done his job properly. The black lettering, stark against the white background looked like a children's word puzzle.

'*H*-something *-o-c-k*' Peter spelled out. 'It says Hock.'

The sign indicated a divergence somewhere ahead, but nothing to show how far.

'Blank-blank-*vices* . . .' he continued. 'Maybe it's a garage. Dad used to have a vice in the garage.'

'You could be right,' Patsy told him, though there was something about the blanks where the letters should have been that niggled at her memory. It looked familiar. She tried to think back, but just then she saw, way off to the left behind the low hills, a moon rising as swiftly as the sun had set. The curve of the hills were ridged in a coppery green as the arch of the moon began to ascend above them.

'The moon's all green,' Peter said, enthralled.

'It's made of green cheese.'

The road swung on a broad bend, coming round to face east, directly at the hills. The verdigris colour, the shade of mould, but luminous, as if it was somehow radioactive, was spreading as the orb swung upwards, fast enough for the motion to be observed.

Patsy was driving straight towards the moonrise. In the mirror, a searing afterpulse of sickly light flared in the sky, as if something had exploded in the sun way down beyond the horizon. She blinked quickly then looked ahead just as the moon cleared the hills. It was as bloated as the sun had been but feverishly phosphorescent, the colour now changing from the mouldy green to a hot red-orange. Despite it being three-quarters full, it was not quite round, but somehow flattened. For a moment the pattern of the shadows of plains and craters on its swollen surface looked like the rugged moonscape she'd known since childhood. Her eyes started to swing away from it then snapped right back.

The face on the moon was different. It was not the vaguely melancholy, somewhat placid countenance she'd always known.

The moon was glaring at her. There was no other word for it.

Rising in an obsidian sky was the flattened oblong of a moon with the face of madness and Patsy's hands clenched on the wheel in a sudden fright that was somehow more intense than the twist of fearsome unreality she'd experienced when she'd seen the hands on the end of the goat's shaggy legs. That had been a mutation, she knew, some sort of witchery, some sort of black magic that had changed the goat to suit this godforsaken place. But the moon was a glaring cretin, somehow mindless, completely malevolent. It reflected the sun's bitter light as a kind of contagion. The luminous reflection crept along the ridges of the low hills, tainting them in noxious splashes.

The crazy moon climbed on the sky. There was nothing vague about the mad glare. Whatever forces had created its scarred and pitted surface, they had combined to make a monstrosity. Two lunatic eyes under distorted brows pinioned her and the squashed head was twisted to one side as if it had melted in some incandescent cosmic cataclysm. The scarred mouth seemed to be pulled back in a savage snarl, and at one corner, a shadow drooled like saliva.

Trick of the light, her rational mind insisted, while the instinctive undermind gibbered in abject fear.

Words of a song sprang into her mind in a weird mental association. The bad moon was rising and there was trouble on the way. The superstitious trickle of foreboding shuddered down her back.

Trouble on the way, Patssseeee. Trouble *all* the way.

So don't go out tonight, the words jangled insistently as she tried to draw her eyes away from the virulent moon. *You're bound to lose your life.* That song had given her a shiver when she'd been small and the words had stuck in the recorder inside her brain, ready for an instant playback when the time was right, when the time was completely *wrong*. The poison light flowed in a tide over the low hills, creeping to fill the hollows with the luminescence of slimy squid in the deeps.

She was out tonight. Out with her children and there was trouble on the way. On the highway.

'It's different,' Peter said.

The moon floated higher, seemed to swing in the darkness and whatever ice or crystal was inside the craters, it gleamed red, the colour of blood in the putrid green of the surface. The shadows swung down from the mouth and she could see the jagged edges of teeth.

Mountains, Patsy insisted. They must be mountains.

But they looked like the teeth of some rabid animal, notched and serrated for rending and tearing. Such a mouth could swallow the car and not even notice. It could take a bite out of the world and burst it like an orange. She shook her head, flicking the idea away. This was witchcraft. It was an enchantment that made her see the moon as an appalling ogre afloat in a pitch-black sky.

It's a moon, she insisted, while at her core the small voice wailed in fear and utter belief, mimicking Judith's fevered whimper.

'Don't like the moon,' her daughter spoke up suddenly. 'Full moon for Erebus.' Her voice had that glassy quality, brittle and sharp. 'Son of chaos, brother of night.'

'Stop it,' Patsy snapped. It sounded like the litany of before, when Kerron had spoken direct through the radio. Judith stopped. Patsy looked up at the purple sky where the moon was rising. It was not full yet and something was nagging at her mind, demanding her attention.

Crandall Gilfeather had spelled it out, the importance of the moon.

She believes it, he'd said. *That's what matters.*

Patsy hadn't believed him then, but she knew now how right she was. She'd heard Kerron Vaunche on the radio, counterpointing the strange litany of names with Judith and she knew that whatever witchcraft the gypsy had begun, it was working here.

The full moon was when everything came into place, the great conjunction, the old man had said. The five dead days and in the midst of them, the Nameless Day.

When was it? When had they spoken? She glanced at her watch and realised the futility of that. The hands were all stuck at midnight now, though the little numbers signifying the date, in the little bubble of glass beside the quarter hour, they were ticking backwards, two for every second. More sorcery, more witchcraft, Patsy assumed. Either that, or time was different here on the road.

They had started out for Broadford House on the sixteenth of December. That had given them five days and Patsy had all her plans in place, a safe haven to hide herself and the children until after the new year when the day Crandall Gilfeather described was long past. Not even Carrick knew where she'd be headed. Patsy did a calculation, trying to work out exactly how long it had been and even that was difficult. So many things had happened since the flight from the havoc at the old house that it seemed like weeks ago, rather than days. They'd been on the road two full days now. This was their third night and the moon was showing nearly full.

She had another two days before the winter solstice, before the moon filled out.

That, Gilfeather had said, is when the Cailleach makes the sacrifice to the Fasgadh, Dark Lord, the guardian of all the ways. And that is the moment of greatest danger for your son and daughter.

She remembered her own question and the reply. *To keep her beauty, to keep her youth and to maintain her enormous power, the Carlin Woman must commune with the Prince of Shadows, and he will demand his price ... the soul of innocence, the seed of life. The Cailleach will use the flesh of her consort. It is the most powerful, most terrible ceremony of them all. Every great sin must be committed on the altar, every one.*

Two more days to go and Patsy knew they were being hunted. Under the glare of the lunatic moon, the sense of pursuit was even stronger. Instinctively she looked in the mirror again, scanning the road behind. For an instant she thought she saw a motion and her grip tightened harder, but it might have been a trick of the moonlight.

'It's just like a big Halloween cake,' Peter was telling Judith who had gone silent. 'Just stick your tongue out at it.'

He made a raspberry sound. 'Isn't it ugly?' Peter asked. He leaned forward and touched Patsy on the shoulder. 'Do you get this moon in America or is it the one we get?'

'I think it's the same as ours,' she said. 'We'll see when we get there.'

'I think we're there already. I think it's all done with computer graphics, like in *Terminator*.'

She wished it was. She knew it wasn't. *Keep going*, Patsy ordered herself. She pulled her eyes away from the noxious sight and the red-lava tinge at the corner of the jagged (*teeth*) mountains. The sickly light rolled across the moorland, flooding the runnels and gullies, washing towards her and suddenly she did not want that light to wash over them. It was as if the flood of luminescence was additional to the actual reflection of the sun on the moon's pocked surface. She shivered as another bolt of premonition went through her and she was instantly certain that if that bane light reached the car, it would infect them with its malignancy. It would melt their eyes out and make their skin drip. The sun had been bad enough, sick and desiccating with those cancerous blotches upon its face, but the moon was different. It was alive with contagion.

She pulled the visor down, hiding its face, and floored the pedal. Somewhere along this road there must be shelter. Maybe an overpass, she thought, or even an underpass. She flicked the headlamps on to full beam. They speared ahead, twin cones that picked out the shimmering condensation from the cooling road surface. The needle swung steadily up towards seventy and the moon rose higher. The leading edge of its illumination came sweeping forward, rippling over the hummocks, drooling through the culverts and ditches. The wheels thrummed on the road and her breath caught at the back of her throat.

There was no shelter. She was on an open road and she was hurtling straight towards that poisonous flood. She felt a groan begin to wind up at the back of her throat where her breath was caught in a knot. Behind her, Judith coughed violently, sending a fine spray onto her mother's cheek.

The car shot forward and the line came sweeping towards them. The engine roared and the wheels sang and Patsy gasped. They were going for it. It was coming for them. The line of light came surging along the road, painting everything a diseased green, flickering on the centre-line, about to swallow them up.

It flicked out and everything went black.

It was as if a curtain had been drawn across the night sky. The field of virulent light abruptly died as a black cloud rolled across the sky and swallowed the moon. The headlamps stabbed out straight ahead, opening the darkness, picking up the white line and the flickering reflectors at the side and the cat's-eyes in the dark spaces between the tracer-line in the centre.

Patsy's bated breath came out in a whoosh.

'The moon's gone,' Peter observed. 'Is there another storm coming?'

She couldn't answer him for a few moments. She was still jittery from the apprehension and her hands were gripped on the wheel tight enough to go into cramps. The muscles of her belly were kinked into knots and under that pressure she felt the real clench of woman's cramp that told her the next period was going to be painful.

'Can't say. It doesn't feel like it,' she finally managed.

'Weird looking moon,' Peter said. 'Like everything around here.'

'That's for sure.' She glanced at his reflection and he looked back, his eyes completely untroubled. The further they went along the road, the calmer Peter seemed to get, as if he, more than any of them, was able to accept the bizarre and the unearthly events of the past couple of days and live with them. His resilience amazed his mother.

'Will we be driving all night?'

'I hope not. We don't have enough fuel.'

'I haven't seen anywhere for petrol. Maybe it is a garage up ahead.'

'Keep your fingers crossed for us then,' Patsy told him. 'We could use some good luck.'

'I can cross my toes as well.'

271

Patsy almost laughed aloud, then bottled it up, because she was unsure just how the laugh would come out. She had a premonition that it would emerge shrill and somehow more like a scream and that once she started she might not be able to stop.

She slowed a little, glanced in the mirror, and froze. Behind her twin headlamps stabbed through the dark.

They were far enough away to be just bright pinpoints of light, and for a second Patsy thought they might have been static until they dimmed then brightened as if the vehicle had gone over a slight bump in the road. It was the first moving car – if it was indeed a car – she had seen in two days, since the massive trailer had tried to swipe them off the road.

She leaned forward and peered into the mirror. The lights seemed bigger, maybe a bit brighter. They had a yellowish hue, the way continental cars shine in the night. Apprehension squeezed at her again. All she could see were the twin points, bright in the darkness behind her, switched to full beam so that despite the distance, they were strong enough to be dazzling. She screwed her eyes up against their glare and tried to estimate distance.

A mile, maybe two behind her.

And who would be driving on this road in the dark? Would it be some lost stranger? Perhaps another family searching for a way off this benighted highway? It could, she tried to tell herself, be another woman, vulnerable and alone and needing help.

It might be, the jittery inner voice nagged. *It could very well be, Patsy girl, but is it likely?* Want to risk it? *Want to risk the children, eh?*

The beams sparkled, brighter again. It was gaining, travelling fast behind her. Her heart did a little flip and then beat harder. If it was a woman on this road, she would have seen Patsy's tail-lights up ahead, and a sane woman would have paused, wondering what to do about the other traveller, because she'd be scared. She'd be wondering the same thing, was there help or was there danger. If she was a normal woman, that is.

Patsy knew if she'd seen the red of night-lights up ahead, she'd have slowed on this road, even if she had never met Crandall Gilfeather, even if she had never heard of the Nameless Day

272

and the dreadful thing the gypsy witch intended. The headlamps swelled. It was moving up fast, trying to catch her.

Run! the inner voice bawled. Her heart kicked again, three times in rapid succession. Her foot went down on the pedal and the car shot forward, roaring round the bend on the road. The lights swept her own shadow across the visor.

'There's a car behind us,' Peter told her.

'I know, I saw it,' she said. 'Sit down and get your belt on.'

Without warning the radio coughed. Static spat and crackled and then the echoing voice came blasting out in a parody of the old Jeff Beck number.

... Everywhere and nowhere baby ... that's where you're at ...

A guitar screeched, raw with distortion then trailed away. All of this happened in the first two seconds. As soon as the sound had blasted out, Patsy jumped so high she almost cracked her head on the roof. Judith let out a searing howl. The guitar music stopped with a sudden click.

Anchor of the shadows. The words hissed and it sounded like Kerron Vaunche, but much older, a dry crackle of a voice.

'Claim your own,' Judith responded automatically.

'Quit that, Judy,' Peter yelped. 'Don't talk to her.'

Patsy reached to hit the switch. As soon as her fingers touched the control a cold spark snapped at her fingers, numbing them dead. The radio light went out and Judith made a small choking sound. The frigid cold seeped up to Patsy's wrist before it began to fade away.

Peter's shape was just a silhouette in the glare of the lights. He ducked down and she heard the safety belt snick home, first on Judith's catch and then on his. The rev-counter swung up the dial as she took the curve on the road fast as she could. The distance markers went from three or two, to one. The lights behind winked out, cut off by the curve. Right then the exit ramp cut away from the main road and without thinking Patsy pulled on the wheel and they soared up the slope. The headlamps, now a pale orange as the distance lessened, illuminated the road behind, though the car was not yet visible round the curve. On an impulse, Patsy killed her own lights and the world went black, but she had got to the top of the slope. The car's own momentum carried them up and over and down the far side, travelling blind. Once in the lee of the hill, Patsy hit the lights again and the beams stabbed out. A crash barrier loomed right in front of them and she hauled on the wheel, swerving away from it and missing the galvanised steel by inches. The road followed a tight curve, disappeared under an overpass that stood on solid concrete pillars and emerged to swoop towards another merger.

About a mile ahead, the lights of a service station beckoned. Behind her she heard the faint rumble of a car moving at speed. She held her breath, listening for a change in pitch. The noise got louder and for a bad moment she was convinced that whatever was racing behind her had followed her up the slip road. The skin on the back of her neck crawled with anticipation. Any second now the yellow lights would blaze behind her, blinding in the mirror. She felt her fingers tighten involuntarily on the wheel and then, incredibly, the noise of pursuit crested and then began to wane.

The gypsy and her people (*it could have been no-one else*) had continued along the straight. The vibration diminished until it faded completely. Patsy steered down the curve of the slope, now able to concentrate on her own driving. Her lights swept across the shadows beyond the verge as the car took the turn, picking out the gorse and scrub alder beyond the barrier, then the straggly birches in a field.

They panned across the twisted steeple of the old church.

Patsy's mouth fell open. They were back on that slope again.

The headlamps swept across the crumbling old church, picking out the cracks and crevices of the masonry, spotlighting the crippled old steeple now hanging so far beyond the perpendicular it was a miracle it hadn't toppled through the sagging roof.

Not a miracle! The inner voice spoke up. Miracles were the province of saints and angels. There was nothing holy about that church. Whatever force kept the steeple from crashing through the ridged slates, it was anything but miraculous.

As the beams swung across the decayed stonework she got a glimpse, nothing more, of the contorted ropes of ivy which smothered the entire tower and much of the roof, tangling it in woody hawsers now growing rampant and reaching out to cover the whole building. In that brief flash, she saw, through the foliage, the arch of one of the gothic windows. The flickering light inside was bright, more powerful, as if whatever was inside of the dead church was stronger now than before. It flared suddenly, sending lines of its bale-light into the sky, tinged a deep red. It was as if the light inside there was shining through glass that was dripping with blood.

The headlamps swept on beyond the church. There was still an afterglow of red in the corner of her eye but Patsy refused to let it draw her eyes back. The beams brushed the ancient cemetery, illuminating the tumbled, moss-covered stones, swung past them across the field.

The scarecrow stood garrotted by her lights, one arm thrown out towards her, one stick leg frozen in mid-stride. It was only ten yards from the edge of the road. The halogen headlights revealed the face in sharp detail. Patsy's open mouth shut with a snap.

It was the face of the mad moon.

The sockets of the eyes blazed in a ferocious glare, and in their depths, something glittered poisonously. The mouth was stretched in a crazed rictus, showing two rows of jagged teeth. Even the ball-shape was oddly squashed. The face on the scarecrow was the one that had glowered from the sky and flooded the land with pestilence.

The lights flashed across it and she saw, in that split second, the motion of the shadows made the jaw seem to open, a jaw carved in a turnip or a pumpkin, and she could look no more. Her hand reached automatically and snapped the lights off. For an instant everything went as black as before and she was driving into infinity, but then the baleful light of the church now behind her, gave just enough sick illumination for her to drive by. She knew she hadn't gone crazy, switching off the headlights on a curve in the road in the dark. Under any other circumstances, to have done so would be the height of madness, risking herself and the children. But if she hadn't killed the lights, she would have been speared on that insane glare, unable to pull away from it. It would have harpooned her and dragged her across the barrier and into the field and it would have had them there forever. The red glare from behind showed the shadow of the car on the road, stretched out in front of her, then rising up on the wall of an underpass. Somewhere to the left, in the darkness of the oak tree field she heard the harsh cawing of the carrion birds. They were fighting and squabbling over something. Probably the occupants of another car lured into the stony field by the mad glare of the scarecrow. She ignored the clamour, drove through the underpass and out the other side.

The lights of the service station were gone. It was as if she had entered the short tunnel and emerged in a completely different place. Above them the clouds parted just a little to let in some of the bleak light of the moon, then closed again like a heavy curtain. Everything went black.

Patsy flicked on the lights again. They stabbed out ahead of her on a long straight road, picking out the cat's-eyes on the broken centre-line. They were past the unholy church and the blood-light flickering in its windows, they were away from the scarecrow that was getting closer every time she passed that field. Gratitude to whatever power was on her side on this hellish road welled up within her. She let her breath out in a long sigh.

And then the cat's-eyes *moved*.

It happened so quickly that for an instant it didn't register. There was a movement on the road, as if one of the reflectors had slipped out of position. Her eyes followed the direction of the motion. One of the reflectors was out of position, right off the centre-line. She was about to look away when the twin glare suddenly jinked, very fast back to the centre and then several feet past it.

'What the . . .?' she blurted.

The moving lights winked out, came back on again and suddenly changed from white to a searing orange.

Beyond it the next set of eyes flickered, went dark and then whizzed almost to the edge of the road. Underneath the reflectors her own headlamps picked out a pale blurring motion. Her foot came off the accelerator, and the car slowed. The first moving cat's-eye stud flickered past her. Something hit the rear wheel arch with a metallic clatter. For an instant Patsy was more puzzled than alarmed. She'd seen the reflectors broken at the side of the road where they'd been jarred free of their housing by heavy tyres, and for that instant she assumed that she'd come across a few loose ones which hadn't been kicked to the edge by passing cars.

'What was that?' Peter asked quickly. 'Did we hit something?'

'Only a cat's-eye,' she told him. He craned up behind her. Patsy looked ahead, down the centre-line. The twin reflectors, exactly like animal eyes in the beam of the headlamps, stretched on down the road until they dwindled beyond the reach of the beams. Apart from the one which had flickered off line, they were all exactly positioned on the lane edges, between the tracery of the white marker lines. She was about to tell him to sit back down when the road ahead simply erupted in a bewildering whirl of lights. As if a special current had been switched on, all of the reflectors went from white to that searing orange-yellow. For a fraction of a second they stretched out in front of the car in two exactly regimented lines on either side of the car, diminishing with distance. A moment later they were wheeling around on the road in a constellation of motion.

For that split second Patsy was completely disoriented. She had been guiding them by the lines of cat's-eyes and then she was plunged into a galaxy of swirling light. Her hands clenched on the wheel and the car plunged into the dancing pinpoints. There was nothing she could do. The whole road ahead was seething with movement, the entire surface heaving. White shapes flickered and tumbled under the orange eyes, pallid outlines barely visible in the glare. Something crunched under a tyre and a stone-saw shriek shivered the car. Another shape clattered against the front end. A third hit the door with a squeal of chalk down a blackboard.

'What's happening?' Peter asked. 'What are all those lights?'

Patsy couldn't answer. She was concentrating on staying on the road, trying to ignore the heaving motion on the surface, keeping her eyes fixed on the painted white line.

'Look at that,' Peter trumpeted, leaning past her, pointing at the phenomenon before them. 'It's like the crabs on Christmas Island.'

A shape scuttered on the roadside just in front of the car and Patsy's stomach tried to loop itself inside out. She gulped against the blurt of nausea. She had only a glimpse of the moving shape, but it had been perfectly delineated in the flat white light and that glimpse had been enough.

Whatever the cat's-eyes had been before, they were now moving on the road like glaring ghostly spiders. The one she had seen was turning in a tight spin, moving away towards the lane-line and then rushing in on a collision course with the front of the car. The eyes, level with the pale body had dimmed, then blared blank saffron. The white stud, the part that had been visible on the road surface, was like a carapace, curved over the eyes. It floated on a clutch of scrabbling and jointed legs and above it, two appendages, finger thick and oddly articulated, flagged the air.

'I saw them on *Naturewatch*,' Peter said, agog with wonder. There was no fear in his voice. 'They're land crabs. Millions of 'em. They live in holes in the ground.'

Patsy was only dimly aware of what he was saying. Ahead of them the road was a seething mass of spidery creatures whirling and wheeling, all of them glaring at the car as it ploughed through them.

An absolute and utter horror welled up in a black tide.

'Oh, Jesus,' she bleated, unaware that she had even spoken.

One of the crawling shapes jumped up from the road, bewilderingly quick, hit the front of the car and went spinning off in a tumbling tangle of pale legs. Another came scuttling in from the side and flashed upwards. She saw it in her peripheral vision moving in a pallid blur. It hit just above the front wheel. A white, sharp shape lanced out and smacked against the flat metal above the engine, loud enough to send a vibration through the whole car. An array of legs scrambled for purchase and she saw that the semaphoring front palp was not what she'd thought. It was a long, jointed arm which ended in a spiked crab-claw. Underneath the flattened carapace, a fat, pulsating abdomen drooped, giving the beast a hybrid appearance that could have been spider or crab or both. The second claw came whacking down, hooking for purchase.

'Oh, please no,' Patsy whimpered. The thing turned and its round, close-set eyes, hooded by a ridge of thick and jagged shell glared at her. There was no intelligence there, only a desperate and mindless hunger. The nearside wheel ran over an obstruction and the car juddered. The thing on the bonnet flicked off, legs scrambling at the air, still trying to get a grip.

'*Spider!*' Judith's screech was so high and crystalline it made the windows resonate in sympathy.

Patsy jerked back at the sound and the car lurched violently as the motion pulled the wheel to the side. A pair of orange eyes were glaring against the window. Stretched out on either side, the thin stalks of legs or claws were scratching at the window for purchase. Under the eyes, a dark space yawned wide.

The violent motion of the car threw Judith away from the thing and she tumbled backwards into Peter, still screaming about a spider.

'Oh, dear Jesus,' Patsy bawled again. Even over the high-pitched screech behind her, she could hear the hard rasp of chitinous legs scratching for a grip. The tyres squealed as the car started to slip sideways and she was thrown against the door. Patsy yanked at the wheel and by sheer change the car did not spin, but came back right on line. Out of the corner of her eye, she saw the white crabby thing flick away from the window. Another one came flying upwards, hit off the pillar at the edge of the windscreen with a crack that made her think the glass had shattered and her fear soared at the thought of the things clambering inside. But the glass did not break. A piece of the crawler broke off and slid right across the glass while the rest tumbled away into the slipstream. A yellow slime drooled across the screen in little trails, blown by the wind and without any evidence – though that would come later – she knew that whatever the turbid liquid was, it was poisonous.

Patsy's mouth opened and closed. Ahead of her the road was alive with the things. There were thousands of them. Their putrid orange eyes glared up from the surface. More of them were hauling themselves out of the pits on the farside lanes, all holding their claws aloft like threatening crabs, while they jinked and scrabbled, not with the sideways motion of the true crab, but with the jittery, rushing gait of a wolf-spider. The glowing, unblinking eyes high up above the swollen abdomens amplified the picture.

'*Spiders,*' Judith screamed again. They were crabs or they were spiders, cat's-eyes come alive by whatever sorcery ruled in this place and there were thousands of them for as far as the head-lamps could reach, hordes of the scuttering things now all focused on their one car hurtling down the highway. It was the very stuff of Patsy's own nightmares, so numbingly frightening that she tried to breathe and found that she could not. A strange little buzz, a little juicy hum, started up in her ears, like a mosquito flying close, the kind of noise made by the blood close to the inner ear when it is under far too much pressure. Judith was screeching hysterically and Peter was bawling at her, panicked by his sister's distress and Patsy was paralysed in the front seat as the car ploughed through the crawling monsters. The wheels crunched through them, flinging them off to the side. Another came leaping upward, quick as a blink, and its pointed front legs hooked on to the air intake in front of the wipers. The glassy eyes glared mindlessly, only inches from her face and this time a semi-circle of mouth opened showing a row of glassy teeth. The claws waved, long serrated pincers that looked as if they could cut through sheet metal. The mouth opened wider and the row of teeth moved in unison, curving outward as if on a hinged jaw. Liquid dribbled down from them and whipped away in the turbulence.

The breath still wouldn't come. The insectile hum whined deep inside her ears and suddenly her heartbeat was a powerful pulse behind her eyes. For a second her vision wavered and blurred. It cleared almost instantly and just as instantly there were three of the things hanging on to the front of the car. Peter shouted something at the top of his voice and his hand came up to smack against the glass.

The crawler closest to her glared and she felt its eyes expand to engulf her. She couldn't look away from it as its claws beckoned to her and its mouth opened wide. She could sense its dreadful hunger. This time her vision blacked out. The car swerved, though she was unaware of that until something cracked against the door pillar with the sound of a gunshot. The car lurched violently. The nose dipped and the offside wheel hit something so hard the front end bounced up into the air again. A black shape, even darker than the background at the side of the road came looping in blindingly fast and batted the three crawlers right off the bonnet. One of them screeched raspingly and the sound faded as it went tumbling backwards over the roof. Peter squawked, came rolling between the seats, both his arms clamped protectively around Judith, although Patsy saw none of this. The blow that had cleared the crawlers from the car had stunned the breath back into her body and she had just realised the car had veered across the hard shoulder, crushing more of the nightmare things into the road surface, crashed through the scrub on the verge and was now skidding out of control through the undergrowth. Shapes whipped past as the car tore reedy branches aside. A gnarled grey tree stump loomed into the lights, then swerved away as the car spun clockwise. She pulled at the wheel, corrected the spin, still not in control. Ahead of them a low hummock rose abruptly. The front wheels jolted hard. The sump clanged on something solid but not enough to crack it. Down on the roadside the cat's-eye demons glared up at the car. The wheels went down another ditch and jarred on the shocks. The offside tyre exploded like a shotgun blast and the nose came crunching down onto soft earth. The car slewed around with a dreadful rasping sound and came to a complete halt with the headlamps out ahead of them, pointing at the black sky. The engine kicked and died.

Patsy's heart thudded hard in her chest and a stream of fire rippled up and down her arm. For a moment she thought she was going to have a heart attack, and if Peter and Judith hadn't been with her she might even have welcomed that.

Below her the kids were tumbled into the foot well, a tangle of arms and legs.

'Don't let them get me,' Judith was screaming uncontrollably, over and over again, so quickly the words were all jammed up against each other. Peter was yelling at her, trying to get her to stop.

Outside the car, something moved with a rasping sound. Patsy's heart kicked again, three times rapid, and the tingling went down to her fingers. Her head felt as if it was going to explode. She had crashed the car and stalled at the edge of the road.

The realisation was so huge it was almost beyond comprehension. They were stalled on the roadside while thousands of the poisonous crab-spiders were scuttling to eat them. A picture flickered across the front of her mind. She saw the pallid things scrambling up the slope towards the car, swarming all over it like soldier ants in spider shape, sharp pincers gouging at the glass and the bodyshell, ripping the car open like a Heinz beans can and forcing their way inside, poison teeth gnashing all the while in anticipation.

The picture was so appalling that instead of freezing her numb, it sent a galvanic jolt through her. She hit the button on her seat belt, scrambled free of the restraint and clambered round on the seat, ignoring her children down on the floor. She patted all the windows, making sure they were completely closed, even touched the windscreen to ensure that it hadn't smashed. She snapped on the courtesy light and saw it reflected from the rear window. At the same time she hit her central locking control and the four buttons plipped down simultaneously.

The car was secure for the moment. She crabbed her way into the back seat, pulled the seat-back down and hauled the picnic box through the opening. Inside, right at the top, she found the butane gas stove and hefted it back to the front. If any of the crawlers made it inside the car, she'd light the thing, turn it to full and fry anything that came near her children. She knuckled the cigar lighter and a few moments later it popped and she knew she could use that to put the flame on.

Down at foot level, Judith was yammering incoherently and Peter was doing his best to help her up. Patsy hadn't had the time to comfort her children. Her whole mind, in those past few seconds, had been focused on a last-stand against the nightmares outside the car. Peter crawled up, hauled his sister onto the seat and turned to his mother.

'Where are they?'

Patsy tried to answer him but the words wouldn't come. Peter loosened his grip on Judith's waist and clambered past his mother to peer out of the window down the slope towards the road. Judith's babbling ran out of steam and for a moment there was a silence of sorts. Patsy could still hear the high-pressure whine inside her ears and thought vaguely she might be about to have a stroke. Her breath was rasping in her throat.

Peter's nose was pressed right up against the glass. 'There's hundreds of them,' he said. Patsy didn't want to look. 'But they're staying on the road.'

She still didn't want to look.

'It's all right, mum. They're not coming up after us.'

She said nothing and he turned towards her. Her eyes were wide and staring, the way Judith's were. His mother was shaking, vibrating like a bowstring and he knew she was scared, though, not being afflicted with the phobia Patsy had for all crawling things, he was unaware of just how utterly terror-stricken she had been.

'Look, mum,' he insisted, pulling her chin gently with his palm until she too was nose-up against the glass.

Down there the cat's-eye spiders danced, claws up in the air, legs rippling and scraping on the surface. Their round, glowing eyes were all fixed on the car. But the creatures stayed on the road. The nearer ones scuttled over the hard shoulder and made forays onto the verge, but just as quickly retreated back to the flat.

They watched them, fascinated, horrified, and eventually the movements slowed down and the horde of crawlers began to drift away, slowly marshalling themselves into straight lines on the road.

'They don't come off the road,' Peter said. 'Maybe they can't climb, or maybe it's just not allowed.'

She looked at him blankly.

'Like against the rules. I think they have to stay on the road. It's like *Dungeons and Dragons* where all the things can only go certain places.'

He stopped and sniffed. 'I can smell oil. Did we break something?'

Patsy's voice came back. 'I hope not. I possibly hit a tree stump or a boulder.' She tested the air. The oily smell was greasy and thick and tinged with rust. That last knock as the car was slewing to a halt could have put a hole in the sump. She sniffed again. It didn't smell like petrol, though it was hard to tell. If the tank had split and petrol was leaking, the car could explode. She cranked the key all the way to the left, switched off the lights and the halogen beams, pointing aslant at the sky winked out, leaving them in darkness.

283

Judith was breathing much too fast. The whoop of asthma was building up in her lungs. The sight of the spider things had scared her so much that for a moment she had seemed to be *normal* again. Patsy reached for her and drew her close, hugging her tight. Both of them were trembling like sparrows. The heat came off Judith in waves.

'They're still keeping away,' Peter said, matter of factly, more interested than scared. Judith cringed against her mother. Patsy turned her head. Far off, the red glow was just warming up the sky and the familiar flicker of lightning lit up the inside of the clouds.

'We'll have to fix the tyre in the morning,' Peter said, taking charge again.

If we get through the night, Patsy thought. Outside the window, below her sight level, the crawlers were moving slowly, making clawing sounds on the hard road surface. They had kept away though, and that was something. Peter could be right, there might be rules here, but on the other hand, they might just wait until later, when everything was quiet, when the car engine had gone cold, and then come sneaking up across the hard shoulder and up the verge. She cringed from the image of the things stalking them. Far away, way beyond the lodestone glow in the sky, a faint rumble of thunder came rolling over the moorland. The three of them sat there in silence. She held Judith tight, while Peter gripped her hand as if to tell her everything would be all right. Eventually Judith's heartbeat slowed down and her breathing lost its panicky rasp and after a while she began to doze.

'You'd better try to get some sleep,' she told Peter.

'Shouldn't we keep watch?'

'You've seen too many action films. You get to sleep and I'll keep watch.' The chances of her being able to close her eyes were remote.

'I'm not tired yet.'

'But you will be in the morning, and we'll have to get moving.'

He clambered into the back again. She heard him rummaging about, then he came back with the blanket which he draped round his mother and sister. Patsy's heart did a weak little flip and she felt like crying. She tucked the comforter around Peter and then settled back, eyes wide and alert as she sat vigil on their third night on the road.

A few minutes after she'd tucked the blanket around him, Peter was snoring softly and Judith was snuffling in against her ribs. Patsy felt the tiredness swell in waves, draining the strength from her, and despite the jangling of her nerves in the aftermath of the fight-or-flight surge of adrenaline, she felt her eyelids droop. Every now and again she'd come alert with a start, head swinging up, body instantly tense with expectation.

Apart from the dull red glimmer in the far sky, the night was pitch-black, though from time to time, a flicker of lightning outlined the distant curves of the vast road network, delineating the swinging curves and the soaring arches. The windows began to mist up and she risked opening hers a fraction so they wouldn't be completely blind in the night. As soon as she did so, the scuffling sound from down by the roadside amplified and she looked down there in immediate apprehension. The pale shapes were still there, dim and insubstantial now that her own lights were off, and if they were moving, it was very slowly. She relaxed a little, leaning back in the seat while thoughts tumbled and cavorted inside her head. She tried to grab one and pin it down, but it danced away. There were too many things to think about. Eventually, without realising it, Patsy dozed off while the cooling engine clicked and pinged and far off the low rumble of thunder rolled across the sky.

In her sleep she dreamed that she was home with Peter and Judith, sitting in the sun in the back garden on a sunny summer morning. They were safe and they were home again and the dreadful journey on the infernal road had been nothing but a bad dream. Peter looked up at her, tawny hair tousled, eyes bright blue in the light. He was whittling something on a piece of wood. Judith had her elbows on the garden table, her summer frock a diaphanous pearly shade, and her black hair glistening. She was smiling up at her and Patsy felt the hot swell of love for them both. In the dream the sun was still rising and the shadow of the big beech tree crept towards them, dulling the shine on Judith's hair first, dimming the sparkle in Peter's eyes, and there was surely something wrong with that picture. In her dream, she sat up, puzzled. If the sun was rising, the shadow would be fading away, wouldn't it? *Wouldn't it?* Judith looked up at her and the smile was gone from her face. Peter said something and his voice was down in the low registers, slowed down beyond recognition. She half turned, in expectation, as a chain-saw roared behind her, racketing against the wide trunk of the tree.

Come to me, the voice whispered in the shadows of the dark bushes, and that too was a puzzle because there were no dark bushes in their garden. *Come to your father, girl and give him your innocence. Give him your power.*

The racketing chain-saw teeth got stuck in the greenwood and began to screech in protest, a harsh and rasping squeal that jittered through the bones in her skull. Judith was turning away from her, turning towards Kerron Vaunche who was floating out from the shadows. The girl opened her mouth, said something in that strange, guttural language and she was reaching for the other woman, but Kerron Vaunche was different in this dream. Her powerful beauty was distorted and corrupted now. Her skin was wrinkled and warty and a great weeping web had opened up beside her nose. Her hair was a tangle of grey, through which spotted scalp showed. A swarm of black flies buzzed around her.

And you, boy. First begotten of the consort. You I will consume to be whole again. What of him is in you will be in me. Her voice was like the scratch of claws on the roadway. Judith was walking away from her, walking towards the woman and she was chanting now in words that Patsy couldn't understand, but were so filled with an evil cadence that the sound terrified her.

She reached out and Peter walked past her, eyes wide and glazed, turning to look at her before swinging away towards the diseased and decrepit figure beckoning them. Patsy swung in slow motion and Kerron Vaunche's eyes followed her, the only part of her that looked strong and filled with vigour. The dark eyes flashed in an ancient wrinkled face and they laughed at her in triumph. The slow motion turn continued as she spun to face the chain-saw which was cutting into the tree, screaming like a cat in a trap. The witch-woman laughed a dry cackle and Patsy's fear soared. She finished the movement, trying to reach for her children while at the same time turning to face the danger behind her, caught between the two.

Paul's forearms were corded and knotted as he forced the chain-saw against the trunk. It kicked and screeched as pieces of wood came fountaining out and then the tree started to fall towards her. The wood tore and twisted in a deafening caterwaul and the big beech tree began to crash down on her, falling down on her children, smashing the roof of the house.

She awoke with such a start her head hit against the window, clawing up through the surface of the dream. For a second or two she didn't know where she was. The shrill wailing sound was so loud it made the bodywork quiver. Judith was struggling in her sleep to free herself from the blanket. Patsy recoiled from the blow on her temple, hauling for breath as the dreadful dream began to fragment and she came completely awake to a night that was riven with noise. Peter was awake and for a bewildering moment she saw his faint outline superimposed on the dream- Peter who had been walking away from her towards the witch that had come from the shadows.

Something batted against the glass with a damp-cloth thud, and left a trail of powder that glistened luminously. Peter's silhouette jerked back a fraction, but not enough to show he was sacred.

'What is it?' she asked. He turned towards her, only one side of his face illuminated by the far glow and the new, now fading, effulgence trailing down the glass.

'There's things out there,' he whispered. 'Different things.'

On Peter's side, somewhere out there in the dark, a big and powerful beast let out a screech and she recognised the chain-saw sound in her dream. Down close to the road, an even bigger thing answered back. Judith jerked in her sleep and Patsy held her tight, cradling her head in the crook of an arm, hoping to drown out the sound.

A pale shape fluttered by, a few inches from her eyes, a moth or a bird perhaps, moving on slow motion wings that were strangely elegant and making a low whirring sound in the air that tickled the inside of her ears. It flew parallel to the glass, trailing that luminescent powder. Patsy peered at it, wiping the glass as she did to clear the condensation. The flying thing turned in the air, hovered for a second, taking two lazy beats to maintain its position.

Then a black and snakelike shape came striking down from the air and snatched it clean away, leaving a puff of shimmering dust drifting in the dark.

Patsy startled back from the window. She hadn't quite seen what had happened, only the impression of a long shape and a wide gape. It had happened so quickly her eyes couldn't follow it. There had been a snap, like a door-bolt driven home and then nothing.

'What are they?' she asked, keeping her voice to a whisper.

'I can't tell,' he replied, just as quiet. 'I don't think they know we're here.'

The smell of oil was still thick and cloying, but over it, there was another, hotter smell that was sweet and greasily rancid at the same time. In front of the car, a dark shape loomed, bigger than the car itself. A sapling cracked and its neighbour whipped about before it fell with a crunch. A deep grunt, so low it made the very ground vibrate, boomed out for several seconds before the shape moved away, heading up from the verge towards the shadow of the ditch. Another flying thing came waltzing on the air, a blanched flicker which swerved, trailing its scatter of magic dust, and came floating right up to the windscreen. It landed with a muffled thud and sat there, a mere foot away from her, stick-like legs spread out on the glass. It was a moth, or something very like a moth, with broad, fanned wings which sat together, butterfly-style, like praying hands, and occasionally opened themselves to display a striking circular pattern on each lobe.

'Look at the size of that . . .' Peter whispered.

As if it heard him, the big insect – though it wasn't because it had at least eight knobbly legs – twisted its body and the wings opened, giving a sudden display of the twin spots. The wings closed, flared wide again, and the pattern flashed into focus. Patsy and Peter both gasped at the same time. The circular marks were eyes, complete with a white reflection spot which made them seem alive and glaring.

Patsy recoiled. The wings flapped again and the mad-staring eyes of the moon transfixed her.

Whatever had evolved the night flyer had uncannily captured the image of the contorted moon, and gave the delicate moth a depraved mimicry. The eyes held her until the wings folded back out of sight. The big insect-thing reached its legs, probing the glass, and its long abdomen pressed against the surface, leaving a ridged pattern of shiny talc. Another fluttering thing, darker and longer, landed on the glass next to Peter, this one more like a dragonfly, with two huge glassy eyes dominating a thin head. An underslung jaw reached out like a clawing arm and scraped against the glass. Peter stayed perfectly still, examining the thing as if it was a specimen in his bug box. Patsy looked away and turned to the flutterer on the windscreen. Its legs pinioned up and down as it made its way across the glass. The wings flashed her a hellish moon-stare, but she realised it was only some kind of protective mimicry and the eyes lost some of their venomous impact. It turned and came back towards her and she saw its head for the first time. Two feathery antennae brushed the air, but there the moth-like appearance ended. The fronds stuck out straight from a round white head. Instead of the blank matt of compound eyes she expected, two glistening, almost intelligent eyes swivelled in deep sockets. Between them, a long and thin, almost human nose protruded, nostrils snuffling sensitively and below the snout a wide mouth opened, showing a row of tiny white teeth.

The head turned on a stringy neck and the little eyes regarded her dispassionately. Between the teeth a pink tongue reached out, uncoiling as it went, and licked against the glass.

It was a human head, wizened and misshapen, like the head of an elf or a leprechaun. The little eyes glittered with some kind of knowledge and for a vertiginous moment, Patsy thought she was going to be sick. The thing on the window was a malformed parody of a human, and its very existence was an affront to her sensibilities. She could feel her gorge rise and tried to swallow the hot bile down, and then, as before, something long and black came slashing out from above. This time it was right before her eyes. A small head, with two glittering eyes on either side of a pointed snout came darting forward and a mouth opened in an impossible gape. She had an impression of a yellow tongue, no more, when the jaws snapped shut on the thing on the window. The little mouth opened in terror and the beady eyes rolled. The legs flexed and scrabbled against the glass, trying to get a grip and pull itself to safety. A high-pitched buzzing drilled the night and she realised it was the fluttering abomination screeching in fear. The yellow pinpoint eyes on either side of the triangular head winked out and then came on again. The head twisted to the side and she saw the long ridged abdomen of the moth-like creature burst open, spewing a blurt of fluid in a trail of blots on the glass and making a sickly little *pop* sound. The prey squeaked again, high and mouse-like. The mouth opened in a perfect circle while the eyes, now wide and repulsively human, stared right at her in dreadful appeal. A piece of wing broke off, fluttered away. The long black neck tensed and pulled back. The dreadful little mutation was plucked off the glass and out into the darkness. Above the whispering trill the sound of even larger wings beat in the air.

'There's lots of them,' Peter said under his breath. Outside the car, the night was alive. Down on the roadside, something big and awesomely fast came darting out from the central reservation, low and long, almost crocodilian. One of the pallid crawlers flicked away from it, legs blurring. The slithering thing twisted like black lightning and the crawler disappeared. Teeth gnashed like a trap and the dark shape spun back into the shadows.

'I don't know what they are,' Peter murmured. 'They're all different. You don't get this on *Naturewatch*.'

And if they did, children and adults would wake screaming, Patsy thought.

Another rasping howl tore through the dark, startling them both. Very close by, a low, fast thing went shooting down the hill, straight across the road and hit one of the other black shapes with such force that it sounded like a hammer-blow on a fence post. A mouth a yard wide opened and closed quicker than a blink. Something gurgled and the two creatures crashed, rolling into the undergrowth.

A moth-flyer flipped past and Patsy could just make out the wizened skull-like face. It was distressing to see something so human on the body of an insect, as if all the laws of the natural world had been broken down and put together by some mad modeller, or as if real creatures – real *humans* – had been monstrously mutated by a black and wicked alchemy.

The flyer winged by, little eyes fixed on her own, while all around them the night was rent and torn by the whoops and cackles and shrieks of a demented horde of things. Patsy looked back at the disgusting little aberration, and listened to the hellish sounds and then remembered a dreadful picture she had seen, a painting by Hieronymous Bosch showing lost souls tormented by demons in hell. The face on the fluttering moth-thing, so deformed and obscenely human, reminded her of one of those lost souls and the shrill cackling and screeching out there in the exterior darkness, they could have been imps of hell or their tortured victims.

The image of lost souls, of evil sorcery stayed with her, while all around their flimsy sanctuary, the night things moved and resulted and hunted. Things rent and bit, others screamed and burst asunder, while inside the car Patsy huddled, praying that the night would soon be over and that the three of them, three lost souls would make it until morning.

18

Peter awoke her by tweaking her ear lobe and for a moment she had no idea where she was.

'Wha. . . .' she began to say as the world came into focus. Over on the left, to the east she assumed, the sky was layering itself in shades of yellow and green as another malignant sunrise began to change the night into a kind of day.

Straight ahead of them, due south, across the wide road, the glow was pulsating in the sky. It seemed closer than it had before and underneath it she could just make out, through a thick and soupy mist of smog, the pillars of one overpass on the vast interchange. Down on the road, close to the barrier where the shadows pooled in inky blots, one of the crawlers scuttled for the centre. It stopped dead, a pale spidery shape, drew itself in tight and then shrank down on the space between the centre markers. A black oblong twitched down by the verge and went still.

The dawn brightened, though that was not quite how Patsy would have described the alien colours patterning the low sky. A flying thing, maybe a bird, but on jagged wings that could have been leathery like a huge bat, whooped away with a harsh cawing. Something leapt up, cat-quick beyond the scrub and almost hooked the flyer out of the sky. A small creature bleated close to the car and made its way to the safety of the scraggle of undergrowth. Gradually the day lightened and as it did, the sound and movement died. The sun came up over the hills, a bleached and sickly ovoid bearing those black cancerous lumps on its face, and painted the world with its fevered light.

Judith stirred and struggled her way out of the blanket wrap. It took a moment for her eyes to focus, then she realised she was still in the car.

'Aren't we home yet?' she asked, voice shaky and still confused. Patsy took her hand and Judith smiled weakly. For the first time since the flight from Broadford House, it seemed as if

Judith was coming round, more aware of what was happening, less under the *influence* of something else. But the bags under her eyes were deeper and a rash was beginning to spread across her forehead where a sheen of sweat glistened. Her breath was ragged, not with the asthmatic whoop, but of some deep infection.

'No, silly,' Peter told his sister. 'But we'll get there,' Peter replied. 'I'm hungry again. And I need the bathroom.'

'Give me a moment, okay?' Patsy's eyes felt gritty and raw and every time she blinked she could feel the need for real sleep drag over her. She wiped the mist from the window and looked out down towards the road. Nothing moved there, except for a couple of tall and twisted stems of grass which nodded agreeably in the breeze. On the passenger side, a bent and buckled fence cut along the side of the ditch and a few yards away, an old low-loader was sunk into the undergrowth. The cab was dented and completely red with rust and on the carrier, two fifty-gallon oil drums were lashed together. One of them was punctured and on the low incline, Patsy could see where it had flowed and seeped into the ground, leaving a dark stain where nothing grew at all. Even now the smell of oil was thick and strong. The stained patch spread outward around the car and a little way down towards the edge of the road. That, at least, was a relief for Patsy. She'd assumed the sump had cracked and left them stranded. With luck, all she had to do now was change a wheel and they would be on their way, as long as none of the night's monstrosities was waiting to ambush them from the bushes. She thought back to the fluttery moth gargoyles with the humanoid faces and shuddered. The light had been bad, she tried to tell herself. She'd only seen the faces in the shadows and she'd probably been wrong.

But she knew within herself that she had not been wrong. That the little monstrosities, preyed upon by other fiends, had been no trick of the dark, no figment of her imagination. They had been all too real.

'Can we eat now?' Peter broke into the memory and Patsy came back to the present. She took a deep breath, steeled herself as best she could though it took all of her resolve, then unlocked the door. She pulled back on the little handle. The door clicked open a fraction. Patsy's heart started to speed up.

'I should go,' Peter said. He was reaching for the handle and she had to reach quickly to stop him. 'But I've got my knife,' he protested, holding his hand up to show her the little red Swiss Army clasp knife with the ten blades including a corkscrew and a spike for taking stones out of mules' hooves. He must have found it among the picnic gear. It had been his pride and joy last summer.

'No,' she said flatly. He saw the look in her eye and shrewdly interpreted it correctly. She held his eyes for a moment, using them to give her strength, then she opened the door just enough. Gingerly she put one foot out and down on to the oil-stained earth. Her shoe sunk an inch into the spongy soil. She froze, desperate to draw that foot back to safety, the way she had always done as a child when she woke and found only one leg dangling cold and vulnerable out of the bed, then steeled herself to keep it there.

Nothing happened. No crab-spider came lurching out from under the wheel arch, legs a-judder scrabbling for her foot. No black snake with a yard-wide gape came striking from the shadows of the spiked gorse. Whatever predator had shrieked in the night, and whatever monstrous hunter had rumbled loud enough to make the ground shake, they had gone.

The moon, she thought. *It's gone and taken them with it.* Whether that was true, she did not know, but it *felt* right. She'd been right to flee from the sick light of the glaring moon as it had crept across the hills and pooled in the culverts. She swung her other foot round and planted it beside the first. In the bushes, something very small squeaked and was silent. Beyond them a cricket chirruped and while its creaking-door call sounded flat and off-key and somehow alien, there was no threat in it. Patsy bent quickly to check under the car. The ground was bare. She stood up again and scanned the road from east to west. Nothing moved, though there were black and ridged pieces of tyre tread scattered her and there on the surface. Between the hyphens of white lane markers, the flat tops of the cat's-eyes showed as white squares. They did not move.

'I'm bursting, mum,' Peter pleaded from inside the car. 'Can I get out?'

She grinned, despite her apprehension and opened her door wide. He came scrambling out, one hand jammed between his legs.

'There.' Patsy pointed at a close-by sapling stump which had been freshly broken in the night.

'Mum!' His face went red. 'Everybody can see me.'

'If anybody comes, I'll tell them to look away,' she promised, unable to keep the smile from her face. Judith managed a wan smile and put her hands over her eyes. The skin on her knuckles was dry and peeling. It made her hands look wizened.

She's sick, Patsy said to herself. *She needs help*. After a minute or so, Peter zipped up his jeans and came back to the car, still blushing furiously. Patsy took Judith out and used the raised boot-lid as a partition then found a dry place for her daughter. She sent her back too, telling her to close the door and when they were both out of sight, she loosened the belt on her jeans and fished the handkerchief from her pocket. It was all she had to staunch the flow of blood that she had felt begin to trickle and drag inside her as soon as she'd swung her foot out of the car.

'God-*damn!*' The words hissed out in a curse. She'd been on this road for three days and three nights without a real wash or a shower and she felt unkempt and unclean. The menstrual blood did nothing to change her self-perception and she could have done without that or been more prepared for it. She wondered how long the little square of cloth would last.

Peter dragged out the cool-box while Patsy checked the area around the car, still wary of stepping down to the road. The oily patch felt spongy and when she pressed her foot on the surface, a little damp trickle puddled out breaking up the light into a red-blue petrol spectrum that reminded her of the unearthly sunset. At the edge of the stain, where the low mossy vegetation struggled to root, the soft earth was pitted and indented. She walked over and bent down, gauging the distance to the car in case anything should move in the undergrowth a few yards away.

The ground was punctuated with tracks. There was hardly an

inch of the churned earth unmarked by the passage of some creature.

She stood quickly, instantly afraid again. Parallel lines showed where big insects had clambered through the mire, making little tractor treads on the surface. Here and there, something with claws like a bird had hopped and close to the edge, something heavy had come out from the bushes and stood facing the car for a while before turning away. She could see the marks of sharp claws, longer than any bear's claws, and she shuddered again. It had come out and stopped. In her mind she heard that awesome low grumble. Had the creature that made the spoor on the mud growled in hunger? Her eyes swept past the indentations, saw a neat trail where a catlike thing had scampered round the perimeter then leapt over a puddle of oily water a yard wide. Her inspection skipped the puddle, scanned the softer ground beyond it and then flicked back again.

The puddle, with the ever-changing colours of the oil-slick patterning its surface, was at least a full yard wide, and it had the shape of a maple leaf. She stared at it and her breathing stopped while her mind began to calculate. It was just the shape of a maple leaf, one long bract with two smaller ones on each side. The colours swirled and merged and Patsy took a step backwards, eyes flicking left and right.

It was a footprint. It was a yard wide and half as much again from claw-tip to heel. It was the biggest claw she had ever seen, bigger even than the dinosaur footsteps preserved in stone on the bottom of that river in Montana. Now she knew what had made the rumbling sound in the dead of night. The foot that made that print could have flattened the bear-sized thing without even noticing. It had come lumbering to within twenty yards of the car and gone on. It could have *stepped* on them she realised, and they'd have known nothing but a brief instant of pain.

Behind her something hissed lightly and she turned again, but it was only Peter lighting the camping stove. She walked towards him, beyond the black stain, to a flat and dry mound of earth which turned out to be the unploughed area between the two gouged tracks made by the low-loader. It had obviously spun off the road just as they themselves had the night before. Patsy thought of the driver careering out of control, scared witless by the crawling things on the road, and she wondered what had happened to him. She decided not to venture up to the rusted cabin to check.

Peter put the little kettle on and had opened one of the packets of powdered soup. He bent over the pot to stir some in and Patsy heard his stomach rumble.

'Feed me,' he growled. 'That's what it's saying.' Judith almost laughed. Her eyes were bloodshot and Patsy wondered if it was this place, this awful road that was affecting her. It might have been that, and it might have been something else. In her dream she had seen Kerron Vaunche, not as she had been at the camp-fire, but old, incredibly ancient.

'*The hag in all her forms*,' Gilfeather had said. In the dreams the gypsy had been a wizened hag. A dread certainly was beginning to steal over Patsy when she recalled the rest of it.

'*I told you the Cailleach is old. Older than any of us. I can't say just how long she has lived. And the dead days are a time of death and rebirth. To keep her beauty, to keep her youth and to maintain her enormous power, the Carlin Woman must commune with the Lord of Death, the Prince of Shadows, and he will demand his price . . . the price is absolute corruption, but there must be a feast at which the Prince of Shadows will feed.*'

That was the ceremony she had planned for the Nameless Day. Patsy remembered every word. She recalled shuddering at the thought, even though belief had not yet arrived.

'*Then there is the dark transference of the renewal. In the ceremony, souls are lost, but the life is transferred and the bargain is made. She needs the flesh of his flesh to make the bargain.*'

She had heard Vaunche on the radio, seen her in her dreams. Was she old now? Was she ageing fast on the approach to the full moon and the Nameless Day? Was the connection to Judith, was that affecting her daughter? Was it making her skin wrinkle and peel? Patsy pulled Judith close, smoothing her hair with a hand. Was it her imagination or was Judith's hair thinning? Was her scalp showing through? She held the girl tightly, ignoring the dry, musty smell that reminded her of her own grandmother.

Dear Lord, let us get through this, she prayed.

'Gimme soup. Gimme *gallons* of soup,' Peter was intoning. 'Feed me *now!*'

297

Patsy listened to him entertain his sister and again her admiration and love for him soared. He should never have had to face any of the things he'd seen on this godforsaken road, but already he was proving to be more of a man than his father was.

'Feed me, too,' Judith mumbled and Peter laughed brightly. Patsy walked around the car. The nearside front tyre was in tatters, ripped right across the tread. A rope of black rubber hung loosely from the wheel rim. The sump, she discovered, was clear of the ground and nothing was dripping, so she assumed it was intact. She made a quick inspection of the car and found nothing but a series of small depressions on the glass of the windscreen where the fluttering monstrosity had burst asunder. She recoiled from the recollection as she hauled the jack out from under the rear seat and got to work.

The soup was ready before she'd finished and she welcomed the break. Already the sun was climbing fast in the sky, and not for the first time, she realised that time on this road was different. Already it was gathering heat, a dry, parching heat that felt as if it would leach all the moisture from their skin. Patsy found Peter's baseball cap and made him wear it, folded a headscarf into a neat headpiece for Judith and tied it on. They sat together on the raised mound of earth and had the best cup of vegetable soup they had ever tasted, followed by reconstituted potatoes and then pale tea with neither milk nor sugar. Judith managed to eat a small amount. Half an hour later Patsy had heaved the spare wheel onto the bolts, fixed it in place and let the car down off the jack. The other wheel was buckled and the tyre worse than useless. She discarded it.

Peter had put the picnic gear back in the box and was sitting with Judith as instructed when Patsy finished the job.

'What now?' he asked brightly, like a keen lieutenant ready for action. 'You've got oil on your nose.'

Patsy wiped the smudge with a finger, quickly smeared the tip of Judith's snub nose and had to hold Peter down to do the same for him.

'Now we're all even. It's warpaint.'

'I think we should go soon,' Peter said when he'd stopped laughing. Judith nodded in agreement.

'Right on, baby,' Patsy replied, holding her hand up for the customary slap. He responded, thought it had been a long time since they'd exchanged the greeting. A small lump swelled in her throat. Peter just grinned and winked.

'First of all,' she said, 'we have to sit and have a think about some things.'

'About how to get home?'

'Exactly. I thought it would have been quicker, so we have to be prepared.'

'In case it takes longer,' Peter stated solemnly. Patsy nodded.

'But we'll get home sometime,' he half-asked.

'Of course we will, but we have to make sure we can get through any delays. We might need more food, so I have to know what's left and it will mean being very careful.'

'Two packets of soup. Six tea bags and two sachets of coffee. Another packet of potatoes. I checked when you were fixing the car.'

'That's all?' She'd expected more. It was hardly enough for another day.

A silent prayer got the engine going first time and another one made sure the tyres didn't spin uselessly on the soft topsoil. She reversed back several yards, then steered between the two patches of gorse down a natural alleyway leading down to the hard shoulder. Just before she reached the level, something white caught her attention and she stopped.

A spider's web, ten feet wide, maybe more, was stretched line a seine net between two saplings. The familiar loop of nausea turned inside her belly and she clenched her muscles until it was gone.

Only a cobweb. She forced herself to whisper it. There was no sign of the thing that had stretched the enormous webbing. The strands were taut and shone like glass and in the tracery she could see pale dusty packages which she knew for certain were things that had been caught and wrapped in silk. In a strand close to her, the delicate wing of one of the moth creatures was held rigid. Beside it, not more than a yard away, the iridescent black wing of a bird spun lazily. The shoulder edge was brown with dried blood and a pearly knuckle of bone protruded into the air. She drove past, keeping a tight rein on the impulse to put her foot down and get away quickly. One guy-line snagged on the headlamp corner and made the whole net vibrate with a low thrum, but nothing moved, apart from the wing which danced on its thread. Beyond the web the natural alley led down the slope to the road. On either side, more of the thick cobwebs were strung on the gorse bushes and each of them bore the little silken packages, but the spiders that had spun the traps were either gone or hiding from the light. The car jostled down the slope and finally got to the edge of the hard shoulder. Patsy felt her heart speed up just a little as she steered onto the flat. The marker line on the edge of the red grit of the breakdown lane arrowed parallel to the kerb. She stayed close to it until she came level with the first of the cat's-eyes and slowed to a crawl, but kept the revs high in case she needed a burst of speed.

It sat squat in its little well.

Patsy peered out, nerves twitching, remembering the way the road had suddenly erupted with life when the moon had risen into the night sky.

The pale glass eyes stared out along the road behind her, forced into a slight frown by the ridge of rubber (*or shell?*) but devoid of expression, empty of life. The thing was snug in the small metal depression, though in her mind's eye she could see it clambering out, drawing its skinny and jointed legs to scuttle on the surface. It fit the way a hermit crab dovetailed into a whelk shell, but in the wan light of day it seemed completely lifeless. She eased the car past, still tense with the expectation that it might spring out of the hole and make a grab at the newly-changed tyre, but it sat still. The next cat's-eye was the same, just two glass eyes staring into infinity along the road behind them, waiting for the night, or the bane-light of the moon to give them life.

Patsy pulled out onto the hardtop and felt the wheel thump on one of the reflectors in the normal way, and her apprehension eased a little. Out on the fast lane, something had been squashed onto the surface in the night. It was just a greasy stain with a splatter of wet spread around it in a small lagoon. A wasp, finger-long and with shivering jewelled wings was sipping at the edge of the wet patch, black and gold belly pumping up and down like bellows. Twenty yards along the road, pieces of ridged tyre-tread were scattered against the barrier on the central reservation. When she reached them, a curved section maybe three feet long was quivering and she saw that it was not a Dunlop steel-belt at all. It was the warted hide of some animal that had been broken in the night. She passed by and one of the smaller pieces, pure black and grooved like the tread of a long-distance hauler tyre flipped over lethargically. It was weird, but not frightening enough, not after the past night. A small furry thing like a weasel was snaking along in the shadow of a large piece, moving with a fluid, hunting gait. It was followed by a line of others and when they reached the quivering black skin they started to feed. She drove on, weaving through the mounds of things that had been flattened, the road-kills of the night. Beyond the broken tyres, there was a stretch of clean road and she pushed the car a little faster.

Without warning the road erupted in a startling black cloud and she almost stalled the car. For an instant she was completely bewildered until she realised what it was. A million black flies had been feeding on the squashed carrion, crawling so densely packed that they had looked just like the road surface itself. They had risen from the kills in a dense, buzzing tornado and immediately, small flying things, so quick and darting they were mere blurs of colour came flicking out from the bushes to snatch the insects in mid-air.

'Flies we can handle,' she muttered to herself, shoving away the memory of the flies buzzing around Kerron Vaunche in her dream, erupting from the chasm in the small form on the stone. She pushed on into the dense cloud. Insects spattered on the windscreen, forcing her to use the wipers and the wash to smear them away. The noise of thousands of them smashing into the glass was like dry hail, and above it the buzz of their millions of wings sounded like the roar of traffic. The sound swelled as she ploughed through the swarm, ignoring the angry buzzing and the scrapy sensation that she could hear her name rasped out under the roar. Finally she broke through into the light and the noise dwindled to nothing, though she imagined she could still hear the eerie undertone calling her name. She drove for half a mile before glancing in the mirror. The flies had settled back down and the road was clear. There was nothing fore or aft, except the dwindling road behind and the line of blank cat's-eyes

301

stretching out to the morning road-mist way in front. Beyond that, far off, the soaring arches and convolutions of the junction could be seen through the smog, ever-present, day and night, and drawing her closer with every turn of the wheels. She had no choice. There was no other way to go.

'Keep them crossed again, you two,' she said, picking up speed on the straight.

'Fingers and toes?' Peter asked lightly.

'Fingers, toes, knees and elbows,' she batted back.

'I can do that,' Judith said, as if she'd just woken up. A moment later she fell off the seat and Peter nearly choked with laughter.

19

The needle was down on the red line.

They were out of fuel and out of water and Patsy knew they were running out of options. She did not know what she could do now to keep them alive. For the first time she had to entertain the possibility that they might not get off this road, and the appalling notion of their impending death sat hunched in the back of her mind like a gnawing tumour.

One packet of powdered soup now, five tea bags and two sachets of coffee. No potatoes. Half a tiny kettle of warm water and nothing else. They were in trouble.

Now the fuel gauge needle had sunk below its horizon and was swimming in the red and they were crawling along the road at twenty miles an hour with the unhealthy sun almost overhead.

They had stopped beyond a bridge over what she took to be a narrow gorge. At first she'd thought she could hear running water and the high call of seabirds and had slowed to a halt right on the bridge and got out of the car, wondering about the possibility of being able to climb down to a stream to fill the flask. Peter and Judith had objected when she'd told them to stay in the car and they had watched as she walked to the railing. When she got there it was clear that she'd been right to keep them inside.

It was not a gorge, not a ravine. There was no running water down there. She leaned over the galvanised balustrade and looked down to a four-lane carriageway emerging from under the bridge.

For a moment she was unable to comprehend what she was seeing, for down below her, despite the light from the sun, the road was in shadow, a kind of twilight, lit here and there by orange flares. She could see the blue, flashing lights of what might have been emergency vehicles, and down on the nearside, two sets of twin-beam headlamps angled out onto the cutaway rock roadside.

What's wrong with this picture, eh? The little internal cynic nagged at her.

The noise of squalling seagulls floated up to her along with the sounds of running water. She scratched her head, leaned further over the barrier, strained her eyes to make out what was happening down there.

Then she froze to stone.

It was not seabirds calling to each other. It was not the sound of running water. The high-pitched wailing scoured in her ears and abruptly the blood seemed to curdle in her veins.

It was human screams. They were high and piercing, echoing against the underside of the bridge and off the box girders, reverberating from the gorge cut in the stone.

What's wrong with this picture? She didn't want to know, but she was forced to look down.

The traffic was not moving. And those weren't orange flares. They were fires. Smoke billowed up in a cloud, dirty on top and fiery red underneath, blown upwards by the intense heat of burning fuel. A breeze blew a space in the smoke and she saw a car, well alight, lying on its side. Something flapped from the top-most window, but then it fell back into the flames.

Patsy's throat closed with a snap against the surge of bile.

A man's voice bawled desperately and a child screeched in agony. A siren ululated and the roaring flames sounded like the rushing of a river in spate.

No water, no birds. Just a vast road smash with flames making their own hurricanes and people screaming as they died. Two shapes lay sprawled at the side of the road. The darkness rolled away again, giving her a clear, though twilight view of the carnage below. A fireman flashed an orange light in their direction and walked across, yellow coat flapping. For some reason she could see the reflection of rain on the surface, though it was dry on the bridge from where she watched and she told herself they must be using hoses down there.

The firemen, whoever it was in the yellow slicker, strode forward. He reached to help one of the people. Patsy was about to call out to him when, without any hesitation at all, he bent and smashed the base of the flashlight against a pale face. The shape twitched and was still. The man in the yellow oilskin bent down and quickly searched the body. The cry strangled itself in Patsy's mouth. A gush of horror blurted within her and she thought, not for the first time, that she might faint.

Down there the road was littered with the wrecks of cars. The sirens wailed and the smoke billowed, but she could not see any of the emergency crews, apart from the one man in the raincoat. There were trapped people screaming for help, bleating in panic. The stench of burning fuel and another sweet and fatty smell that she knew was roasting flesh, came billowing up on the smoke which only reached the level of the bridge, like an inversion layer and flowed along in a turbulent river, following the direction of the road below.

A real mess, I can tell you. There's blood and guts and bits of bodies all over the place.

The words came back from the first night, when she was still fleeing from Broadford House. The coarse face of the man she'd taken for a traffic cop floated in her memory. *It's like a junkyard, and you don't want the kiddies to hear the screams, that's for sure.*

If that hadn't been three nights ago, he could have been describing the scene below. *It's a bad night to be out here at the junction*

Patsy leaned over again and saw a line of cars directly below, all shunted one into the other and she couldn't tell whether there were people inside these or not, but the road was blocked. Completely.

A dark shape moved between the cars, clambered over the crumpled bonnet that was billowing steam and for an instant, his shadow cut off the glaring, upside-down reflection of the moon. He passed by and the red, squashed circle of light snarled up at her. She jerked back as if dodging from its sight, then stopped instantly. She forced herself to lean back over the barrier again.

It was the moon all right, more distorted in the reflection than it had been the night before – *and that had been bad enough* – but it had the same baleful orange-red tinge and she could see the contorted brow framing the glaring eye sockets. She looked up at the sky. It was still day-pale. There was no moon overhead. She peered down again and saw smoke level off just under the bridge span, then she checked the reflection once more. It was definitely the crazed moon reflected from a windscreen. Patsy swung back, away from the carnage in the strange dusk below. It was still dark down there and it was daylight up where she stood, and for some reason that was eerily unnerving. She backed away and beyond the barrier a woman screamed long and high and wavering, and the sound tore at Patsy's heart.

Back in the car she started the engine and drove off the bridge, still hearing that wavering cry in her ears.

'What was it?' Peter asked.

'I thought it was water. I heard seagulls.'

'I heard people,' Judith said. 'They were crying.'

'No, it was birds. Sometimes they sound like children. In the distance.'

She glanced round at Judith. Her daughter was looking at her and Patsy knew that she knew. A patch of skin on Judith's cheek had crinkled. It looked as if it was about to slough off. Her lips looked raw and a weeping scab was forming just under her eyelid.

'Okay, let's get a move on,' she said, turning away from Judith's eyes. Two days before the midwinter and they were still running and Judith was getting sicker. 'Wagons hoh-oh!'

Peter looked at her askance.

'From an old TV show when I was knee-high,' she explained. 'About a wagon train.'

And it had been rolling along forever, week after week, with no end in sight, she recalled. Maybe the writer had dreamed about this place.

She got them moving again and drove for another mile when a dark shape got her attention not far along the road. Patsy recognised it instantly, a black cycle helmet hanging from a pole. She told the kids to wait and walked towards it, staying close to the edge. The helmet swung by its strap from a branch that had been shoved into the ground and propped up with two kerbstones. Beside it, a mound of smaller pieces of concrete had been piled up in a low oblong. Patsy lifted the helmet down from where it swayed in the breeze. Inside it a scrap of paper was tucked into the webbing.

Eight days. Buried Sally Bowman here and it's no hallowed ground. She got bit in the night and died in the morning. Said my prayers for her and me and God help me now. Heading towards

306

the junction, but it's a long way off and I don't know if I'll make another day. If anybody finds this note, say a prayer for Sally. She was a good woman and shouldn't have suffered like she did. God help all of us. Billy Walker.

Patsy held the letter in her hand and stood there beside the low mound of broken concrete, waiting until the dreadful twist of sadness washed away from her. Silent tears coursed down her cheeks and dripped from her chin. Sally B had loved Billy Walker and he had watched her die out here in this godforsaken wilderness. For some reason, the unknown woman's death affected her desperately. Eventually, she said a prayer for the soul of Sally Bowman and another for the man who walked alone on the road. She wiped the tears and went back to the car.

Two hours later she was creeping along the road, eking out the last of the fuel, knowing she'd soon be drifting on vapour and that the engine would choke to a stall and they'd be stuck. The road was on a long curve, punctuated by small rises and alternating dips and disappeared from view five miles in front and maybe six behind. Here and there, dotted at random, she could make out the shapes of other vehicles. Most of them had that russet shade of old rust. She rolled the window down and found it was hot, but not killing. She urged the car onwards until she reached a low rise which gave her the impression of it being a vantage point, pulled in on the short scrub at the side and stopped the car. The engine wheezed a little and coughed in pre-ignition before it stopped. A faint hiss under the bonnet told her the leak in the hose was getting worse.

'What's wrong?'

Patsy folded her arms on the wheel and used them to cushion her head. A trickle of sweat ran down under her armpit and her hair felt dirty and greasy. The little handkerchief she'd stuffed inside her pants was chafing against her and she knew it would be sodden.

'I need petrol,' she finally told him.

'Oh.'

'Oh is correct,' she breathed. 'Oh says it all, my man.'

'What will we do? Will we have to walk?'

'No, we won't have to walk. I want you to stay here.'

'What do you mean?'

'Dive in the back and get the flask and the kettle,' she told Peter. He looked at her for a long moment, wondering what to ask, then did as he'd been told. He fished out both containers and watched while she poured the rest of the water into the empty drinks bottle. When she asked, he dragged the cool-box through and she smiled tightly when she saw that the plastic tube which sealed the lid could be removed. It was a clear flexible tube. She pulled it free without difficulty and he cut it for her with one blade of his knife.

'I want you to look after Judith. There's a few cars along the road. With any luck, one of them might have some fuel we can use, at least to get us another thirty miles or so. I can suck it out with this tube, and if we get some petrol, we can get to water and that's really important. Without either of them, we're in a whole lot of trouble, so you have to be solid for me.'

'I think we should all go,' he said, face impassive, and she knew that was for Judith's sake.

'Under any other circumstances you'd be right. Come here.' She opened the door and stepped out. He clambered out behind her and she hunkered down, putting both hands on his shoulders.

'As I said, that would normally be best, but you have to remember that here things are pretty screwed up.'

He nodded slowly.

'If something comes out of the bushes, or along the road, I could probably get away. Your old mum's a pretty fit girl, you know.'

She got a grim smile with that.

'But if Judith's with us, then it's a different kettle of fish. She's pretty sick. I'd have to carry her and that would slow us down a lot. Don't worry, I won't be long. As long as you're here, you'll be fine, and I'll be back pretty soon, an hour tops, okay?'

His eyes told her he was not happy with her idea, but he was not going to fight her. She gave him a tight hug and he got back in the car. Judith just looked at her blankly.

Patsy walked down the slow lane, turning back every now and again to wave to them, trying to give them some reassurance. Beyond the sloping verge, she could see the tops of all trees shivering in the light breeze. On the far side of the road, the rocky hillocks were like islands in a sea of dry scrub which

308

rustled like shingle on a beach, reminding her of the crawling things of the night before. Just as that image came back to her, her foot came down on one of the cat's-eyes. It shifted under her weight and her heart almost burst in fright. She jumped back, whirling as she did to face the thing, almost tumbled to her knees and caught herself before she fell. The little reflector did not move. For almost a minute, until she got her breath back, neither did Patsy. When the pounding in her temples eased off, her muscles unfroze. She leaned forward.

The thing stared blindly back at her, just a reflector, made of two glass eyes under a rubbery shield fitted into a cast-iron well. It was only a reflector, only a cat's-eye. It was wholly inanimate in the light of day. But she could see the little scalloped edges on the sides of the shield which would hide the articulated legs under the body, and she could make out the curved line underneath the bulging glass orbs where a mouth could open in a slit and show jagged teeth; and she knew that in the night, no matter how inanimate and lifeless it looked now, this thing and the other ones stretching out over the brow of the hills in front, would blink in the beams of a car's headlights and their pale stare would turn orange and poisonous and they would haul themselves up from the road, hunting in the light of that moon.

Another hundred yards down the road she found a two-foot piece of angle-iron stuck into the ground and she pulled it out. Its weight felt good in her hand and she turned to wave back at the distant car. About a mile away, the first three wrecks were angled in to the side of the road.

Down the lee of the hill, the vegetation was different, as if she'd crossed yet another time zone, another geographical boundary. The rocky scrub gave way to what at first seemed to be more fertile land in this dip. The air here smelt moist which made her think there was a chance of another stream. Further down the hill the trees petered out to a marshy sphagnum bog lined with tasselled willow-herb crowding the edge of the road, competing for space with glue-thistles and a strange sundew on the edge of the bog where insects buzzed and hummed among the sticky spines. Patsy caught a slow movement in her peripheral vision and slowed to look. A flying thing, maybe a small bird or a large insect was struggling against the sticky grip of one of the viscous flowerheads. Beside it another hand of sundew was closing like a gelatinous fist, entrapping another dark shape which shivered and trembled in its struggles to be free. She walked on, past a clump of bindweed crawling up a stump, and as she passed, for one disquieting moment she thought she actually *did* see it crawl. It bore white trumpet flowers like death lilies which smelled of putrid meat and attracted pus-coloured flies in swarms. There was no water at the bottom of the dip where the road levelled out, despite the promise of the marshland. Ahead of her the cars were closer and she walked faster, reluctant to leave the children alone for longer than she had to. Staying close to the edge and hefting her piece of metal, she passed a clump of nettles which were just like the ones back home but had leaves a foot long and were spiked with shiny spines from which tiny drops of fluid dripped to the concrete edge. She could see little holes there like burn marks and when she passed by she got a whiff of something violent and bitterly caustic.

The first car was an old Model T, or something similar, with running boards and flaring wheel arches and a little yellow indicator arm which stuck out from above the door. If what she knew about old Henry Ford was true, it had once been black, but now there was not a lick of paint on its entire surface. The rcar end was angled in against a cluster of the venomous nettles and from bumper to wheel arch, the whole of the back had disintegrated completely. She passed it by, edging alongside the mottled bodywork through which twisted some sort of creeper bearing wide, orchid-like flowers patterned like mouths opened in silent screams.

Only twenty yards ahead, another car was canted against a shattered tree stump. The rear bumper had sheared off and was lying at the side of the road and as she approached, Patsy could make out no further damage. The paintwork was dirty, as if the car had been left in the open for a month or more, but it was intact. The boot lid had sprung open an inch or two and it was swinging gently in the breeze, banging against the lower edge with a not unmusical chime, and trailing several pieces of white frayed twine. She approached it quickly, ignoring the minute rustlings from the undergrowth. The filler cap resisted at first, then twisted off and immediately she was breathing in fumes. Patsy unfankled the plastic tube, fed it down into the tank, and unscrewed the top of the flask. She was about to siphon the gas when a thought struck her and she got up, went to the back and lifted the tail up.

A carry-case and a kluge-bag were tumbled at the back, among a shower of dried flower blossom. Right in the corner a bright red plastic container was strapped to the bulkhead.

'Wonderful,' she said to herself and her spirits soared. Finding a petrol can would save the flask, and it was the first piece of luck she could recall in days. Patsy grinned and the little boost made her think she might yet win through.

'I'll beat you, bitch,' she shouted out loud and she laughed triumphantly. Her laughter echoed along the road and came back to her from the flat face of a distant rock.

The little tube reached into the tank and she sucked it hard, not realising how quickly the fuel would rise. It hit the back of her throat and she gagged against the foul taste, eyes watering. Some petrol spilled on the ground, making a little refraction pattern like the oil on the water earlier in the morning, but she managed to get the end into the opening of the container and watched as the level rose. The red canister would take a gallon which would give her fifty miles if she drove slowly. She'd find water in fifty miles and she'd find food too, even if she had to catch something and kill. Something inside her tightened and she knew, despite her revulsion, that if push came to shove, she'd catch and eat one of the road crawlers before she let them eat her children, and the knowledge that she could do such a thing, *would* do such a thing, gave her added strength.

She twisted the top to seal the canister and straightened up, feeling stronger – despite the hunger – than she had since the flight from Broadford House.

'It's about time you took control of this,' she scolded herself. 'You've lasted three nights and this road hasn't beat you yet, so get your backside in gear, Patsy Havelin and beat those *bastards*.'

She was about to heft the fuel and go back when another thought struck her. She'd had some luck and there might be more. If there was petrol and a can, there might be food, maybe a tin of something, even a bag of sweets. Both cases in the back were locked. She went round to the front and as she reached the driver's door something rustled in the undergrowth beyond the snapped-off sapling. Patsy scanned the tangle of thorny runners, not alarmed but wary enough, as she reached for the handle, turned it down and pulled the door open. She swivelled towards the car, still checking the greenery, then turned to look inside.

A grinning skull lunged right at her.

Dry air wheezed out of her throat. The shock was so great that the scream never reached her vocal chords. Patsy's mouth opened so wide the muscles creaked under her jaw.

For an instant her vision wavered on the crest of the unbelievable fright. She reeled back, tripped on her own feet and landed on her backside with a jarring thud. Her vision cleared, snapped back into focus and she raised her head to see the grinning skull come looming down at her.

'No!' One single word was all she could blurt as she scrabbled backwards, heels kicking for purchase on the stony ground. The horror came leering down, a dreadful brown mask over which a thin membrane was stretched. Two dry slits were cut across the eye sockets and a strand of dirty-fair hair hung down to the teeth in a mouldy rat's tail.

The skull stopped with a jerk and the mouth lolled open in a six-inch gape.

'Jesus,' Patsy bleated.

She stopped moving, frozen to stone, bulging eyes fixed on the sunken hollows. A miasma of putrefaction wafted from the shrunken cadaver, so powerful and foetid that her throat opened and she retched the last cup of tea onto the ground in an acid trickle. The reaction broke her paralysis. Her stomach clenched twice in painful spasms and her eyes swum with tears and when the moment was over, she could move again. She blinked her vision clear and looked at the corpse.

It was a body, that was all. Nothing to be afraid of. It leaned half out of the car, disturbed by the opening of the door, caught by the seat-belt that had snagged a withered shoulder. The skin covering the skull was paper-thin and ripped in places. Two gashes on the cheeks, caused by the sudden lolling of the head, allowed the jaw to swing wide, showing a powerful array of teeth above a scrawny neck through which brushed the ridges of the windpipe.

Patsy forced herself to be still and look at it. She'd never seen a dead body before, not a recently dead one, and on the geological scale she was used to, this was recently dead, though it had been drying in the heat of the car for months, maybe years. The smell had passed and she got to her feet, made herself move closer and inspected the mummified cadaver.

The skinny, elongated arms were still stretched out in front, attenuated fingers hooked onto the steering wheel. A gold bracelet dangled from the gristly junction at the wrist beside an expensive looking watch.

'It's a woman,' she heard herself say, though there was nothing feminine, indeed hardly anything *human* about the dried-up corpse.

It was wearing a bright dress in a vernal Paisley-pattern swirl. Whatever the original colour of her hair, it was now a greenish shade and most of it had fallen down onto the scrawny shoulder. The dress had crumpled where the body had sagged. The low neckline boasted two horribly wrinkled pouches. The stick-like legs, knees grossly swollen as the muscles had shrunk, ended in a pair of expensive patent shoes. Just below the collar, a withered nest of dried leaves was stuck to the material and Patsy realised it was a corsage.

It explained the luggage in the boot, covered in dried apple blossom.

She stepped back and her disgust was replaced by a wave of desolate melancholy. The blossom had been confetti. The odd pieces of string dangling from the trunk lid had been cut to stop the noise of clattering tin cans.

The woman had been a bride.

She'd been married and had come from the reception with her new husband, just a young girl maybe, though the wizened body made her look like a crone, and she'd been happy. They'd have stopped somewhere to cut tin cans away, heading for a hotel or a motel for their first night as married people.

And they'd found themselves on this road.

For some reason, this was worse than the graveyard of cars, where there had been no people, at least as far as she had seen, just dead and abandoned vehicles. It was even worse, in a strange way, than the scenario below the parapet of the bridge, because

313

despite the horrifying destruction it had not seemed completely *real* to her, more like a flickering scene being screened for her benefit, like a moving picture show, repeated for anybody who stopped on the bridge.

This was different. This was a body, somebody who had been alive and was now dead, killed by this road.

Patsy stepped back, squeezing down her own body's sudden need for extra oxygen. She slowly sank to her haunches Indian-style on the hard shoulder and stared at the corpse, trying to visualise what had happened.

Had it been a jealous lover?

If any here present know of any reason why this couple should not be lawfully married, let him speak now, or forever hold his peace.

She visualised somebody tall and black haired with olive skin and hawk's eyes come striding down the aisle, while the guests gasped themselves into a hushed silence.

Forever? I give them forever! Let them travel together on the low road that goes forever and never ends.

Her mind conjured up the scene, making it up as she went along, but it fit, it felt right, though the bride could have simply taken the wrong turning.

She thought not.

Had he spat in church, in front of the altar, challenging their God? Had he wanted her as much as Kerron Vaunche had wanted Paul? As much as she wanted Judith?

She raised herself up again, having gone from despair at the thought of their impending death, to savage elation when she'd found the spare tank, and back to foreboding in a matter of minutes.

'Be brave, woman,' she berated herself. 'You have to be strong.'

The wind carried her words away over the leprous birches.

The passenger seat of the car was empty. A dusty champagne bottle lay in the foot well, the cork beside it. They hadn't known, she could see that. They'd been laughing, sharing the champagne. *Don't get it on my dress!*

And at some point they must have realised they were lost. They hadn't run out of fuel, but they had run off the road. The twin shallow gouges on the ground and the crumpled fender testified to that. It might have been the cat's-eye crawlers, or some other monstrosity of the night. Had he left her to search for help in the morning, telling her to wait until he came back? Had she sat with the window up, listening to the screams in the night and the howls of dying lives, slowly getting weaker from thirst and hunger, eyes scanning the road, hoping and praying that she would see her man come back for her?

'It won't happen to me,' she asserted. 'I'll damned well make sure of that.' Her voice rose strongly and her mood flipped back to defiance.

As soon as she spoke the words, lightning flickered way off down the road. She turned and saw a huge dark cloud rolling up into the pale sky and a moment or so later, thunder rumbled across the undulating rocky plain, vibrating the ground. She turned back to the car and as she did so the corpse wheezed.

Patsy almost died.

The slit in the stretched skin covering the eye opened with a slight ripping sound and a flash of blue glinted in the hollow. The eye rolled. A big sapphire-blue beetle crawled out of the socket, mandibles clicking a chitinous morse. The jaw opened wider and the thing wheezed again.

Ghhh. . . . atseeee. . . .

'No!' She shook her head. 'No way!' She backed off.

The skull turned, making a little creaking sound. Something moved in the shrivelled neck. The skin broke with a nasty little pop and a maggot, sluggardly undulating and enormously fat, came squirming out of the rip.

Its black head rubbed against the windpipe and the sound came again, just like a hoarse, choking whisper, calling her name.

Her heart kicked again and went galloping hell for leather. The smell of putrefaction came wafting strong again and a big scream began to evolve inside her. The corpse's other eye started to wriggle behind the parched lid and the chest hitched once. It was full of bugs, her mind told her, but underneath conscious thought, the insistent voice was yelling: *It's alive. It's coming to get you!*

A far-off howl broke the paralysis.

'Peter!' Her voice came back and suddenly the twitching

corpse could have come alive and done an Irish jig. She had left them too long. Something dreadful had happened. The gypsy had found them. She spun away from the car, one hand gripping the handle of the petrol tank, while the flask went spinning away. It tumbled on the flat of the road and crunched its innards to shards, but by then Patsy was haring it back along the road towards the car.

20

She reached the car and skidded to a halt, almost collapsing with the effort. The nearside door was open wide. Judith's scarf was fluttering by the roadside. The children were gone.

There was no sign of a struggle. There were no other cars on the road except the wrecks ahead. Panic flooded her. The children were gone. She gasped for a breath that would not come, felt her vision waver. Had Kerron Vaunche sneaked up on them when she was getting water? Had she snatched them again to take them back to Broadford House and that dreadful stone?

Patsy tried to recall if she had heard the distant sound of an engine. Her heart was thumping away inside her as if it was trying to break out.

Then she heard the cry from beyond the low ridge of the embankment. Without hesitation she staggered up the final few yards and looked down a short steep bank. Thick, rubbery-leafed bushes clumped darkly. Beyond them pools of water gleamed, throwing back reflections of tall trees with buttressed trunks planted in deep pools.

That wasn't here before, she thought vaguely. Some of the low vegetation had been trampled down showing where two sets of feet had passed. She couldn't tell if they had been made by her children. She didn't know enough. It could have been animals. It could have been monsters come down the ridge to snatch them. *Oh, Jesus* . . .

'Peter! *Where are you?*'

Her cry racketed off the tall trunks and broke up in the dim reaches of the swamp. A black dread bubbled up in the pit of her belly. Without hesitation she went plunging through the gap in the foliage.

The bank was steeper than Patsy had realised. No sooner was she over the lip than she was indeed plunging down the slope. The land fell away for about thirty feet on a mossy gradient that offered little traction. Two yards down, she lost her footing, slipped halfway and then rolled the rest. She landed heavily on her shoulder, knocking her breath away, half submerged in a decaying pile of leaf mould. She rolled over, badly winded and her foot burst an enormous multicoloured mushroom, sending a cloud of green, evil-smelling spores rolling into the damp air. The fungus was the only colour down in the shadow of the swamp. Everything else was in grey shadow.

'Peter?' Her cry reverberated out in broken shards of noise. 'Come on, Peter. *Answer me!*'

She stumbled forward, a-jitter with panic and plunged up to her knees in tepid water. Grey bubbles juggled to the surface and burst with moist plops. Their gases stank. In the tall trees, a bird called hollowly, a jungle sound from a hundred movies and in her peripheral vision, something rolled under the surface of a slick pool, disturbing the layers of dead leaves floating there.

'Please, Peter. If you can hear me, shout out,' she bawled, voice heading upwards to a scream. The schizoid little voice yelled incessantly. '*Oh God . . . they've drowned. She's under the water. Oh please no . . .*'

'Mum'.

Off to the left. Not a shout, more a whimper, and a pulse of joy almost burst her heart.

'Oh, thank God,' she whooped. Little sparks danced in front of her eyes. 'Peter. Call out again. Tell me where you are.'

She waded through the glutinous swamp. Small things like little fish, maybe eels, squirmed under her feet.

'Mum. Help.' Peter cried again in a strangled voice.

'Keep talking, son. I'm coming for you.' She got to the far side of the pool and reached a little ridge that was formed from the long-dead trunk of a fallen tree. A slithery shape wriggled against her leg and sped away. She got a hand to the mouldering log and a sticky sundew closed gelatinous fingers around hers. Pins and needles ran up to her elbow and she pulled away. The plant's tendrils waved slowly. High overhead in the dim canopy, the bird hooted again. Something moved between the trunks somewhere to the right and she ignored it.

'I'm almost there,' she babbled. 'Call out to me.'

'Please ma . . .' It came out like *fleas wa*. Patsy clambered over the ridge, down into another basin and stopped motionless. Peter was squashed down between the flanges of the buttressed roots of a giant swamp tree. His head dipped below the scum on the stagnant surface, then bobbed up again. He gasped for air, face slimed with muck. A hand came up from the water clutching his penknife, waved in the air. He came right out of the water, struggling to his feet, then slipped back down again into shallows which came up to his waist.

'Peter, what's wr. . . .' she started to say. The words froze.

The green coil around his neck seemed to squeeze.

Snake.

The word hissed in her mind.

Peter's eyes blinked open, startling blue against the dark brown mud. He struggled back to his feet, tugging against the green coils. His hand came down and jabbed at the thing constricting his neck and it spasmed galvanically, so fast that both his feet came up out of the water and he was smacked back down. An arc of mud splattered the tree and Peter disappeared completely under the surface.

Patsy leapt into the pool, heedless of the sharp branches that jutted upwards. Something snagged the cuff of her jeans and she pulled away with a grunt of effort. Peter's foot broke through the slick skin. She gained a yard, fighting against the suction of the mud under her own feet and reached him, gasping for air. His hand came up again, swinging the knife and without thinking she twisted it out of his fingers. A gurgling bubble of air broke the surface above where his head disappeared.

He's drowning. Oh Jesus, he's swallowing water.

She plunged down, right under the water, got a hand to his head, an arm round his shoulder and heaved upwards. A muscle twisted under her shoulder-blade but she didn't even notice. A powerful convulsion jerked her back. Her right hand came down and stabbed just under the algae and something as thick as her arm jolted in a powerful twist. A green coil came looping out, rolled around her wrist, started to tighten and in a flash she saw it was not a snake. It was some kind of creeper, ropy and sappy and slithering fast. She dragged her hand backwards before the noose closed on her and the blade ripped through the rind.

Green sap blurted over her arm. The loop opened with a snap and Peter came breaching out of the water.

She hauled him over the edge of the tree root and got him to the bank. The creeper, moss-hoared on the top and bearded with tiny squirming rootlets underneath, came slithering after her and Patsy simply hacked at it in two vicious chops which severed it completely. The amputated section went wriggling away like an eel and disappeared under the water, while the thick remainder glupped its sickly sap in pulses to the beat of a giant, invisible heart.

'Got you,' she gasped, dragging him further away from the water and turning him over. A leaf stuck to his face like a leech and she scraped it away, revealing his wide blue eyes staring blankly at her.

'Come on, son, get up.'

He flopped to the ground, arms spread lifelessly.

'Peter,' she urged. 'Get up.'

Beyond her, in the depths of the waterlogged forest, Patsy could hear the creaking of branches, the cracking of twigs as if something was moving towards them. Judith must be there.

'Get *up*, Peter. *Get moving.*'

For a second he lay completely still, eyes still staring blindly. Then he coughed so violently his whole head and chest came off the ground and a thick gobbet of mud went flying over Patsy's shoulder. She clasped him to her chest and he coughed again, hard enough to shake her backwards but she held on to him, slapping his back hard to help his lungs clear.

He shuddered in her arms, hawked roughly and then spat deliberately. 'It got me,' he spluttered. 'It just came down from the tree and grabbed me and I couldn't get away.'

'We have to get Judith,' Patsy interrupted. Somewhere ahead of them she could hear the sounds of footsteps. She had no time to listen to him.

'She just got out of the car. I tried to catch her.'

'Tell me later,' she insisted, dragging him up off the damp leaf-litter. Beyond, in the shadow, another branch broke with a gun-fire crack. Patsy looked up, expecting, but there was nothing but deeper shade.

Peter coughed again. Two brown trails of slimy mud formed

on his upper lip and he wiped them away with his forearm. Patsy half-dragged him back through the pool, all the time sweeping the shadows for any sign of Judith. They got to the far side, feet sucking up from the mud and freeing the foetid marsh gases which bubbled up through the soupy liquid and burst in flatulent little stenchy explosions. At the buttressed base of the next tree, something thin and green came snaking lazily towards them. Patsy batted it with the knife, almost casually, and hauled Peter over the ledge and down into the next pool. It was only a dozen feet wide, but deeper than the last and beyond it was the steep muddy bank they'd have to climb to get back onto the road.

Judith stood stock-still at the edge of the bank, eyes blindly fixed beyond them, staring at the depths of the forest swamp. A cloud of iridescent dark flies was buzzing about her head. Some of them were tangled in her hair. Patsy started down the lip of the pool.

'. . . *Who dwells in the roots in the dark beneath the earth* . . .'
The chant was clear in the still air. Judith's face was expressionless, like a mannequin. The rash was spreading down past her temple. Beside her ear the skin had cracked into fissures. Something inside Patsy broke. She went plunging across the soft earth, crashing through the succulent plants, drew her hand back and simply slapped Judith as hard as she could. The child's head rocked back. Peter gasped. Judith made a little squeaking sound. Under their feet the ground shivered as if lightning had struck and the massive swamp tree trembled.

Judith fell backwards. Patsy caught her and the child simply burst into tears. The glazed look disappeared from her eyes and she looked up at her mother as if she had woken up. Patsy wanted to burst into tears. Instead she swept her daughter up and pulled Peter behind her.

She was just about to slide down into the water when something moved just below her and she pulled back.

'Something's coming,' Peter said, urging her forward. 'I can hear noises behind us.'

Patsy tried to make her feet move, but without warning, every nerve in her body was suddenly stretched taught in dreadful alarm.

'What's the matter?' Peter asked behind her. He turned round to look behind them. Something moved in the shadows, just a flutter of dark on dark, with no real shape. He nudged his mother, trying to gain her attention.

'Quick, mum. There really is something coming.'

Patsy tried to go forward again, senses now quivering in alarm. The water boiled suddenly and a big bubble swelled more than a foot in diameter, green and shiny with algal sheen before it burst in a reek of dank rot. For a second the surface-slick was swept clear and a pale oval came floating to the surface. It turned over, becoming momentarily darker, like the waning of the moon, then brightened as it rose upwards to within a couple of inches of the surface.

A pair of white eyes stared at her from the water.

'Come on, mum,' Peter jittered beside her. 'There's more things coming.' He was still looking back anxiously, gripping her arm. She jumped back and he turned, saw her eyes, followed their direction and saw the bleached face of the corpse come rolling up through the greasy skin of the water. A yard away, another bubble swelled and burst. Another pale shape came wavering upwards. Close to the far edge, two immense bubbles expanded, shimmered in the still air and then winked out simultaneously with loud pops. A grey hand came twisting limply into the air. Peter's breath drew inwards in a loud gasp.

Just below where they stood the white face broke through the slick, propelled upwards by the rising gases, and her eyes were snagged by the dead stare of the dead man. Dirty water poured from his chewed nostrils and a little blanched piece of skin fell away from under his eye. Something flat and wriggling came out from between his frayed lips and went undulating down into the depths.

'We have to go,' Peter said in a stage whisper, as if afraid the floating thing would hear him. 'Honest, mum. We can't stay here.'

He pushed at her urgently and the shove was just enough to make her feet slip on the downslope, and that was enough to break Patsy's paralysis. She slid only six inches, but it was half a foot closer to the water-bleached face rising up in the stinking pool. She turned and saw something move on the far side of the shallow pool. It looked like a shadow which quickly merged with the other shadows at the base of a broken trunk. The shallow tarn they had come wading through was now bubbling violently as gases under the mud came rolling upwards. Beyond it, between the pillars formed by the thick trunks, shapes were moving towards them.

'It's ghosts!' Peter yelped. Up against Patsy's shoulder, Judith's breath had begun to whoop.

Grey forms came wading through mud and slime. Whatever they were, they were too substantial to be ghosts. A branch creaked underfoot off to the left, a piece of rotted log crumbled with a muted crunch straight ahead. Somewhere to the right, a foot came out of the mire with a hungry sucking sound. Right behind them, a small grunt rumbled and Patsy whirled so fast she almost tumbled them both down the embankment and into the water. Another corpse had come floating upwards, its rotted belly bulging with gas. As it turned, a blurt of vapour gurgled out of its open mouth, making it sound as if it was struggling for breath.

She grabbed Peter by the collar and hauled him along the narrow causeway formed by a dead trunk, heading for the steep bank. They hit it at a run and scrambled their way upwards, slip-sliding, gaining two feet and losing inches while behind them shadows and shapes came steadily squelching their way through the swamp.

Let her stay . . .

The whisper sounded inside her head. The words had the texture of damp mushrooms, jellied and mouldering in a lightless cellar.

Uanan . . . stay with us.

Judith stiffened. She lifted her head from Patsy's shoulder. Her mother reached up and slammed it back down again. She hit Peter on the backside with the heel of her hand, driving him up the slope. In her own head she could hear the slithering exhortations and a picture of Gollum came flitting into her mind, pale and amphibious, slinking through the marsh where the souls of the dead flickered and glowed under the surface.

'It's a dream,' she told herself, and for a moment, she could have believed it was a dream, some kind of hallucination, until Peter slipped backwards and his heel dug into her instep with

323

enough force to cause a shriek of hot pain and the notion that she was dreaming vanished.

Ssstay down here ... bring the offerings. The slithery voice wheedled and she shook her head, trying to push it away. She got a hand under Peter again and gave him a hard push which sent him up and over the lip of the bank. He yelped in surprise and disappeared into a flaccid cluster of water-iris. She heard a splash, followed him through and plunged into a hole of clear water. She got to her knees, then to her feet and through the patch of reeds, up the incline, beyond the straggle of low bushes and on to the verge at the side of the road. She bundled them into the car and got moving, all the time expecting to see swamp wraiths come loping down the slope, but nothing moved out from the dark of the trees.

They reached the wrecked car and she stopped, still breathing heavily. Peter tried to explain what had happened but she hushed him up. No explanations were needed. Something had reached out from the dark and tugged at Judith. It had been Kerron Vaunche or one of the dreadful things she worshipped in the dark of the cellar.

The idea of slapping her daughter, striking a sick child, was an appalling one. But it had worked. For an instant it had stopped that chant, that black litany. For an instant it had silenced the wheedling thoughts that reached and scratched inside Judith's fevered brain.

Two more days. The moon would be full. *They must be getting desperate.* Patsy knew they would hound them without cease, without peace.

The flask was lying on its side in the middle of the road, one side crumpled and she knew it was beyond repair. The kettle and the petrol can were where she'd left them. Peter and Judith stayed in the car – she didn't want either of them to see the mummified thing in the wreck – while she poured fuel into her own tank. She gathered up the kettle and the piece of angle-iron and dumped them on the floor in the back.

One gallon of fuel was enough for thirty, maybe forty miles, even more if she drove slowly. Patsy debated trying to drain another gallon from the car, wondering if she could kneel down beside the filler-vent while the dead and rustling thing inside squirmed with maggots and crawled with beetles and those black flies. She picked up the can, realising with some amazement that she could do it, *would* do it, when Peter rolled the window down.

'Mum?'

She halted just as she was heading for the other car.

'Look.' He pointed behind them. The road stretched away into the distance, curving gently around a low rise of rocky hillocks and stunted trees. A flash of light winked at her and she raised her hand to shield her eyes, scanning the distance where the road disappeared into the dusty haze.

'What is it?' she asked. Peter came out of the car and stood beside her, unconsciously mimicking his mother's stance.

'It's a van.'

The dark shape, indistinct in the wavering distance, gradually resolved. It was moving along the curve of the road, sending up a little cloud of dust in a slipstream which marked its passage. Sunlight flashed against glass again. It was a black transit van. They stood there, staring into the distance, watching as the van cleared the curve and headed onto the straight. Headlights, dim in the daylight, flashed a weak yellow and instantly Patsy recalled the car that had pursued them the previous night before they had run off the road. It went over a slight bump on the road and the lights flashed again, and they were clearly a yellow-orange colour, not white. The shape of the van was clearer. It swelled as it neared, though it was still a couple of miles distant. Of a sudden, Patsy knew it was the same one that had tailed them, gaining fast, before they'd gone up the slip road and lost it. That seemed like an eternity ago, though it was only a matter of hours.

The same van was coming up behind them, getting closer. The instinctive little voice started bleating inside her head. *Kerron Vaunche.* She was coming now. The trail of dust rolled up into the pearly sky, causing its own shimmering mirage. A low insectile hum became a bluebottle drone as the sound of a fast-revved engine got ever louder as the black van approached.

Patsy pivoted on her heel. 'Back in the car,' she ordered Peter and this time there was no hesitation. He scrambled into the back beside Judith. Patsy started the engine with one hand while she slung the empty petrol can down into the foot well on the passenger side. The gears ground, bit and then they were spurting forward, sending up their own cloud as the tyres spun on the red grit. The needle on the speedometer swung up past sixty, then seventy, and they were racing down the highway, past a jumble of cars which clustered in a tangle, all crumpled into each other, round a tight curve and away.

Patsy put her foot down and the car accelerated to eighty, guzzling their gallon of fuel. She knew she couldn't keep the speed up for long, but there were no choices now. They were coming for her children.

Another tight bend and a rising slope, through an archway formed by the reaching branches of trees and Patsy realised that she was now no longer on a motorway. Again the road had changed, becoming a two-way secondary road, though she couldn't recall seeing any sign. The narrow road twisted and turned, snaking left and right while the forest crowded up against the tarmac. Patsy drove on, not letting her eyes wander because she was certain she'd see movement in the depths of the forest, and if she did that she'd hear the scratchy supplication in her head and that would be enough to make her jerk the wheel and kill them all.

The road dived under another dark alley of foliage, came out again into sunshine and then, almost miraculously, a square sign flickered on the verge, a white flag on a striped pole. It bore the simple thick black cross which denoted a crossroads ahead. She slowed, now past the trees, touched the brakes a little. A tall angular construction loomed ahead, a wooden gantry set, it seemed, in the middle of the highway, but when she neared it, she saw it was a circular patch of bare ground which formed the heart of the intersection. Four roads, including the one she was on, fed away from it. She slowed almost to a halt, peering right and left, wondering which direction she should take. She glanced up at the gantry, expecting to see a signpost. Four arrows, carved roughly in paint-peeled slats of wood, pointed down all four directions, but there was nothing to identify what or where they indicated.

'What's that?' Peter asked. He leaned forward and pointed up at the framework of timber. Patsy was too busy to listen. Behind her, though it was still out of sight, the black van was following fast. It could burst out from the trees any second.

'Make a decision,' she told herself angrily. 'Just *choose!*'

Left? The left-hand path? It didn't sound right.

'There's something up there,' Peter insisted. Patsy's attention was grabbed just for that moment and she looked up. In the far side of the wooden construction, a fluttering bundle dangled from a heavy timber plank. It looked like a twist of rags. She looked away, and somehow, the shape resolved itself in an after-image. Her eyes snapped back to the dangling thing and she saw the fretwork of black wrought iron, like a tall bird cage dangling from a rusted chain. Inside the cage, crumpled in a slump, the white of bones contrasted starkly against fluttering black rags.

'What is it?' Judith asked again.

A corpse in a cage dangled from the timber pointing straight ahead. She looked left and something squeezed within her, telling her *no*. She swung the wheel hard right, gunned the engine and went haring down the single track, all the while expecting to see the black van come shooting out from the archway of trees. A mile along the narrow road, it bent to the left, cutting off the dead-man's crossroads from sight. Inside her, she could feel the scrape of something dark and scabrous, and again she got a mental image of *Gollum*, snuffling and sniffing, searching for the ring, and she knew that she had been right to flee the black van. Kerron Vaunche's contact was like the touch of disease. The withering mental touch faded out almost immediately and instinct told her she'd taken the right turning. They had gone the other way. So certain was this impression that she eased her foot off the accelerator and let the car coast down to below fifty.

Rolling hills, vividly green stretched as far as the eye could see, dotted here and there with the tall clumps of odd trees. In her mind, the danger had receded, faded to silence. She drove for another five miles, now taking it easy, keeping alert for any signs of a car whose tank she could drain. The road twisted to avoid a low hummock and when she was past that she could see it stretch, arrow straight into the far distance. The needle was heading back down towards the red again. Somewhere along here, she told herself, she must find another car with fuel. She estimated she'd about twenty miles left before the car stalled.

Judith murmured dopily, but it was no mindless chant. Patsy remembered they'd no water left. She drove on, eyes fixed on the far distance, looking for any sign of an abandoned car.

She was past the man sitting back from the side of the road before his shape even registered. Without thinking, her foot hit the brake and the car screeched to a halt, sending up a little shower of grit. Patsy twisted in her seat to look out of the rear window.

He appeared not to have seen them. A thin waver in the air beside him told her he'd a fire going. Indecision clenched at her belly. The man sat hunched at his fire, not moving, neither looking up or down. It was as if he was carved from stone.

She didn't know what to do and the kids said nothing. Here was a strange man on a strange road where everything she had seen so far had been dangerous, if not downright deadly. But she was alone with two children and she had no water and little food and only enough fuel for a few more miles. Almost without thinking she opened the car door. Peter spun round at the sound. She held her finger up to her lips, tension suddenly tight as a violin string within her. Very slowly she eased herself out of the car, groping as she did for the piece of angle-iron behind the seat. The smell of burning wood came drifting on the air, along with the scent of something cooking and without warning her whole mouth was filled with thin saliva. She stood up and slowly swung the door half shut, leaving the keys in the ignition just in case.

For what seemed like an eternity, she stood there beside the car, watching the motionless form beside the fire. After a while she started to walk forward, holding the piece of metal up in front of her like a sword.

21

He didn't look up and she had no way of knowing if he'd seen her, though unless he was stone deaf he couldn't have failed to hear the car. She turned quickly, once again swithering in an agony of indecision.

Was he one of them? One of the gypsy folk? She couldn't tell. He could be anybody.

He could be any *thing*.

The man did not move. Patsy's hands started to quiver. If she approached him and he looked up and his face was a skull, she would die. If he reached and grabbed her and turned into the policeman creature, she would drop like a stone.

Peter and Judith were watching, both of them kneeling up to peer over the back seat. She forced herself to move away from the car towards the man, one step at a time, fingers clenched on the piece of metal. She had to find out, find out if he was real, if he could help. Every step of the way she expected his hunched shape to writhe and change. If he made one wrong move she'd club him, club him hard on the side of the head and then she'd get back to the car when he collapsed to the ground.

Ten yards from the car, the man raised his head up. He was wearing a brown hat with a wide brim. Underneath it his eyes were hidden by shadows. He looked like a dirty, dangerous tramp.

The image of the man in uniform came instantly back again and she stopped, one foot forward, one back. He'd reached in and grabbed her breast with hard and horny hands scraping across her skin, and when she'd fought him off, when Peter had screamed at him, the shadows had flitted across the man's face and she'd thought he'd begun to *change*.

She looked back at the children then turned to face the tramp by the fire. He was fifty yards away, no more. She was about to move forward when he reached down close to the fire and picked something up. Slowly, almost leisurely, he got to his feet and walked towards the road. Patsy backed off, but he didn't even look at her.

Ambush. Get out of here. Every nerve was jangling.

He strolled maybe ten yards, head still lowered, as if he was looking for something that had fallen and put the object down on the white edge-marker line. It was a tin can, opened in a jagged curve at the top. A wisp of steam curled upwards. The stranger walked back to the fire and sat down again with that same, unhurried economy of motion. There had been nothing threatening, nothing tense in the way he'd moved.

He'll kill you. Kill the children. The internal voice was hysterical now. The man had walked with a lazy arrogance, as if laying bait for vermin. Despite the dreadful fear, Patsy made herself move forward until she was close enough to see what he'd put on the road surface. It was a tin of beans. Immediately her mouth watered so much she had to swallow quickly.

He looked up at her then and waved a nonchalant hand in the direction of the steaming tin, letting her know in the simple gesture that she should take it. She stared at the fingers, checking to see if the hand was thick and calloused, the fingers horny and covered in red hair. From where she stood, it just looked like a grimy hand. She forced herself to walk closer, pinning him with her eyes, alert for the slightest movement. He had gone back to his original position, head bowed, hidden by the flopped brim, so that she couldn't see his eyes. He huddled into a tattered leather coat and she had no way of knowing if he was drawing an axe or a big jagged blade. She reached the beans, shaking with strain and feeling as if she'd run a marathon to claim a prize, bent down and groped for it, never taking her eyes off him for an instant.

The plain smell of baked beans rose up and filled her head with heady fumes. The saliva trickled again and insistent internal muscles squeezed in anticipation. The can was hot, but not enough to burn. She grasped it and stood up. He didn't react except to reach in to a big bag and bring forth another tin which might have been the same as the first, or any of a whole range of varieties. As she walked back to the car she could hear the little squeaking sound as he used the blade of a knife to open it.

Peter fell on the beans like a wolf-cub and Patsy tried to feed spoonfuls to Judith, all the time looking back to the huddled shape by the fire, the way a she-wolf would stay alert when the cubs fed. She took two spoons from the top, scalding her tongue and it was the most delicious food she could ever remember tasting. The tin was empty in a few minutes.

'Who is he?' Peter asked her, mouth full, jaws working overtime. A little red trickle of tomato sauce escaped for a moment of freedom before being recaptured by his tongue.

Patsy shrugged her shoulders. 'I don't know. We have to be careful.'

'What are you going to do?'

She looked from Peter to Judith who was gazing up at her blankly. The sheen was back on her forehead and the dry fissures were spreading out across her cheeks. Underneath the skin a tracery of fine veins gave a false blush. She had hardly eaten anything and her breath was sour now. Patsy leaned her gently back in the folded blanket.

'I'm going to speak to him. I want you to stay in the car, and make sure Judith does, too.' She gave Peter a long look which told him she expected to be obeyed this time and he nodded guiltily. Patsy backed out of the car and looked back at the stranger. He was turning a stick which bore a dark cluster along its length. She closed the door as quietly as she could, hefted the piece of iron again, just in case he turned out to be unfriendly, or in case he turned out to be something *other* than what he seemed to be. She walked along the edge of the road, once again jittery with the expectation of fight or flight, or maybe just plain fright.

When she got to where she'd picked up his offering she stopped and he looked up. His eyes were still in shadow and he'd a straggly beard that might have been red. His coat was tattered and covered with dust. On the stick over the fire, the dark mass, she could see now, was something charred.

Instantly she had a vision of the imbecilic girl with the eyes of mould hunched over the smoking black thing on the table that had looked like something dragged from a burned car. She shrank back, mind whirling again. Was it meat? Was it something dragged from a burning car? Patsy tried to speak, gulped, started again.

331

'Can you help us?' she began.

'Don't know, ma'am.' His voice rumbled out from under the shadow of the brim, rough as the singer on the jukebox at the mad way-station.

'We're lost,' she said, and even as it came out she realised how plaintive she sounded.

'You and everyone else, lady. Nobody got directions on this godless place.' He raised his head and she got a glimpse of eyes that might have been blue and a grimace that could have been a wolfish grin.

'I've been on this road for days now.'

He nodded, reaching towards the fire to turn the mass of stuff on the stick balanced between two small slingshot-forked branches. She smelled meat. Two thin bones poked out from the black mass and she realised it was a small animal. That brought a small wash of relief.

'Do you know where we are?'

'Nope,' he said in a drawl that made her think of a marshal in an old western movie. American or Canadian, she couldn't tell which. 'But I've a good enough idea.'

'Where?'

He reached for his hat and took it off, using his sleeve to wipe his brow as he did so. His hair was long and dirty-fair, caught in a tangled pony-tail at his collar. He looked down at the fire and then back up at Patsy.

'Lady, I believe this is the road to hell.'

She opened her mouth to ask another question, then closed it again. He took the opportunity of her silence. 'You want to put that thing down, or maybe you're aiming to crack my skull, huh?'

The angle-iron was still held *en-garde*. Slowly she lowered it until the end touched the road.

'Do you know how we get off it?'

'If I did, then I'd be somewhere else, that's for sure.' He grinned again and she saw a flash of strong teeth. 'Anybody with the sense the Lord gave them would be well out of here.'

The man reached to stir the second can which was now steaming as enthusiastically as the first. 'The beans to your liking?'

'Yes, thanks.' He looked normal. She took a tentative step forward, wanting to believe he was a normal human being, a

332

man of good intent. As she took her step he reached inside his tattered jacket and when he drew his hand out again it was hefting a big black handgun with an enormous barrel.

'Oh!' The little sound came out in a gasp. She jerked backwards, head turning to look at Peter who still watched from the back window, ready to call out a warning, while a part of her mind screeched: *Stupid bloody bitch!* She'd walked right up to this man on a road where everything was hostile and deadly, armed with a piece of metal. What did she expect? He was going to kill her and she had to tell the children to get out of the car and run and keep running.

'Can you use one of these?' he growled.

Patsy stopped in mid-turn. She spun back to the stranger, dimly aware of a nerve jittering just under her knee. He was holding the gun by the long black barrel, butt presented towards her.

'I . . .' she started. 'I thought . . .'

'Have you ever fired one?'

She shook her head, unable to get her mouth to form the words.

'I reckon you ought to learn,' he said. He laid the gun down on the short dry moss and gave it a little flick with his hand. It slid for several feet and came to rest a yard or so in front of her. Patsy dropped the length of metal, bent down immediately and snatched the gun up. The weight took her by such surprise that she almost dropped it, caught it before it fell and hefted it to shoulder height, aiming at the stranger.

'Don't move,' she said through clenched teeth, trying to sight along the barrel. It wavered unsteadily, left to right.

'Nowhere to move to, not until I've eaten, and even then I might just sit here and rest up a while,' he said. 'You go right ahead and wave that thing around in the air and when it gets too heavy, you can settle down here and share my meal, you and your passengers.'

'My children,' Patsy said. The gun just wouldn't stay still and already the weight was bearing her hand down.

'You'll probably break your shoulder,' the man said, and he gave a rumbling laugh as if he was witnessing a joke. 'That is if you manage to fire it, which you can't because it's not cocked, and I can't remember if it's loaded. Maybe even sprain your wrist into the bargain. But one thing's for sure, you won't hit me nor anything else five yards on either side.'

He picked his hat up and flicked some ash off the brim.

'Having said all that, I'd just as soon you didn't point it right at me, even if it's gettin' too heavy. It's against my principles to be a target, and on this road, there's just too much of that.'

The gun took over the decision-making and lowered itself to point at the ground.

'You weren't even looking,' Patsy said truculently.

'You have to have eyes in the back of your head on this damned road, and anyway, I'd probably have done the same if I was you.' He looked up at her again and then glanced at the car. 'You got kids riding with you?'

'My son and daughter. We're lost.'

'That's no lie, ma'am. You want to bring them along for a bite to eat? Or maybe you want to leave it until you're sure you don't want to bash my head in or blow my brains out. Either way, there's food enough here for everybody.'

Patsy lowered herself to her haunches, embarrassed, somehow relieved, but still apprehensive. She laid the gun down on the moss. He'd been right. She'd seen a thousand guns like this in the cinema, but she had not the faintest idea of how to make one fire.

'Do you know where this road goes?'

'As far as I can tell, it goes on and on forever, though there must be an end to it somewhere. I've never found it, and I don't know if I ever *want* to find it.'

'I've been driving for ages. We must have taken the wrong turning four days ago.'

'Four days, eh?'

She nodded and he reached towards the fire again and nimbly snatched the other bubbling tin from the coals. 'You've done pretty good so far if you've got a pair of young ones with you, and I admire you for that, but,' he paused and shook his head. 'You'd better learn how to use that handgun, or maybe a rifle would be best, for there's some bad things on this road.'

'I know. Nothing's right here. It's like Dante's Inferno. I think somebody put a curse on us, I really do.'

'That figures.' He lifted the can and sniffed. 'Ravioli. Hate the damned stuff, but what the hell. Beggars can't be choosers.'

'Can you help us?'

He shrugged, but the gesture told her he didn't know if he *could* help, not whether he would.

'Like the blind leading the blind,' he said slowly, gingerly fishing a piece of hot pasta with his fingers. He blew on it to cool it and then took a bite. 'I can tell you things to watch out for, show you what you can eat and when to stay off the road. Like tonight, for instance, when it's getting close to a full moon.'

'How did you get here?'

'It's a long story, and it was a long time ago.'

He stuffed the rest of the pasta into his mouth and chewed briskly. His beard was dark red, and tangled as if he hadn't had a shave or a haircut for a long time. A thin red scar that looked freshly healed ran down from his ear to the side of his mouth and Patsy could see another much deeper and more ragged whorl of damaged skin on his forearm when he reached for another mouthful.

'How long?' she finally asked.

'Near as I can tell, as much as anybody can tell in this god-damned place, it's been about three years. Maybe nearer four.'

Patsy's jaw dropped wide. The words went echoing around in her head. *Four years. FOUR YEARS!* She shook her head, trying to deny what she had heard though she knew she couldn't deny it. Four years. Those two words went ricocheting and bouncing around like bullet fragments, out of control, ripping through her mind.

'No,' she finally gasped out. *Four years?!* 'You don't understand. I have to get home. I've been travelling for days with my children. There's somebody following us in a black van and there's things at night and the cat's-eyes come alive and try to get us.' She heard her voice gabbling, almost out of control *Four years! Oh Jesus.*

'Been trying to get home myself awhile,' he said, and despite the turmoil inside her own head she heard an enormous sadness and a helpless regret in his voice. He lifted the stick from over the fire and swung it between them. A sweet smell of charred meat came wafting up from it.

'You ought to bring your little 'uns for a taste of this. Not quite rabbit, but not far from it. A kind of highway cousin maybe. You snare them on the margins where folks can live. Got to cut the heads off first, though. Got more poison than a toxic dump. Kill you near enough just by looking.'

'Four years?' she blurted, ignoring his explanation.

He nodded and the corners of his mouth turned down.

'But I can't. Honestly. I can't do that.'

He gave her a slow smile that said a lot of things and for some reason told her he was not a bad man.

'Maybe you'll be one of the lucky ones,' he said, though inside herself she could tell he was only trying to make her feel better. 'You don't meet many people on this road, not outside the cars that is. Not real folks. Maybe some of them find a way off and I met one or two folk who knew their own way back, but that was for them and nobody else. If there's black magic, there must be good stuff too, know what I mean?'

She nodded again. Kerron Vaunche had been black magic. There had to be a white. *Hadn't there?*

'That junction?' She pointed behind her, past the car where Peter's pale face hovered inches from the glass, at the distant arch of the intersection. 'Do you know where that is?'

He shook his head. 'I can't say, but I got a feeling that's where all the roads lead to. You can always see it, no matter where you are. You keep on going, and I think maybe when the time's right, you get to it. It's been getting closer now for a while, so I reckon I must be heading there. I met an old fella on the road, a bit addled in the head, but not stupid when it counted. He had a name for it. It'll come back to me in a while but its name don't matter much anyway. He believed that all lost souls ended up in the centre of it, going round and round forever.'

Patsy shivered. 'What do you believe?'

'I believe you have to keep your eyes open and learn how to use that big handgun there and try to do the best by your kids. I never saw young ones on this road and maybe you're going to tell me how you got here. Whatever sent you down on this road, they must have had a real mean streak to set children's feet towards the junction and that's the truth.'

He leaned forward and held out his free hand.

'Name's Christopher Deane. Chris to everybody except my old mother. Wish we could have met in better circumstances.'

For some reason she reached out and took his hand and it was only after his fingers clasped hers that she realised how she'd walked right into it. He could just pull her forward and grab her by the throat. He squeezed her hand quickly, firm enough to let her feel his strength and the hard workman's skin of his fingers, then let it go. He must have felt the sudden tension in her, or maybe read it on her face.

'That's good,' he said, smiling broadly. 'Stay scared and stay alive. Got a name?'

'Patsy Havelin,' she murmured. *Four years?* The enormity of it started up the echo inside her head.

'You want to go and tell the kids they can come and eat?'

She looked at him blankly, while the mental ricochet faded, came back to the present and slowly got to her feet. Back at the car Peter had a million questions in his eyes. Judith's were dull and the whites were tinged with green.

'Who is he? Is he dangerous? Is he a *bad man*?'

'I don't think so. He's got some food.'

'Is that a gun? Did you see the size of it? It's a Magnum, isn't it?'

'You want more food?' He nodded enthusiastically. 'Well, we'd better give him the benefit of the doubt.'

'Hunker down here and have something to eat,' Chris Deane told Peter. Patsy had Judith in her arms. It had only been days, but her daughter felt almost weightless, as if she was drying like a husk.

'What is it?' Peter asked, eyeing the blackened lumps on the makeshift spit. The ragged man looked up at him.

'It's um, pork. Like pork chops. You like them?'

Peter agreed that he did. The man rummaged in a big rucksack lying on the ground behind him, turning his back to them and Patsy saw that his leather jacket was in fact a long coat with the hem roughly cut back. When it fell open she saw two big leather knife sheaths strung on his belt. He turned back with a tin plate in his hand.

'You'll like this tinned stuff,' he said, tipping some of the ravioli onto the plate and handing it across to Patsy. Peter squatted by

337

the fire and accepted a piece of meat, gingerly passing it from hand to hand until it cooled enough to hold. He bit through the blackened crust and as soon as he did so the smell of cooked meat came wafting across.

Chris Deane winked at him and hauled another piece from the spit. For five minutes nobody spoke.

When they'd finished, he produced an old canvas-covered flask and passed it around. The water was clear and cold and Patsy made Judith drink as much as she could.

'She don't look too good,' the man said. 'She been stung maybe?'

Patsy shook her head. 'Something from before.' She didn't know how to explain. Kerron Vaunche had contaminated Judith, and maybe the touch of the waxing moon had spread the contagion. Chris Deane shrugged.

'We're short of water,' Patsy told him.

'You have to know where to look. There's some near here, so you can drink all you like. Won't take but a minute to fill the bottle.'

'Can you show me?' Peter asked.

'You have to be careful here, Pete,' Chris Deane told him, speaking softly, making it man-to-man. 'All the trails here, they can go different places, like sometimes there's a choice and you have to guess. You can take the wrong turning and it can be pretty wild out there beyond the road. You have to learn to see where the trails go.'

'Can I see your gun?'

'Maybe in a while. You have to be even more careful with guns. I got a slingshot you can use. They're good for pulling down the roost-birds just before it gets dark. Very delicious. Better than Colonel Sanders, believe me.'

'Is that like McNuggets?' Peter asked, and Chris Deane laughed aloud.

They finished the meat, which, underneath the crisp and carbonised skin was tender and pale, a tangy cross between chicken and pork, and Patsy just listened to Chris Deane talking to her son. Judith's head began to nod and in a few minutes she was fast asleep, with her head on Patsy's lap. Her dark hair was dry and wispy. The pink of her scalp showed through. Behind her ears, blisters were forming.

'You should bring the car back here and get it off the hardtop,' Chris Deane said. He looked up at the sky to where the sun was sinking towards the horizon. 'Going to be dark soon and you have to be up on the bank before moon-up. Closer it gets to full, the worse it gets here. Whole place is going crazy.'

'It's a conjunction,' Patsy said. 'It's going to get worse. There were things last night. They were on the road.'

'I've seen them. Crazy little fuckers. Pardon my language, but they're beasts from hell. You have to stay off the road when it gets dark.'

Patsy thought about what he'd said, debating whether to stay or move on. Chris Deane had a wild, unkempt and maybe untamed look about him. The scar on his face gave him even more of a rascally aspect. His leather jacket smelled of days on the road, and many a meal by a wood fire. She remembered the smell of smoke from Paul's clothing, that musty, somehow exciting scent of night and flames. The comparison annoyed her, more because of the fact that she had thought of it after all that time.

'And you have to put up your perimeter on the margin,' he said, breaking into her thoughts. 'To keep the night-walkers away. They can be pretty scary.'

'I know. They were all round us last night.'

'Well, you were lucky. You get the car and bring it back here. The fire keeps them away for a while, but there's other things.'

Patsy gently laid Judith down on the ground, pleased that the motion had not wakened her. She got to her feet and was about to turn towards the car when the thought struck her that she was leaving the children with the stranger. She looked down at him, but he was busy gnawing on a thin bone while Peter watched him askance.

'You're like Crocodile Dundee,' Peter said, and Chris Deane laughed again.

'Can even do the accent, if you give me some practice,' he said. 'I had a pal who was Australian, a real Aborigine, and he was a lot tougher than Crocodile Dundee, that's for sure.'

For some reason, this little exchange drained Patsy's misgivings. She turned and went to the car and reversed it back to where her son and the travelling man sat by the fire. She drove it off the road, up a small slope and onto the level. Beyond the margin, the land rose steadily towards a distant rocky escarpment where dense gorse-like scrub formed an impenetrable matt below the crags. The sky over there was turning that deep cobalt blue, shading to purple as the pre-dusk colours began to blot out the light. She managed to get Judith into the car without waking her completely, and wrapped the blanket round her. Peter began to yawn, even though he tried to hold his jaw closed to hide it from his mother, but he couldn't disguise it when his head began to nod. Every couple of minutes, while Patsy and Chris Deane shared a tin cup of coffee, he would jerk up, eyes blinking.

'Time for some shut-eye,' she told him.

'Not tired yet,' he protested sleepily, typically boyish in wanting to stay by the fire with the grown-ups as long as he could. She led him to the car, while their new companion gathered up some broken branches down towards the ditch. Patsy eased her son in beside Judith and folded the rug down from his chin.

'Get some sleep,' she told him. 'I'll be with you in a minute.' The sky beyond the scarp was even darker when she got back to the fireside. Chris Deane had stuck the branches into the ground in a rough circle which encompassed the car and the fire and was now drawing a long roll of string from a canister. An acrid smell made Patsy wrinkle her nose as he passed by and completed the loop.

'Oil and some battery acid. That and the fire helps keep away the night things. The road crawlers, they'll go for anything moving on the road. Except the black trucks. Nothing touches them. But the crawlers, they come out of their holes when the moon's getting to be full. It makes things change, as far as I can tell, but it's worse now than ever. You can feel it.'

'We stayed on the verge last night. I skidded off the road and a tyre blew out.'

'You were lucky, that's for sure. The crawlers can cut your tyres wide open. Don't know how you made it through the night, though, up on the margin. You need something to keep the other critters away.'

'Did you say you put oil on the string?'

'Just like creosote for carrot-fly.'

'Where I stopped last night, it was on a big black patch where oil had drained into the ground. I can remember smelling it and thinking I'd broken the engine.'

'That must've been it,' Chris Deane said. 'I didn't want to tell you in front of the kids, but there's some pretty bad shit out here, pardon my language. I didn't want to scare them any more than they are just now, but I reckon you should know. You've got the kids with you and I never saw any children on this road before.'

'I just want to get home.'

He glanced across, filled the coffee cup from the blackened pot and handed it across.

'You and me both, ma'am. I ain't been home in a long time.'

They sat in silence as the light faded further. Through the open window of the car, Patsy could here Peter snoring and envied him his boyish resilience. Chris Deane put some wood on the fire and sparks flew upwards in a brief constellation and a waft of heat blared.

'You said something about being followed,' he finally said.

'They want the children,' Patsy said flatly.

He leaned over, lowered his voice so that even if the children were awake they wouldn't hear what he said. The sun was almost gone from his eyes and the flames of the fire lit one half of his face, sending the other half into darkness.

'Maybe you'd better tell me what you did to get sent down this road.'

Patsy sat until the heat of the cup had drained away, wondering where to start. Chris Deane sat motionless. Finally she began to tell him about Kerron Vaunche and Broadford House.

22

'I don't think you *can ever* get off,' Chris said. 'That's the long and short of it, like my father used to say. I'd rather be able to tell you something different, but I won't tell you a lie.'

He had woken her just after sunrise by tapping softly at the window until she'd stirred. At first, when she saw his craggy face peering in, she'd thought it was the man in uniform, now caught up with her, about to reach in again and maul at her. She pulled back in alarm, then recognition dawned. He motioned to her and she eased herself out from under the blanket, letting Judith's frail form rest tight against the door. She quietly depressed the handle and got out into a morning where purple clouds harried each other across a bleak sky and the air carried the stench of corruption.

The fire was well alight, red flames crackling up, giving off hardly any smoke. The wind carried a heavenly scent of coffee towards her and she sniffed in, savouring the aroma.

'Always best to get started early,' he said. 'Days are pretty short round about now for some reason. Thought you might want a coffee before the children wake up.'

'I'd kill for a coffee,' she said, stretching the kinks out of her joints.

'Let's hope it won't come to it.' He poured some out. 'Only got the one cup, so you'll have to share. No milk, but there's some sugar in the bag.'

She took a first sip, hot and strong and amazingly tasty. 'Wonderful,' she sighed, eyes closed, letting the heat trickle down inside her.

'Gets the engine started,' he agreed. He reached for the cup and took it from her, gulping down a big mouthful that she thought must have scalded his throat, before handing it back. There was no ceremony, and he didn't even bother to drink from the opposite side of the cup. In the light of day, she was able to get a proper look at him and noticed his hair was fairer than she'd at first thought, roughly pulled back and tied in a short pony-bob. His beard was a coppery colour, thick and wavy. He'd left his hat off and she could see his eyes. In the morning light, they were quite a startling blue, narrowed against the early morning sun. The crow's-feet on either side showed he'd been heading sunwards for some time. The scar was still red which meant it had to have been a recent wound.

He was aware of her scrutiny, but he didn't react.

'Thought we'd best have a parley while the kids are a-bed. Might be a good idea if I didn't scare them none.'

'Are you American or Canadian?' she asked impulsively, knowing she'd changed the subject.

'US of A. Born and raised, but my father was an army man so I was marched all over. Had an uncle went to Canada to avoid the draft, but I haven't seen him since I was knee-high. Wouldn't mind going up there some day, though. Up in the tall timber, fishing the lakes. That would be fine.'

He had a faraway look in his eyes when he spoke. 'Nothing up there but maybe a grizzly or a rattlesnake and they're pussies compared to what comes snuffling on the verges of a night.'

'I just want to get home,' Patsy said. 'I've just got Peter and Judith back, and I have to get them away from here. Everything was all set to get better and now it's gone to hell.'

'You said it. That little girl looks seriously sick to me. Your gypsy lady sounds like one mean bitch.'

Patsy had told him the story and he hadn't said a word. There had been no sidelong glances as if she was crazy, as if she was telling a fairy tale. Chris Deane had just nodded now and again, encouraging her to go on.

'I have to get them home, because she's coming after them. She can connect with Judith and that's what's making her sick, I think.'

'This thing about the full moon,' he said, brow furrowed, 'I reckon that's what's making things really get worse. I didn't know anything about that.'

'Only two days left. If we can get away, there's nothing she can do. Crandall Gilfeather said she won't have time to prepare somebody else, so we have to get where she can't find us.'

'I hope you get there, I really do. But I've been trying to find

343

a way out of here for a long time. It could be there's no end to it, though I reckon it's at the big junction. He nodded his head to indicate the far-off spirals of elevated roadway barely seen through a gossamer mist. 'That could be where all roads go. I met a man who called it Havock Junction and he was half crazy, but the name seems to fit.'

The name brought back a memory of the service station.

'We found a place. The sign said it was Havock Services. I thought it was like a filling station, but it changed into something else.'

'I've seen that place a couple of times. You want to stay out of there if you can. I reckon what lives there are what's left of folks who've stopped and stayed. It's like a trap. I've been in there, a while back, and it's like a piece that's broken off the world and gone bad. I didn't stay long enough to get to know the place, but it was like all time was mixed together, so you could be in yesterday and tomorrow just the same as today. I reckon the folk who've stayed there, they stayed too long and got changed by it.'

'Have you really been here four years?'

He gave a brief nod. 'Near as I can tell, but you have to realise that in here time's different. Sometimes it goes backwards as well as front.'

'Have you met many people?'

'Damned few, that's the truth. At least, damned few that you could say were alive. I know that sounds mixed up, but there's a lot of bad stuff going on hereabouts. I've crossed paths with some folk who were crazy, and whether they were crazy first or this place made them crack-brained I couldn't tell. First time I came on the road proper, and it took me a while to get here, I met an old black fella. Not black like an American black, but like Australian. You know, an Aborigine? That's why I laughed when your boy said I reminded him of Crocodile Mick, because the old black man, he showed me how to live in this place, and I reckon if he hadn't, I'd have become one of them things that comes crawling out of the cars now the moon's getting full.'

'What do you mean?'

'There's a way to survive here, if you want to survive that is.'

344

'No,' Patsy interrupted. 'What do you mean the things that come out of the cars?'

He looked her up and down, as if gauging her strength, and while he did so he poured another coffee. 'I'll tell you another time. You're going to find out pretty soon anyhow,' he said, 'so you might as well be prepared for it. Hey, do your kids like eggs? There's a big bird like a coot down in the marshes, lays an egg big enough to split it in two.' He handed her the cup.

'Tell me,' she insisted.

'I got the eggs. Can scramble them up. Anyway, you've seen the moon over here?' He didn't even wait for a reply. 'Can't have missed it. Looks like it's dripping blood and it's got a face that would give you nightmares. I've been watching it this past couple of days. Everything's got a whole lot worse and I reckon your old man Crandall, he's hit the nail right on the head. There's something bad brewing up. It's bad enough at any other full moon time, but this is worse. I can feel it tugging away inside my own head.'

He turned to look at Patsy. 'You have to keep away from all the cars and trucks, even those horse-drawn wagons, because what's left of the folk inside them, the moon gets them awake, and sometimes they come wandering down the road. You don't want to be on the highway when that happens.'

Patsy put the cup down. 'I don't believe this,' she said flatly.

'I had the same problem myself, far as I recall. When I heard you coming down the road, that gave me a turn. On this place, anything that's moving on the road is out to get you, or it's something out of the *Curse of the Mummy*.'

'I don't believe this,' she said again and he looked over at her. The wavering air over the fire made his face shimmer.

'It could be this place is like purgatory,' he said. 'I had a friend once who told me about this place the Catholics believe in, where you have to stay until you've paid your dues. It could be this is like that. Maybe a branch office.'

He laughed ruefully. 'I've been telling myself that ever since I got here, that maybe I would work it out, pay it off or whatever. I told myself there had to be a door, some place I could find and say something like *abracadabra* or *open sesame* and I'd walk through and find myself in Vermont.'

'How did you get here?'

Chris leaned forward and picked up the cup, took a manly drink and sat back against the big canvas rucksack.

'I got on the wrong side of a little guy with no clothes and plenty of make up.'

'What, a homosexual?'

Chris laughed again, this time a spontaneous bark. It took him a minute to find his voice again.

'No. I don't think so. He was a bit like your friend the gypsy woman. At least, they had something in common. To cut a long story short, I was with a geology team down in Central America, doing a survey. One of the Indians came out of the trees and asked for help for a sick kid. The doc was away and I was the only one with any medical experience. By the time I got there, the kid was pretty far gone. Half his face was eaten away by some infection. I gave him painkillers, everything I had, and he died in the night. A couple of hours later, this little old guy came out of the forest and started pointing and jabbering at me. I got the feeling he was the local medicine man. The Indians, they got pretty scared and went back to the hut, leaving me and the ju-ju man in the rain. He took his stick and stabbed at me with it and for a second, it wasn't a stick. It looked like a snake. I felt a sting in my arm and then a whole world of pain and then everything faded away.'

He took another drink, his eyes far away, looking back.

'I woke up in the middle of a circle of stones, all standing up like teeth. The village had disappeared and my whole arm felt like it was on fire. I remember thinking I had to find water or the pain was going to kill me.

'I got out of the ring of stones and stumbled into the trees. The jungle was different. Trees the likes of which you never saw before, hundreds of feet high. And weird birds with wings like skin, like something out of a dinosaur book. I remember getting along the track, banging into trees and falling over creepers. Trying to find my way back.'

Patsy looked at him. *Four years.* He must have thought he was going mad.

346

23

'And I've been walking ever since,' Chris said. His eyes had that long-distance stare that told her he was looking far back inside his memory.

'At first I didn't realise what was going on. Hell, it took me a long time to figure out that I wasn't in some kind of nightmare, though thinking on it, its pretty much the same thing. I walked on the track for two, maybe three nights, and I was lucky that nothing killed me. It was just like I'd landed on another planet. My arm swelled up and got really septic and I must have had a fever for a while. I fell asleep in the bottom of an old hollow tree and when I woke up there were ants all over me, over my arm. That's what saved me, for they were carrying little maggot things that were squirming all over the slash on my arm, cleaning all the poison out. Things were a bit hazy for a while, but the arm healed up and I got out of there and kept on walking. I still had the idea that I had to find the village again, but I never did. After some more time, I can't say how long, the track got wider and wider and I found myself on dirt road and then a stone path and finally onto the blacktop. That old Indian, he sent me on this way, and I've been trying to find my way back to those standing stones ever since.'

He sat back against his rucksack. 'Coffee's gone cold,' he said. He bent to put the pot back on the coals again. Patsy watched him, still trying to take in what he'd told her. His narrative had been so plain, so succinct, that she could see the story unreeling, like a film.

'But why did he do it?' she asked him. 'You hadn't done anything to him.'

'Could have been he thought I was stealing his job,' Chris said. 'But I think it was because I touched his magic stick. It was like grabbing a lightning spike at the height of a storm and my arm still jumps a bit when there's a squall heading in. I reckon that was taboo. So he sent me here and I've been here since, just trying to get by, one day at a time. Once I read about an inscription carved on one of the caravels Columbus sailed in. It said: *Following the sun, we left the old world*. Kind of fits with what happened to me.'

Something jarred in Patsy's memory.

'You said there were standing stones?'

'Big things, all carved I think, but at the time I wasn't thinking about archaeology. Can't say how many there were, but there was a ring of them, that's for sure.'

'There was a ring of stones where the gypsies came to stay, and Lisa Prosser, the girl who escaped from Broadford, she said there was another ring inside the grounds, surrounding the house. Maybe there's a connection. Crandall Gilfeather said all the places with standing stones were connected by the *ley* lines.'

'Could be he's right. I know I've crossed a couple of bridges here, some of them over water, and another over a long stretch that took me nearly a day to get over, and you don't ever want to be stuck on a road you can't get off, believe me. None of the bridges were big enough to cross an ocean, but I must have done if I started halfway to Brazil and you started out in Scotland.'

'If there's a way in, there must be a way out.'

'Oh, there is, so I've heard. They say you have to find your own way. That's the secret, but whether that's true or not, I can't be certain. It would be fine if anybody would give you a hint. Old Leather, the Aborigine I told you about, he showed me a couple of things, plenty of things, but while he could go back up to the high track as he called it, he couldn't show me how to do it. Said it was against the law. You have to have the magic or you have to fight, is what he said, but when I asked him about it, he couldn't explain. He said his people called this the dream path that was made by some spirit way back in the past. He said all roads lead to every other road, but you have to have a sense inside your head of where you were. He tried to explain that to me, but I never ever got it.'

He was about to say something else when the car door opened and Peter came out yawning widely and stretching for the sky.

'Hey Pete, how d'you like your eggs? Fried sunnyside, sliced or diced.'

'Eggs? Have you got eggs?'

348

'Sure. There's a big bird down in the marsh that lays an egg . . .'

'Big enough to split it in two,' Patsy finished for him. He grinned at her.

'You have to drop it in water to make sure its fresh. Old ones float and they taste like . . . bad anyway.' He caught her look and smiled again.

He opened a small leather pouch and brought out two green eggs, each as big as a baseball which he cracked into a fire-blackened pan. Patsy went to the car and lifted Judith out. She was mumbling in her sleep and her clothes were saturated with sweat. She opened her eyes but they didn't seem able to focus. Patsy carried her close to the fire and wrapped her tightly in the little jacket with the red hood. She didn't know what else she could do.

The pink egg yolk fascinated Peter. Chris mixed them in with some powdered milk and water and in five minutes he'd made enough eggs for them all.

'Needs bread. I haven't had fresh bread in . . .' He looked down at the children who were sharing one spoon, and thought better of being precise. 'Don't get too much of it around here. And cheese. Sometimes I'd shoot my granny for a piece of cheese.'

'That's Benn Gunn,' Patsy said absently, rocking back and forth.

'Was he in *Bonanza*?'

'No. *Treasure Island*. He was marooned on an island and he was desperate for cheese.'

'Ma'am, I know just how he feels. I get to the stage when sometimes I even dream about Big Macs. That's when I know I'm going Section Eight.'

Peter looked up at him, the question evident in his eyes.

'Looney tunes,' Chris explained. 'Nutso.' He twirled his finger at his temple. Peter grinned and went back to his scrambled eggs. He put away two spoonfuls then came back.

'Are you going to help us? Can I get a shot of the gun?'

'If I can, that's the answer to the first. Certainly not, is the answer to the second, but you can use the slingshot anytime.'

Less than half an hour later they were on the move. Chris Deane unhooked the oil-laced twine from round the campsite

349

and stashed it in a small plastic container. His big rucksack only just fitted beside the picnic box and he made a quick inventory before he closed the lid. The big gun wouldn't fit in the glove compartment, but the smaller pistol was just short enough. Peter watched enviously as their new companion handled the firearm.

About five miles down the road, they came across two cars stranded just off the road and a heavy van stopped in the slow lane. The van's tyres were completely shredded. Pieces of frayed rubber strung out in solid splashes around the wheel rims.

'I need more petrol,' Patsy said, slowing to a halt beside the two cars. One of them was a long fifties-style saloon with elaborate tail fins and a spectacular array of tail-lights.

Chris got out of the car first, and when Patsy joined him she saw he had pulled out the gun. It was big and menacing and looked as if it could blow a hole through a wall.

'Just in case,' he said, pulling his hat brim down over his brow, the way a television gunslinger would. Patsy almost laughed. He unlocked the trunk, fished in his bag, and pulled out a small ribbed plastic hose.

'One of my best ever finds,' he said. 'The taste of gasoline makes me sick. Found it about a year ago.'

In moments the little siphon handpump got the suction going and the fuel was flowing. While Patsy worked the pump, Chris explored the other two cars. Peter rolled down the window and watched him.

They got moving again, while the sun climbed steadily.

'It doesn't look right,' Patsy said. 'What are those black marks?'

'I reckon they're sunspots,' Chris said. 'It's been getting worse this past while, and the days are getting shorter. It's some kind of weird seasonal thing, maybe those dark days you were telling me about. The more patches you see, the more the moon changes. It's like one's getting stronger and the other's getting weaker.'

They were half an hour down the road, on a long, straight stretch raised above the surrounding countryside which was flat and boggy and glistened with oily sink-holes and tarns, when he tapped her gently on the knee.

The touch was so unexpected that she jerked in surprise, turning to face him as if was about to molest her.

He had a finger to his lips and was indicating behind them, with a small backwards motion of his head. For a second she didn't understand, but then he reached out of the window, as casually as if he was yawning, and pointed at the wing mirror.

Patsy glanced in the rear-view mirror. Far behind them, another car was travelling on the road.

'What's wrong?' Peter asked. He'd been watching Chris and had seen the little motion of his head. He scrambled up on the back seat and peered out.

'Too far to see.'

Chris reached inside his jacket and pulled out a small black cylinder. With a quick flick he pulled the end and it lengthened into a neat telescope. He twisted in his seat much as Peter had done and put the glass to his left eye.

'Is it a car?' Patsy asked. The twist of intuition suddenly wound up tight. It wasn't a car. It was a black van. Kerron Vaunche had sniffed them out again.

'Doesn't look like it. I think it's a van, but it's still too far away.'

'Let me look,' Peter demanded, reaching for the telescope. Chris handed it to him and the boy whirled to point it through the rear screen. Judith watched the whole thing silently, her head cocked to the side as if she was listening for something.

'It *is* a van,' Peter exclaimed. 'It's the same one.'

'You must have eyes like a hawk,' Chris told him and Peter visibly swelled with pride. Patsy's heart just dropped.

Chris pulled the gun out and checked the cylinder, reaching into another inside pocket to bring out a few shells which he thumbed into their chambers. Patsy revved the engine and the car surged forward. Far behind, the van's yellow lights flashed once. She speeded up and within a minute she was doing almost eighty. In the mirror the van dwindled. They got to the end of the straight and she had to slow down for a curve. The road rose up another incline, crested and in front of them, the vast confusion of roadworks stretched into the distance.

'It's closer,' Chris said. Peter clambered up between the front seats to see.

'It's like a road-puzzle,' he observed. 'They've got streets like that in LA or San Francisco. I've seen them on television.'

The road swooped down on a curve, went across a short bridge which spanned a narrow ravine and a couple of miles on, a big roadside sign showed another junction ahead. Patsy looked at Chris, but he shrugged. Behind them, Judith muttered something.

'What's that, honey?'

'No. I can't,' Judith said aloud. 'I don't want to.'

'What's the matter?'

The girl sat upright in her seat, head cocked to the side. The skin on her cheeks had gone crusty and the black marks under her eyes were expanding downwards. She looked as if a poison was spreading inside her.

'What?' she asked, a puzzled expression on her face.

'I said, what's the matter,' Patsy repeated. She glanced over her shoulder, and saw her daughter's dark eyes, wide and blinkless, the irises ringed now in a fungal green, gazing into the far distance.

'Want to stay with mummy,' she said quite emphatically. 'Want to go home.'

A cold quiver went down Patsy's spine.

'Who's she talking to?' Peter demanded.

'Don't want to come back,' Judith said, voice rising. 'I don't like it.'

Chris looked at Patsy. 'Is she all right? Maybe I should drive.'

She nodded, slowing the car down. Judith was still wide-eyed, her head still cocked to the side, listening for a voice none of them could hear.

'Oh-oh,' Peter chipped in. 'It's still behind us.' He was kneeling up in the back again with the small telescope jammed against his eye.

'What's wrong, Judy?' Patsy demanded, though she knew that a dreadful communication was happening, that a malignant link had arced out and hooked into her daughter. She twisted in her seat and reached behind her to grip Judith's knee and as soon as she did so she felt the singing vibration shuddering within the girl as if every nerve was shaking with tension. Fever-heat radiated into her fingers.

'Jesus,' she gasped. 'She's burning up.'

'It's getting closer,' Peter said.

'What can I do?' Patsy cried, torn by her need to stop and

352

help her daughter and the urgent imperative to get away from the pursuing van.

'Keep driving,' Chris told her. He got his feet up on the seat, and managed to turn around to face the back and then, with no small difficulty, he clambered in beside Judith. 'Keep going, fast as you can.'

In the mirror she saw the black van visibly swelling as it caught up with them. It looked like an ordinary van, but there was something about it that radiated enormous threat. She floored the pedal and willed the car forward. Up ahead a ramp exited from the straight. Behind her the van's horn blared and the headlamps flashed. It was coming up fast, too fast for any normal transit van. Peter kneeled up again, cutting off her view and she almost screamed at him to get down. The yellow lights flared again, baleful and poisonous, like the cat's-eye things in the night.

'Daddy wants me,' Judith said. Patsy's heart turned to stone. 'Kerron says my father loves me.'

'Come on, kid,' Chris cajoled her. He got an arm around her, not quite sure what to do. The girl was trembling like a leaf. Her wide eyes were completely blank, as if all her attention was focused inwards. A small dribble of saliva slid down her chin and dripped to her knee. He pulled her in towards him and felt the heat coming off her in waves. Her breath smelt of decay.

'Keep your tainted hands off me, worthless fool,' Judith hissed, and in the space of one sentence her voice dropped an octave. Instantly the hairs on Patsy's neck stood to attention and began to crawl in unison.

'Come on, Jude,' Chris started again. 'Your mom's . . .'

'You are not my father, unbeliever. Less than the sand beneath my feet.' The words came rasping out in a growl that was almost animal, full of venom.

Peter shrank back from his sister. 'Mum, she's talking all funny again . . .'

Judith spun towards him, twisting right round so that the belt pressed against her neck. The green rim on her iris flared, giving her a snake-like and completely alien stare. The smell of rot was suddenly choking.

'That *gadge* creature is not my mother, *Tavartas*. My father is

353

Thanatos who is Taimat the Footless, brother of night, and my mother was *Cailleach the Morrigan* who is in me and who will eat your heart.'

'Oh, Jesus,' Patsy pleaded. The van was gaining on them, hounding them along the road, and inside the car her own daughter's mind was possessed and a sense of complete and utter evil clamped itself upon Patsy.

'Our Father, who art in heaven, hallowed by thy name . . .' she started to pray, desperately battling the sensation of foul power pressing in on her consciousness.

Judith screamed, raw and hoarse, grinding like a stone saw.

'My father is the *Fasgadh*, who dwells in Hades, in the darkness under the roots of Yggdrasil in the uttermost pit. He will drench himself in the blood of yours and his power will shake the foundations of this world for a thousand years. His legions will glut themselves.'

Judith arched up in her seat. The restraining belt creaked under the pressure. She snarled like a cat and hot spittle came flecking out. Patsy felt it spray on her cheek and it burned bitter as acid.

'. . . Thy kingdom come, thy will be done on earth, as it is in heaven.'

'My father's will!' Judith screeched the words and Patsy heard Kerron Vaunche in the harsh rasp. She swivelled the mirror. Chris was trying to get his arms around Judith who was squirming and writhing, her face purple, eyes rolling wildly. Peter was up against the back of the seat, panic slack on his face. Judith stopped moving. She glared into her mother's eyes. Her mouth opened and when she spoke again, Patsy heard Crandall Gilfeather's voice.

'A child has to die as the blood of rape is spilled on the stone. A child must be consumed while the Carlin and her consort consummate their evil. The price is absolute corruption, but there must be a feast at which the Prince of Shadows will feed.'

'Give us this day our daily bread and forgive us our trespasses. . . .' Patsy pleaded with her God.

'Take this and eat it, all of you,' Kerron Vaunche's witch voice crackled from the little girl's swollen mouth. 'For this is the body of *Uanan* the lamb and the blood of *Tavartas* the offering. My

354

father *Dracul* will mount her and impale her upon his spike and his seed will burgeon within his offspring. My father will cleave the offering and feast on its heart.'

'As we forgive,' Patsy gabbled. Judith's face had gone almost as black as the careering van. Peter was white with dread. The dream came ricocheting into her mind and she saw again the writhing bodies on a stone and the pale shape lying trussed, arms and legs spread and a wet chasm cleaving from chin to crotch. The monstrosity snuffled again, gobbling down there in the wet mess of the chasm, and when it rose again the flies came bursting out in a fog and Judith's dead eyes fixed accusingly on her.

'. . . Those who trespass against us.'

'And trespass within us and burst us asunder so that the legions of *Be-elzebub* the Lord of Flies that feed upon the dead, the ravening swarm will feast.'

'And deliver us from evil,' Patsy cried out, voice rising to a scream. 'Please Lord, deliver her from this evil.'

Kerron Vaunche's screech rose to match, to overtake it. Judith's back arched like a bow. Something creaked wetly, as if muscle was tearing. Threads of the seat-belt webbing burst in a series of whipcrack snaps. Chris simply grabbed her in his arms and forced her down onto the seat. Her hand came up and hooked at him. Three little red striations immediately dripped blood.

'Christ on a Cadillac,' he bellowed.

Without warning all the fight went out of the girl. She flopped back down on the seat.

'*No!* she squealed suddenly, in her own voice. 'Don't *want* to go with daddy. It's *bad*.'

'It's catching us,' Peter yelled. He was pressed up against the door. 'You have to go faster.'

Ahead of them the distance markers counted down to the ramp. Judith screeched, high and searing in the confines of the car. The shrill cry died away and then she began to sob.

'Mum, *mum!*' Peter cried. Her eyes snapped to the mirror. The van had disappeared. A shape loomed on the other side and she spun so fast her neck muscles creaked in protest. In the wing mirror the van was pulling up on the outside. It had come up unbelievably fast. It was jet black, almost completely black, even

355

the windows. The only colour was in the strange orange glow of the headlights and a red splash just above the grille. It looked like a splash of blood.

Judith shrieked. 'She's coming, mummy. *She's coming for me.*'

Patsy's panic erupted. The van was almost alongside her. Chris was trying to clamber back onto the front seat, drawing the big gun from inside his jacket. The horn rapped the air again. It was pulling level with them. Peter was down beside, trying to get his arms around his sister. Chris was shouting at her to open the window. The big black barrel of the gun was right in front of her eyes, pointing through the window.

The van swung in and clipped her wheel arch the way she'd seen happen in car chases in the movies, but instead of a gentle bump which would rock them from side to side, it felt as if the car had been hit by a colossal weight. Her head snapped to the side and banged against the glass. Chris was thrown backwards against the far door and tumbled to the floor.

Patsy instinctively stepped on the pedal and felt the car jerk forward. The van's horn blared. It fell behind, very briefly, and she got a glimpse of it in the wing mirror. It wasn't blood on the front, it was a customised fire-burst in orange and red, showing flames licking up from the front to lap around the edge of the black windscreen. It lurched forward out of view and came alongside again. She looked to the side, but the windows were too dark to see through though she thought she could make out a pale shape in the cabin. With one hand she frantically rolled down the window, fingers slipping on the winder.

'Shoot it,' she screamed. 'Come on, quick! Shoot the bastards.'

The van came veering in for another sideswipe. Patsy felt it coming. Behind her Judith screeched like a hurt animal and then the cry was cut off as if she'd been hit. Immediately, above all the tumult, Patsy heard the rasp in her daughter's throat as she fought for breath. Peter was bawling at her in a panic.

'Get the puffer,' Patsy shouted. She leaned to the left, flipped the glove compartment lid. The small gun came tumbling out and hit Chris on the head with a loud *clunk* sound. Patsy grabbed the ventilator and slung it behind her. Peter's fingers snatched it from her. She heard the hollow hiss as the fine spray hit the back of Judith's throat. She couldn't stop, couldn't turn, but somehow, on a very high level, she was completely aware of everything, every sound, every movement, as if the world had gone into slow motion or she herself had been geared up to super-speed. She pulled the wheel, sliding away from the black van as it came angling in towards her. Peter shouted again. He triggered the inhaler another time and Judith suddenly whooped for breath. Patsy's heart leaped. Judith coughed twice, harsh and rasping and then she took a deep breath.

'She's all right, mum,' Peter shot back. 'She's breathing fine.'

The van came wheeling in again and she swung away. Something scraped inside her head, like the rustle of dry holly leaves, like the growl of a beast in a cave and she shuddered, almost driving up onto the sloping verge, sending everyone rocking again.

Chris was hauling himself up from where he'd fallen. She heard him cock the gun with a metallic click. Ahead of her the entrance to the ramp loomed. She was driving straight ahead, hurtling past it. The black van was closing fast, charging in to batter them off the road.

At the very last second, with only a yard to spare she jerked the wheel and the car soared up the ramp, missing the barrier by scant inches.

The van tried to follow. It came swerving in and the driver – *whatever it was behind the wheel* – must have seen the gap was too narrow. The black transit pulled away with a sudden screech of tyres and over the rattle of the engine Patsy thought she heard the panicked whinny of horses. The tail end hit against the barrier and a shower of white sparks fountained upwards. It bounced off twice, hit the fence again, then shot across the road heading for the far side.

By this time Patsy was skidding at the edge of the slip road, scooting up the slope. The fence loomed, right in front of them. Chris yelled a warning and she managed to pull the nose away before she hit. Gravel spewed up and rattled under the wheel arches. Peter fell off his seat and landed with a thump. Chris banged his head on the dashboard as he bent to pick up the gun which had tumbled down under the glove compartment. Judith let out an unbelievable scream and then they were up on the shoulder of the hill. The road below them, the road they had been travelling on, sunk away. The black van's tail was just a dark flash as it swerved under the arch of the overpass and it was gone. The ramp continued up in a circle, levelled off and they found themselves on a clover leaf junction.

Two hundred yards away, the mirror image of the road they were on curved in the opposite direction. Below them the main routes criss-crossed. For an instant, everything was quiet and still.

'Damned women drivers,' Chris finally said, rubbing his temple. Peter snorted.

24

The clover leaf was now just a distant concrete flower. Chris had asked her to pull over on the two-way highway when they came to a suspension bridge with tall black towers and a spider's web of dark cables bearing its weight. He got out of the car and went over to the railing – much as she had done the time when she'd seen the hellish carnage below – and bent to look down. Patsy got out of the car and opened the back door to let Peter scramble out. He immediately ran for the nearest pillar, turned his back on them and relieved himself quickly. Judith lay dozing in the back of the car, breathless and hot. The skin on her hands was peeling like sloughed scales. Patsy knew that she had to do something, find some antibiotics, though within herself she wondered what would combat the contagion that was sweeping through her daughter.

Chris was leaning on the balustrade, his old hat shoved back on his head. His jacket was ragged and scratched and had seen plenty of better days, and his boots were worn down at the outside of the heels.

'I thought there might be a river or a stream,' he said. 'I've got some line. You can catch fish from the bridges in some places, though there's other things in the water that'll cut through the line. I was hoping we could get some water before we go further.'

'Wasn't there plenty in the bottle?'

He shook his head. 'It's half full, or half empty, depending on your point of view, but you don't take chances.' He pointed ahead. 'Those mountains, they might be an illusion. We could be heading into desert country again. If we find a river, there's a bush with berries that will help your girl. They take the heat out of the blood.'

Down below, a road snaked through a narrow gorge which looked natural, as if the earth had cracked and separated. It was a single-track road, dimly shadowed. The sun was too low to reach into the depths. Nothing moved down there and there were no cars crashed by the side of the track. Purple-leafed bushes crowded onto the surface, almost meeting in the middle in some places. 'It's a bush like that, only darker,' Chris said.

'She needs something,' Patsy said. Judith was still holding her hand, leaning listlessly against her, and she was still hot, too hot. 'Can we get down and have a look?'

'No point. It'll be different down there. Don't worry. We'll find what we need.' He fingered the three red scratches on his cheek and Patsy was instantly reminded of the weals on Paul's back when he'd come home, stinking of woodsmoke and the musk of the woman.

Peter came back to join them, his face now back to its normal colour. Chris reached into his jacket and brought out his slingshot, an old black *Diablo*, which he handed to the boy. He pointed below them to the road down in the gorge. Just against the edge, a single hub cap caught enough light from the sky to show a pale circle.

'Can you hit that, Hawkeye?' Chris asked him. Peter grinned with pride at the nickname.

'Sure I can,' he answered. He searched along beside the barrier for a smooth stone, and when he found one he nestled it into the leather grip. There was a ledge at the iron railing that allowed him to lean over and point the catapult downwards. They all watched him take aim. He let go and the stone, a white pebble, whirred in the air, aiming straight at the hub cap.

It dropped about twenty feet and then it vanished. One second it was tumbling in the air and the next it disappeared completely.

Peter pulled up in consternation. 'Where'd it go?'

Chris said nothing. He scouted around, further along the bridge, until he found an old green bottle half buried in the road dust at the edge of the barrier. He hefted it in his hand and then threw it up in the air. It caught the weak light of the sun as it rose, poised on its apex and then started to plummet. It fell quickly, heading for the edge of the road. And as soon as it reached the shadow, it winked out of existence.

'Boy, that's a neat trick.' Peter was impressed.

'No trick,' Chris said. He pushed his hat further and for an instant Patsy saw the resemblance to Crocodile Dundee, who was Peter's all-time-favourite character next to Indiana Jones. He grinned as if he'd shown them magic.

'That's why there's no point in going down,' he said. 'The different levels are on different times over the roads. I thought I'd get off the turnpike and onto a track like that a long while back. I got some rope from an eighteen-wheeler and tied it together. Let myself down fifty feet and by the time I got there it was winter. You don't ever want to climb down if you can help it.'

'What makes it do that?' Peter wanted to know.

Chris shrugged. 'Time's all different, I reckon. Maybe its warped. I don't know whether it goes backward or forward, but in a place like this, you always want to know what you're getting into.'

Peter nodded, man-to-man, understanding another rule of the road.

They headed back to the car. Peter scrambled for a handful of smooth stones and held on to the slingshot. Five miles on they stopped by a small black stream and Chris lit a fire. He opened a tin of hot dogs and let Peter cook them.

'We're getting closer,' Chris said. He pointed out beyond the little stream where they'd stopped, across the rolling hills towards the distant tangle of the intersection. It was still hazy, either from a low mist or from the road fog of exhaust fumes, but the bee-hum murmur of traffic was louder.

'Maybe that's a good thing,' Patsy said, though in herself she knew she was wrong. Peter stirred the food in the can. Judith was sagged in against her mother's side, head drooping. Her breathing was laboured and a line of warts was swelling in rough mounds down the side of her jaw. To Patsy she felt as if she was hollowed out, like a dry husk. Her sweat smelled impure.

She's dying. The thought she'd been shying away from sneaked up and grabbed Patsy. Her daughter was sickening to death, she was dying from the touch of Kerron Vaunche or whatever it was that the witch obeyed. Judith was sickening and she was ageing.

Crandall Gilfeather's words came back to her now. 'The dark transference of the renewal,' he'd said, earnest eyes holding her own. 'In the ceremony, souls are lost, but the *life* is transferred and the bargain is made. She needs the flesh of his flesh to make the bargain.'

It was as if the youth was being sucked out of Judith, to be replaced by something old and mouldering and decayed. Kerron Vaunche had spoken through Patsy's daughter and her voice had the decrepit rustle of terrible age.

'Death and rebirth,' Gilfeather had insisted. 'To keep her beauty, to keep her youth and to maintain her enormous power, the Carlin Woman must commune with the Prince of Shadows, and he will demand his price.'

Was it already happening? Was some appalling transference taking place as they fled down this road?

Patsy twisted her wrist to look at her watch, but it was a useless gesture. The little numbers still subtracted themselves, two days for every second, but she needed no watch to tell her how close it was to the midwinter. The moon would be full and it would glare down its madness from malevolent sky. The *Nameless Day*.

The closer they got to that conjunction, the more Judith seemed to wither. Was Kerron Vaunche getting younger now? Were the wrinkles smoothing out, the cracks and fissures of the hag mellowing to the creamy skin of youth?

Or did that witch still need to perform her obscene ceremony? Judith moaned and a drool of ropy saliva dribbled from a sagging mouth. The vision came looping back to her mother.

Kerron Vaunche, shrivelled and dry, as if she'd been drained of all humanity. The witchety thing cackled at her and pointed to the stone on which the pale shape lay trussed, arms and legs spread and a wet chasm cleaving from chin to crotch. A monstrosity hunched over, snuffling and gobbling down there in the wet mess of the chasm, and when it rose again the flies came bursting out in a fog and Judith's dead eyes fixed accusingly on her.

Would there still have to be a sacrifice? Judith held tight to her child. Chris had turned to her, answering her statement.

'Don't count on it,' Chris said. 'I don't mean to be pessimistic, but I've been heading in that direction for a long time, and the nearer I get the crazier this road's become. That's why I've been travelling on foot. I reckon it's going to get a lot worse between here and there.'

'So what should we do?'

'Nothing much you *can do*. There's no other way to go. I've tried it a dozen times, just turned on my heels and tried to get back the way I came, but no matter what direction you take, you end up with that darned thing in front of you. A couple of times I made the mistake of getting off the road and trying to go across country, but there is no cross-country. All there is out there are badlands and believe me, you *never* want to get lost in there.'

'What's in the badlands?' Peter asked. He'd stopped stirring at the can and was now practising with the catapult, missing a rusty hub cap by a good yard.

'Nothing you want to tackle with that slingshot, Hawkeye,' Chris told him. 'Hell, nothing I want to face even with this big bazooka.' He dropped his voice and turned to Patsy. 'There's nothing for it but to keep on moving. I read somewhere it's better to travel hopefully than to arrive, and here that makes a lot of sense. You're damned if you stay and damned if you go.' He stopped and looked straight at Patsy. 'But you've come so far and you've had some luck.'

'Will you come with us?'

'Sure I will,' he said. 'But you've got to learn to shoot the gun,' he said. Peter ate most of the sausages, then some soup. Judith drank some water, just a few dribbles that Patsy coaxed past her lips. Chris Deane used some spare water to give himself a shave. From one of his inside pockets, he fished out a big open razor and used the pink perfumed soap to work up a lather. It took him ten minutes to whet the blade on his belt and twice that to scrape the beard away. When he was finished he had metamorphosed into a man in his early thirties, not a tramp in his mid-forties as she'd first thought. The scar on his cheek stood out red against the untanned skin which had been covered by his beard.

They got started again, while the sun was still low in the sky. The road descended through dense evergreen forest, a place of shadows and movement and strange, harsh calls that might have been birds but could have been anything. They kept the windows up as they drove past the trees after the first sparrow-sized bee had come buzzing in on thrumming wings to clatter on the inside of the windscreen. In its frantic search for escape, it kept butting the glass and its abdomen pulsed up and down, every movement displaying its needle-like stinger. Chris managed to hit it a lucky blow with his hat, just enough to eject it from the car and immediately rolled his window up. They all did the same and within ten seconds another monstrous insect cracked itself to death on the glass, leaving a six-inch greasy smear which completely defied the best efforts of the wipers.

The forest ended abruptly on the lip of yet another curving slope and they emerged on an unbroken gradient so straight that the road disappeared into the distant haze. Beyond it the arches and curves of the intersection caught the wan sunlight, making them look eerily insubstantial, like an optical illusion in the distance.

They came on the first of the cars ten miles along the straight and Patsy slowed down automatically. A Rolls-Royce, once sleek and silvered had tumbled off the straight and crashed into the back of what could have been an army jeep. Glass had spread like hail in every direction, crunching under their own tyres as they passed. A shape slumped over the wheel of the big limousine, and a dark brown stain, like old paint, had splashed outwards to soak the crumpled paintwork. Patsy drew her eyes away and scanned the road ahead.

It was littered with cars as far as the eye could see.

'It's another car cemetery,' Peter observed from behind her.

'That's what it looks like,' Chris agreed. 'It's like the place all the wrecks go when they die.'

'Except they didn't come here as wrecks,' Patsy said.

Mile upon eerie mile, they continued, past old coaches and newly abandoned trucks. At one point, there was a multiple pile-up, a tangle of ten, maybe a dozen cars all wrapped around and crumpled into each other and almost blocking the entire throughway. As they steered around the mess, Patsy smelled the metallic scent of new blood. She rolled up the window and drove on. They passed another old stagecoach, this one with all its wheels but one rotted to splinters, sitting at a crazy angle, swaying in the slight breeze. A mile beyond that, an ancient cart, with solid wooden wheels, was rotting on the verge. In front of it, still attached to a carved wooden yoke, the dried carcasses of two immense oxen lay slumped in twin heaps of bones and torn hide. Each pair of horns had a huge six-foot span.

A mile beyond that, they came across a travois of latticed saplings, canted up against a rock. In front of it, a crumbled pile of bones was all that remained of the primitive native, Indian, Aborigine, Patsy couldn't tell, while on the woven trellis of thin branches, the whitened, clean-picked skeletons of an adult and a child lay exposed to the sun, and Patsy knew it had been a mother and her baby, pulled through this wilderness by her husband who had tried to save them and failed. She drove on through the seemingly endless conglomeration of hulks and wrecks, and as the clouds began to pile up to darken the sky, she felt them gathering within her. The thought of the man dragging his family along this track on a primitive travois kept echoing in her mind. He had tried and he had failed and they had died. A wave of melancholy swept into her heart, the way it had done when she'd seen the dead bride in the car.

She forced the black feeling away from her. She was no blushing bride. She had made vows and they had been thrown back in her face, not once but twice, and the second time they'd been thrown back on the curse that had sent her here. She was no primitive, dragging the family on a bower of sticks.

'I'm Patsy Havelin,' she whispered, not realising she had said it aloud.

'Beg your pardon?' Chris asked. Patsy steered around an old flat loader still piled high with massive unmilled timbers. Another time she would have blushed; this time she took her eyes off the road, turning to their new companion.

'I'm Patsy Havelin. I'm not going to let this road beat me.'

'Glad to hear it,' he said.

'I mean it. I'm going home.'

She drove on and for more than an hour the array of crumpled, rusting hulks of cars and vans and lorries and buses flickered past on either side, interspersed with the occasional gleam of a sporty roadster or the flapping canvas of an ancient carriage, some of them festooned with huge spiders webs, others crawling with insects, while the air smelled of corruption and decay. Clouds of black flies rose up when they passed, eerie and dense swarms which buzzed angrily before settling back down to feed.

'You've come this far,' she told herself. 'You've come further than any of those poor devils.'

Ahead of them, the vast junction beckoned, drawing them ever closer. The clouds rolled and thickened and a flicker of lightning sparked and flashed in their depths. Eventually they came to the end of the straight and the line of wrecks petered out. Beyond the shoulder of a low hill, the character of the land changed to an undulating moor, punctuated by jagged stones poking up from the peaty ground, and by black and shadowed pools which reminded Patsy of the swamp where the gas bubbles had wobbled up from the depths, bursting with the reek of putrefaction and where the corpses had come rising, bloated and leached. If they stopped here, she knew instinctively, things would come clambering out of the dark water, things that had been lurking below the mirrored surfaces, waiting for the unwary to stoop to drink or to bathe.

She passed by, and the burgeoning power of her own perception picked up the shadowy voiceless thoughts out there in the moorland beyond the roadside. She sensed insatiable hunger and a strange, feral anger reach out from the hidden pools. The car began to drift, almost of its own volition, towards the edge and she had to fight the queer magnetic influence drawing her off the road. Chris did not react at all, but in the back, Judith moaned softly. Whatever strange sense was blossoming inside Patsy, Judith had it ten-fold. She was like a living radar, Patsy realised, picking up everything that was hellish in this place. It was another reason to get her baby out of here and get her home.

The lightning stabbed down from the clouds in a series of juddering strokes which punched into the tussock grass on a low hill a mile away, leaving the travellers with jagged after-images dancing in their eyes and blasting the air with an enormous crack of thunder.

'We should find shelter,' Chris suggested. 'We're pretty exposed here.'

The lightning tore the air again and cleavered a gash in a narrow bank beside one of the pools, sending up a spray of red earth. The hit was closer, more threatening. Something down in the water let out a mental grunt of fury and fear which twisted like a corkscrew into Patsy's consciousness. Judith squealed aloud and Patsy reached a hand behind the seat, grasping her fingers tight. Rain lashed the screen and then hail came again in jagged little chunks, dropping like bird-shot from the rolling black cloud above them. Patsy kept the car in the middle of the road, gave the engine more fuel and started to outrun the storm.

The road curved slowly across the moorland as she built up speed, changing down a gear to speed up on a slow slope and quickly flipping the lever on the downside. The lightning stabbed again, this time a quarter of a mile away, in two bolts of fire which went rolling across the bracken, setting alight the ferns in twisting tracks of flames. Ahead of them, just appearing through the rain, a tall stand of trees huddled beside the roadway.

'Head for there,' Chris said. A solitary tree, out in the open, would attract the lightning just as surely as a single car moving on a bleak road would, but a forest of them would spread the risk.

'I don't want to go off the road,' Patsy asserted. She floored the pedal again and the wheels hissed on the wet, sending up a spray behind her. The trees flickered past in peripheral vision and then were gone. Ahead of them, beyond the edge of the storm cloud, the moorland gradually changed to a rough brush as it sloped gently towards another plain. She could see veils of rain falling just ahead of them, so thick it looked like low cloud. She ploughed through the wet, sending up crests of water now on either side, going too fast for safety, but willing to risk a skid rather than the sudden final explosion of lightning. The car reached the demarcation line marking the edge of the storm and popped out of the rain like a squeezed pip.

The drumming lash of rain stopped instantly and the hissing sound of the tyres became the whirr of rubber on dry tarmac. Behind them, she could see in the wing mirror, the spray of their wake was like a tumbling cloud completely obscuring the road. A flicker of light snaked through it like an adder in the bracken and then exploded in a blinding flash. The after-image, forked like a trident, floated in her vision, changing from orange to a fuzzed purple. An enormous explosion crashed instantaneously, making the air expand so fast the wind of it buffeted the car like a powerful kick from behind, throwing it forward.

'Shit,' Chris barked, forgetting to ask for pardon. He swivelled in his seat just in time to see the entire stand of trees erupt in a firestorm. One moment the copse of craggy pines, grey silhouettes through the film of rain, were huddled against the storm and the next they were blasting up and outwards, shattered to matchwood by the force of the lightning-strike. A ball of fire ripped out in an expanding globe of heat. It caught the car in a second kick. For an instant a weird St Elmo's fire rippled and writhed over the bodywork and arced between the mirror and the wipers. A burnt scent of ozone came smoking through the ventilators. Pieces of burning twigs trailed smoke as they fell from the sky, rattling on the roof and tumbling to the road. A large section of tree-trunk went whirling overhead like a baton thrown by a colossal cheerleader, whooping through the air to land with a splintering crash against a boulder. Patsy ducked instinctively.

'Did you see that?' Chris asked, just as excited as Peter had been. 'The whole lot's gone. Must have been fifty, a hundred trees in there and there's nothing left.'

'Just as well we didn't go in there,' Patsy said shakily.

'Believe it,' Chris breathed. 'We'd have been . . .' He let the sentence trail away.

'How did you know?' he finally asked.

'I didn't,' Patsy said, though that was not entirely the truth. The little internal voice had been responsible, scratching at the underside of her mind, just enough to make her drive on. She had obeyed it unquestioningly and it had saved them again. 'I just had a hunch we'd be better to keep going.'

'Well any time you get a hunch, you go right ahead,' he told her.

The lightning struck again, now well behind them, as if it was having a final stab at the burning coppice. Patsy drove on, keeping up her speed until the storm was a mile or more behind before slowing down as the urgency declined. The fuel indicator was edging downwards again, which meant that they would soon need to start scavenging again. She scanned the road ahead, hoping to find an abandoned car which might yield what they needed. For some reason she had not been tempted to stop in the vast conglomeration of wrecks she'd passed by only an hour before. There had been something about the place that was eerie and somehow expectant, as if the cars, or the mouldering things in and around them, were not entirely dead. The feeling was insubstantial and hard to explain, but it had been there, making her wary enough to keep on going.

She smiled grimly to herself now, aware of how close they had come, yet aware that they had won through. Kerron Vaunche, that witch, had set her feet on this road, but there was something, surely some higher power, that had let her survive for so long. She drove on, while the fire of the blasted forest flared in the mirrors, sending up billows of smoke and steam that finally obscured the flames and rolled on the road behind them. Patsy stayed in the middle lane, heading for the curving slope ahead that would take them over the brow of the next hill. She looked in the mirror one last time at the destruction caused by that trident-bolt, was about to draw her eyes back to the road ahead again, and stopped.

The black van came hurtling out of the smoke, charging behind them like an enraged bull.

Her hands jerked on the wheel in an instant of panic but she clamped it down. Patsy tapped Chris on the knee and motioned to him to look behind them. He flipped the visor and peered into the vanity mirror. Without a word he reached into his coat and drew out the big gun. She speeded up before they hit the slope and let the momentum carry them to the brow. They crested the rise and raced down the lee side on a tight bend. Something caught her eye and she glanced to the left.

The old church spire leaned hard over the sway-backed roof. The ivy clambered up the entire length of the steeple and over the nave, knotted and hoary and full of unnatural motion, as if it was strangling the stone. In the daylight, there was no glow behind the windows, but somehow this was just as eerie. The dark shadows behind the stained glass were tense with expectancy. The crumbling masonry seemed to expand and contract, as if it were alive and taking a slow, rasping breath.

'We've been here before,' she whispered.

'Me too,' Chris said. 'And you want to get far away from it. It's a warped place, and it'll draw you inside, that's for sure.'

She nodded. The van hadn't appeared round the curve, but it must be halfway up the slope by now. Over at the little church-

369

yard, through a gap in the collapsed dry-stone wall, she saw the open graves, mounds of freshly-dug red earth piled beside the narrow trenches. There were four of them, waiting and inviting, ready to swallow the dead. She dragged her eyes away from it, away from the church. They rounded the curve, past the field. The scarecrow was almost at the edge of the road, narrow face now wide in a ferocious frozen scream, jagged teeth ready to clamp and rend. It was in the middle of taking another timeless step, and she knew that the next time she passed this little black warp, it would have reached the road. She felt the whispering rustle of unnatural lust scrape in the back of her head with the touch of festering rot and she recoiled from it. Judith whimpered like a small animal in pain.

In a second they were past the gargoyle figure, hurtling down the curve. She felt the cold of its bane even when the scarecrow was out of sight, and above that she still felt the filthy emanation that oozed from the profane black church where a godless thing lurked in the dark, waiting to be worshipped or fed. Overlaying those dreadful mental touchings, she heard the buzzing of flies and the cat-hiss of the mind of whatever pursued them in the black van. She could feel it reaching out, malignant and hungry and sensed its need, not for herself, but for her children.

She accelerated round the bend, feeling the steering protest. The tyres shrieked on the curve before she brought the car back into line. On the barren field, the crows were huddled over yet another piece of wreckage which had left the tell-tale ruts on the earth to show where it had ploughed off the road. The immense birds were squabbling over the red thing lying some distance from the little sports car which had finally flipped over and landed on its back. One of them turned to look at them and Chris watched it open its beak. A slither of meat swung wetly. He cocked the gun quietly.

The underpass was different from below. It rose quickly over another road then dived below a third. It separated without warning, forking left and right. Her instinct rejected the left track which descended into a narrow tunnel. The right rose up in a tight arc. At the top, she had a view of a smaller interchange and about a mile away, she saw the welcome sign for the service station.

Welcome to Havock Services it beckoned from its rusted paint-work. It swung away to the left and Patsy knew she'd chosen correctly. She risked a look at the station, set high off the road, its neat little mall dressed up in olde-worlde stone and tile, and lensed glass panels. Its quaint prettiness sent a shudder up and down her spine, for it conveyed the message of pure night-mare; a snare for the unwary, a gingerbread house baited with good things which were only a thin disguise for the corruption and malignancy under the veneer. As she drew her eyes away from it she saw its outlines waver and run, rippling together and merging, darkening into a place of shadows and old worn stone and rickety, wormholed shacks.

Just out of the corner of her eye, she saw the black van scoot up the track towards the huddle of wasted buildings and she let her breath out in a long exhalation. She'd beaten it again, but it would be back behind them, harrying them on the road, that she knew without doubt.

Chris followed the van's progress up towards the way-station, turning his head as the car took them further from it until the road curved away and the group of buildings was lost to sight. He uncocked the gun and put it back in its harness.

'That's another place you have to avoid,' he said softly.

'I know. We were in there on the first day.'

'It's like there are whirlpools here, the way you get black holes in space. Places where the bad is that much worse, and they've got their own special gravity that pulls people into them. Once you get stuck in a place like that, I don't think you can ever get out, and there's a few of them along this road, let me tell you.' He gave Patsy a sidelong glance. 'That station and the church, they're both the same, like black quicksands, always looking to suck something down.'

He paused, as if searching for his words. 'I suspect that the junction way ahead is the same kind of thing. If the way-station pulls people in with its own gravity, and if that church acts like a magnet, then that intersection is just the same, but I reckon it's the daddy of them all.'

'You mean like a big spider's web?' Peter asked astutely.

'Like that. Like a big magnetic spider web.'

'But there's no other way to go,' Patsy said, though her inflection made it a question.

'None that I ever found and I've looked, swear to God.'

'So there's nothing we can do?'

'Doesn't look like it.'

'So we might as well face it,' Patsy said, drawing her lips back from her teeth in a grimace. The words came out, almost of their own volition, surprising Patsy herself. If she'd said that four days ago, she'd have thought she was mad, but right at that moment, she realised there was more to herself than she had imagined. The unrolling nightmare of the past few days had crystallised some strength within her, a diamond core which had demanded that she fight like a savage to save her children. Even as that realisation came to her she felt the clench of cramp again, almost as if her body was trying to remind her that she was only a woman.

Her lips pulled back again from her teeth. Sometime in the past few days she'd stopped thinking of herself as *only* a woman. That had been the way she thought in her previous life when she had allowed herself to be subsumed into Paul's scheme of things. She had been *only a woman* when he'd dropped her for the wildness of Kerron Vaunche, *only a woman* when he'd stolen her children away. The hard, crystalline centre within her encapsulated every facet of her being and the woman within her was only a part.

You are a mother, the inner voice told her. *You're a survivor*, it asserted. *You're going to bring them home.*

They drove on until they were well away from the abominable way-station. Patsy estimated she had another eighty miles in the tank and the sun was still high and after a while she pulled off on a flat space beside the road and demanded that he teach her to shoot the gun. She tied her hair back with the scarf as a headband and for an hour, until her arm was numbed to her shoulder, he made her shoot the handgun until she could put a hole in the hub cap at twenty feet. It may not have been the answer to everything that moved on the road, but it made both of them feel better.

Peter watched enviously, matching her shot for shot with the catapult, and initially achieving a much higher score than she did. When she'd finished, and Chris had shown her how to clean the still-warm firearm, her son had sidled up to her, eyes fixed on the gun. Chris had ruffled his hair and complimented him on his shooting. Peter had looked up at his mother with open admiration.

'You look just like Sarah Connor,' he told her.

Patsy raised an eyebrow.

'She's the heroine in *Terminator*,' Chris explained, smiling. 'Everybody knows that.' He looked her up and down, though with a different admiration from Peter's. 'He's right,' he added, snapping the reloaded cylinder closed. He stashed the gun in a small handmade holster and put it back in the glove compartment. They went back to the fire where Patsy had tucked Judy into the old bedroll Chris had spread out. The coffee was boiled to thick tar but it was good enough for both of them. Peter devoured both drumsticks from the big water-bird and looked as if he could have finished a third. Judith listlessly sipped the last of the reconstituted soup and fell into a slumber. Patsy reached to check her forehead. It was beaded with sweat, but it felt strangely dry, like old paper.

They broke camp and started along the road as the sun sank quickly towards the rolling heathland in what they assumed was the east, and the sky to the west began to darken with the onset of dusk. Out in front, the glow from the vast junction began to brighten in the diminishing light and the hum of traffic was now clearly audible on the still air. They drove for twenty miles on a road that had come down from three lanes to a single carriageway and began to twist and turn around eroded bluffs of jagged volcanic rock. Peter was whittling on a scrap of wood while Chris scanned the road ahead for signs of somewhere to stop, eyeing the sky every now and again, gauging how much time they had before nightfall and a possible moonrise. The clouds overhead were thick, but there were patches showing darkening sky which promised the chance of a clear night. Despite the basalt plugs of rock, the land on either side of the road was too flat between the hardtop and the ditch to pitch a camp.

Come to daddy. It came in a harsh whisper from the shadows of the back seat.

Nowhere to hide on the open road. Judith mouthed the words, but the voice, the tone, it was Kerron Vaunche.

And you, boy. Your daddy needs you. You better come on back.

Chris looked at Patsy who was slowing the car down, pulling in to the tussock grass. She killed the engine and twisted to kneel on her seat. Judith was slumped against the door, head at an odd angle. Her eyes were closed under gummy lids. Her mouth was open and already her breathing was fast and shallow. Patsy clambered into the back again.

Don't touch me, stupid Gadge *cow.*

Patsy recoiled. A wave of heat came radiating out from the child. She reached again. Her hands went automatically to Judith's forehead. Her daughter's eyes snapped open and glared at her, black as coals, somehow afire.

Keep your unclean hands off, chattel.

'Judith,' Patsy snapped, ignoring the caution and reaching for her daughter. She got a hand to her shoulder and almost drew it back again. Judith felt as if she was on fire. As soon as the girl felt the touch, she flinched backwards, pushing herself against the door.

Keep off. Judith shuddered and then went rigid, back arching up from the seat. *Send them back.*

'It's Kerron,' Peter blurted. 'It's Kerron's voice. Why is she talking like that?'

Patsy didn't seem to hear. She pulled Judith towards her and held the stiff little body tight. Her daughter was shivering violently and so hot her face was lacquered with sweat. Her eyes were glazed and unfocussed. Patsy drew her in and held her tight and immediately the stiffness collapsed and Judith slumped into her arms. Her eyes blinked into focus again, only briefly, but in that moment, she was back with them again and whatever had spoken through her – Kerron Vaunche, Patsy knew, that bitch, the *witch* – was gone.

Judith whimpered weakly.

'We have to cool her down,' Patsy told Chris. Without hesitation he got out of the car and hauled his backpack out onto the roadside. The bottle was full. Patsy tore off a second corner of the travelling rug and soaked it before applying it to the girl's forehead. For an instant she thought she heard a hiss of steam as she put it to Judith's skin, but it was just her imagination.

'What's wrong with her?' Peter asked.

'She's sick,' Patsy told him. 'Some kind of bug.' She reached under Judith's chin and palpated her neck. The glands under the jawline were swollen and rubbery. Whatever dreadful contagion she suffered, she was also really ill.

'We need antibiotics,' she said to Chris. 'Even something to bring her temperature down.'

'You can find almost anything on this road,' he said, 'but we'll have to travel.' He looked up at the sky, now deepening to a violent purple.

'She needs medicine,' Patsy said. 'We can't stop until we get some.'

The sun dropped like a weight beyond the horizon, sending up its sickly aurora of alien dusk and then night fell. It happened so quickly that for an instant Patsy was driving in the dark. She flicked the headlamps on and the beams stabbed out on the road ahead. Chris checked the other horizon. There was some low cloud, hardly visible in the gloom, but lined with a hint of red, like cooling embers. Judith moaned deliriously in the dark of the back seat and Peter mumbled something in a comforting tone. Patsy kept her eyes fixed on the road ahead. The headlights coned outwards, picking up the white line marking the edge and the stuttering tracer fire of the lane dividers.

In the dark interstices between the markers, the cat's-eyes threw back the glare of the lights with their own blind stare.

She drove on, watching the reflectors, staying in the centre of her lane. They travelled four miles and the night got darker. The cloud was building up in the west, where the sun had set, but in the east, over the low hills, a clear patch of sky showed the twinkling of stars in tight, unfamiliar constellations. The edge of the cloud was brighter, now a light-infused scarlet, the colour of thin blood. Chris kept his eye on the patch, willing the clouds to blow in to cover the clear sky. Patsy drove on, feeling the tension rise inside her, knowing something was about to happen. She kept her eyes on the far reach of the headlights, hoping to find a car or a truck with a travel-pack of medicines.

Without warning, the screaming moon rose up from the low

375

cloud, rising like a malignant red balloon showing its twisted face. In that same moment, there was a *twist* in the air, a palpable wrench of change. Chris dived his hand inside the jacket and gripped the butt of the gun. Patsy hadn't seen the baleful moonrise, but she had felt the sudden transition, as if they'd passed through a freezing curtain.

The cat's-eyes changed. They blared orange. Then they were up and moving, scuttling from their pits, pale and spidery, caught in the beams.

Patsy gasped. Chris sat up. The first of the cat's-eye crabs disappeared under the front. A noise like a tin can kicked hard rang out. The second in line jinked to the side, thin, sharp claws raised high and eyes blinding. The car ploughed over it. There was a sharp *click*. A shape darted out from the hard shoulder, black and sinuous, low on the ground and moving in a blur. It crossed right in front of them, snatched one of the crawlers in the flick of an eye. A black mouth gaped, closed with an audible crunch and the scuttling thing was gone. The car ploughed on. The tyres thudded over a small obstacle and a grotesque shriek tore the air. A piece of dark rubbery stuff went whirring up into the air, bounced on the window, leaving a slick smear, and tumbled off into the night.

Ahead of them the road was alive with movement. The car rolled on, faster now as Patsy tried to batter her way through the scuttling road things. The moon rose higher and as it did, a thin vaporous mist crept in from the edges of the road, glowing with the red light of the burning moon, completely obscuring the verges. For a vertiginous moment, Patsy had the weird sensation that the road had taken another one of those mysterious turns and had left the ground altogether. There was nothing to be seen on either side. It was like driving through clouds.

Except that the cat's-eyes were swarming on the road, grabbing for the car, pulling her eyes with their basilisk stares, and black slithery things with skin the texture of truck tyres were darting in from the rolling mist, snatching at anything that moved. The wheels crashed over one of the scuttling pale crabs, flattening it into the tarmac with a satisfying crunch. Patsy drove faster. Something huge reached in from the haze, a great black head on a long black neck and seized one of the sinuous predators. It bit the thing in two, leaving one half wriggling headless and frantic on the roadside. The tyres trundled over it with a sickening squelch.

'We've got to get off this,' Chris said.

'We have to find something for Judith.' Patsy's eyes were fixed on the road, ready to swerve to avoid anything that came lunging for them. Her mind was fixed on her need to find whatever medicine she could to get Judith's temperature down. Behind her, as if in emphasis, her daughter whimpered again and then shouted aloud, a babble of delirious gobbledegook.

One of the cat's-eyes came lurching out from the centre-line, claws raised. It leapt upwards the way a jumping spider would, all legs flexing at once and hit the side of the car with a clatter. Another came whirling in and was mashed under the offside tyre. In the roadside mist, vast shapes, no more substantial than shadows, but somehow solid and threatening, towered just out of reach. Patsy recalled the grunts and snorts and the bellows in the dark on the night they'd careered off the road. She remembered the monstrous footprints sunk into the earth. If one of these things stepped out onto the blacktop, it would squash them flat in an instant. There was nothing she could do but drive on.

A white shape caught her eye. Chris was looking out of the side window and she had to elbow him to get his attention.

One of the crawlers scuttered up across the bonnet, hard jointed legs digging into the bodywork. Out of the headlights, its round blank eyes glowed pure red. It moved quickly, with the rolling, jittery gait of a spider, but its claws, held up and away from the flat carapace, were pure crustacean. It came lurching up, right on to the windscreen. It had a small mouth which opened in three segments and inside small, needle-sharp rows of teeth ground hungrily against each other and its legs, impossibly long and with too many joints, spanned half of the glass, blocking their view.

Complete revulsion brought bile rolling up inside Patsy in a searing heartburn. She was trying to swallow it back, which made it impossible for her to cry out in alarm when Chris wound his window down. He reached his hand out to bat the thing off the windscreen. Without warning, the creature whirled and lunged for him. He snatched his hand back but in the flick of an eye one of the claws had whipped out so fast it was impossible to follow. It pincered his hand, dragged itself forward. The mouth opened and the needle teeth sank right into the heel of his palm. Chris grunted. Excruciating pain drilled up to his elbow and he snatched his hand back. The crawler tried to hold on, A sliver of his skin peeled away and he pulled free, raised his hand again, quicker than before and smashed the butt of the gun down on the shell. All eight or ten legs untangled instantly, splayed out flat against the screen and then the slipstream whipped the crawler off and into the night.

Chris dragged his hand back, gritting his teeth against the awesome shriek of hurt in his hand and arm. Without hesitation, he dropped the gun to the floor and fumbled with his free hand for the open razor. He had to use his teeth to open it, holding his other hand in against himself, trying to concentrate the pain away. Patsy only saw the flicker of movement as he slit the skin on the heel of his hand. The warm metal smell of blood filled the car, along with the scent of something bitter and caustic. He squeezed his arm in a tight grip and drew down towards the wrist. She heard wet drips on the floor mat, and his compressed breath as he worked on himself. A few minutes later he was breathing again, fast and shallow, but normally enough. He wrapped the thin cut tightly with the neckerchief.

'Are you all right?' Peter asked from the shadows.

'Sure I am, Hawkeye,' Chris said. Patsy heard the strain of pain in his voice. She drove faster. Ahead of them the road curved to the left, still bounded by the ethereal mist which cut them off from the rest of the land. Another crab thing came scrambling in towards them and leapt for the car. It hit low down and the offside tyre burst with a bang. The car jolted and the rim bit into the tarmac. For an instant they were slewing to the left, heading into the mist. Patsy put all her weight on the wheel and brought them out of the skid just before they went off the road. Sparks flew up where the wheel was grinding into the surface. A crawling thing leapt up on the bonnet, scuttered round to the side and came clambering upwards, hooking its spiny legs over the top of the glass of the driver's window.

Patsy was too busy trying to prevent the car from somersaulting to look at it, though she felt the red eyes burning into her.

Judith screeched. The thing flexed, all of its legs drawing in towards each other. The window shuddered downwards, leaving a three-inch gap just above her eye level. A white and jagged claw came reaching in, questing blindly, opening and closing with a chitinous snap.

'Fuck this,' Chris rasped. He fumbled below him for the gun, brought it up. He reached his hand past her forehead, forcing her to duck to see where she was steering. The gun went off with an almighty roar. Wet droplets splashed the side of Patsy's neck, burning like battery acid. The claw vanished. Bits of the creature went cartwheeling away into the mist. Peter yelled something but Patsy never heard a thing. Her ears were ringing painfully from the noise of the big gun. She steered them round the bend, having to use all of her strength now that the tyre was gone. Ahead of them the road rose sharply. In that moment the clouds rolled over and smothered the moon, cutting off the poisonous red light.

The car clanked and rumbled up the steep incline.

'Stop here,' Chris said, laying his free hand on hers.

'Can't stop,' Patsy gasped, breathless with the effort of holding the car on the road.

'It's a flyover. We'll be safe here.'

They reached the summit of the overpass. Two cars were parked nose to tail. She pulled in some distance beyond them and killed the engine, breathing heavily. The car canted to the side, hunkered down on the bare wheel. The headlights picked out the nearest of the cat's-eyes. They were just reflectors stuck in the gaps in the road.

Chris opened the door carefully, wincing at the stab of pain in his arm. Very quickly he retrieved his oil can and stretched his barrier twine from edge to edge behind and in front of the car, defining their perimeter. In the headlights, she saw him move towards the two cars. A door opened and he leaned in. He checked the other one and after a while he came back with something in his hand.

'There's a couple of aspirin, but I can't say how old it is.' He handed the bottle over to Patsy who clambered into the back seat again. She crushed two of the tablets, mixed them with some water in the cup and forced it down Judith's throat.

The cloud stayed thick for the rest of the night, hiding the malignant moon. Outside, in the night, shrieks and grunts broke the dark. Things flitted on leathery wings and unseen carrion birds cawed and croaked. In the deep of night, heading for the black shallows before dawn, something so monstrous it made the roadway shake, marched past them, off in the badlands beyond the road. Below them, Patsy thought she heard the screams of people in pain, but it could have been anything. After a while, she was sure Judith's temperature began to fall, and she herself began to doze off. Peter curled into a ball and snored through the night. Once or twice Chris Deane groaned, loud enough to wake her, and she reached across to the front to squeeze his shoulder, letting him know she was grateful for what he had done, letting him know she knew of his pain.

For most of the night, Patsy ran with her children through dreams where a dreadful hag pursued her, eyes blazing red, clawing for Judith and Peter, trying to drag them away into the shadows where Patsy knew she would devour their flesh and rip out their hearts. It crashed after her, hissing and snarling, close on her heels while Patsy urged the children on, pushing them in front of her until she came to a cliff wall across the path, barring her way. A cave opened in the stone and she moved towards it until she saw the red furnace glow flickering in its depths and she heard the hollow, echoing cries of humans in torment and she realised she could not take her children in there. In her dream she turned to face the gargoyle that was hunting her. It came hurtling towards her, a writhing black shadow with the red eyes of the mad moon. It came whispering inside her head with the scrape of cat's-eye claws on the road and she pushed the children behind her, taking a dreadful step forward, hands raised to fight the thing.

It came closer and she saw it had the wizened face of something old. The features began to waver and run, resolving themselves into something else, and she knew it would metamorphose into Kerron Vaunche and she braced herself for combat.

In her dream its features ran and fused like hot grey wax, but when they reformed it was not Kerron Vaunche.

Paul stared at her, his face contorted out of shape. His eyes

380

were tinged with scarlet and he looked as if he was riddled with disease.

'Give me the children,' he said in a hoarse rattle. 'They're mine.'

She woke up, whooping for breath, just as the tumorous sun was lightening the pestilent sky. The smell of rot and absolute corruption hung about her like a veil.

25

'I'll have to climb,' Chris finally said, leaning on the galvanised steel barrier to look below them. They were on the crest of a long flyover which twisted fore and aft, merging into a complex knot of roadways. From where they stood the ends of the bridge couldn't be seen, but below them, however, a road cut from east to west, as far as they could make out, its surface completely hidden by a mass of entangled vehicles.

'Looks like one hell of a smash,' he added. 'Every time I see something like this, I can't figure it out. It's like they all piled into each other, hundreds of them, just for no reason, keeping on coming, one after the other.'

The image sparked another, a memory in Patsy's mind.

Too late for those down there, even if the fire brigade was here. They're held up along the road with the other lot, and that's a real mess, I can tell you. There's blood and guts and bits of bodies all over the place.

That was before the man had reached in with his calloused hand to paw at her skin.

It's a bad night to be out here at the junction. It's like a junkyard, and you don't want the kiddies to hear the screams, that's for sure.

She'd already heard the screams.

The dark had finally given up its hold on the road and the sun was now well above the horizon. Downslope on the bridge, pieces of the tyre-tread salamander things were scattered across the surface, each piece an island in a greasy, bloody puddle. Clouds of those black flies swarmed and buzzed over the morsels of strange carrion and she thought of the febrile chanting, the gypsy's voice scratching out from Judith's mouth.

The legions of Be-elzebub the Lord of Flies that feast upon the dead, the ravening swarm will feast. No doubt about it, they were feasting now.

The cat's-eyes, in the pale light of day, out of the madness of the night, were back in their pits on the centre-lines, blind and lifeless. Below the span, in the snarl of rusting cars and trucks, there was silence. Nothing moved.

Chris leaned over the barrier again and she could see the twist of concentration at the corners of his mouth as he gritted back the hurt in his hand. As soon as there had been enough light, he'd got out of the car and sat by the edge as the morning aurora had wavered on the low sky just after dawn when the screams and shrieks of the night were dying away, and he'd stitched the gash on the inside of his wrist with a casual dexterity that told her he'd done this before. When he'd finished and rebound the wound with the twist of rag, he'd walked off alone, first to one end of the bridge and then to the other, walking quickly and frowning with concentration. When he came back he'd a pocketful of black, greasy-looking berries. In half an hour he'd mashed and boiled them into a thick liquid which he let cool then partially drank. He gave the rest to Patsy, telling her it would help lower Judith's temperature for a while. Judith screwed up her face when her mother spooned it into her mouth, but she was too exhausted to protest and within minutes she was in a fitful sleep again.

'Can't find a way down from the bridge,' Chris said. 'So it'll have to be a climb.' His face was pale and pinched and despite the bandage that he'd cinched tightly around his hand, she could see his fingers were badly swollen and curved into paralysed hooks.

'You can't go down there,' she protested. 'Not with that hand. And you said before that you should never climb down if you can help it. It's too dangerous.'

'Nothing else for it,' he said. The coffee-pot had replaced the gelatinous berry mixture on the stove and he was cradling his tin mug in his good hand. 'That stuff won't last long, and it won't cure what's burning her up. Down there,' he nodded beyond the barrier, 'there's sure to be a first aid kit, and we need some more food.'

'I could climb it,' Peter chipped in, as bright-eyed and enthusiastic as ever, as if he'd spent an untroubled night in his own bed. His freckles stood out like paint spots.

'Sure you could,' Chris agreed. 'But you've got to stay here and look after the lady-folk, it's a law of the wild Northwest.'

383

He looked up at Patsy and winked. Peter didn't know whether to swell with pride or deflate with disappointment.

'And anyway, the reason I have to go is that we don't know what's down there.'

'It's just a bunch of old smashed-up cars.'

'From up here it is,' Chris told him. 'But once you get down there, you don't know *when* it is. Remember the bottle I threw over? And when you fired the slingshot? You thought it was a neat trick.'

'But I could help,' Peter protested weakly.

'I know, pal, and don't think I'd rather have anybody else go along if I could help it, but it could be the dead of winter down there and you could freeze your ass off.'

The rope Chris drew from his rucksack looked too fine to take even a child's weight, but he assured Patsy that it was strong enough. He tied it in a complex knot to one of the stanchions, cut a segment off the end, and threw the main line over the edge. It snaked away, unravelling as it fell, dropping fast towards the tangle of wrecks. Then the unfurling loops disappeared. The rope looked as if it had been cut neatly some thirty feet down from the railing. Chris gave Patsy a glance that conveyed as much disappointment as anything else. He tied another complex knot, fixing the segment to the main line, looped his belt through it, and explained to Peter that it was a mountaineer's safety rope. Finally he tethered his tin cup to the line so that it was pressed against the barrier.

'When you hear this rattling, pull the rope up. But don't forget, you'll have to drop it back down again. Put something heavy on it so that it comes down straight.'

He climbed over the safety rail, winked at Peter, then lowered himself down, bracing his feet against the slender concrete pillar, kicking outwards from the surface and dropping five or six feet with every swing, holding tight to the line with his one good hand.

'How will he get back up?' Peter asked. Patsy shrugged. The same thought had crossed her mind. Below them, Chris pushed himself outwards, arcing into the air on the slender rope. He came swinging back in towards the pillar, dropping quickly as he did so, feet braced for the impact.

And he vanished.

It happened so quickly that it took both of them by surprise. It was as if he had winked out of existence, disappeared into another universe. The rope juddered, an odd, stiff rod of fibre, swaying in and out like a pendulum, ending in mid-air. The sound of feet slamming against the concrete pillar had vanished just as completely. Below them, there was only dead silence.

Patsy stood looking down for a long while, wondering what really was below her feet, below the twist of air through which their new friend had disappeared. Behind her, Judith was talking in her sleep, shaking her head from side to side, as if she was backing away from something in her dream. Patsy turned and went back to take her in her arms, aghast at the papery insubstantiality in her child, wondering what monsters haunted her daughter's sleep. Peter sat at the barrier, loaded slingshot at the ready, glancing each way on the bridge, keeping guard.

The membrane, like the surface tension on water, squeezed at Chris in a surreal twist, as if for an instant he'd been turned inside out, and then he was through. There was a snap of noise, like a plucked string and a faint vibration in his ears and he was *elsewhere.* Above him, the rope rose for six, maybe eight feet, a thin braided rod wavering only slightly with the swing of his weight. Its end was severed as if slashed by a razor, leaving a straight edge pointing to a bruised sky. A wild and freezing wind shrieked around him, moaning as it vibrated the taut cable, driving a hard sleet into his face. He spun quickly, getting his back to the wind, listening to the shrieks, not sure whether they were all caused by the wind; afraid they might be coming from below him.

The cut end of the rope was eerily unnatural, unnerving and wrong. He was suspended from nothing, his whole weight hanging over an abyss with nothing to support him, hanging by one hand on a rope standing in the air. An instant of vertigo swelled and he clamped it down.

Walking fella, has to look-see with the other eye. Old Leather the Aborigine had tapped him on the forehead, his flat black face like tanned hide, strong nut-cracking Neanderthal teeth showing in a wide grin.

Only way you find track you git back along home you bilong.

The pain in his hand was a twisting hot corkscrew running right up to the crook of his elbow, despite the berries which should have numbed it a couple of degrees and he cursed himself through his gritted teeth for being a damned fool for swiping at the thing with his hand. He could have blasted it off the front of the car with one shot. The hurt helped damp down the rolling vertigo of utter disorientation at his own predicament. The fear of falling, the instinctive certainty of it, began to fade. The wind plucked at him with insistent fingers, fluttering the open ends of his jacket and swung him around. He risked a look down. A savage flash of lightning speared from the roiling sky and cast everything below him into stark relief. A hundred, maybe two hundred cars were crammed and crashed into each other, trucks and buses and pick-ups, all intertwined. A stale smell of oil and smoke blew up on the cold wind, and inside it was the bad smell of rot. A huge storm was wheeling around, whipping the clouds into a circle of purple and green, a whirlpool of angry sky.

He looked back up and saw the black rainbow of the bridge far overhead, as if it spanned a deep chasm. There were no lights up there, no signs of life, and he was back to being completely alone in this world.

Chris Deane took a deep breath, gripped the safety rope and braced for another descent. He thought he'd got used to it, after all this time, imagined he'd become self-sufficient, able to look after himself despite the terrors of the road. Travellers were few and far between, encounters with living people so rare that they were fraught occasions of wary circumspection.

Then this woman and her children had screeched to a stop on the road and they had made him not alone. But for them he would not ever, under any circumstances he could imagine, be hanging there, suspended between two regions of purgatory, lowering himself into the unknown.

Down and down, eight, sometimes ten feet at a time, a human spider on its guy rope, Chris Deane dropped to the mad tangle on the bottom road. He braced himself for the last swing, keeping his back to the storm, until his feet boomed on the roof of a white delivery van. It was not night yet, though it was certainly dark enough. The storm clouds were so thick that they shut out the daylight. Lightning lanced again, three twists of blistering light sizzling from the low clouds to stab on the road in the distance, sending a coruscating fountain of sparks into the air. The rank sear of ozone came rolling down on the turbulence, bitter enough to make his eyes water, but not sufficiently strong to overcome the smell of putrefaction. A heavy gust sent him lurching to the right, making him grab at the rope with his injured hand, sending another jolt of pain up his arm and then he was down, huddled between the van and its neighbour, a big black police wagon, stove-in on its side and paint-bubbled where the fire had almost melted the bodyshell. Rain drummed on the panelwork in a steady rhythm. He tied the end of the rope to one of the bars on the window, pulling the hawser tight and tying a double knot that would be impossible for the wind to pull free. The rope was his only lifeline. If it snapped, he'd be stuck on this road and he'd never see the woman or her children again. For some reason, though he had known them hardly more than a day, that was a situation he wanted to avoid. Something about them told Chris he should stay with them and help them on their way. He'd long given up hope of finding a way off the road that led to nowhere – or led to somewhere he did not want to go – but now he was not so sure. Patsy Havelin, travelling down the highway with her children, was determined to find her way home. He would help her, and maybe she would help him, too.

The safety line unshipped with a quick, skilful twist and he lowered himself down to the road level. The lightning sputtered and hissed again, searing the mess of wrecks. Thunder blasted on its heels, so intense that the police van thrummed in the shock wave. Over by the concrete pillar, a shadow wavered suddenly and his eyes instinctively flicked towards the motion. He waited for twenty seconds, but nothing else moved. He squeezed himself past the van and down to the level of the road, crawling under the unnatural bridge of a flat-loader's broken back. The stench of oil and foetid decay was thick enough to clog his throat, but there was nothing he could do about it. He pressed on, edging his way to the side of the road where he could make some progress and find a truck or car which hadn't been completely crushed. It took him ten minutes to get to the crash barrier and clamber over it. Underfoot the verge was a squelching mess and as foul as a slaughterhouse dump. He forced himself on, while the pain wound up in his hand and the storm wound up in the sky.

It took him fifty yards to find a car with enough clearance to swing a door open. The windscreen was completely gone and the front end so badly crushed the engine had pushed right through to the footwell. He flicked open the glove compartment, checking inside first, before reaching to scoop the contents, discarding the sunglasses first, then pocketing the unopened packet of mints and the bottle with six loose aspirin rattling inside. Aspirin wouldn't fix the girl, he knew, but it would be better than nothing. Here, on the road, Chris also knew, you took everything you found.

Three lengths back, a stylish limousine yielded a mouldering corpse with his head stove in on the dashboard and the neck of a bottle of whisky still clutched in a skeletal hand. The rain was pouring in through the smashed sunroof, cascading into the hole in the skull and then pouring out in twin cataracts through the empty sockets. The power of the water made the jaw rap tinny morse against the fascia in a grotesque deathly chatter. He pulled back, turning away from the image of wet death and tried the next door. It swung wide and a dead woman slid gracelessly from the seat, summer dress flaking, skinny, meatless legs splayed wide. Her head turned slowly, as if to look up to tongue-lash him for the disturbance, except she had no tongue behind the two perfect rows of teeth. Most of her hair hung in rat's tails, still stuck to the back of the seat. The stench was thick as syrup. He ignored it and leaned past her, grabbed a big handbag and hauled it out in the space of one tightly-held breath.

He opened the catch and emptied the contents down on the road underneath a tilted trailer where the road was not completely awash. The money he chucked away, letting the wind take the useless paper. A small leather-bound diary with a pen stuck down the spine told him the woman's name was Penelope and that she was diabetic. A little plastic box gave him six unused hypodermic syringes and ten vials of insulin which he took anyway. Another box was packed with tampons and he stuffed that in his bag too, though he didn't even think of Patsy when

388

he did so. The little towels made handy little field dressings when you were stuck and hurting.

Three cars down the line, very close to the barrier, a silver-grey stretch limo with the boomerang antenna of a portable television was squeezed between a delivery van and a timber-truck. One of the timbers had rolled at some stage and crushed the back end enough to spring the lock. Chris checked there first and found a kilo of cocaine stuffed into a golf-bag. He toyed with the idea of taking a snort, just to get rid of the fire in his hand, then decided against. The pain might go for a while, but he needed something to get rid of the infection he knew was digging in through the cut edges where he'd slit the skin to get rid of the spider-acid. In a day, two at the most, the burn would be up to his shoulder and his whole arm swollen like a marrow. He jammed one small bag into his pocket and went back to the front. The car was empty, and every bottle in the stowaway drinks cabinet was smashed to shards. A puddle of something which had been blood was scabbed over on the floor. Beside it, an expensive briefcase turned up a silver box of big cigars, and a handful of negotiable bearer bonds which could have bought a life of ease anywhere, but which were only firelighters on this road. Underneath them, a leather wallet lay beside a silver hip-flask. The flask was full and it contained overproof vodka. The wallet was a hypochondriac's travel-pack, complete with amoxyl capsules, painkillers, antiseptic creams and insect repellent.

Chris grinned widely to himself. He washed two capsules down with a mouthful of liquor which burned almost as fiercely as the fire in his arm, and after a while, he clambered out of the limousine and into the rain. The delivery van door swung open creakily. Something small and fast scuttled into the far shadows, and as long as it was moving away from him, Chris was not concerned. Red hamper-boxes held a treasure of canned foods. He picked out a dozen and stuffed them into a plastic carrier bag before crawling back out into the rain, heading back towards the bridge.

The storm was whipped up to a rage by the time he reached the rope and already the pain was smoothing down. Clambering in from the edge, negotiating the jagged edges of the burnt-out hulks of the trucks and cars was more difficult on the inward journey, but he persevered, keeping himself low against the driving rain and the shrieking wind, cringing every time a bolt of lightning speared down from the black sky to stab at the edges of the road. Twice, on his way to the centre, shards of lightning sizzled overhead, dancing from the antenna of one truck to the exhaust stack of another in a juddery arc of power, sending silvered light dancing on every surface. It rippled up the rope, a thin glowing thread of light and for a moment his heart did a double jump, imagining his lifeline burning through like the filament of a lamp. Thunder clapped in a deafening crash of sound and the fire fizzled out. Rain fell in sheets and poured along the road under the crumple of cars in streams red with rust and black with ash and muddied with other things it was not wise to dwell on.

He tried both hands on the rope, but his left was still swollen stiff and pulsing with pain, and he realised there was no chance of climbing upwards. Even with two good hands and on a dry day, it would be an exhausting ascent. One-handed, whipped by the winds and slathered in rain, it would be impossible. Chris scouted around until he found the broken-backed trailer again, crawled underneath and assembled his spoils in the plastic carrier bag. He wrote a detailed note in dead Penelope's diary and attached the lot to the guy rope. He loosened the hitch on the paddy wagon and gave the hawser a couple of vigorous flicks. The wind shrieked around him and he had to hold on, like one of the bloated spiders, waiting for the tremble of a reply.

The cup rattled against the barrier, a sudden jangle of sound that startled Patsy awake from a baleful daydream. It was well into the afternoon and while she didn't know how long Chris had been gone, it seemed like a long time. The sun was halfway down the sky again and clouds were rolling in across the gnarled and rocky landscape stretching out on either side of the bridge. She felt exposed here on the bridge and she wanted to be on her way, rolling along.

Peter had kept vigil, over at the barrier. Every ten minutes or so, he'd haul himself up and lean over to look downwards where the tangle of wreckage was rusting in the dim light. The rope hung there, motionless for the distance from where Chris had tied it to where the end was sheared off at whatever point of reality – *or unreality* – it passed through. Earlier, he'd been scanning the horizon with the small telescope and had called her across to the balustrade. She'd peered through, following the line of the road until it forked far off where the mist was just beginning to evaporate. A light twinkled in a double-pulse like sun on glass. Patsy had strained until she could make out a slight movement. The blink of light came again and then the shape resolved itself.

The black van, tiny in the distance, even magnified through the glass, was beetling along the road, kicking up its own contrail of dust.

'Is it coming this way?' Peter had asked, and she had shaken her head, indicating that she didn't know. The road forked in the distance and the van was on the left side, coming roughly in their direction, but whether or not the road it travelled would cross the bridge, she couldn't say. There were several bypass connections at both ends of the bridge, little spiral junctions that seemed to lead to nowhere.

'She keeps on coming,' Peter said. 'Why can't she leave us alone?'

Patsy knew the answer to that. The gypsy must be getting desperate now. There were only hours left until the midwinter. After that, if Crandall Gilfeather was right, she'd have missed her chance.

The van was hurtling along purposefully, with a motion that was somehow animal, like a questing hound. It reminded her of the shadow-wights hunting Frodo Baggins, sniffing for signs of the ring. She remembered the strange sound of horses when she'd jinked up the slip-road, forcing the van to drive on the straight. That could have been her imagination, or it could have been something else. The black van was as much part of this eerie place as the spider things that crawled from the cat's eye mountings, or the tyre-skin snappers which slithered out to eat them. There were always pieces of truck tyres scattered on the roads back home, but here they were different. Here they took on a life of their own. The black transit van with its custom-styled flame-burst licking around the black headlights and the dark grille, that too was part of this place, a changing thing charged with its own

391

unnatural life. It was sniffing them out, hounding their progress, baying at their heels.

Cry havock and let loose the dogs of war. It was an old quote from somewhere, *Hamlet* maybe, but she thought it was appropriate. A bitch was on their trail. It would not stop until it found them.

Patsy handed the telescope back to her son and crossed to the car. She flipped the glove compartment open and drew out the handgun. It was heavy in her hand and she broke it to check that all the cylinders were full. Peter was scanning the distance and had his back to her, so she slipped the gun inside her jacket, hitching the little holster to the belt of her jeans so he wouldn't see it. She went back to the railing just as Peter pointed out in the other direction to where the van had disappeared round the curve.

Without a word he handed her the scope and she panned this way and that until the image jumped out at her. An even section of highway arrowed straight for several miles before it reached a circular junction fed by a number of smaller roads. Hulking dark shapes were angling along the lesser routes. As she watched, they turned, almost in unison, and fed onto the straight. A faint moan came drifting on the air, just loud enough to tell her it was the *whonk* of a big haulage rig's horn. She drew back and blinked, hoping she'd been mistaken.

The black trucks. Chris had mentioned them. *You always want to avoid them.* As soon as the line of trucks impinged on her consciousness, his words came back to her, superimposed on the memory of the big haulage rig rumbling alongside her on the storm-tossed road, tarpaulin flapping like a devil's wing, and she recalled how it had tried to bat her into oblivion with a vicious swipe of the trailer. She kept the telescope still and counted them. There were at least five now, maybe six, though on the straight, with one behind the other, there might have been more of the things. They were monstrous trucks, black as coal, powerful things that could have been built for a road in this godforsaken place. They rumbled on, heading in their direction, as the van had done, sending up a fug of road fumes and blue exhaust.

For an instant Patsy wanted to get into the car and drive,

taking any route off this exposed crest of bridge, taking any turn to get away from the menace of the dark transit, away from the threat of the convoy of black trucks. She pulled Peter back towards the car and got in, knowing she had no option but to stay. They would get nowhere with the tyre torn to shreds.

She squeezed in beside Judith, letting Peter crouch on the front seat, and sat waiting. For half a hour, nothing happened and despite her apprehension, she fell into a nervous doze. The jangling cup startled her awake and her first instinct was to grab for the gun. She whirled round, expecting to see the line of black trucks come roaring up the curve of the bridge, night monsters in the pallid daylight. The cup rattled again and she almost giggled with relief. Judith stirred and groaned, but she did not waken.

The cup rattled a third time as she reached the barrier. She gripped the rope and gave it three swift tugs, one after the other. Down below, unseen beyond the straight-edge cut of the rope, the line twitched in response. Without delay she pulled on it, hauling it hand over hand. A weight on the line told her he'd tied something to it. A few moments later, the white plastic bag appeared from nowhere. She heaved it over the fence and was about to set it down when Peter pointed to the far side of the bridge. Immediately she grabbed the telescope and looked.

The line of trucks was heading away from them. She could see the rear of the last one, tail-lights winking that sickly orange, shrouded in a whirl of exhaust. A very faint rumble carried on the strengthening wind. The lead truck went up an incline and the rest followed, a black road-serpent, before they disappeared down the lee side. As soon as they were out of sight, Patsy hunkered down and opened the bag, shaking off the droplets of water on the plastic.

Some penicillin (he'd written, though the words were blotted and water-marked and the paper in the little diary was damp.) *Should help along with painkillers. Can't climb until morning. Set up perimeter again and send bag down pronto. Use a weight. Hope kids are okay*

A quick tear burned in the corner of her eye and she blinked it back, fumbling for the bottle of antibiotic capsules.

Chris watched the bag dwindle as it was drawn up on the rope, until it silently vanished. He waited for what seemed an age until it came slowly descending from the dimly-seen arch of the bridge. She'd understood his message and weighted it with a heavy section of kerbstone, but even so, the buffeting wind swung it away from him and he had to clamber over the jagged hulks of the wrecks to grab for it. He tied it tightly to the paddy wagon again.

Thanks (she wrote in a neat, rounded script.) *Gave Judith medicine. It should work. Trucks on road in distance. Did you take pills for hand? Be careful!!! Hawkeye is eating hot dogs. He says How!*

He read the note by the fading light, and smiled to himself, though the mention of the trucks was a worry. He'd seen the black rigs hammering on the road and instinct had made him crouch in the scrub on the verges when one had overtaken him. There was a menace about them that was as chilling as it was inexplicable. It was something sensed in the marrow, in the long nerves in the spine. They juddered past, making the road vibrate, fumes roiling from tall stacks, great wheels pounding, sending up sheets of spray. The windows were smoked, too dark to see through, which made them look as if the trucks were driving by themselves; but when they passed, there was a sense of baleful perception, a bleak awareness, as if a tainted conscious-ness had reached out and made contact.

Down here, there was nothing he could do. The storm was whirling in an immense anti-cyclone which made him feel he was in the bottom of a rolling barrel. Clouds of purple and blood-red were whipping round in a glowering galaxy stirred by some vast and brutal force. The wind shrieked and moaned through the broken fenders and the glass-shattered window frames and under the popped trunks of squashed limousines. The rain came down in rods and every now and again the poisonous lightning would stutter to send up clusters of sparks where it hit and thunder clapped the air in deafening blasts. He crawled through the wrecks of a couple of nearby cars, found a depleted medi-pack in the trunk of a small car and took the sticking plasters and a bottle of surgical spirit which he slung in his pocket.

He was cold, but not frozen, not yet, though the wind-chill was fierce. Chris crawled back to the trailer again and squeezed further in beside the big double wheels, getting his back to the rear panel of an old army transporter. The ozone smell of the storm was doing its best to smother the stench of rot all around, which was the only blessing, although the bitter lightning ions stung his eyes and nose. From above, the wreckage was old, a year, maybe two of rust; he could tell from experience. Down here, though, the pile-up was only months old, if that. He didn't understand whatever principle was involved here. All he could do was accept the fact that he was perhaps two years in the past when viewed from the bridge, yet he had passed up a bag of medicine and food to Patsy Havelin who was on the span overhead. If he thought about that sort of thing for long enough, it would drive him crazy, he knew, so he tried not to think about it, or the kind of force that could twist and rend a normal reality so violently. There were plenty of other things not to think about while he wasn't thinking about the worm-holes in time. The dead and mouldering bodies in the cars; the cars themselves. How they had come to be smashed and entangled on this road was beyond his comprehension, but he'd walked the road so long he'd been able to close his mind to it.

Yet now, closer than ever to the vast interchange he'd always seen from the distance, he sensed a change in the power and a surge of mutation that was different from before. Somehow, he sensed, they were getting closer to a destination. Whether that was good or bad, he did not know, but instinctively he sensed it was far from good.

The ache in his hand was settling down to a hot throb and already the edges of the gash were itching madly, a sign that he was healing fast. Time was different in this world, whether on the flyover or underneath it. He'd passed through some regions where a cut would have bled for two days. Here, his healing process was speeded up, and that was a good sign. He'd washed the wound in surgical spirit, wincing at the bite in his flesh, but now the painful pressure of septic infection was dwindling, and the real fear that he might have to open his flesh again receded. Chris opened the other tin of hot dogs and ate them cold. They were greasy and slick with brine, but they filled a space. The eye of the storm passed by, whipping up the winds to a crescendo as it rolled along the road, and then it began to fade. The clouds were still piled up, bruised purple and somehow alien. For a while they rolled in the sky and then they went black. Night fell so suddenly it was as if a mighty hand had shut a door on the world.

The squall raced away past the bridge, a spinning carousel of screaming winds and rain, and then it swept westwards, heading towards where Chris knew the tangle of roadways lined the horizon. In seconds, the winds died, dwindling from a shriek to a moan to a whisper. Overhead the clouds began to clear quickly and above him, the fine arch of the bridge curved across the coal surface of the sky which shimmered red, like a banked up fire waiting to burst into heat, and he knew the moon had risen, though it was hidden form his view by the concrete ribbon of the flyover. Through a narrow gap between the wheels of the big twisted flat-loader, the sky in the distance was the same colour, though much brighter and pulsating like a blast furnace. It could have been a volcano spewing lava over where the intersection wheeled and twisted, or it could have been a colossal forge where twisted and misshapen things, the badlands equivalent of *morlocks* pumped the bellows of dreadful fires. That glow had been with him, somewhere in the sky, every night since he'd first found his feet on the track through the rainforest. The breeze, the tail-end of the storm carried the throb of distant traffic, of great wheels rumbling on a roadway, the growl of transmissions and protesting gears, and the oil scent greased the already foetid air.

It was night and the moon was risen and the far furnace was pulsing with its own life. Chris Deane squeezed himself back against the perished rubber of a truck tyre. A creak of movement jarred a few yards away beyond the police van and Chris came to suddenly, completely alert.

A shadow moved within a shadow and he slowly drew out the big gun and laid it on his knee. He inched a hand inside his poacher's pocket and found the little flashlight on its lanyard chain. He waited, breathing so slowly, so quietly he might not have been breathing at all.

Another movement, this time to the right, high up in the

crumple of wreckage. His eyes flickered that way, though not another muscle in his body so much as twitched. He was safe here from the cat's eye crawlers, that was for certain. They came scuttling out at moonrise, but they avoided the scent of oil, and here, in the pile-up, the air was thick with it. It wouldn't be the crawlers or the creepy things that fed on them, Chris knew that, but he'd walked the roads long enough to know that the night always brought the hunters and the hungry. He slowly pushed himself further back into the recess, becoming one of the patches of shadow.

Something squeaked, close to his foot. Two pinprick red eyes flicked on then winked out. Another squeak responded, high-pitched, like chalk on a blackboard, just enough to set his teeth on edge. A tiny flurry of movement and a small, fast thing clambered over his boot. Two pairs of close-set eyes glared again, swivelling towards him. He slung the gun back in its holster and lifted the torch.

Teeth ground on his ankle-bone in a sudden flare of pain. His leg kicked reflexively and a small shape went tumbling away. A squeal became a high shriek. Another one chittered right next to his ear. Small horny feet pattered up his thigh and onto his jacket and he jerked away from it. Whiskers brushed his cheek and a red eye blinked only inches from his own, too close to be in focus. He pulled back, cracking his head painfully on a metal spar. He thumbed the flashlight and saw the weasels.

That's what they looked like, for the first couple of seconds, in the white electric glare. Two of them looped towards him with that familiar mustelid gait, thin and sleek, but bigger than weasels. They could have been the size of stoats. One of them stood on its hind legs, sniffing the air. Its red eyes reflected the light of the torch, gleaming like polished rubies, giving off a feral light of their own. The standing creature looked almost cute, except for the bulging eyes set high on its head, and its long, rat-like tail. It whistled, almost bird-like. And then without warning, it darted, quicker than the eye could follow, towards Chris's boot. It dived in and its mouth opened in a gape which was almost impossible to comprehend in a creature so small. It was as if its whole head unhinged, like a viper's jaw. It struck, blurring fast, before he could react, and sank its teeth into the thick leather.

Right at that moment, Chris was unalarmed, even though his ankle-bone was throbbing from the first nip. Two seconds later, when the little sinuous creature's jaws clamped like a vice on his foot and a white river of pain went rolling over his toes, and six other little weasley things came snaking out of the shadows towards him, he realised he was in real danger. One of the creatures ran right up his leg, heading for his crotch. Panic blossomed. The mustelid opened its mouth, only inches from his testicles. He swung the torch. Shadows waxed and waned as the light spun. The edge of the flashlight caught the thing on the jaw just before the mandible snapped shut. A little splash of blood hit his leg and the animal went tumbling away without a sound, its head squashed flat. Chris crawled to the side, out of the corner where he had crept at the first sound. The little brute on his foot was chewing away, eating into the leather. Tiny needle-like teeth were through his skin and ground on his bones. He drew his foot back, stamped it down and felt the animal crunch wetly. The pain in his toes flared hot, drawing a groan from him, and then it faded. A shadow came jittering up the old tyre, zigzagging in a grey blur. The bulbous eyes flashed at him and some instinct made him raise his hand. The thing came leaping towards him at shoulder height, leaping straight for his neck. The mouth yawned, showing an impressive array of teeth. His free hand lashed out and smacked the thing from the air, sending shards of agony up to his elbow when the wound from the previous night tore at its edge. Chris dragged himself, both feet kicking frantically as more of the things came squirming out of the crannies and fissures in the snarl of wrecks. He panned the flashlight and saw an array of red, swollen eyes, all of them fixed on his own. He clambered out, hauling himself up on top of the police wagon and climbed over an old station wagon that had burned to a shell. A series of piping squeals, like rats in the dark, followed his progress. Christ leapt on top of the flatbed, struggled over the broken back and down the other side. Another truck, this one an old petrol bowser loomed ahead. A convenient ladder gave him access to the top of the tank which had crumpled like a beer can and he reached the far end, where he could take one step to reach the cab of another delivery truck. He made a grab for the door, not sure whether he could still hear the squeak of the crazy little weasel monsters. The handle clicked down and he tugged. The door creaked open with a dreadful protest of twisted metal and he hauled himself inside. He was pulling the door closed when suddenly ever nerve in his body sizzled in alarm. The hairs on the back of his neck stood up and rippled in unison and the enormous surge of pure dread rocked him back against the door. He spun so fast he almost fell to the floor.

The driver turned his head to look at him.

The sick red moonlight was far from bright, here under the bridge, but it was enough to show Chris Deane the outline of a man propped up against the big, old-fashioned steering wheel.

The head had turned with a dry creak, and a mouth slowly opened. The temperature in the cab plummeted. The air froze. A rime of flowery ice raced over the windscreen. A plume of scent so foul it was almost solid, invaded his nose like a contagion.

The driver, a rustling skinny shape, swung slowly in his seat and a long scrawny hand came off the wheel.

Goin' my way? An arid voice scraped the yard between them. *Goin' all the way, good buddy.*

Some word tried to blurt its way out of him, but Chris, in that instant, was as frozen as the air in the cab. He couldn't breathe. He couldn't move.

The angular thing with the shingle voice leaned towards him and Chris heard the scrape of bone upon bone.

Gotta keep right on goin' to the end of the trip. The jaw opened wide and a thin, dry laugh came bleating out of the dead space. Empty sockets were turning towards him and Chris suddenly knew that when they were facing him, he'd see the mad red light of the moon shining in their depths and that he'd be caught in the bane light, speared in the headlights like a deer on the road. Fright kicked him in the belly. He jerked back, as scared as he had ever been in his life, and his hand hit the door-catch. He spun, shoved at the door with all of his strength and tumbled out. Something snagged the back of his jacket and he almost screamed for his mother. He jumped forward and the snag gave with a small rip. Chris landed on the roof of a little Volkswagen Beetle jammed up against the bowser, clambered over it and onto an open-top tourer from the forties. He stepped over the passenger seat and into the back.

A corpse in a black dinner suit groped its way up, white wing collar still fastened, but the bow-tie askew. For an instant it looked like Fred Astaire, just as lean in the red luminescence. But the face was longer, the cheeks more prominent, and it was missing two teeth on the top row. A hank of jet-black hair hung down from the forehead, giving the skeleton a drunken look.

Going the wrong way, my good man, the bones gibbered at him. *You'll have to join the party. We're all getting there in the end.*

Chris didn't stop. He batted the thing with his flashlight before it could swing its sockets round towards him. Underneath the rickle of bones, a dry woman's voice giggled. Chris glanced down and saw another mouldering body with its head jammed against the first one's pelvis, an obscenity caught in a lewd act.

He leapt over the back of the tourer, almost put his foot through a travelling truck lashed to the caddie and swung up through the empty windscreen frame of a single-deck tourist coach. Instantly he knew that was a mistake. Down the aisle a series of pale heads leaned outwards in a parody of curious passengers checking the new arrival.

Join the mystery tour, creaky voices whispered inside his head. *You don't know where you're going until you get there.*

Chris dropped the flashlight, letting it dangle on its chain, and pulled out the gun. One of the nearby passengers reached a long hand out towards him. A shiny watch swung gently, clicking against the wrist. He backed away, grabbed the window-spar and went straight out the front again.

The bus driver was impaled in a scaffolding pole sticking out from a pick-up truck. Chris pushed past the body. It twisted on the spike and creaked its head round towards him.

Stick with us, mate. Come on the busman's holiday. We've plenty of space.

'Fuck you,' Chris bawled. He raised his gun and jammed it against the head of the corpse. The turning motion stopped.

Be a sport.

A hand touched him on the shoulder and his heart vaulted into the back of his throat.

I'm lost.

A young woman, naked but for a thin raincoat spattered with blood was leaning from the step of a truck.

I only wanted to go home. I only hitched a ride.

The girl's skin was alabaster white and her hair dark and lustrous and for an instant Chris was reminded of Judith.

But they took me away and hurt me and now I'm on the road. Can you help me?

'Sure,' he blurted. He reached a hand to help her down. She gripped his with cold fingers. He turned towards her. The air froze and the rime frost ran crackling up the sides of the truck and Chris saw the red glow begin to light in her shadowed eyes. She sighed and a stench assailed him, so foul it stopped his breath. She was turning her head towards him. A tiny motion by her ear caught his eye. A maggot, almost two inches long, squirmed out, blindly questing the air.

'Jesus,' Chris cried, gagging. He snatched his hand away, skin tingling with the horror of leprosy. He raised the gun again.

'Get away from me!'

She was turning towards him, the fat maggot still squirming out from inside. A patch of white skin peeled away from the corner of her mouth as she began to speak.

He hit her with the butt of the gun. It made a dull crack and she went tumbling away from him. There was no blood, just a blurt of some liquid that stank of putrefaction. The girl dropped between the two trucks and smacked on the road surface. Chris gagged. Hot bile came rolling up. His throat spasmed against it and an acid burn scored on the inside of his throat. His eyes filled with water and for an instant everything swam in red puddles until he used the heel of his hand to wipe them clear. When his vision returned he clambered to the top of the pick-up, then hauled up over a big container rig. From there he could see his rope, a thin black line stretching from the bridge. Beyond it, right across the width of the road where all the wreckage was packed together in a tortured mass, he could see the slow, slumped motion of things on the move. Whispering sounds invaded his brain, arid entreaties, dry as sticks. He tried to clamp his mind shut against them. Little red eyes glared up from down in the depths. He ignored them.

401

It took five minutes to get back to the low-loader next to the overturned paddy wagon. He holstered his gun quickly and untied his lifeline. It swung free. A scraping sound came from inside the Black Maria and a long, white arm came questing out into the night air.

Gonna fry us all, cockroach. Gonna all take the walk together. 'Not me, pal,' he heard himself retort. A pale shape came climbing up onto the loader. Chris ignored the staggering pain in his hand and gripped the rope. He hauled himself up, one hand at a time, muscles shuddering with the effort. He made it to six feet, eight feet. Something reached up and snatched at his foot. He kicked hard, hit something solid but brittle and used the impetus to snatch another four feet in a quick scramble. The next six feet took longer. A tug jerked at the rope and he twisted his leg around the line until there was enough friction to take his weight, then he reached down and snatched at the section below him. It snagged, then pulled free and he reeled it in, looping it as it came.

For a while, he swung there, suspended between the bridge and the world of dead travellers, listening to their appeals and barren entreaties while they crept from the shadows and crawled over the wrecks, heading in the direction of the glow in the sky. Chris dangled on the rope until the pain in his hand dopplered down to a bearable throb. With great difficulty, he managed to fish a faded handkerchief from his pack and wrap it around the weeping wound. After a while he began to haul himself up under the black arch of the bridge until he could climb no more.

26

Morning broke, humid and sultry under a strange obsidian sky. Pulses of what might have been lightning arced in sizzling streaks from ground to the molten glass vaults above, and the air was tense with an expectant energy on the skin and sent goose-flesh crawling on Patsy's arms. She had woken suddenly from a fitful slumber, disoriented and confused.

She looked at her watch. A crack like a spider's web frosted the glass. Behind it the hands were lying in a little pile. There was something different about this day, an importance that she should know. Patsy shook her head and swallowed the taste of sulphur and burnt ozone.

December twenty-first. It came to her now. Despite the heat, it was the midwinter, the solstice. She had woken to the shortest day, the *Nameless Day*. Thunder growled behind the pulses of baleful lightning. The fast-rising sun seemed to have lost all of its power. The sunspots were like tumours, like the warts risen on the side of Judith's face.

Judith. Patsy turned to her.

Patsy had made Judith swallow two of the antibiotic capsules before dark. An hour later, her daughter's temperature had soared so high her skin felt as if it would blister and she screamed and whimpered as if all the demons in hell were clawing at her dreams. Patsy considered crushing some of the Amoxil into boiling water and using one of the syringes to inject it directly into a vein. If that's what it took to save Judith's life, she'd have done it, but within twenty minutes, as she mopped Judith's fiery brow with the last of their water on a cloth, the fever broke. It happened so suddenly that at first Patsy couldn't believe it. One minute her daughter was shivering against her, radiating heat and dripping with perspiration and the next she was in a deep slumber, and the burning fever was draining away. Something was battling what was eating away at her, but despite that, her skin was still peeling away like old paper and the darkness underneath it had spread down to her jawline. Her hands were like withered little paws and the tendons stuck out like shoelaces.

Nothing had attacked them during the night, even here on the exposed curve of the flyover, but all around them, the dark had been filled with screams and cries of things which had sounded not quite animal, but not human. It was as if something waited for the right moment.

Some time in the night, a big truck had roared somewhere on one of the roads close to the flyover, making the bridge vibrate as it passed, waking Patsy up from a dream where Chris Deane lowered himself down from the parapet into a burning hell in which demons with forked tails and gargoyle faces reached up clawed hands to tear and rend at him, and when she tried to pull him up on the rope she saw it was not Chris, but Peter who was dangling like bait on the rope. She came awake, gasping for breath, and the roar of the truck echoed through the night, drowning out the shrieks and yells in the dark. Even in the aftermath of the dream, Patsy could sense the dreadful presence of the juggernaut, as if it was something alive, and she crouched back in the seat, drawing her children closer to her, until the shuddering vibration died away. Peter turned in his slumber, opened a sleepy eye and wriggled to get comfortable. Patsy sat alone with her thoughts, wondering what was happening to their companion down there beyond the parapet where the crumpled shells of cars and trucks and buses seemed to stretch forever.

Judith woke up with that feeble slowness of the infirm. Peter got the stove going again and opened a tin of tomato soup which was warm enough to drink in five minutes, but his sister couldn't touch it. The camping kettle started to boil and Patsy made a cup of coffee, thick and black and she could have killed for a spoonful of demerara sugar.

'Chris ain't back yet?' Peter asked.

'*Isn't* back,' she corrected automatically, before she realised how silly she was to worry about the pedantry of English on this road. She worked up a smile for him and ruffled his hair. 'No. But I don't imagine he'll be too long.'

'I like him,' Peter said, slurping at his soup.

'I know you do. I think I like him too.' That was true. They'd picked up a complete stranger on a road where all strangers

404

were to be avoided and in hardly more than a day, he'd become part of the travelling party. Even more, he'd gone over the side of the bridge, swinging on a rope that looked hardly thick enough to take his weight, and gone dropping down out of sight into the complete unknown, just to find medicine for Judith. Without the antibiotics, her daughter would be close to death by now. Closer anyway. She was still far from well, but if he'd come climbing over the barrier just then, she'd have hugged him until his ribs cracked.

'Can he come and stay with us?'

'I think he'll want to go home. To his own home.'

'He doesn't have one,' Peter said. 'He says his dad moved around a lot and he's never had a real place to stay.' Patsy could hear the hero-worship in Peter's tone. Chris Deane had a big black gun in a holster, a battered leather hat that spoke of many adventures, and he'd the lean, lived-in look of every action hero who'd stalked across the screen. She remembered his lazy grin as he showed Peter how to use the catapult, holding the boy's wrist steady while Peter pulled back the rubber, and she wondered how he'd managed to stay sane on the road. He'd been alone in purgatory a long time.

When she finished her coffee, she crossed over to the railing again and looked down. There was still no sign of movement. The mouldering wrecks were red with the slanted light of a low sun, which told her it was early morning down there, just after dawn, at least from her point of view. Down below the cut-off rope, it could be any time, any season. Peter was using the telescope to scan the distant weave of low roads. Nothing moved. They went back to the car and she let the children sit by the stove in the cool of the morning while she inspected the front wheel. Pieces of rubber had split off from the tread and the entire wall had been sliced through by the wheel rims. It was beyond repair, and she'd left the spare back at the stump where she'd first come off the road so there was nothing she could do. Until Chris Deane came back, she was stuck here with no transport. Without his big gun – and, she conceded, his presence – the long walk on the road was inconceivable. She came round to where she'd tucked Judith into the blanket, out of the light, and hunkered down close to the open front door of the car.

Peter had been saying something, but now he fell silent. Judith was staring blankly into the distance, fingers working on something held tightly in the palm of her hand. Her head was cocked to the side, as if she was listening to something.

Patsy followed her gaze, down the forward slope of the bridge to where it forked right and left, spiralling down to whichever routes it joined. She listened, holding her breath. For an instant she thought she could hear distant moans of distress, the kind you would hear on television when it showed a newsflash of some distant tragedy. The moaning sound faded away and she assumed it had been the wind. She was still listening when the voice whispered in her head.

Patssssseee.

She snapped upright.

Losssst now, Patsssseeee.

Judith made a little gulping sound. Peter was in the act of turning. Every nerve in Patsy's body was suddenly thrumming.

The radio blared so loudly the three of them jumped in fright. A gravelly voice, deep and rough as a gravel track came booming out on the crest of a jarring power chord on an electric guitar.

You're on the road, it told her. She'd heard the song before. She knew these words. She knew what was coming next. Heavy bass beats came thrumming out.

You're on the road to hell.

A guitar rasp slid down to thump against the bass and for an instant, despite the sudden fright when the radio had come blasting on, Patsy was completely bewildered. The sound was coming from the speaker close to her, but inside her head she could hear a phased echo, just out of synch with the radio, as if the music was reverberating from somewhere else. Peter was in the act of turning and the radio was booming at her. Judith turned over, hauled herself to her feet without a sound and stumbled round the front of the car.

Patsy scrambled after her, then reached for her daughter's arm just by the offside headlamp. A dark shape caught her eye. Her hand snagged on Judith's sleeve and missed its grip.

The black van was hunched on the centre of the road, no more than fifty yards away.

It shuddered like a big animal, a crouching predator. It was only a van, black and dust-streaked from days on the road, with the stylised flames curling up from the fender to lick round the sides and over the wheel arches. The music thundered from invisible speakers, fast, frantic guitar riffs and chord slams counterpunched by deep drumbeats. It was a song she knew, but played differently, as if the van's sound system had distorted it. The black eye of the windscreen glistened. The glass was opaque, like obsidian, reflecting the low clouds behind her. It made the van look empty, and her mind tried to tell her it was *only a van* but her antennae were quivering, her instincts wound up so tight they could snap and she *sensed* a presence.

It's her. *She's here.* Patsy could feel the proximity of Kerron Vaunche, the way she had sensed her in the gloom of the basement in Broadford House. It was the scrape of stone, the rasp of thorns, the rustle of age. The witch had caught them on the open curve and there was no way to run.

The transit glowered, quivering with the shudder of the engine as the music faded. An invisible foot stamped on the pedal and the thing growled, low and throaty.

'Mum,' Peter said, a bleat of panic. He was behind her but she couldn't turn. Judith had stumbled, surprisingly quickly, beyond the front of the car, almost to the middle of the road. She was slightly ahead of Patsy who now had her hand reaching for her daughter's shoulder, frozen to immobility.

The gun, her rational mind exclaimed. It was in the glove compartment. Jesus, she told herself, stupid *bitch*. Everything was happening in a rush, every thought clear as quartz in the immediacy of danger. The driver's door was close enough and she debated dragging Judith towards it, throwing both of them inside, and snatching the gun from the shelf.

The music died. The engine revved again, rasping and gruff, as if reading her mind.

Forget it, kid. We've got you now. No true words, but the growl of the engine was just as eloquent.

'Mum, come on,' Peter wailed. He'd come round to where she stood and was tugging at her belt. 'It's . . . it's *bad*.'

She started to turn toward him, moving, it seemed to her adrenaline-driven senses, as if through treacle. Somewhere off to her right, a bird cawed, maybe a crow pecking at a decaying

407

corpse. Peter's foot kicked a small stone which tumbled across the blacktop like a marble, taking forever to get to the other side. A note of music came singing out from the car. Not electric guitar, not drums. It was the sound of a pipe, clear and hollow. The drawn out note floated on the air, a mystical sound, before it faded away to be followed by another, higher note that soared upwards in a sudden glissade of music and warbled when it reached a plateau.

Judith nodded. A simple inclination. She cocked her head again, listening. Patsy heard nothing but the eerie hover of the pipes. Judith shook her head.

A dry whisper, like the rustle of dead grass, scraped on Patsy's mind. She strained, willing herself to hear it. Judith shuddered. Behind them, Peter began to say something and then gulped the words down.

Come, children. Come to your father.

The words were in no language Patsy understood, but somehow she could comprehend them. Her blood curdled, turning to slush. Her throat was so tight it felt as if a fist had clenched over it.

The van shuddered again and the custom-painted flames seemed to writhe and flicker. Inside the curling tongues of fire, pitiful things with agonised faces twisted and turned in the heat.

Come now, Uanan. Pray to the father. Oh lord Thanatos ...

Judith nodded like a sleepwalker and as she did so, she took a step forward.

'Who calls from the depths in profane splendour ...'

'*And calls in eternal night ...* '

'My heart to hold ...'

Patsy heard the scratching words counterpointing her daughter's replies, and behind them all she heard the urgent instruction.

Walk now. Come willing. Walk fast Uanan.

The word was foreign and carried no meaning in any normal sense, but in her mind, Patsy got a picture of a white lamb. But that was not the whole picture. The imagery was crowded, subtle and immense. It was a lamb, and it was the daughter of a horned thing and it was a vision of purity offered for power. She saw the lamb on a flat stone dripping with blood and in that instant she knew what *Uanan* meant. She started to turn towards Judith, feeling her body move so slowly it turned at a snail's pace. A blurt of denial was lodged in her throat, stillborn, unable to fight its way free.

'Don't go near it,' Peter bawled, high and urgent voice cracking with fear.

Silence, Tavartas. A hiss of anger and another meaningless word but Patsy's inner perception gave her a picture of a bloodied heart, still pulsating, gripped between two gnarled and taloned hands.

The pipes trilled, echoing from the metal barriers on either side, becoming a sudden cacophony of fragmented sounds.

Judith took another step forward, pulling away from her. Patsy lunged to grab her, but her hands snatched the air. She tried to scream, but her throat had locked. Some pressure had cut off her own air, some force was strangling the words in her lungs. She tried to reach again, but her arm wouldn't obey her. A movement caught the corner of her eye and Peter walked slowly past her, moving like someone in a dream. His head was shaking back and forth, very slowly, almost imperceptibly, but his feet carried him inexorably past his mother towards the growling van.

Come now. Come back. The scaly words scraped inside her, but she could do nothing. She was locked in the act of reaching for her daughter. Judith took a slow step, walking like an automaton, the movement jerky and alien. Another, and another. Now she was nodding her head, agreeing with the words behind the music. Peter almost stumbled, caught himself. His head half turned, trying to swivel towards his mother. She could see his eyes, wide and staring, absolutely terrified. Inside her, she could sense the dreadful fear shuddering through him.

The van vibrated and the engine growled and the chitinous voice, cold and hard as two millstones grinding each other to dust, urged the children on. Judith was ten yards away, now twelve yards away. Peter was following behind her, rubber strings of the slingshot dangling from his hip pocket.

'Oh Jesus, please,' she prayed. Her mind jabbered the words. 'Oh, holy mother, stop them.'

Behind her the clouds parted and the diseased sun reflected in the black windscreen of the transit van. The dark blots were right across the milky surface. The weak light sent the painted

409

flames curling and twisting and for an instant they did not look painted at all.

A dry snigger rippled over the surface of her mind, a scaly slither of gloating venom.

Lost them now, Gadge *woman. Lost forever.*

She couldn't speak, couldn't move. The strange echo of the pipes had trapped her in a wreath of sound while her children were pulled towards the beast in the shape of a black transit van. Judith was halfway there, a tiny figure on the middle of the road. Behind her Peter dragged his feet, but he kept walking his dream-walk while all the time the voice beckoned them forward.

The van juddered again and the engine revved. The front door on the nearside opened with a hard shunt of metal and in that instant, the headlights clicked on and Patsy felt herself speared on a glare so cold she felt her skin turn to ice.

There was no light at all. The twin cones stabbing out from the smoked glass units were not light. They were fields of darkness, so pitch-black they were the antithesis of day. She felt the dreadful frost in them, as if they sucked out the heat and the light from the world, leeched the warmth from her very soul. A numbness crawled through her and she felt the dark power in the black lights. It slithered into her, invading her every pore, wrapping her up in its sorcery.

Now you know the power. The whisper scratched inside her mind. *The Nameless Day has dawned and a new order begins.*

Kerron Vaunche cackled and the foul glee ground like glass in Patsy's mind. The sound of it was overpowering her. Judith was getting close to the van, a small emaciated shape, shoulders bent like a crone. Behind her Peter was being reeled in by the awful traction. The cold sent a hoar-frost creeping over Patsy's skin, stinging her eyes, numbing her muscles.

She was aware of everything, every beat of her heart, every shuffling step her daughter took. Inside the darkness, her own senses were stretched to encompass them all. She could feel Peter's terror as he tried to pull back from it. Underneath the witchety cackling, she could hear Judith's own voice chanting the litany of names, a cataract of apalling profanity.

The door reached its full extent and slammed against the side of the van with a boom like a vast gong.

410

A buzzing hum, like power in a high-tension cable, came vibrating in the cold. In the cone of obsidian black it swelled louder.

Father of darkness . . . the gypsy led.

'Accept this offering, flesh of my flesh,' Judith responded. Her voice was hollow and reedy. She took another step forward, slowing down now.

Lord of the carrion-flies and the worms of corruption . . .

'Despoil this innocence on the darkest day.' The words were in a strange, guttural language, but the meaning came clear into Patsy's mind.

It's beginning, she realised. Fear and despair dragged at her. She reached forward, desperately clawing her way towards her daughter. Judith had no more than twenty paces to reach the van. She took another step, and as she did so, a shape moved in the doorway. Peter groaned, loud and shuddery.

Kerron Vaunche came leaning out. A cloud of black flies swarmed around her head like a dark veil, a dusky halo.

Her beauty was gone. It was still Kerron Vaunche, that much Patsy could sense in the merciless contact that arced between them, but there was no resemblance to the haughty perfect creature who had strutted around her in the forest clearing.

Crandall Gilfeather had said the Carlin woman was old, but even he could not have had a full comprehension of how ancient was the thing which came stalking out from the black van.

Behind the shambling thing, a pale shape moved behind the windscreen. Patsy got a glimpse, no more, but she knew it was Paul and she could feel the dreadful change in him. All she had seen was a pallid, bloated face and the image of *Gollum*, sickened and warped by the proximity of great power and great evil, came strong in her mind.

Power corrupts. And he had been corrupted. Absolute power of absolute evil corrupts forever. He had flown too near.

The shape behind the glass turned away just as the Kerron-hag turned forwards, a hideous, shrivelled ruin. For an instant, though she knew who it was, Patsy thought back to the mummified woman in the car where the dried confetti had stirred in the breeze. The witch held up both hands and the skin on them was stretched so thin it looked as if it might shred into ragged holes. In the dark of the beams where everything was obscured and shadowed, the dreadful apparition that Kerron Vaunche had become was clearly visible, every wrinkle on her cleated skin, every pustule on a long and narrowed face. Her nose was warted with wens from which spouted coarse bristles and her hair was scraggled and thin, showing clear patches of shrivelled and peeling scalp.

'She's desperate,' Patsy thought. 'She's dying.'

But Crandall Gilfeather's words came back clear and strong. *The dark transference of the renewal.* Judith was half turned now, her profile just inside the dark cone of the black lights. The van shuddered and Patsy heard the low, feral growl of some beast. Judith twisted away, mouth open in the chant. The cracks and corrugations on her skin were like lines etched in ink. The surface was ridged and peeling. She was raising a hand up towards Kerron Vaunche and the fingers seemed long and crooked, gnarled at the joints.

It's started, Patsy's thought blurted again. *The transference.* In another part of her memory, Gilfeather leaned forward and took her free hand. 'It is her chance now, and she will take it, and I'm afraid she will take what is yours.'

In the black glare, where even time itself and all true reality seemed twisted and distorted, Patsy saw the change in her daughter and knew that Kerron Vaunche was taking what was hers. Peter's cry came echoing from ahead.

'*No.*' She shook her head in desperate denial. The gypsy came sloughing towards the children. The hollows of her eyes swivelled and fixed themselves on Patsy. A terrible cold shunted through her. The gypsy's eyes blared their mouldy green. The van shuddered again and Patsy knew nothing here was real except the black light and the dreadful vortex of complete evil. It followed the blast of cold and seeped into her skin and flesh and bones and a dark part of her own self opened and welcomed it.

Yes. It flooded through her and she was swimming in dark surf. The cells of her body were singing with the power. Black jolts of electricity sizzled in her veins, stripping her motherhood from her, scouring her humanity. She felt the affinity and the hunger and necessity. For an instant nothing else mattered.

The hag pointed a gnarled hand that looked as if it had clawed its way out from the shale of a graveyard. The poison in her eyes flared again; it seemed to sizzle like acid, burning the distance between them. For an instant Patsy was impaled on a hellish barb of contact.

See . . . the apparition hissed.

A black flash exploded in the back of her head and everything was gone. She was alone on a bleak and barren moorland where a wintry wind moaned and howled as it blew between the grey teeth of standing stones. A miserable dampness leeched into her bones. Snakes and creeping things slithered in the dank moss and ripples of submerged things shuddered the surface waters of black tarns. On a spike of stone a great black crow cawed and pecked at the eye sockets of a ragged skeleton tied to the pillar.

The wind whooped and shrieked and it was not the wind at all, but a high and glassy cry from inside the ring of stones. The sound drew her forward, a fish-hook in her brain and she felt the need to chant in the strange tongue which was alien and sorcerous, but somehow completely comprehensible. The mist parted and she flowed between the first two stones and overhead the sky darkened and lightning jagged like spears, and on the stone she saw the dark and massive thing thrusting on the pale shape and she heard the rend of flesh and the crunch of bones.

Take them . . . The words came unbidden, trying to make themselves heard. In her ears the hoarse buzzing of flies became a whine, a crescendo.

On the stone she saw Kerron Vaunche with blood on her face and as she looked she saw her change and contort and become Judith with blood in her eyes, and when she reached to touch the Judith thing snarled at her and spat poison and ripped at the body of her own brother . . .

The black power rolled through her in a tide and she felt herself dying inside and knew that the ripping sound was her own soul torn from her being.

All of it, everything your heart desires . . . a dreadful voice so deep and low it was the sound of mountains collapsing . . . *if you will fall down on your knees and worship.*

NO!

The voice was her own, the voice which had nagged and urged

and forced her onwards. It came up from the very centre of her being.

Fight it. The voice shrieked. *Fight the damned thing or you'll lose them.*

The cold twisted inside her, but it was a foul cold, not a charge of magic. Patsy shivered and felt the clamp of ice in her own soul.

Fight them, you fool. Deny it, deny the dark!

She felt as if she would split in two. Enormous forces pulled at her, dragging her one way and then another. A sizzling screech drilled into her ears. The black light pulsed, buffeting her this way and that. The music of the pipes blared, soared to a crescendo. She was caught in the black lights. Her children were in there and she couldn't see them and she needed the power and it was killing her.

Fight it, you stupid bitch. Her own mind blared at her. She screamed and the scream echoed in the pit of blackness, wavering on and on and on, and the force was too strong. It had her tight and it wouldn't let go and she felt her mind begin to fragment as the cold scoured the centre of her being with jagged shards of black ice and she started to plunge down the well that went on forever.

27

A crack of thunder exploded, so loud and close that a needle of pain stabbed into her eardrum and Patsy was tumbling down the dark well.

A sear of harsh lightning burned in her eyes and she cried out. The thunder crashed again and the lightning flared a second time and she was sent reeling and tottering, blinded by the glare of light. A dreadful shrieking sound was tearing in her ears and she did not know whether it was herself or her children or something else. She fell heavily and her hip cracked against something solid. Her vision swam dizzily but the hurt in her pelvis drew it back into focus and Patsy could see the darkness had vanished. The blinding glare was the cold pale light of day. The screaming sound, like metal torn asunder, went on and on and on. A weight slammed into her shoulder and she was dragged off her knees in a violent jerk. She spun, arms flailing for balance, lurching backwards.

Chris Deane was moving fast, striding towards the black van, his big gun held up at eye-level. A bitter smell of burnt powder billowed behind him.

The headlamps were blown out, completely shattered and the anti-light which had blared out from them was gone. Instead, a red vapour seeped out from where the glass had been, quickly dispersing in the slow breeze. The ululating scream pulsed on without a pause.

Chris went running forward. The hag had clawed her way back to the van door. He raised the gun again, following the fluttering motion of the thing that looked shrivelled and dry but was still alive and able to scutter like a gaunt mantis. Two pale hands had reached out, hands the colour of a frog's belly and just as amphibious, and the crone had reached for them. They pulled her in. The door started to slide closed and as it did two tendrils of filmy darkness, as insubstantial as smoke, but somehow appallingly powerful, had come reaching out from the side window, twisting and curling in the air, probing towards the children. Peter and Judith stood motionless, as frozen as Patsy had been in the black beams. It was as if they could not see the vaporous tentacles weaving towards them.

He reached Peter and leaned beyond the boy, getting a hand to the collar of Judith's jerkin. One of the tendrils struck like a snake, whipping out in a blur. The gun roared and the van lurched heavily. The side window imploded in a crash of glass and the whipping tentacle exploded into a buzzing swarm of black flies which fell to the ground in a foul hail and twitched on the road. The other tendril drew back for a strike and Patsy could see the individual insects all buzzing madly, spreading out and then condensing again to form a close-packed mass. Chris pulled Judith back towards him and fired again. The tentacle collapsed under its own weight and fell to the ground with a strangely heavy thump, breaking up into millions of black insects spinning uselessly on their backs.

Patsy stumbled forward towards her children. The shriek from inside the van was now sharp as glass. Chris was down on one knee with the girl clamped in against his side. The gun was up high and bucking in his hand, roaring like an animal, spewing smoke. The front of the van rang like a gong and craters as wide as fists appeared as if by black magic beside the grille. A venomous green steam gushed out and condensed in the air, dripping to the tarmac which immediately bubbled and sizzled. A reek of sulphur and melted stone drifted over them.

The gun kicked again and a corner of the windscreen starred like a spider's web. The screaming stopped dead. Chris was bawling at the top of his voice, though Patsy couldn't make out a word of it. She reached Peter and got both of her hands under his armpits, intertwined her fingers in a locked grip and dragged him backwards.

Sparks exploded from the grille on the van, where the painted flames licked round the misshapen little figures. The door shut with such a slam that the whole transit rocked on its springs. Inside her head Patsy heard a savage scraping protest, completely incoherent, completely venomous and altogether comprehensible in its hate. She ignored it.

416

Chris was moving backwards, like a soldier under fire. Judith was flopped in against him and he struggled to his feet.

Real flames winked into existence in the bullet holes and a thick grey smoke came belching out. Without warning, the engine revved, so hard it sounded just like the crazy screech that had suddenly died. Chris moved instinctively. His shoulder dropped and he threw himself to the side, dragging Judith with him. The van lurched forward, leaping like a black boar, like a mad buffalo. The tyres screamed, leaving blistered trails and a stench of burning rubber. Patsy tried to yell a warning, too late. Peter was already bawling, twisting to get free of her grip as they both stumbled sideways to crash against the barrier. The black van seemed to leap off the road, bulleting towards Chris and Judith. He rolled, cradling her tight, protecting her from harm. His hip smacked the rough surface the way Patsy's had when she fell, but if there was any pain, he did not feel it then. He swivelled and the black wheels crunched past him, inches from his face.

Patsy saw the van streak towards Chris and her daughter. In her mind, she heard the crunch as the black wing smashed into them, the wet creak as the heavy-tread tyres ground them into the road. She was shoving herself away from the barrier, trying to keep a hold of Peter. He was down on the ground, scrabbling in at the edge. She pulled him upright as the transit roared past and she knew she'd find a red smear on the road spreading out from two crushed and broken heaps.

The van swerved to the side, careering towards the barrier. It missed her and Peter by mere inches and slammed against the galvanised railings, sending up a whole fountain of red sparks. It bounced out to the centre of the road again, trailing a cloud of filthy fumes. Small flames, bright orange and strangely intense, were licking up from under the wheel arches.

Peter bawled ferociously and pulled away from her. Chris was lying against the far barrier with Judith tucked against him, both her arms tight around his neck. Peter leapt to the centre of the road, pulling his slingshot from his pocket. He raised the catapult, pulled the rubber back way beyond his chin and let fly. A white stone, bright as a star went shooting forward. It smacked against the smoked glass window on the nearside rear door. Instantly it starred into a maze of cracks and then fell inward.

The pale and ghostly face that Patsy had seen behind the smoked glass appeared briefly in the gaping space, then flinched back quickly as if the daylight caused it pain. Just before it did so, Paul's eyes, piggy little pinpoints of coal against a yellow-white background of bloated and distorted features, stared out at his own son. They glittered with a kind of insane malignity. Orange tail-lights winked and the pallid shape drew back into the infinite darkness. Peter loaded his catapult again and drew it back. He was yelling incoherently, and it would be several days before the exact content would come to Patsy and she would wonder where he had learned some of the curses which he spat at the black transit van. He let go and another rounded pebble went whizzing forward. The van was moving fast, but the stone was faster. It went straight through the blank window.

A shriek of anger and pain came searing out, shivering the air, so loud it could be felt rather than heard. By this time, Patsy was halfway across the road, sprinting towards the slumped bodies of her daughter and Chris. She threw herself down, screaming Judith's name, reaching for her. The girl's dark eyes were blank and staring. Chris was slumped against the steel framework, eyes closed, head twisted to the side.

Patsy fell against him in her rush to grab Judith. Her elbow slipped down and slammed against his crotch. Chris snapped upright, as if he'd been electrocuted and a loud grunt escaped him. His arms loosened reflexively and Judith went flopping out. Patsy grabbed her.

'Jesus Christ, lady,' Chris groaned. 'What did I ever do to you? I think you've killed me.'

She spun towards him, unable to speak, and fell against him once more.

'Don't hurt me, please,' he pleaded. 'I'm going to pass out.'

Patsy got an arm around his neck and pulled him in against her, completely dumbstruck, swamped in a maelstrom of emotion. She held on to Judith and to Chris until her arms ached.

The black van went roaring away down the lee slope of the bridge and disappeared, leaving only a fading fog of fumes which were slowly dispersed by the warm wind. Peter stood in the centre of the road, legs braced apart, watching until the van was

418

out of sight. Finally, satisfied that he'd seen it off, he came striding across to where the others were sprawled.

'Great shot, Hawkeye,' Chris told him through clenched teeth. 'Damned fine shot.'

'Would have been better if I'd had the gun,' Peter said, as nonchalantly as he could, though his chest was heaving and he was panting like a greyhound. 'I could have really wasted those suckers.' He looked down at Chris. 'You don't look very well. Is there something wrong with your voice?'

A sudden and unexpected laugh bubbled up inside Chris and he tried unsuccessfully to fight it down. It was the most painful laugh of his life.

'They'll be back,' Chris said. 'Nothing's more certain.'

'I know that,' Patsy agreed. 'She's desperate, they both are. Gilfeather was right. This is the only day. She's wasting away, worse even than Judith. It has to be now or she'll wither to nothing. I'm sure of it.'

They'd started the car and let it roll down the slope on the flyover, getting them off the exposed curve. With one tyre gone, even travelling slowly was difficult and Patsy had to use all her strength to keep them going straight. The car lurched and the wheel rim ground on the surface and she knew they couldn't travel far. Down at the bottom, she eased round the little junction and onto another road which, after a quarter of a mile, led to a second flyover. Chris asked her to stop at the far side. Above them, a bridge curved to connect two adjacent routes.

'Is that where we were before?' Peter asked. Chris shook his head. 'It's getting more complex the further we travel. There's a lot of connections here.'

They got the stove going again and made some breakfast, and Chris lay back against his rucksack. He pulled his hat down over his eyes.

'Give me half an hour, not much more. If I don't get some sleep I'll drop.' Two minutes later he was snoring loudly. Peter gave a tired grin. Judith lay in against Patsy, her own breath dry and soughing, shallow as a bird's.

Chris had hung under the dark rainbow span of the bridge, twisting in the wind, every muscle creaking with cramp and

419

spasms of pain, while the wound in his hand throbbed with the fiery hurt of serious damage.

Below him shadows lurched and stumbled, hauling themselves out from the carcasses of crushed vehicles, while the light of the dreadful moon cast a bloody glow over the confusion of wreckage, pooling in dark and secret deeps, reflecting venomously from shards of shattered glass, picking out a movement here, a twitch there as the bodies crawled and clambered, all moving forward towards the far glow in the sky.

Come down, come on down. Tinder dry voices rustled.

'No chance,' he grunted aloud. The scent of rot rose up in a cloud. Bone knocked against metal, scraped against glass. Directly below, a thin piece of bodywork caved under pressure and popped back out again like a giant thumb-clicker.

No escape, a hollow voice told him, booming up from the deep dark right under him. *No turning back now.*

Somebody cried, low and shuddery, a girl's tone sobbing despair. Beyond it, near to where he'd found the limo with the briefcase, something moaned and the sound was picked up by another crawling thing closer to hand. The shapes were indistinct, merging with the sharp angles of the mass of wreckage. The whole tangle seemed to be crawling with motion.

Please help me. The naked girl whimpered up at him, though her speech was blurred and rubbery, as if spoken through bleeding, frayed lips. *They took me away and hurt me and now I'm lost.* The litany went on and on and Chris felt a desperate sadness try to overcome his revulsion. Something had put the girl on the road, dragged her here, kicking and screaming, or maybe too numbed and scared to do more than shiver in fright. But she'd been brought here and she'd died here. Now she was crawling with all those other corpses, broken bodies now switched into movement, clambering in a nightmare procession of corruption and rot, heading for the eerie glow far along the road.

Chris had climbed until the muscles in his arms had seized up and simply stopped working. He was halfway up the rope, suspended between the hell above and the hell below while around him the dead voices sailed and whimpered and the seething horde of dead travellers forced their broken bodies ever onwards. He had managed to wrap his legs around the trailing

420

loop, twisting the rope around his ankles, then relaxed, bending his knees until he was seated on a precarious swing. With some effort, he managed to get the short length of safety rope connected to the main line, threaded through his belt and back to the hawser again. The thin rigging dug into the muscles of his legs, but at least he wouldn't fall. There was nothing for it. He couldn't climb further and he couldn't go back down, not while the insane moon was sailing the sky. He risked a look down and saw the pinpoint pairs of red eyes, winking on and off as the little stoat-creatures darted in and out of the shadows and in that instant, he knew they were feasting on the mass of dead travellers as they clambered by, stripping the mouldering flesh from their bones as they blindly trekked on. In his mind's eye he could see the little serpentine bodies wriggling faster than the eye could follow, squirming up the raincoat of the pale, cold girl, pausing only to dart their flat little heads in and bite out chunks of the white flesh. The image stayed with him for some time as he hung there, waiting for the moon to set.

After a while real fatigue began to set in and while he could not sleep, could not risk closing his eyes in case one of the moving dead things found a way to clamber up and grab at him, the exhaustion brought its dark visions, pictures in the night, looming in at him from the dead shadows.

Please help me, the girl pleaded again and a big maggot came chewing its way out of her glazed eye, hooked pincers opening and closing in a blind search for food. *Gonna fry us all, cockroach. Gonna all take the walk together.* The hard little jaws scraped against each other, grinding out the words that had come from the dead man in the police wagon. The girl's dead face winked out and another came wobbling in from the shadows under the bridge.

What kept you? Patsy Havelin's eyes burned into him, fiercely accusing. *We waited and waited and you never came back and now we're dead.*

He shook his head in denial.

We've got to walk now, all because of you. Her face came wavering in towards him and he could see the flat look of death in the glaze of her eyes and the little rips of early decomposition around the corners of her eyelids.

'No. I couldn't climb any more,' he protested and Patsy screamed, mouth opening so wide that it became a gaping hole which could have swallowed him up, and he started falling towards it.

The safety rope jerked him back, jerked him out of the dream and he came fully awake. The face had gone, but the scream lingered in his ears for a long time. Something told him Patsy Havelin and her children were in some kind of trouble. Down below, the shadows deepened as the moon started to sink towards the horizon and the sky on the other side was streaked with the purple of strange dawn.

He unfettered the top end of the safety harness and started to climb again, inching his way higher and higher. Down below him the wailing and groaning, the rasping and knock of bone on metal, began to abate. He got to within feet of the edge of the bridge span just as the mad moon sank out of sight and a sickly light began to spread along the road. A noxious waft of putrefaction billowed upwards and then the dead world down there fell silent. He climbed several feet more and then his head was through the membrane and into the light of a different day. He strove harder, ignoring the quiver in his muscles, until all of him was up from the deeps, struggling, panting to get a hand to the edge of the barrier. He grunted with pain and effort, raised himself up onto the guard-rail and flopped over, falling hard on the gritty surface. He rolled over, almost sick from the exertion, drew in a huge breath, and stiffened.

Patsy Havelin was wreathed in a filmy blackness reaching out from the headlamps of the black van. For an instant his vision wavered and the van seemed to *change*, its outline running and blurring, becoming something else, something that was not metal and not machine, something that was squat and rippling and shuddering with a kind of life. He blinked and it was a van again, black and shiny, its engine growling and the black un-lights reaching out to snare the woman, while in front of her, much closer to the van, something hunched and raddled came lurching towards the children. He hauled himself to his feet, drawing the big gun out of its holster, then made it to the centre of the road close to the edges of the black lights. Immediately

422

the temperature plummeted in the fringes of the dreadful influence of the beams. He felt his skin pucker with goose-flesh.

Chris stepped forward, raised the gun just as he was closing with Patsy and aimed at the headlamp unit. He squeezed the trigger, felt the gun buck in his hand. Patsy came reeling out of the darkness. The gun went off again with a noise of thunder and a dreadful shriek tore the air. Glass shattered and the black lights winked out. Something hit Chris on the shoulder.

He woke up, jolted back to the present. Patsy was shaking him gently.

'You've had an hour,' she said. 'You looked as though you needed it. I've made some coffee, but it's the last.'

She handed him the hot cup and he drank it, shaking off the shuddery aftermath of sleep. He rubbed his eyes with a knuckle and then stretched until his back protested.

'You were snoring,' Peter told him. 'Really loud.' Patsy knocked him on the shoulder.

'Thank you, Henry Kissinger,' Chris retorted.

'Who?'

'Never mind.' He took a long drink, savouring the burn as it scoured his throat, grateful to be back to reality again, even if it was a reality as twisted and malignant as the road they now travelled. Above them the clouds in the bruised sky were wheeling in a great circle as a monstrous storm stoked itself up.

'They'll be back,' Chris told her. 'Nothing's more certain.'

Patsy agreed. She pointed at the side of the car where the wheel was digging into the road surface. 'That won't get us far.'

'And we'll have to get moving, away from this little junction, unless you want to wait.

'We can't wait. If we stay here they'll catch us and I can't let them do it. We have to go on, but on foot we'll be too slow.'

'And it'll catch us in the open. I reckon there's only one option, but there's no guarantees. We have to find wheels, and quick. Can you climb?'

28

Peter disappeared. A cold hand clamped around Patsy's heart and squeezed hard. A void opened inside her, a space where the perception, the very identity of her son had been, but was now as empty as the space between universes. Peter had dropped through the membrane below the parapet of the bridge and in an instant, he was excised from her motherhood. The pain of the most intense loss twisted in the depths of her soul.

'Bring him back,' she told Chris, voice tight. 'Do it *now*.'

They had emptied the car. The rucksack Chris carried and their little picnic box, the old siphon and the spare fuel tank were piled beside the barrier.

'We just might get lucky,' Chris had told her, 'but if I go down there, it's a one-way ticket. I'll never make it back.'

'I'll go,' she'd offered, but he shook his head.

'Too heavy for me to pull back with this hand,' he replied with an apologetic shrug. 'I hate to ask, but you'll have to let Hawkeye do it.'

Patsy had quailed at the thought and Chris hadn't pushed her. He'd just stood there, elbows on the railing, looking down into the gloom below. No sound rose up towards them. Above them the storm was winding up and the sky was darkening. Huge forces were at play up there and she could feel the tingle of electricity in the air.

The Nameless Day. It was here and it was now. She recalled the bleakness of the bale-light from the black van and the sudden unearthly yearning within her, the ripping apart of her own psyche. She could not risk that again. She might fail them all.

Christ waited without saying a word, watching the emotions play across her face. They had no choices; both of them knew that. They could only try to run, try to battle the odds. Ten minutes later, Peter was hooked to the line and sitting on the rim.

'Just like a bungee jump,' he said, with a grin.

'But a lot slower, and you won't be going far,' Chris said. He'd wrapped a thick piece of cloth over the cut on his hand, which let him hold the rope with both hands. Peter braced himself, feet tucked in on the ledge. He leaned back, took a step backwards and was suspended in space. He lifted a hand, cocked a thumb and flashed them an excited smile. Chris lowered him ten, maybe twelve feet. Peter looked up, waited for his signal, then drew the small gun from the holster. He gripped it in both hands and without any hesitation, Chris lowered him out of their lives.

'Bring him back!' Patsy ordered, a sharp edge of panic tightening her voice. The rope thrummed. Chris unhitched a loop from the stanchion, waited another ten seconds, and then hauled backwards, drawing in the line hand over fist. Peter popped back again and the void in Patsy's soul filled instantly in a violent, hot *twist*.

'It's all right,' Peter yelled up at them. 'There's some cars on the sides, but not on the road.'

His face was red from the tension, but alive with excitement. He'd gone down into the unknown and it had been like exploring another world. Chris pulled him up quickly and Patsy grabbed him by the arms to help him over the rail.

'Nothing moving?'

Peter shook his head. 'There's big trees on one side, going for miles, but there's no other bridges except this one.'

'What time do you think? Remember what I said about the shadows.'

'They were going that way,' Peter said, still breathless. He pointed to the opposite side from where the sun had risen. Time might be different on another level, but the direction was always the same. The vast configuration of roadways was always ahead of them, where the glow flared in the night sky. All the roads pointed that way.

'Long?'

Peter nodded and Chris grinned. He punched the boy manfully on the shoulder, the way comrades do, and Peter swelled. Patsy swallowed down the anxiety she'd gone through and smiled. Peter wanted to be just like Chris Deane. She smiled even wider. Given what Chris had done for them, what he'd risked for them when he'd gone down into the dark on the other road, she would not mind in the least if her boy turned out like the man who'd

425

been, until that morning, a fellow traveller, but was now their friend.

'Good man, Hawkeye.' Chris turned to Patsy. 'It's morning down there too and the road's clear. If we find a recent set of wheels, I can maybe hot wire it. With a bit of luck, with a *lot of it*, we should get some sort of head start before they come sniffing after us again.

The decision was made there and then. Patsy was first over the edge. A dismaying dread rolled through her as Chris's face disappeared above her head. She experienced the vertiginous wrench as she went through from *then* to *now* and in an instant her whole being was swamped by the most melancholy sense of utter bereavement as she lost her spiritual connection, her extra-sensory perception of her children. A cold, early morning damp breeze ruffled her jeans and swung her gently on the line as she dropped further. This bridge was not as high as the other one had been, a small flyover arching across a two-lane road. She looked upwards and saw, not Chris and Peter leaning over the balustrade, but a blank railing. Just below it, the top of the rope ended abruptly in mid-air. Purple clouds scudded past overhead. The storm was rising here too. Way in the east, the sickly, blotched sun was just rising.

Patsy bent her knees just before touchdown and her feet hit the ground with a soft thump. Down here the sense of empty loss, of amputation, was even stronger, more dismaying. Without hesitation she unslung the rope and tugged hard. Immediately, it started snaking up and away from her, shortening as it climbed. She hefted the gun he'd given her in both hands, looking up until the rope vanished just under the bridge and in an instant she was alone; completely, utterly alone.

A physical tremor shook her. Here, in this world and at this moment, there were no connections, no threads, nothing at all which linked her to any other human being. Peter and Judith did not exist here. They were not part of her. The void inside her was vast, infinite. She closed her eyes and tried to shuck off the awesome feeling of abandonment, the sensation of being marooned. Her nerves jangled in panic and for a moment, the world spun crazily. She sat down quickly, feeling the surface of the road with both hands, feeling the breeze on her cheek and

426

scenting the smell of oil and road fumes. A distant drone told her the conjunction of the interchange was still ahead of her. Her strange new sense felt out on all sides, striving to make a connection. Nothing came back. Patsy gritted her teeth, blinking back unwanted tears.

Then Judith came plunging into the world.

It was as if a high-tension jolt had rushed through her. Patsy had been sitting, head bowed, trying to keep her own self from unravelling, when Judith suddenly arrived above her, wrapped in the blanket like a baby in swaddling clothes. Pure joy bloomed in her heart and she arched back as her daughter came gliding down towards her. Patsy scrambled to her feet and held her hands up, needing to touch Judith to appraise her with another of her senses. Seconds later Patsy had her daughter in her arms. The unwanted tears came sparkling into her eyes and she could not keep them back.

Patsy had to loosen rope from the makeshift sling. She tugged it, felt the response on the far end of the line. Peter appeared in the air and the warmth of her completeness surged through his mother. He came spinning down, deliberately twisting on the rope like a plane out of control and landed nimbly on his feet. He unhitched the harness and sent the signal back up. Moments later he was untying the knot on the travelling blanket to reveal all their belongings and then Chris came sliding down the hawser. He still looked tired, but otherwise cheerful and he seemed to have got over the painful blow to his groin. As soon as his feet hit, he loosened the harness, turned quickly, tugged hard at the line he'd brought down with him and immediately the whole rope fell out of the sky and landed at his feet.

'That's a great trick,' Peter told him. 'How do you do that?'

'An old mountaineering trick, from an old mountaineer, and there's darn few of them.'

Chris winked at him, took his battered hat off and plumped it down on Peter's head. The boy looked as if he would burst with pride.

'Which way?' Patsy asked, though she knew the answer. There was only one way to go, no matter which direction they took. They would always end up heading for the interchange in the misty distance. She shrugged. Chris hefted the bag along with his rucksack. Peter carried the stove. Patsy lifted Judith into her arms. She weighed nothing at all. The freshening wind could have blown her away. They started walking along the narrow road with the sun on their left side and the hazy junction in front of them. The road went roughly straight across an uneven plain dotted on one side with a moraine of huge and craggy boulders. On the other side a thick broad-leaved forest crowded the verge, barely held back by a slow-moving stagnant runnel.

Little knots of cars, ones and twos, the odd truck and an old buckboard buggy dotted the edge of the highway. The little group plodded forward while the sun rose; a pale, diseased disc festering with dark, spreading blotches.

An hour later, with the same sun swinging quickly overhead, they were on the move again, rumbling along in a big four-wheel drive utility jeep with impressive whip antennae swinging like marlin rods on the back. It was bashed and dented and had seen better days, but the engine had cranked and coughed into life. It was the fifth abandoned vehicle they'd tried, and the first to start. There had been no sign of the driver, nor any passengers, and they were grateful for that.

'You'll have to show me how to do that sometime,' Patsy told Chris.

'Hot wiring? I've only ever seen it in the movies.'

She looked at him and saw the lie in his eyes. Without thinking she slapped him on the chest, the way a woman can do with a man when they're close. She'd travelled two miles further when she realised what she'd done and she felt a warm blush creep up from the neck of her shirt. She sneaked a glance at him and saw he was smiling to himself.

The rocky land on the east side gave way to smoother undulating countryside covered in dense shrubs at first and then progressing to tall forest which crowded in against the road on both sides. Patsy was reminded of the swamp-land where she'd almost lost Peter. Chris couldn't help but recall the jungle on the Guatemala border where he'd started out on the path that had become a track and evolved into the endless highway. The jeep rumbled past on its big heavy-tread wheels. The shadows in the trees were deep and fathomless. Patsy looked in once and then kept her eyes on the road. As ever she sensed the unseen gaze fixed upon her. Whatever moved in there, she did not want to see.

They breasted a rise where the trees crowded so densely they formed an almost complete arch over the road and on the other side of the hill the forest stopped dead, bounded in by an old stone wall.

In front of them, the road went straight, widening as it descended the slope, aiming dead south. It lost itself in the vast conjunction of roadways. Patsy's foot pressed on the brake and the car slowed to a halt on the centre-line. They sat there, all four of them, staring ahead in complete silence, stunned dumbed by the immensity of the interchange.

For days, Patsy had caught glimpses of the network, hazily seen through distant mist. It had always been there, a confusion of arches and loops, beckoning them ever onward.

None of them had been prepared for the vastness of the junction. From their vantage point high on the rise, the whole complex weave of highways spread out before them, stretching to infinity, a maze within a maze within a puzzle. The road they travelled headed across a flat plain, curving as it went, but aiming in the general direction of the web of concrete and steel. Here in the heights, the air was still relatively clear, overlaid though it was by the scent of oil and exhaust. At the junction itself, a vast sprawl of serpentine flyovers and diving underpasses, the fumes were thick enough to become clouds. Even in the daylight they flickered red, as if lit from within. A hum of unseen traffic was like the drone of insects in a mighty hive. Even here, they could feel the pull of the junction, drawing them towards it.

'I don't like the look of that,' Chris finally said.

'Me neither. Can we avoid it?'

He shook his head. 'Only if we stop here forever.'

'Might be better than going in there,' she said, but she knew there was no stopping. Already she could sense the prickling of the hairs on the back of her neck and knew Kerron Vaunche was hunting them again. Patsy let off the brake and they started to coast slowly down the slope. Nobody said a word as they crossed the plain, every turn of the wheels putting them closer to the junction. The road curved round in a slow sweep, rose over a gentle incline and then they were there.

A shiver rippled through Patsy as she steered the jeep down the incline and over a wide box girder bridge that spanned a broad highway. The sound of the traffic was louder and the scent of oil was thick and toxic. They crossed the bridge, spiralled up a ramp to a higher level, took a left turn that brought them to a short overpass and then they were down the slope on a straight road which crossed over a series of lanes. In mere minutes they were lost on the junction.

Great concrete pillars bearing the highways at different levels flickered past them as they travelled. Here and there, the rusting remains of a car would be crushed up against a bulwark or decayed to a red crumble of rust in the breakdown lane.

'It *is* like *Termight*,' Peter whispered, voice filled with wonder. 'It just goes on forever.'

'You could be right, kid,' Chris said. He was sitting up, both hands on the fascia, looking ahead. They were exposed here, though the crowding arches and columns gave a false sense of concealment. They couldn't see where they were going, because every route twisted and turned, spiralling off or onto other levels, or snaking down into unexpected subways. Anything could surprise them here and that gave him a twitching sense of unease. Patsy drove on, keeping, quite wisely, to the centre-lines, dropping a gear to go even slower. Chris could sense her own apprehension and he wished there had been a way of avoiding this place. The sense of wrongness here saturated the very air.

An hour after they had plunged into the maze of roadworks, they were climbing up an enormous flyover which soared in a stunning curve above a complex tangle of lanes. They broke out of the fog of fumes into clearer air. Patsy slowed down on the crest and stopped close to the edge. From inside the jeep, they could see very little beyond the balustrade and the sounds of moving vehicles was deflected away. She shut off the engine and opened the door. Chris got out the other side and Peter made to follow him. Judith lay back, breathing shallowly. Her eyes were blank and the skin around them was crusted and raw. Patsy ordered Peter back into the car, overriding his objections. They leaned over the chest-high palisade. The noise hit them like a blow. Patsy's jaw dropped.

Below them, packing every lane, was the biggest traffic jam

either of them had ever seen. Cars, pick-up trucks, great double-trailer rigs crammed every inch of roadway in an enormous grinding gridlock. Directly underneath the flyover, a four-leafed clover junction was crawling with vehicles, like a plant infested with ants. The combined noise of the engines was like a thunder in the air and dense clouds of exhaust blanketed the entire level, throwing everything into shade. The heat from the engines rose up in a searing thermal wind which carried in it the stench of burned hydrocarbons, the eye-watering scorch of pulverised and molten rock and the sickening stink of rotten flesh.

Patsy had travelled the road for six days and she had come through encounters which were more frightening than her worst nightmares, but somehow the sight of all those cars, every one of them following the same route, was more terrifying than anything. It took her breath away. Chris leaned his elbows on the parapet and took in the scene, his mouth clamped in a tight line.

'Where are they going?' Patsy finally said shakily.

Chris took out his neat little telescope and put it to his eye. She saw it move in this hands as he followed the line of traffic, up one loop and down another, under a flyover and over an underpass. Finally the motion stopped.

'What is it?'

He handed her the glass, standing close to point down, between two pillars, some distance away. A thick road mist had rolled over the road there, obscuring the line of vehicles. A waft of the hot air began to thin it out. Patsy brought the lens up to her eye. For a moment, the blue-grey cloud roiled and the greasy hot fumes caught in the back of her throat. The cloud dispersed and she saw the tunnel.

'Oh, my *God*!' The words came out in a shuddery whisper.

Down there, magnified in the glass, but needing no magnification, an immense tunnel yawned. It seemed to plunge deep into the earth, right underneath the whole conjunction of roads. Patsy adjusted the focus and swept the telescope right and left. The cavern gaped like a mouth, like the maw of a giant predator. It was vast, wide enough to take ten, fifteen, maybe even twenty lanes. She couldn't tell because her view was obscured by the loops of closer intersections, but the part she could see was sectioned off by columns dividing two wide highways. The pillars were white and conical, like colossal teeth. Both highways were crowded, bumper to bumper and wing to wing with traffic. Even in the distance, the humming roar of engines rolled like a deadly thunder. Patsy could not draw her eyes away. The tunnel was a vast cave, an enormous hole in the ground. She could see that the entry roads did not glide down a shallow concave as they would on any man-made underpass. This road swooped in a convex curve, as if once under the rim, the cars were plunging down a vast well, swallowed up by the biggest tunnel in the world.

She slowly panned the glass, picking out a truck here, a small saloon there. A great black carriage pulled by shapes that might have been horses, but in the rolling fumes could have been anything, waited behind a touring bus. As she watched, the bus jerked forward a few feet and the *diligence*, the great wooden-spoked nighthawk trundled forward. That movement sparked another, just within vision. Patsy swung the glass and saw a black squad car inch forward. Beside it, a squat Zyl limousine, something straight out of Red Square, eased forward two yards to put its leading chrome edge against the tow-bar of a camper.

The traffic was moving, crawling along, inching on the highways, edging ever closer to the incredible tunnel. What she had thought was a gridlock jam was just a queue of traffic, all of it in motion, all of it heading inexorably for the yawning maw in the distance.

'That's where the roads go,' Chris said.

Patsy didn't hear him. Her whole attention was fixed on the gaping hole which was swallowing cars and trucks in their hundreds, in their thousands. Fumes spewed out, roiling as from a furnace, obscuring much of the entrance, but now and again a whirl of wind, an eddy of hot turbulence would thin the cloud and she could see the red glow. It reflected off the pillars, turning them into bloodied teeth. It was like the swelling brightness of a well-bellowed furnace, pumped by a monstrous ogre of legend. The black clouds rolled back and the red glimmer would expand to gleam on the windscreens and the mirrors of the cars on the clover leaf junction, sending a coruscating glitter of red up into the sky to reflect on the heat-tumbled clouds above.

Way down in the tunnel, the roaring growl of the moving traffic was punctuated by a deep vibration which shivered the road under their feet; a sound so deep and so vast that it could not simply be heard, but was felt as a pulsing vibration. It was like the strike of a colossal mallet against white-hot steel down there, under the ground, and it was like the pulse of a monstrous heart.

'I was right all along,' Chris said, almost dreamily. 'It's the road to hell.'

'I'm not going down there,' Patsy said. A dreadful fear came bubbling up inside her, the kind of fear experienced in the nightmare hunts in the depths of sleep when the dreamer is running from an unseen beast which slavvers and growls and in the moment before wakening the dreamer knows, with absolute certainty, that the monster is gaining and that its claws and jaws will rip and rend. That was the nature of the dread which percolated up from the centre of her belly, but there was one difference. Patsy knew that she was not asleep, that she would not wake up from this.

'I'm *not* going down there,' she said again, shaking her head violently. From the car Peter and Judith watched her and both of them knew something was wrong.

'Now you know why I was walking all this time,' Chris said, trying to sound light, though the sight of the traffic being swallowed by the tunnel had shaken him. 'I wanted to get here later rather than sooner.'

Patsy could feel the tremendous *draw* of the pulsing red well. It tugged at her, pulling her towards it. She raised the eyeglass again in horrified fascination and slowly followed the line of traffic nearest them as it crawled round the steep curve of the flyover and then down the slope towards the opening. A separate motion caught her attention and she panned to the left, gasped and froze. Chris heard the sharp intake of breath and waited for a few moments.

'What is it?'

Patsy said nothing. She backed away from the wall and handed him the eyeglass and he looked down. She saw him stiffen too and knew he'd seen the dreadful line of pedestrians on the narrow walkway.

433

There were hundreds of them, thousands of them, all packed together on the little fenced ramp, shuffling along like slaves, like the pitiful wretches of Auschwitz. Even in the distance she had been able to see that some of them were limping, some lurching and some crawling. And worse, she had seen the flaps of clothing, the tattered rags that fluttered in the heat breeze, and her heart had almost stopped when she saw that some of the fluttering shreds were not that at all, but flaps of dried and peeling skin; and she had seen that the queue of lurching things were not living people at all, but dead and mouldering corpses, like the ones she'd seen in the crashed cars along the road, somehow foully animated and drawn by the enormous force of the red tunnel.

In that instant she knew Chris Deane's instinct had been right and that her own had not been wrong. She could not go down there, not into that hellish queue crawling towards the red depths. She could not take her children into that awful pulsating tunnel. Her skin squirmed with the horror of finding out what great beast could cause those apocalyptic hammer-blows that shivered the world, or had a heart that beat in a way that made the ground shake.

'*Beelzebub*,' she whispered through tight lips. 'The lord of the flies'.

In a moment of dreadful clarity, she utterly believed what Crandall Gilfeather had told her of what Kerron Vaunche had planned in Broadford House.

Down there in the red tunnel, was the power that Kerron Vaunche had worshipped, the awesome black force that had drawn Paul in with her and turned him into the bloodless and bloated thing she had glimpsed in the black van.

The heartbeat pulsed on, rolling under the ground in a slow, ponderous rhythm.

'Are we dead, Chris? Is that what this is?' She put her hands to her temples and squeezed. 'Are we just like those things down there?'

'Not me,' Chris said. 'I'm still kicking. And you look a shade pale, but you're still hooking and jabbing as far as I can see.'

'But it could be an illusion.'

'Sure it could, but we're both having the same one, unless I'm

434

imagining you.' Chris grinned tightly, but not without his laconic, almost fatalistic humour.

She turned away from him, trying to pull herself together and when she reached the car she caught a glimpse of Judith's face, eyes bloodshot and skin cracking. The fear and dread came back to her, but the anger came back with it and held onto that, the way a drowner will cling to anything. She grabbed the anger and felt its heat and the horror was pushed back a little.

'I'm not going down there,' she said. 'I'm not going down there, and I'm going to get my children home.'

'I'll go along with that,' Chris said. 'But I think it would be a good idea if we started pretty soon.'

She looked at him and he gave a quick twist of his head. She followed the motion and he saw her eyes widen. Down at the bottom of the bridge the black van was back. It was moving very slowly, somehow stealthily, like a stalking panther towards the point of the curve where the flyover began to soar upwards. The lights were still smashed and the side of the windscreen was crazed over. Behind it, forming a barrier right across all four lanes, was an array of huge black trucks. They shuddered with restrained power and their exhaust stacks breathed out black fumes. The smoked glass of the windscreens made then look somehow feral and the tarpaulins, loosely tied over their humped loads, looked like the folded, creased wings of giant bats.

'We might be in a spot of bother,' Chris said, edging towards the car.

29

The jeep shuddered, coughed and then kicked into life. A blue cloud belched out from under the tailgate and they were moving, rolling on the big rough-country treads on the crest of the arch. Peter was kneeling up in the back and for a moment, the road behind them was clear, thanks to the curve of the flyover. Within five seconds however the roof of the black transit van appeared over the rise.

'Faster, mum,' Peter urged. 'They're coming for us.'

She knew that already and she wished they'd found a Ferrari instead of this old four-wheel drive with valves that rattled like dice and a cylinder head gasket shot full of holes. It was a strong old workhorse, well used by whatever unfortunate had found himself on the black highway and got stuck there, but it was not a racer, not a car to be fleeing in.

They began to roll down the slope. Ahead of them, maybe a quarter of a mile down the enormous arch, the road split and forked, one side rising again to double over the main route and the other diving down in a crazy corkscrew. She kept to the left, foot jammed to the floor, listening to the protest of the engine. Down the hill they went, Patsy holding on to the wheel so tightly her palms were almost welded to the rim. Judith was strapped in, swaddled in the blanket. Chris and Peter just held on.

The van loomed larger in the mirror and behind the van, the mass of the huge trailers appeared, all of them in a line, keeping pace with each other. She could feel the vibration of their wheels on the road, hear the grind of their gears. The smokestacks belched fumes as black as the paintwork on their ancient cabins. The fenders and grilles were oddly gothic, like wrought armour of a bygone age. They breasted the rise, seeming to grow taller as they made it to the top until they completely blocked the skyline in the rear-view mirror.

Whonk. WHONK.

One of the rigs blasted its air horn, like a maddened beast. The light from the hellish tunnel beamed through a gap in the balustrade and reflected from the transit's windshield a feral eye glaring at them as it zoomed closer. The other trucks, trundling and rumbling abreast of each other sounded their own horns until the air thundered, masking the road noise of the crowded lines of traffic on the roads which fed the red underground. For a few moments all that could be heard was the mindless and somehow hungry blaring of the blind, black trucks and the dull, physical pulse which shivered through the spinning wheels and into their bones.

'I can't outrun them,' Patsy cried, trying to make herself heard over the noise. Defeat was beating down on her.

'We'll have to lose them,' Chris said. 'Otherwise they'll scrape us into the concrete.' He slammed his hand down on the metal shelf in front of him.

Patsy willed the jeep forward, concentrating hard as the fork in the road loomed closer. She was aware that the van was gaining on them, angling across the road to the left lane to get right behind them. She could hear the grinding whine of the engine. It sounded like big cats fighting.

'Come on, mum,' Peter pleaded. 'Go faster.'

She tried to reply but the words wouldn't come. All her attention was fixed on the junction. The rigs blared again, all in unison, a deafening blast that conveyed triumph and power. She flicked a glance at the mirror, wishing she'd cleaned the greasy back window, though it was clear enough to see the dark shape swelling behind. The shot-out headlights were like sharks' mouths, one on either side, rimmed with jagged glass shards for teeth. The flames on the paintwork were blistered and bubbled and almost as dark as the rest of the bodyshell. The fist-sized holes were scabbed over, as if the black transit was somehow *healing*. It zoomed closer and the whine of a turbocharger – or what Patsy assumed had to be a turbo – rasped like grindstones. She pressed her foot down, getting the ball of her foot hard against the metal plate and the jeep engine rattled in protest. She was going as fast as she could, as fast as the jeep could achieve. The line of trucks towered behind the van like the battlements of a black castle, billowing oily smoke from their stacks.

The division was ahead of her, getting closer with every second. Peter squawked something which was lost in the noise and confusion. The transit came charging up, yards away, now feet away, swinging in to swipe them against the concrete edge-wall, and behind it came the phalanx of trucks in a monstrous cavalry. She held her breath, clenching her teeth, clamping her hands on the wheel, gauging the moment as she had done before. She was heading down the spiral, taking the plunge that would lead them ever closer to the nightmare red tunnel. The fork was only yards away and she was heading down into the loop. The big rigs blasted their horns again, as if to confirm her mistake.

Patsy hauled the wheel and the jeep veered abruptly from the left-hand lane right across the road, tilting onto two wheels, wobbling so violently Chris thought they were sure to roll. Peter went crashing against Patsy's seat. Tyres screeched like fighting pigs. For an instant Patsy was convinced she'd misjudged it. She felt the whole thing totter beyond its centre of gravity and she knew she was losing it, sending them into a tumbling pirouette that would smear them against a solid pillar; but she could do nothing about that because she'd calculated it right down to the last foot and if she swung the wheel at all she would spike them all on the narrow metal wedge that separated the two routes. The jeep went careering across the road. The black transit reacted a second too late. It came swerving after them, horn blasting and engine screeching furiously. The truck nearest it started to turn and crashed against its neighbour. Instantly the air was ruptured with the protest of brakes and the tortured squeal of scraping metal as the trucks, all of them travelling abreast, shunted and slammed broadside into each other. The violent contact sounded like the clash of armies.

Patsy held her line, feeling the jeep lean out on its two wheels until it was getting to the point of no return. The paintwork nicked the edge of the separator barrier just enough to scrape paint and then she was right off the main route, scooting on the upward slope on the right. The raised wheels came slamming down onto the road again and Peter went rolling on the floor, arse for elbow. They went zooming up the clover leaf while the van and its massive cohorts dived below them, making the road shake in their passing. Peter scrambled up to the seat, completely unhurt, and pressed his face against the glass on the tailgate.

'You did it again, mum,' he breathed. 'You lost them.'

'And us, near enough,' she mumbled raggedly. She steered them upwards and round the horseshoe curve, hands only now loosening their grip on the wheel. Below them, the oily fumes from the big gothic trucks were rolling in the air, gradually dissipating, but they could still hear the roar of their engines, diminishing with distance as the black cavalcade swooped down the left-hand spiral into the depths.

Patsy let out a long breath, freed her fingers from the steering wheel and wiped her sleeve across her brow. Perspiration was dripping into her eyes, making them sting and smart. Chris handed her a dry rag and she knuckled it to clear her vision. The road swung round, doubled back on itself and headed along a straight section which paralleled two immense raised highways supported on slender columns.

'How did they find us so quickly?' she asked. Chris had no answer to that.

'Maybe they've bugged us,' Peter said. 'They can do that, y'know.'

Despite the beating of her heart, Patsy smiled, risking a quick glance round. Peter's face was open and earnest. 'Maybe,' she agreed with him, giving him a wink.

'I think whoever they are, they know these roads better than we do.'

'We don't know them at all. I wish I'd never seen them.'

'Amen to that,' Chris said softly. They were trundling along on the straight with the tall supporting struts flickering past on either side, like an avenue of tree-trunks. The ghastly tunnel was out of sight, but they could hear the rumble of massed engines and the air was still thick and greasy with their fumes.

'I think we're heading away from it,' Patsy ventured and Chris nodded his agreement.

'For now. But it'll find a way of heading us back again. I reckon we should go a bit slower, so we don't get taken by surprise.'

No sooner had he spoken when the old, dented radio bolted

under the shelf spat loudly, startling them all. A crackle of static coughed harshly, a rasping assault on the ears. It went on for several seconds, a deafening electromagnetic hiss.

The Witch. Patsy reached to turn the switch and cut it out. She grabbed the knob, but it wouldn't turn anti-clockwise. She twisted it in the opposite direction and it clicked. A little green light came on, showing that the radio had been off in the first place. The interference soared to a crescendo, as if she'd tuned into a recording of a vast waterfall, and then, abruptly, it cut off with a sharp snap.

A silence lasted for five seconds and then they heard the sound. It was the deep, booming thump that had emanated from the tunnel, but now was coming from the speaker, the double-beat of a gigantic heart. The whole chassis shivered in sympathetic resonance.

The beat went on, even when Patsy switched the receiver off. For half a minute, that was all they could hear and then, underneath the deep pulse, a whispering came, soft as the chittering of insects in the night, but swiftly gaining in intensity until it crackled all around them. It reminded Patsy of the cloud of insects that had come reaching, cohesive as tentacles, from the side door of the black transit and the image of *Beelzebub* came leaping into her mind. *The insects in her dream had buzzed up from the crevasse in the small corpse on the stone.* The rustling whirr soared up to a deafening crash of sound and suddenly stopped, leaving Patsy shaken by its intensity.

In the back seat, Peter jerked back, pressing himself against the door. In his mind's eye, he saw a long and bony hand reach out to clamp on Willow's cheeks. The woman's shuddering mouth opened and something black and shiny had come scrambling up inside her throat and he had seen the fly. Its head turned, swollen eyes staring blankly. Another followed, and another, until the mouth was filled with them. Willow's face was just a mass of crawling insects and then, all at once, they took off with an angry buzzing, flew into the shadows and disappeared.

The buzzing hiss went on and on and for a moment Chris was back in time, to the jungle beyond the stone pillars. On the raw earth, something long and rotted was covered in a mass of crawling black flies which erupted into a buzzing cloud as he approached. What might have been a grinning skull flashed whitely before the flies descended again to feed. The swarm hummed busily and suddenly he was scared to look in case he saw a face staring up at him from the mass of insects.

The crackling hiss went on for a long moment, then

Patseeee.

The voice dropped into the silence. She jumped in her seat. Behind her, Judith whimpered.

Got you now, Patseee. Nowhere to run, no place to hide. Going down the hole, Patseee.

'Who the hell is that?' Chris demanded angrily. He reached out and thumped the radio. It made a jarring crackle but the voice came back again.

Smell your blood. Follow the trail. Hounding you all the way down.

'It's dad,' Peter blurted. 'It's dad talking. But he sounds different.'

Patsy shuddered. She'd recognised the voice, and the fact that Peter did too only confirmed it. Chris turned in his seat and looked at her, the question open on his face. Judith moaned, high wavering.

'Don't want to come, daddy,' she whimpered. She pulled back, pushing herself into the rear of the seat. Patsy slowed down again and turned. Judith was shaking her head in dumb denial.

'Want to stay with mummy,' she mewled, and then she wheezed. Her dark eyes, flared and unfocussed, opened even wider as she suddenly hauled for breath. The mottled discoloration under her skin deepened as her face was suffused with blood. Her chest hitched but nothing happened.

'Get the inhaler, quick,' Patsy cried. 'It's in the bag.' Peter scrambled over the back seat and started rummaging. He seemed to take forever and then came up with ventilator. Without hesitation, he slid the nozzle into Judith's gaping mouth and thumbed the trigger. A little hiss spat.

He did it again and Judith convulsed. Her hand came flying up and something hard hit off the roof, bounced against the window inches from Chris's ear and rattled on the ledge under the windshield.

441

He reached for the small object. His fingers grasped it and then jerked back.

'Jesus,' he yelped. 'It's red hot.' He snatched the rag he'd given Patsy and tried again, lifting the thing and turning it around. A scorching smell came off the cloth. Chris held it up to show Patsy and she saw the heavily carved ring. It bore the leering face of a gargoyle, or something deformed enough to be one. The eyes were two orange polished stones which glared blindly out from the tarnished sockets and in an instant she recognised the sight-less, ferocious stare of the cat's-eyes which crawled up from the road.

'Where did that come fr . . .' The sentence dried in her mouth and in slap of comprehension, her mind flashed back.

'Just thought I'd give a hand,' the man's voice said. It sounded more like an animal than a human. In that hazard light's glow, she saw his face for the first time, long and grey with a huge, almost dog-like nose, lips pulled back over narrow, blackened teeth. Not human! Not human. She pumped on the handle, feeling it grind up against the reaching arm. Something ripped and there was a crack like a bullet-strike, then a metallic tinkle and the man, the thing whatever it was, had gone.

She'd heard the noise, the hard ricochet and for an instant, back then, a lurch of nausea had rippled inside her when she'd thought she'd amputated his finger. She recalled the shivery panic as she imagined it down in the dark of the footwell, beckoning gruesomely. It had been a ring, an old, heavy signet, set with a grotesque grinning head with glaring blind eyes and suddenly she knew without a shadow of doubt how they'd found them so quickly, how they could reach out and touch them. Judith must have picked it up from the floor somewhere along the road. Peter had been right when he'd said they were bugged. The ring was tainted with the poisonous witchery of this place. She remembered thinking of *Gollum*, slinking along after the ring of power, and that had only been half right. The black transit van and its cavalry of monstrous trucks must have been trailing them by locking in to whatever emanations the ring gave off, but it was not the old circle of tarnished metal they wanted. They wanted the power of innocence they could only find in the children.

442

'Get it out of here,' Patsy rasped. 'Get that thing away from us.' Even as she said it, a memory was tugging at the edge of her mind, trying to show her something. She reached for it but it danced away from her, leaving her with an odd sense of failure.

Chris rolled down the window. Judith was breathing again, but her breath was hoarse and strangled. She was shaking her head violently from side to side, as if trying to escape an invisible bond. The cloth rag smouldered and then caught fire. Green flames licked up in a sudden flare. Chris yelped, pulling back from the scorch of heat, twisted and slung the burning rag out onto the road. The wind whipped the flames into long tongues and the ring tinkled heavily along the hard surface before rolling into the dusty corner beside the guard rail.

Judith sighed heavily, took in a deep, clean breath of air, then burst into tears. Patsy could say nothing, but Chris reached back to take her hand. Peter put an arm around her sister. The sobbing went on for a short time until Judith sniffed the tears away and wiped her eyes.

'I heard daddy,' she said in a shaky little voice. 'He wants me to come back, but he's all different now and he wants to do bad things.'

'I know, sweetheart,' Patsy said, wanting to stop, but unable to slow.

'And Kerron, she was speaking inside my head and she wants to take me down to the stone and she's *old*.'

'But they're gone now.'

Judith nodded. 'I can't hear them now.' She sniffed again and Peter wiped her eyes with the edge of his jerkin, taking care to avoid the cracked skin of the red rash creeping outward from the hairline. Chris was still reaching back to hold the girl's hand. Slowly he let it go and turned to face forward. He edged over to Patsy and whispered in her ear. Patsy glanced in the mirror.

The van was swooping down from the level above on a steep ramp. Behind it, the line of trucks rumbled in a midnight avalanche. Patsy craned round. The side window on the transit was darkly smoked, but she could see a shape through the glass, pale against the darkness and she knew it was Paul, or whatever Paul had become here on the *Ley Road*. The slip road came angling down beside the straight they were rolling on. She followed the direction and saw the junction ahead. The transit and the phalanx of black monsters were racing to cut them off. She put her foot down again and her gratitude swelled when she felt the thrust in her back as the jeep responded. The van was parallel with them now and the rigs right on its tail. She flicked another glance and saw the nearest lorry, tarpaulin flapping in its own slipstream. Its cabin was high and dark, the windows like insect eyes and the wheel arches and girders oddly smoothed, like rippling muscles.

They're alive, she thought to herself. They were like the false policeman. They could look like trucks, as he could look human, but they were *not* what they seemed to be. Underneath the image, she sensed life of a kind, and enormous, evil power. At the black way-station, she had seen them as great black night-hawk stagecoaches drawn by nightmare horses. Was that how they really were? The road shuddered as they came rumbling down the ramp.

The radio clicked again and a screeching voice, completely incomprehensible, came yammering up through the static. Chris did not hesitate this time. He leaned back in his seat, lifted his foot and stamped down on the little set. The metal squealed and the whole receiver came right off the mounting. A small bolt went leaping up to strike the glass. Without hesitation he bent, grabbed the box, pulled the wires free with a violent twist of his hand and chucked the lot out of the window. It hit the road with a crash which faded instantly.

Patsy drove on. She had the wheel in a death grip and her heart was somewhere in her throat, kicking away like an angry mule. The trucks were rolling down that ramp, the van now ahead of her, heading for the intersection where they'd pour into the straight. There was no way out, just this long section flanked by the enormous pillars of the upper viaducts hemming them in. Ahead of them, the road dipped and she could not see where they would get to beyond the slope. She was losing the race. The pale face behind the glass turned towards her and while she could not make out the features, she sensed the emptiness and corruption within him. Somewhere inside her she felt Paul's touch, and she squirmed because it felt now like the touch of death.

'*Bastard*,' she hissed under her breath.

'Don't worry,' Chris said. He reached over and put a hand on her shoulder, letting her know in that small gesture that he was with her and he believed in her, no matter what happened. Despite the fear that was winding up inside her again, that touch, that message, gave her such a hot surge that she almost yelled. Chris Deane did not see her as an adjunct, as a chattel, as a weak little woman.

Chris looked at her and in that crazy moment he saw the profile of the moon goddess. Patsy's teeth were clenched and her lips were drawn back and her brows pulled down in a fierce, desperate grimace, her eyes nailed on the junction ahead of them.

She shoved the ball of her foot down so hard she felt the plate give a little and she *willed* the jeep onwards.

'Come on, *damn you*,' she grated.

'You'll make it. You'll beat them,' Chris said, more in awe than in true belief.

Patsy howled, though she never heard it, and miraculously the jeep surged forward. The black van came angling down, straight for the junction. Patsy pulled ahead and the van came right off the ramp, aiming to cut her off. She jerked the wheel to the right this time and the transit went flashing in front of them. A huge truck, right on its heels loomed inches from her, sliding right across the road. Instinct told her to go straight and she held the wheel steady. The jeep leapt forward through the gap between the van and the first rig and she was in the clear. The dip was just in front of them. The van went careering across to the side and slammed against the barrier, slapping the metal in ever decreasing curves as it tried to compensate and get back on line. The rear truck clipped its tail and sent it swerving back into the railing. Sparks fountained in a pyrotechnic display and a piece of the transit's shiny wing was peeled right back. Patsy hit the dip. Below her she had a choice of three lanes which wove around each other, all taking different directions. She didn't even choose. The jeep went squirting straight into the one ahead of her. She went down a slope, turned a narrow corner, leaning over with the centripetal force, angled round one of the monstrous pillars and came to another fork. She took the right again, instinctively playing on her luck once more – instinctively refusing to take the left-hand path – and emerged on the top road, high above the straight where they'd almost been trapped.

A glance in her rear-view mirror told her the black cavalcade was still behind them, though it had lost some time lining up to squeeze into the first gap. The black van, now battered and crumpled on its nearside, was rumbling its way up towards them and she kept her foot down, trying to summon whatever it was that had given it the miracle kick. She went hurtling along on the overpass.

And night fell.

There was no warning at all on the impossible junction. Night simply dropped on them. For an instant Patsy was driving blind. She fumbled for the unfamiliar switch, heart sinking at the possibility that the lights might not work and cursing herself for not having checked them when she'd started out. Her fingers found a bank of toggles and she pulled them all down. The beams stabbed out ahead of her, parallels of light.

The road was alive.

The cat's-eyes were up and moving. Overhead, up in a rolling sky, the red furnace-pulse flickered in the clouds and behind them, the blood-light of the moon glimmered feverishly. Crabbed things came angling in on pinioning legs, pale claws held aloft, scarlet eyes blazing in the lights. The big treads went crunching through them. Something flicked up and sizzled on the glass, bubbling a groove down the pane.

Behind them, the truck-lights flared, inflamed scarlet eyes staring mad. They formed an aura around the blind van, which had no lights to shine, sending it into silhouette. The road rumbled under their wheels as the motorcade came powering in their wake.

They hammered along the overpass, looking down on the level where they'd been hunted. Beyond that, lower down, between the soaring supports, the glow of the tunnel waxed and waned in time to the ponderous beat. The lights of moving traffic, as red as blood, winked down there in the fumes as the unceasing line of vehicles crawled ever onwards into the maw.

Something big and black came whirling in from the side. Through the glass and over the rumble of the chase, she heard the whoop of giant wings and could not help but flick a glance to the side. A great black bird with flat red eyes banked just beside them. Its scimitar beak came spiking down and stabbed at the roof of the car in a rapid series of blows. Peter looked up and saw the line of dents, smooth and evenly spaced appear on the panelling. A darker shadow peeled away from the underside of the parallel flyover and came snaking across the road, a moving piece of night, and snatched the flyer away in a snap of jaws.

They raced through the night, soaring up a ramp and down a slip, wheeling on a curve that took them looping over a six-lane highway, and everywhere, amidst the death that was creeping and crawling towards the preposterous underground tunnel, there was an abundance of eerie life. The cat's-eyes crawled and grabbed at them, but the jeep's wheels crumpled them into the surface and squat amphibious things with the tractor tyre skin came slithering out to snatch them up. The road was filled with the flare of blinkless red eyes and Patsy simply held the wheel and kept going. She angled the jeep up a slope and down a bend, roaring headlong down the hill.

Overhead the sky was a maelstrom, a vast whirlpool of a storm spinning and whirling while jagged forks of lightning arced from one edge to the other, curving round the edges of the cyclone's eyes and sending clots of baleful luminescence searing into the banked clouds. But in the centre of the storm, in the clear, stygian darkness, the moon hovered.

The full moon . . .

The memory she'd been reaching for danced closer then spun away. The mad moon was full; now, blinding and poisonous, its face demented and raving, mountain range teeth sharp as daggers, crater-eyes red with hot lava. It glared down into Patsy's eyes. She felt it tug and draw her. For an instant her eyes left the road.

A rip of hailstones battered the windshield and it was not hailstones but a swarm of flies. They rolled in the headlight beams and for that instant there was nothing to be seen. The front fender slapped against a brittle barrier that might have been wood. She heard it splinter and crack. The tyres rumbled over a soft, rough surface which was not tarmac and she knew she had run them off the road. The moon glared down and she could hear a growling voice inside her head. Peter let out a cry of alarm.

They crashed forward, blinded by the flies. A light appeared straight ahead. Judith rasped in the shadows of the back seat. The jeep jostled and bounced. The light flared, widened like opening curtains. The buzzing of the flies became a searing shriek. A shape loomed ahead and Patsy stamped on the brake. The sides clattered against unseen objects which were simply scattered.

'What's happened?' Peter demanded. All around them the air was thick with the swarm. A foul smell came billowing through the vents. Chris felt his throat constrict against it. Judith rasped again, as if she was clearing her lungs.

'I think we've gone off . . .' Patsy started to say when all of a sudden the swarm lifted, as if it was one single organism.

All around them lights flickered, reflecting back from tall, stained glass windows. Straight in front, a marble altar stood squat under a gilded tabernacle. Above that, an inverted crucifix hung suspended.

'Oh, sweet Lord . . .' Chris heard Patsy's whispered prayer.

'Fuck you,' Judith rasped. Peter drew in a sharp breath. In the twist of the moment Patsy hadn't heard it.

On the crucifix, a black shape was impaled. Its skin was tattered and peeling, showing white in places, reflecting red in others. Its head hung over a wide receptacle on the altar. Quite clearly they heard the drip of blood draining into it. It tugged at Patsy's attention and she saw it was not a black chalice or a bowl. It was a smooth biker's helmet, slowly filling with the blood of the impaled man on the cross.

Billy Walker. It had to be him. He had buried Sally B in a shallow roadside grave and started walking, and this is where he had reached. Patsy recalled his scrawled prayer. *If anybody finds this note, say a prayer for Sally. She was a good woman and shouldn't have suffered like she did. God help all of us.*

She had run them off the road and they had been snared by the dreadful black church. For an awful moment Patsy's heart stopped dead in her chest with such a pain that she thought she would just die.

Billy Walker shouldn't have suffered like this, but the foul magnetism of the decrepit church had reeled him in and he had died upside-down, nailed to a cross while his blood dripped into the cup of his helmet. Behind the black bowl, a shadow flickered and writhed.

'What in the name of . . .' Chris started to say.

Welcome to my house. The voice ground out, cold as millstones.

'Into thy hands I commend this spirit, *Father*,' Judith rasped. Chris turned towards her. Peter yelled. Judith fought her way out of the swaddling blanket. Her pale, emaciated hand thumbed the catch on the belt. Chris reached for her, but in a surprisingly quick motion she twisted away.

'You are not my father,' she shrieked. 'My father calls me now.'

It was Kerron's voice, mixed in with Judith's in a strange bi-sonance. The girl pulled the handle and the door opened. She tumbled out into the aisle. Patsy screamed in pure panic. Quick as a flash Peter was out beside her. Over at the altar, the dark shape laughed in gleeful expectation.

'*Come now, innocence.*' The walls shivered. Blood plinked into the helmet.

Peter made a grab for his sister and she reached out to claw at him. As she did the flickering light from the candles caught her face. The dark hair was lank and rat-tailed. The skin stretched tight as parchment across her forehead. In the shadows of her eyes a verdigris green glowed.

The transference! Patsy's mind screeched. *It's happening.*

She was twisted in her seat, watching as her daughter's hand came up to slash at Peter, and she saw Judith's face twisted into a snarling rictus. She recognised the look of Kerron Vaunche. Underneath the scabbed jaw, on the scrawny neck, a black spider clenched.

The connection came loping in, right at that instant. It was not a spider. It was the amulet she'd glimpsed on the thong when she'd reached for Judith in the shadows of Broadford House. Only now did its significance reach her. It was not a spider, it was a small, skeletal hand. It could have been a monkey's shrivelled paw, but Patsy knew it was the hand of a dead baby.

The hand of glory. The hand of innocence. The little black and gnarled fingers were squeezed onto Judith's throat so tightly,

Patsy could see the skin begin to rip. Any moment now, blood would spurt from her throat, the carotid artery would rupture and her daughter would be gone.

Peter was reaching again and Judith was fighting him off.

'To hell with this,' Chris bellowed. Without hesitation he slammed open the door so hard it hit the bodyshell with a clang like a gong. In two strides he reached the girl, just as Peter was reeling back from another vicious slap. He snatched for her and she twisted away from him. By sheer accident, or guided by a counter-force to the black power behind the altar, his fingers snagged at the thong. It snapped with a rip and the little skeletal hand was jerked off the girl's throat. It flew like a flicked spider across the nave towards the altar. Under the tabernacle, the black shape roared, and the ground shivered under their feet.

Judith screamed. Chris grabbed her and slung her into the car. She hit the far door with a bang. Patsy reached and held her shoulder, forcing the girl to stay still. A squat and amorphous thing came lumbering out from the shadows behind the overflowing helmet. Chris felt its rage and outrage like a blast from a furnace. It came scutting over the marble, rocking the biker's helmet and splashing blood to the flat stone.

'Shit,' Chris grunted. He reached into his pocket, fumbled for something, drew out the bottle of surgical spirit. Without any hesitation he slammed the neck against the wheel arch. The glass shattered and the top went flying away. The tingling scent of spirit bit at him, combating the gagging reek of rot. He spun and threw the bottle out towards the altar.

'Quick,' Patsy cried. 'Get in.' She had the engine revving. Peter yelled at the top of his voice, a high and urgent plea. Chris turned away from them. He clambered over a tumbled pew, reached a twisted gothic candlestick and plucked a candle from its holder. It felt greasy in his hand and he knew it was not wax but some kind of fat, and instinctively he realised it was not animal. He whirled again and threw it right at the dark shadow scuttling over the broad altar.

The surgical spirit caught with a *whump*. Flames blossomed, white and searing. They licked up to an old tapestry which immediately caught fire. The dark shape roared in pain and fury and drew back towards the tabernacle. The flames swelled and the dreadful black thing squeezed its way into the receptacle and slammed the door shut. Instantly, all the candles flickered and died.

Chris clambered blindly over the scattered pews, groping for the jeep. He found the door, climbed in and told her to drive. Patsy slammed the gear into reverse. Judith was screaming, but it was her own voice again and her scream seemed to be real fright and not that dreadful contamination. The doors were creaking shut, but when the rear fender hit them they smashed to powder. At the altar the flames roared as they consumed the tapestry and the crucifix and the offering nailed to it, cleansing everything in a searing catharsis. The jeep came ramming out of the church. Patsy twisted the wheel and they went lumbering past the awful little graveyard with its four empty holes. They skirted the tumble-down wall when the old steeple finally reached its point of no return and slowly toppled onto the roof of the church. A noise like an explosion blasted out and the church collapsed in on itself. Yellow flames burst from the windows and reached for the sky.

She put her foot down and went rumbling across the field. Out of the corner of her eye she saw a movement. She turned and a gaunt shadow lurched out from the hedge.

The scarecrow reached for them, branch hands elongating, horned and twisted. The face screamed at them, eyes glowing mad-red, mouth agape with jagged teeth.

'Fuck this,' Chris said. Patsy jerked the wheel, pulling the nose round to the right. Chris leaned out and the gun thundered. The scarecrow's head disintegrated and the mad scream vanished.

'Pardon my language,' Chris said. Patsy's ears were still ringing and she never heard him. She drove on and made it to the road, crashing through a small barrier and bouncing over a kerb. She sped forward on the blacktop, taking the dips and the turns as the crazy night deepened. Chris kept his hand on her shoulder, letting her know he was willing her on. Somewhere above them the clouds rolled in, hiding the demented moon from sight while the moon goddess in Patricia Havelin battled her way through the night.

Patsy drove like someone possessed, determined to beat the black transit, knowing she *could* beat it. She drove on, steering

451

them up and down and round while the massed trucks ground and roared somewhere in her wake, sometimes behind her, sometimes on a parallel road, and the night wore on as the lightning flashed and stuttered continuously, giving the roiling sky a flickering glow. Patsy reached another crest on another overpass high above the twisting confusion of connections on the junction. She slowed her speed and let the jeep coast to a halt.

Behind her, there was no sign of pursuit. 'Want me to take a spell at the wheel?' Chris asked. 'I reckon we should keep moving.'

She yawned, forcing the stiffness out of her joints and trying to push exhaustion away from her. 'I thought you didn't drive.'

'You've been doing well enough so far. I never mess with success.' He gave her a smile that told her she'd done good. She knew that anyway but appreciated it.

After a few minutes, they got rolling on again. The needle was edging down to the red on the fuel gauge and Patsy realised they were getting close to the end. Unless they found an abandoned van or truck with some fuel left, they would have to walk it on the junction, and she knew they would never survive until morning. How much time they had left until morning, until the end of the *Nameless Day*, she couldn't tell, because here, as it had been on the road, there seemed to be no natural span. She eased a hand down to the worn little holster on her belt and felt the butt of the small gun. She would not let her children suffer more in the night.

They came down off the height, swerved on another spiral access road and reached a flyover which was almost as high as the one they'd crossed. Over to the right, now somehow further away than it had been before, the maw of the vast tunnel gaped and in the rolling black clouds down there, she could see the incessant crawl of the mass of vehicles. Somewhere there, she knew, the staggering line of walkers were edging down into the depths.

She would not let her children suffer in the night, and she would never let them join that dreadful, lurching rank.

They breasted the rise and came across two abandoned trucks and an ancient patrol car that could have driven straight out of a Chicago gangster movie. She slowed down at Chris's suggestion and let the jeep stand idling in the middle of the road with the headlamps lighting up the wrecks.

'What's wrong?' she asked, feeling the tiredness push in at her, fuzzing the edges of her vision, though she was still determined to keep driving.

'I've got an idea,' he told her. The nearest truck was a long trailer bearing a load of steel pipes, piled high on each other. Its cabin was crumpled against the tail of the next one, a payload dumper still filled with rubble from some site clearance. A river of fuel had spewed out from underneath and stained the road surface in a slick, greasy patch.

'If I can get those pipes off, we can set up a barricade. It could slow them up.'

'What if they come the other way?'

Chris shook his head.

'I reckon they've got to follow the same rules as we do. The road only goes one way, and eventually they all get down there,' he said, indicating the pulsing glow in the depths.

'It's worth a try,' she said. 'But after that, we need fuel or we'll be stuck.' A small whinge of despair told her none of it mattered any more, that they'd come to the end, but behind that, the stronger voice overrode the objections. She'd fought this far and she could fight a little more. It was the longest night, but it could not go on forever.

Chris swung his legs out and dumped his rucksack on the ground. He rummaged inside and came out with a pair of pliers and a small monkey wrench. Peter eased himself out beside him and stood watching. The trailer was angled up against a caved-in section of crash barrier just back from the crest of the arch. The steel sewage pipes were grey and flaked with red rust, big heavy cylinders straining against the braided hawser which kept them in place. Patsy got out and arched her back to ease the cramp setting in while he worked at the connection, clamping the wrench onto the retaining nut and tugging down hard. He grunted with exertion. The nut didn't budge.

'I might have to saw it,' he said, panting. 'That could take half an hour, maybe more, but it could be worth a try.'

'Put some oil on the nut,' Peter suggested. 'That's how I fix my bike.'

Chris stood up and scratched his brow, leaving a red rust mark angled across it. He grinned at Peter and flipped the brim of the hat which the boy had worn since the day before. 'Good man. Excellent advice.' He went back to the bag and drew out his barrier twine in its canister, dripping with oil. He daubed some on the steel nut, rubbing it down into the join and waited a few moments before applying the wrench.

He grunted again, sweat beading above his eyes to trickle the rust down his nose. The nut gave a fraction. He strained again and it turned a little. Another heave and it made an eighth of a turn.

Chris looked up at Peter who gave him an *I-told-you-so* grin. He heaved again, braced for another, when Peter drew in his breath.

'Chris, you'd better hurry up,' he said fast. Chris looked up, saw Peter staring behind him, turned and saw the deadly convoy on the pass above them, silhouetted in the flickering storm-light. Their orange headlights reached out ahead of them, sweeping across the concrete pillars.

'That's where we were before, isn't it?'

Chris nodded. 'Get your mother in the car.' Peter looked at him, mouth agape. Chris shoved him.

'Move it,' he told him. Patsy turned, eyes wide. Peter came charging across the road. He almost barged into his mother. Chris was wrenching at the restraining nut. He saw the boy point, then pull at Patsy. They went running towards the jeep and dived in. She leaned over and opened the passenger door.

'Come on,' she shouted. 'Get in.'

Chris didn't stop. He started pumping at the wrench. The nut was spiralling now, a half turn with every pull. It was rising up, squalling dryly as it came.

'Go on,' Chris called back. 'Get a move on.'

He saw her shake her head.

'Chris. Please. They're coming.' Her voice was sharp and urgent.

He waved his free hand, the one still bound in the rag. 'Go, for Christ's sake. *Get going.*'

The black transit was swinging down the connecting road they'd followed. The line of huge trucks were rolling behind in

454

a thundering charge. He pumped the wrench, willing the metal to free itself.

The nut swung up. Too slow. *Too slow.* The trucks were coming, thundering down on him and he was going to be too late.

Patsy had started the engine. She screamed at him to forget the pipes, to get into the car. The jeep inched forward in a series of little jerks. The engine gunned. Patsy was leaning across the seat, yammering dementedly. Peter was bawling. Judith was crying now.

Above them, the clouds parted and the moon leered down, but it was low in the sky. Behind them, the greasy colours of dawn were swirling in the turbulence of the storm. The moon was losing its fierce glare, but it still had that poison. Patsy could feel it on her skin.

'Jesus, woman,' he roared. 'Get the hell out of here.'

The van was swooping down, hammering along towards the flat. The great trucks blasted smoke and sparks from their stacks and rumbled behind it, a solid wall of motion making the road shiver.

There was a fraction of an inch to go. If he'd got the thing started twenty seconds earlier, he'd have freed it. He eyed the distance between himself and the jeep, between himself and the line of trucks. For an instant he thought he could make it, but that would still leave Patsy and those two kids on the run and they were out of fuel and he knew none of them would make it.

'Go,' he bawled. Patsy looked in the mirror. She'd waited until the last possible second. He heard the handbrake smack off. Tyres squealed and the jeep launched itself forward. His heart kicked hard and in fury he threw his weight on the wrench. The metal tip of the nut cracked and the hawser parted with a gunshot crack. The bolt bulleted out and hit him across the temple so violently that he was thrown back. Blood gouted and he rolled over the pile of pipes.

A noise like a bell clanged out. One pipe shifted and batted him to the side. He flopped, rolled, fetched up against the tyre under the cab and the first pipe came lumbering off the trailer. It bounced twice, rolled across the road, curved and went trundling downhill. The second followed it, the third swerved, bounced

455

against the barrier then clattered down the slope. The fourth, and the seventeen other three-ton pipes simply slid off and thundered down the road.

The third one caught the black van and swiped it up into the air. It did a perfect somersault and landed on its wheels. One side was stove in and the windscreen disappeared in an obsidian explosion. Something flew out of the front and landed with a flop on the roadway.

It twitched, got to its knees. Patsy saw a white face topped by dark hair and the thing turned. Paul's eyes, like coals in snow, snagged her across the intervening distance. A trickle of blood drooled from his mouth. His face was fat and doughy, as if he'd lost all of the resilience, like a maggot in human form. He shivered in the light of the moon and wisps of steam came spiralling off his skin as if the light was burning him up.

He turned towards the van. It was damaged, but still mobile. It reversed away from the barrier then lurched forward.

Another pipe came lumbering down just at that moment and smashed the van into the wall. Flames gouted and spread out onto the road. A dark shape came scuttering out and Peter saw the Kerron Vaunche apparition he'd seen on the day Willow had died. It came tumbling outwards, just ahead of the flames. It was screeching like a banshee, a papery, wizened thing with skin the colour of parchment and eyes like mould.

Judith cried out and then flopped in the seat, her whole body twitching. Peter hauled her up and saw his sister's eyes turning green again. He could sense the sizzling connection between Judith and the scuttering thing that crabbed along the road. Kerron Vaunche passed the white and bloated figure which stood on the edge of the flames.

The fourth pipe lumbered over it and squashed it like a road-kill into the tarmac. The gypsy turned, mouth agape. The river of flame came rippling along the road and simply swallowed her up. She screamed again, a dreadful fluttering thing of fire. Above her the clouds tumbled and an arc of lightning came stabbing down, connecting the pillar of flame with the sky in an instant of searing power. The tumbling figure exploded and the scream they heard inside their minds died instantly.

Judith hiccuped, her whole body went into a spasm, arcing like a bow, then all the tension went out of her.

In the mirror Patsy saw the load shift. She slowed the jeep and brought it to a halt again. Chris was flopped against the wheel. Patsy saw him get to his feet. He staggered towards the trucks, as if dazed, seemed to shake himself, and lurched in the direction she'd taken. Peter was screeching desperately, telling him to run. He was up against the back window, bawling at the top of his voice. Chris started to move towards them, though whether he saw them or not she could not tell.

The line of trucks was just hitting the straight. One of the pipes went tumbling like a Scottish caber, end over point and plunged through the back of the nearest one. The vast truck heeled over and fell onto its side, sending up a cascade of sparks. The next rig crumpled into it, swerved violently, travelling on its right set of wheels and slammed into the van. The black transit went right into the air, spinning as it went. Its nose hit the low restraining wall and it tumbled over the edge, somersaulting as it went. It slammed against a concrete wall and a bright flare on the underside of the overpass showed when it exploded in flames. The third lorry hit the second and came ramming right along the road. A black cylinder of pipe speared through the cabin and both of them went hurtling through the barrier.

Chris was moving, stumbling away from the cataclysm. Behind him the pipes were rumbling and tumbling down the hill, one black avalanche challenging another. Patsy was two, maybe three hundred yards away. She hit the horn, leaned on it, sending out a message, pleading with him to run. He was trying, she could see, but he was moving awkwardly, as if he was hurt. She leaned out of the window and saw the red of blood on the side of his face.

'Come on, Chris. Come on.' She slammed the jeep into reverse, started to go backwards. Chris shouted at her, waving his hands, telling her to go forward.

Behind her, two of the trucks went flying through the gap left by the first. From where she was, on the turn, she saw them leap into space, twisting and turning, great juggernauts flying through the air like mad locomotives, but they seemed to change and contort as they flew, lines and edges running and mutating. For an instant she saw great beasts, bunched muscles rippling, black dragons twisting in the air. The first hit the slender pillar of the overpass they'd travelled and exploded in a ball of flame and smoke. It dropped like a stone, but when it did, a jagged crack appeared in the pillar. The second truck went flying past and broke in two on the other pillar and the third came ramming down to strike where the first one had battered the concrete. The slender column simply broke in two.

Without warning, the overpass canted to the side.

Chris roared again. He was stumbling away, heading towards them, but a black truck was bearing down on him, its metallic lines rippling and mutating. It growled like a beast and its grille was like an array of teeth. Behind it came two others that had escaped the avalanche of pipes.

A shadow loomed and Patsy turned. The road above simply sagged. Another pillar broke in a puff of debris and the whole section dropped. It landed smack on the lower road and sent a vast whipping pressure wave along a mile of highway. The earthquake hit the supports of another overpass and flipped the box girder span into the air. It twisted, fell and went through three levels of viaduct, dropping them like dominoes in a roar of destruction.

Patsy had no choice. Ahead of her a pattern of cracks snaked, crackling like fireworks along the side of the road and she could see the surface torque and twist as the shear pressures contorted the supports of the road she was on. Tarmac bubbled. A series of retorts cracked in the air close by and a fusillade of foot-long bolts came flying out of the girders sixty yards away and embedded themselves up to their hex-heads in the concrete on the far side.

She stamped on the pedal, tears streaming down her face. Over the tumult she could hear Chris ordering her to go, to get moving. He was ahead of the lead truck, maybe fifty metres in front, now running fast. She could wait no longer. A snaking crack came rippling up towards her. The jeep moved forward over the gap. It widened to six inches and she could feel the tyres slam in the groove. Peter was crying real tears, jabbering inconsolably.

The jeep surged forward. Ahead of her the road tilted and

they were all thrown to the side. A huge explosion blasted away the barricade on the side. Straight ahead a crevasse opened, six inches, nine, a foot. She stamped down and they zoomed forward. The fissure opened wider. The far side dropped a foot, dropped three. She accelerated, willing the jeep faster, making it fly.

The lorry was gaining on Chris. He stumbled, regained his footing. A piece of concrete as big as a house fell away from somewhere above and hit the truck on its side, batting it in a casual flick which sent it into space. She saw the chasm in front open wide, could not stop. Chris made a desperate lunge, moving amazingly fast now, seeing the slimmest chance. She couldn't stop or she'd plunge into the crevasse. He couldn't make it. The jeep went over the edge and the section slipped and the fissure yawned. He was reaching and then they were falling. She saw him skid, arms pinwheeling right at the edge, saw him slip, tumble through the air. Peter screamed and they were falling.

Darkness slammed down. The red of the tunnel pulsed on her eyelids. The night was filled with scarlet eyes and reaching hands and they were tumbling down from an impossible height into the dreaded mouth of the abyss.

Something hit one of the pillars a tremendous blow and she saw it was the fallen truck twisting and writhing and alive. The pillar collapsed, knocking the next, smashing the third, in another domino-strike. The noise was apocalyptic, like the end of the world. Patsy heard someone scream and didn't know which of them it was, though it could have been herself. There was an explosion that sent fire all around them and then the red mouth, the pulsating tunnel snapped shut, collapsed on itself and real darkness fell.

For an instant, dizzying moment, there was a numbing silence. The moment stretched out, elongated. They were frozen in time. The scream was echoing in Patsy's ears. In her mind she saw Chris Deane running behind them, trying to make it, skidding over the edge, cartwheeling as he plummeted into space.

The silence went on and on and on and they fell in the darkness. She started to turn in her seat to reach for her children, to hold them one last time, moving as though through thick jelly.

Peter's mouth was open so wide she could see the back teeth. His arm was gripped around his sister whose eyes were rolling wildly in her pale face. Patsy reached for them, knowing they were all going to die. Her fingers clutched at her children and drew them in. Judith's eyes suddenly focused. The lightning flickered in them and Judith recognised her mother. In a matter of seconds, the warted growths which had crept onto her face seemed to evaporate. The black blotches under the skin drained away like ink.

An enormous sense of love flowed between Patsy and her children. Some instinct made her turn in her seat. Judith reached and put a soft hand on her shoulder. The lightning stabbed down once. It was lancing down through the absolute blackness, like a rip in a black curtain. There was a sound like a mountain rising up from solid rock. The sky ripped wide open as the lightning came arcing down at them.

And then they were in daylight.

Blinding light flashed in front of her eyes. Instinctively she grabbed the wheel. The tyres thumped and the jeep bounced into the air, fell and hit again. Her foot thudded on the brake and rubber shrieked. Ahead of her a small car suddenly changed lanes and she had to twist violently to avoid crashing into it. A taxi travelling in the adjacent lane slammed its horn. Somebody bawled a curse. A lorry gave a *whonk* that sent a chill through her bones. Behind her, headlights flashed. Ahead, the sun was blinding.

For a second, a sick, looping sensation of vertigo rolled through her. A sign whizzed past and she thought she read *Birmingham* at the top end of a directional schematic. The road was crowded with cars and trucks and they were all going in the same direction.

But over on the other side, across the low barrier, they were heading the opposite way.

There was a scent of road fumes in the air, but it smelt like a real road.

They were back in their own world again.

After a stunned mile, Patsy came to a ramp which led off and she pulled up and into a highway service station. Some children were climbing a jungle gym. She heard their tinkling laughter. She found a parking space and pulled in. Patsy stepped out of the jeep, opened the back door and grabbed for Peter and Judith and then she burst into tears.

She held them tight, shuddering with the force of her tears of joy and tears of grief. After a while, a little girl with fair curly hair came up and tugged at the torn and dirty leg of her jeans.

'Are you lost?' she asked.

30

On a country road in high summer, a year after Patsy Havelin and her children dropped back into the world.

Peter was a year older and as mischievous as ever. Judith was still shy and though she'd suffered a painful trauma of repeated nightmares in which she heard her father calling her name as clouds of black flies came buzzing to snatch her, she had survived and would survive.

According to the newspapers Paul Thomson had died, along with Kerron Vaunche and others of their sect in an explosion -- blamed on a methane leak from an archaic sewage system – which had ripped through the basement of Broadford House with such force that the three storeys above it had slapped down like cards, crushing everything flat, including the round stone table with its intricate carvings. None of the bodies in the basement could be identified. Only Patsy Havelin knew the real truth.

Carrick Thomson, Paul's brother, had broken three ribs from a kick he received from one of the followers on the night he'd helped rescue Peter and Judith from Broadford House. He'd also broken two fingers and fractured his wrist from the series of punches he'd thrown to great effect. The man he called McGregor had taken a stab wound in the thigh, but there had been no serious damage. Crandall Gilfeather had a burn which puckered the skin all down his left arm. Nobody but he knew how it had happened.

Patsy had disappeared and Carrick had been convinced she'd gone into hiding to ensure her children were safe, though two months after she vanished, he'd begun to get concerned when there was no contact.

She and her children had travelled on the road for six days. When the old jeep had slammed down on the busy road south of Birmingham, it was in early summer, six months after the day Kerron Vaunche had cursed her and sent her on the road to hell. Things were just beginning to settle down. Patsy mourned the loss of her husband for her children's sake, but to herself she cursed him and hoped he was twisting in flames. At night, sometimes she'd have a vision of that hellish tunnel and in her dreams she'd be fleeing on a dark road under a mad moon with the cat's-eyes coming out of the road and that dreadful thing scrabbling over the altar in the malignant old church. On such nights she'd wake up hauling for breath and shivering with fright. Just as bad, in a way, was the persistence of the memory of Chris Deane running after them, racing to catch up while the black pipes went rolling down the hill. In her mind's eye she still saw him run, face twisted with effort, saw him slip, stumble, roll forward and begin to slide over the jagged edge of the crevasse in the road and begin to fall. In her mind's eye she saw him tumble helplessly as he fell into the darkness. Her memory left her with an empty sense of loss.

A country road in high summer with the windows open and the new car taking the turns easily. Peter and Judith in the back seat, playing with the little hand-held game. Every now and again she'd hear a bleep and look in the mirror, catching a glimpse of Judith's tousled black hair and the old battered hat that Peter wore when they went out into the country.

They had been driving for an hour, along the narrow little road that would take them to the quiet valley where they'd picnic on the short grass beside the stream. The air was warm and insects hummed in the trees. Patsy drove along, a half smile on her face, feeling that the summer should never end.

She stamped on the brake.

Peter and Judith were thrown forward, held back only by the seat restraints. Immediately Peter asked her what was wrong and she head the tight alertness in his voice that told her he was always ready.

Patsy turned in her seat, mouth agape. Peter unhitched his belt and knelt up to look behind him. Judith followed suit.

The man sat on the short grass close to the stream. A smokeless fire flickered under an old blackened can. His head was down, but she got the impression he was aware of them. Very slowly she got out of the car and stood there at the side of the road, unable to walk forward, but wanting to.

After a while, he lifted the can from the fire, using a forked stick, and slowly got to his feet. He limped heavily, using a gnarled stick to get to the side of the road and placed the steaming container on the verge before going back to sit by the fire again.

BANE

There is a town called Arden. Nestling in the Scottish hills, its tranquillity masks a terrifying, chilling secret.

There is a journalist called Ryan. Drawn back to Arden by forces he cannot comprehend, he is the victim of nightmares that seem all too real.

Then there is the watcher who waits for whatever it is that sleeps beneath Ardhmor rock to wake . . . and destroy.

Gripped by a horror as ancient as night, Arden will become the gateway to ultimate evil, to a deadly legacy from the mists of the primeval past that will create a hell on earth.

And only Ryan, accompanied by a ten-year-old girl and a brain-damaged man, can stop it.

THE SHEE

Kilgallan – a small, quiet community on Ireland's west coast. Things at Donovan's Bar get a little raucous sometimes, and the people carry their share of Ireland's tragic history, but in Kilgallan, the fights are happy, the songs are sad, and the days are as rich as slow-poured, peaty beer.

It happens first to the children.

To little Mikey Boyle, whose auntie takes off all her clothes, takes off his too, and persuades him into the river . . .

To sweet Marie Lally, barely sixteen, when Mike O'Hara ties the cord around her neck and slides up her night-gown . . .

Village tragedies. Casual eruptions of horror . . .

But at the heart of a nearby hill, something turns in its sleep.

Breathes . . .

Awakes . . .

The Shee will put her fingers into your dreams, and leave you crying for more.

SHRIKE

Levenford had seen its share of horror, with the strange and bloody deaths in the old house in the centre of the town some thirty years before. Now a new round of deaths has shocked the town. And they are more brutal than anyone could have imagined.

Levenford is at the mercy of a superhuman, remorseless killer that, *whatever it is*, loves the dark places, the high places the old town offers. Evil has been given flesh and blood. And this evil *demands* more . . .

The slaughter has turned the town into a pressure chamber of dread. Jack Fallon has no leads that will help him stop the carnage. But soon the bizarre visions of a young Highland woman begin to make some kind of weird sense. Only she can unlock Levenford's terrible secret. Only she can lead Fallon to the Shrike . . .